Special thanks to:

Amanda Kay Smith, Anij Fallows, Azia MacManus, Burning Spear Comix, Carl W Bishop, Catherine Leja, Chris Call, Christine Gourley, Collin David, Courtney Cannon, Damion and Cathy Gilzean, Daniel Groves, Dave Baxter, DeWayne Copeland, Earl Hall, Elizabeth Nohelty Romano, Emerson Kasak, Erin Congdon, Jake Schroeder, Jason Crase, Jeff Lewis, Jimbo, John Mead, Joshua Bowers, Katrina Roets, Ken Reich, Kimberly Lucia, Laura Reed, Mark Byzewski, Mark Hill, Massimo Piras, Matthew Johnson, Michael H Bullington, Nick Smith, Nikres, Odile Purcell O'Byrne, Paul Rose Jr., Peter Anders, Rob Fowler, Rob Steinberger, Sammy G., scantrontb, Schreuka, Scott Kilburn, Shannon Carlin, Sherry Mock, SwordFirey, Talinda Willard, Thomas Werner, Venron, and Walter Weiss.

ALSO BY RUSSELL NOHELTY

THE GODVERSE CHRONICLES
And Death Followed Behind Her
And Doom Followed Behind Her
And Ruin Followed Behind Her
And Hell Followed Behind Her
Katrina Hates the Dead
Pixie Dust

OTHER NOVEL WORK
My Father Didn't Kill Himself
Sorry for Existing
Gumshoes: The Case of Madison's Father
The Invasion Saga
The Vessel
Worst Thing in the Universe
The Void Calls Us Home

OTHER ILLUSTRATED WORK
The Little Bird and the Little Worm
Ichabod Jones: Monster Hunter
Gherkin Boy

www.russellnohelty.com

THE MARKED ONES

By:

Russell Nohelty

Edited by:

Amy Cissell and Chris Barnes

Cover by:

Paramita Bhattacharjee

BOOK ONE

"Marked"

PROLOGUE

The Royal Military Police pounded their feet on the sidewalk above the sewer where I cradled my newborn baby. They had been on our heels since we entered Madrid, and with every step I took, the threat of the RMP finding us multiplied.

Breathe. Breathe. Breathe. Keep calm. You knew the risks when you came here. It will be okay. Just put one foot in front of the other.

I looked down at my sweet baby's face, resting so peacefully. I didn't want to give her Nyquil, but I needed her to sleep until we dropped her off and got out of Madrid. She would forgive me in time, if she ever found out who I was, that is. If all went well, that wouldn't happen until her eighteenth birthday.

"Hey!" Tom said, slinking down into the sewer. His curly black hair fell over his ice blue eyes. I loved him so much it blinded me to the world we brought our baby into, and now we all suffered the consequences.

"What did you find?" I asked breathlessly.

"I found a way through the RMP blockade. Let's go."

I squeezed my baby tightly in my arms and ambled down the sewer behind Tom. This would be my last chance to hold her tight. The next time I saw her, she would be an adult.

"Wait," Tom whispered, hearing the footsteps of RMP soldiers above our heads.

It wasn't an easy decision to leave my baby, but she had a better shot at living here, with the Normals. It was a risk.

If they found her, they would brand her a traitor to the crown, but concealing her identity was her best chance for a real life.

The sun on the side of Tom's cheek glowed as he beckoned me forward down the grimy sewer.

"Turn that off!" I whispered forcefully to him.

"We need the light," Tom replied as he inched down the dark sewer in front of us.

"They're going to see!" I said.

"Nobody will see, Susie," Tom replied with a smile. "Trust me."

He didn't make it five steps before he regretted those words. Something ripped off the sewer grate behind us, and a robotic Goliath peered down at us. Ten feet tall and crewed by Royal Air Force pilots, Goliaths were the most lethal weapon against magic users. They were built to take us down by the dozen.

"Halt!" it shouted. "You are in violation of statute 20.986 of Her Majesty's charter."

"Cover your eyes!" Tom shouted to me.

Tom held up his hands, and the sewer went white. The man inside the Goliath covered his eyes as he stumbled backwards against the stone wall of the sewer, momentarily dazed. Tom grabbed my arm to pull me forward. I looked back at the destruction as we disappeared into the darkness.

*

"I thought you knew the path, Tom!" I scolded after a half hour of aimlessly wandering through the sewers. "We've passed the same dead rat a half dozen times already!"

"How do you know it's the same rat?" Tom asked. "Maybe it's another dead rat. Ever think of that, huh?"

I sighed. "I don't want to have this discussion. Really and truly, I don't. I just want to get our baby to safety."

I looked down at the baby. She breathed heavily in my arms and tossed back and forth as if trying to break free of a nightmare. Soon she would wake up, and if we weren't safely hidden by then, she would cry and blow our cover. I kept a pacifier in my back pocket just in case we needed it, but she hated pacifiers; and even if she took it, I couldn't promise it wasn't covered in sewer sludge.

Heck, I couldn't promise she wasn't covered in sewer sludge. I could barely see anything in the tunnels.

"Which way are we going?" I asked.

"I don't— We have to go up, Susie. It's the only way. I can't find my bearings down here. We should be at the Plaza Mayor, and if we are, it's only a few more blocks to the drop point, but I have no idea if that's—"

He stopped talking as helicopters landed overhead. That wasn't a new sound, and it might not be for us, but more soldiers milling about was never a good thing.

The Royal Military Police were always hunting for Shiners like Tom and I. Ever since the war, we couldn't go anywhere without the RMP or the US Army on our tails, but it had gotten worse of late, and I didn't want that for our baby. She should have a real life.

The baby's eyes fluttered open. There was no keeping her silent now. I kept her pressed to my chest, but she squirmed out, and let out a deep wail.

"Shh shh shh shh shh," I said, rocking her with my arms. "Shhhhh…"

But she wouldn't stop crying. She wouldn't stop wailing. I reached into my back pocket to grab the pacifier, but it was gone. I searched the ground around me; I'd lost it in the sinewy labyrinth of the sewers.

"What do we do?" I asked Tom.

He looked back at me. "I have an idea, but you're not going to like it."

I caught his eyes for a moment. I knew he was going to give himself up before he pushed open the sewer grate.

"No. No. No." I blubbered as the tears filled my eyes. "Please, Tom. Don't"

"Just get ready to run."

He leapt out of the sewer grate and held up his hands. The glow of his cheek brought the attention of a half-dozen RMPs and three Goliath mechs that surrounded the square above us. Then with a little nod, he turned back to me and unleashed a fire ring around his body that knocked all the guards to the ground.

"Remember," I said to the baby. "Mommy loves you."

The crescent moon on my cheek glowed a bright blue. I gathered all the sewage I could and pushed it out of the grate above me with all the force I could muster. The bile jettisoned me forward out of the sewers and into the air. When I hit the ground, I was already running away as the mech suits were rebooting their systems after Tom's attack.

"Tom!" I shouted.

He was already halfway to me by the time I shouted. We sprinted down the nearest alleyway, running as fast as we could, with our baby screaming loudly into the night.

"That was so stupid," I shouted. "You could've been caught."

"But I wasn't caught," Tom said, pointing backwards. "And did you see the statue in the center of that square? It was Philip III on horseback. This is Plaza Mayor, just like I said. We're just a few blocks away from the drop point."

I turned to look at King Philip III on horseback at the center of the square and realized Tom was right. We were close. I couldn't believe we might actually pull it off and give our daughter a chance for a real life. I wanted to smile, but that was before the mech suits stomped toward us. Their steps quaked the ground under our feet.

"Run!" Tom shouted, but I was done taking orders.

"No!" I shouted back, stuffing my crying baby into his arms. "You run."

I kissed our baby's sweet head as I gave Tom one last glance, then I turned back toward the mechs towering over me. The soldier piloting the nearest suit sneered at me from her protective bubble, enjoying her job a little too much for my taste.

The moon on my cheek glowed bright blue. I pulled my arms close until the pipes in every building burst into the street, creating a wall of water between the mechs and my baby.

The water rose into the air, and I shot it as fast as I could at the approaching mechs. I turned back to see Tom frozen in horror, unable to move his feet. The baby in his arms wailing for comfort.

"Run!" I shouted. "Don't stop!"

We would never see each other again. I would be arrested, detained, and tortured…at the very least. At worst, I would be executed as a lesson to all other magic users. I wanted to live and meet our baby again, but that wasn't possible anymore, and it didn't matter. All that mattered was that we got our baby girl to safety.

I teared up as Tom turned the corner, and my salty tears mixed with the water bursting from the pipes around me. I shot as much water as I could at the mechs, but they were ready for the blast the second time.

They locked their feet into the ground and stepped forward one after another. It was slow moving for them, but they would eventually be on me. Every slow step of their boots brought me closer to my demise.

"Enough!" A modulated voice screamed from the other side of the streaming water.

A metallic claw burst through the water and wrapped around my head. I couldn't hold my concentration. The water fell around me, splashing harmlessly onto the stone.

The metallic arm pulled me close to the bubble cockpit that encased the driver inside, who smiled a maniacal grin at me. She enjoyed the chase. She enjoyed hunting Shiners like me. It was written all over her face. And she would enjoy hunting my child, too. I wouldn't let that happen.

In one last burst of energy, I flung by hand up, and the water around me shot up from the ground into an icicle which crashed through the bubble and stabbed the driver in the stomach.

I fell to the ground, coughing, as ten MPs with machine guns surrounded me. In that moment, I lost the will to fight on and passed into unconsciousness.

CHAPTER ONE

I always wished I had magic powers. Sure, magic users lived in ghettos all around Ambrosia…but they could do things nobody else could. They could breathe fire, control rain, see into the future, and create beautiful illusions with the snap of their fingers.

Once I saw a magic user leap fifty feet into the air onto the top of a building to save a kid's balloon. He got arrested for that, so maybe it was a dumb idea. Still, it was nice. Magic users could do that all the time as if it was nothing—as if they were taking a leisurely stroll.

I didn't have any of that. I didn't have any powers or cool stories, and my cheeks didn't light up when I wanted to breathe fire out of my mouth or look deep into the future.

I was just a normal kid with straight, dirty blonde hair and an overbite, who hunched over when she walked and had to wear orthopedic shoes through middle school to straighten out my foot. There was nothing magic about that, or me.

"Rosie!" Mama said, calling up the stairs through the thin floorboards of our row house. "Breakfast!"

If I had magic, I could get my clothes to dance around the room and dress me by themselves…but no. I had to be a Normal, which meant I was stuck putting on my school uniform myself, like a sucker.

"Coming!" I shouted to my mother as I pulled the blue vest over my hair. As I did, I caught a glimpse in the mirror, and I couldn't help but think that I really was a Normal. There was nothing special about my reflection. Average height, average hair, average looks. So very normal.

Stupid Normals. We were the worst. No magic. No powers. Just…like machine powered electricity and junk. I heard the Light Wielders once used their magic to power the whole grid before stupid Alexander Graham Bell spoiled it…just like a Normal.

I flipped the light off in my room as I picked up my backpack and ran downstairs. Our townhouse was small and cramped—too cramped for even just the two of us—but we managed. Mama and I didn't need much, and we didn't get much, so it worked out.

I hopped over the banister and landed on the creaky wooden floor. Mama sighed at me from her seemingly permanent spot huddled over the kitchen counter. "Would you be gentle. You're gonna snap those floorboards one of these days."

"Good," I replied. "We need new ones anyway."

"Oh yeah," Mom replied, sliding scrambled eggs on to a plate. "And who's gonna pay for them. You?"

I ran forward and kissed her on her cheek before sitting down at the kitchen table. Mama was a plump woman, and she kept rounding out with age. With every year that passed, her cheeks grew rosier and plumper. She didn't care though, she was happy, and that was what mattered…to me at least.

"You're gonna miss the bus," Mama said, laying a plate of scrambled eggs in front of me.

I sighed. This was the thousandth day in a row she'd made scrambled eggs for breakfast. "Do I have to? Can't I have a Pop Tart or something?"

"No," Mama said. "They're bad for you. Now, eat up."

I grumbled as I stuffed the scrambled eggs down my throat. If I had magic, I wouldn't have to eat scrambled eggs.

*

Televisions blared out onto the street as I walked down the alleyway toward the bus stop. Ambrosia didn't use school buses. We had to take the city bus just like everybody else, but at least we got passes which made riding free.

The narrow and windy streets of Ambrosia were crafted from the remnants of Madrid that remained after the war. Remnants of the old language spoke in old Madrid still clung to the city like bits of flotsam.

Businesses sometimes still had their signs up in Spanish, and you could get tapas on just about any street corner, but people only spoke Spanish in the darkness now, in the same corners that magic users practiced their powers. Here, and in all of Europe, people spoke English. Anything else meant you might be plotting against the queen.

"Hey!" my friend Anabelle said, running up as I walked down the cobblestone streets that lined the back alleys of Ambrosia. Anabelle wasn't like me. She wasn't normal. She was a Normal, but she was anything but...long silky brown hair, bright green eyes, and a million-dollar smile that shined for days. She could pal around with anybody, but she chose me...or she was stuck with me. After all, we had lived five houses away from each other since we were babies.

Our bus picked us up on the main street, Queen Anne Boulevard, that once took people to and from the Prado, and other Spanish cultural touchstones. Many of the buildings were repurposed after the war.

"Are you with me?" Anabelle asked.

I had been zoned out since I walked out of the house this morning, just like every morning for the past few months. I wasn't sure why, but I had trouble focusing ever since we'd started high school last fall.

"Yeah, I'm fine."

"You sure?" Anabelle asked. "Cuz you look like you are a million miles away."

I wished I was a million miles away, flying over Paris or Berlin with my hair fluttering in the wind, but I couldn't tell that to Anabelle. She had no desire to leave Ambrosia and was quite content with going to school, playing piano, and being doted on by older boys.

We couldn't be much more different, and yet we could finish each other's sentences. Even when she grew half a foot in the middle of eighth grade and could suddenly sit at the popular table, she never abandoned me. She insisted I be included too, even though people looked at her weirdly when we were together.

"I said I'm fine—" I scoffed, but I couldn't finish my thought. My eyes turned to the television screens lining the alleyway. They installed screens on streets and alleys all over Ambrosia that blared propaganda out of them 24 hours a day, in case we weren't aware that every citizen sat on the knife's edge.

"Last night a pair of Shiners were arrested trying to sneak past Plaza Mayor with their baby," a reporter said. "Luckily, our wonderful RMPs caught them before they could carry out whatever horrible plot they had planned. Hip hip hooray for the brave men and woman of our military."

I hated that term…Shiner. People used it all the time, but I saw what it did to magic users when you called them that. Their eyes fell low, and they lost their breath for a second. They were powerless to stop people from saying it, but they didn't have to like it, either.

"Good riddance, I guess," Anabelle said with a triumphant smile on her face. "Hip hip hooray."

It was one thing Anabelle and I disagreed on, though she never knew it. She had more tolerance to magic users than most people in Ambrosia, but there was this latent magicism that still reared its ugly head from time to time.

I tried to broach the topic with her several times, but it always turned into a catfight. She was adamant that she wasn't magicist, but that didn't change the fact that she said some really magicist stuff from time to time. Still, she was the best friend I ever had, so I quietly bit my tongue around her for the sake of the friendship. After all, she was a good person otherwise, and it didn't affect me, right?

"Yeah," I replied halfheartedly, noticing the 235 bus, which would take us to school, pulling up at the end of the alley. "Come on. We're gonna be late."

"Wait!" I shouted, flailing my hands in the air as we ran toward the bus. "Stop!"

The driver was used to halting his route due to our tardiness. There wasn't a week that went by when we didn't have to rush to catch up to a departing bus at least once. Of course, if I had magic, this wouldn't be a problem. I could fly us to school. Then I wouldn't be able to go to school, either, though. At least not mine—as it wasn't integrated.

Some schools still let magic kids and Normals interact together, but they were few and far between in the city. Most magic users were schooled by their own kind in the ghettos of Ambrosia.

"Please!" Anabelle shouted behind me as the bus pulled away. "Stop!!!"

The bus jerked to a stop, and the door swung open. "Come on, then."

I hopped onto the bus and showed my school ID to Trevor, the kindly old bus driver who always smiled at us when we came on board.

"Thanks, Trev," I said, sucking wind. "You are a lifesaver."

"Oh, think nothing of it," Trevor replied from the driver's seat, smiling at me.

The bus was packed. There wasn't an empty seat anywhere. I passed a pregnant woman wearing a red plus sign on her tattered jacket. Her matted hair hadn't been washed in days, nor had her muddied face.

She was a healer, endowed with the ability to fix others with her magical hands. Magic users weren't supposed to sit at the front of the bus, especially not when Normals needed a seat, but I didn't mind letting her stay.

"Can I sit there?" Anabelle said sweetly to the woman.

"Please," the woman replied in a thick Irish accent. "Don't make me go up the stairs to the back. I just worked a twelve-hour shift, and I'm so tired."

"Look, I don't want this to be a thing," Anabelle said. "But you really shouldn't be up here. I mean, I personally don't care, but like, just let me sit there okay. Your place is in the back."

"Just let her sit there," I said. "It's not that far."

"It's the principle of the thing, Rosie. I mean, without rules society breaks down."

"Come on," I said, pulling her arm.

"No!" she shouted back. "Quit being a wet blanket!"

"I'm sorry. I'm sorry," the healer said, crouching down in her seat. "Please, I don't want to move."

"Hey!" Trevor shouted in the rearview mirror at the woman. "Get to the back of the bus!"

"There's no room back there, sir." She looked up at me. "Please, don't make me move."

"I don't mind standing," I said, grabbing on to the metal pole.

"I do," Anabelle scoffed. "I wasn't trying to make a scene, but well, here we are. Get up."

The woman winced at the sound of that word. That horrible word. I spun around to Anabelle. "She's pregnant."

"Yeah? And that's just one more shiner baby we gotta take care of, ain't it?"

"Wow," I replied. "I thought you weren't magicist?"

"I'm not!" she replied before she lowered her voice. "But it's true."

I leaned into her with a sneer. "Who? You? Personally? Are you paying for her to eat and sleep?"

"Not today," Anabelle replied. "But one day I'm gonna be outta school and then yeah, I'm gonna be paying for the lot of them."

I turned back toward the woman. "It's okay, miss. I'll go to the back."

"No, you won't," Anabelle scoffed. "Not with me. I want to sit in the front of the bus like I'm supposed to, and I want her to sit in the back like she's supposed to. That's not so much to ask, is it?"

There was a step up to the back of the bus, and behind the guard rails sat dozens of men, women, and children, all wearing tattered clothes embroidered with one of the seven magical signs.

The bus stopped again, and the woman went to stand. "No, don't. I was just leaving."

I hopped off the bus. Anabelle shouted at me. "Where are you going?"

"I feel like walking!" I shouted back. "Tell Mrs. Fritz I'm on my way. Or don't. I don't care."

I watched Anabelle's confused look as the door jerked closed and the bus pulled away. I really didn't want to get into it with her, but sometimes I had no choice. I just hated how she treated magic users.

*

Seven types of magic and Normals hated them all equally. Air, Light, Water, Eye, Ground, Mirror, and Health. Each magical user glowed with a hidden emblem on their cheek, which lit up when they used their magic, but otherwise stayed hidden from view. They shined, thus the term "Shiner." I preferred to think of it as a gentle glow. Before the war, people called it the Glow.

When they weren't using their magic, which was like 99 percent of the time, magic users were just like everyone else. You couldn't even tell they could use magic. However, that 1 percent was enough to make them a pariah—and made people like Anabelle hate them.

There was a time when I might have understood the hate. After the Great War, where magic users like Hitler, Franco, and Mussolini revolted against the Normals and tried to take control of the world, executing everybody that didn't have powers, forcing them into concentration camps, and burning them alive—after that horror, I understood the hatred toward magic users. I understood why the UK and the US chose to subjugate magic users.

They were scared—terrified even. Magic users could do things us Normals could never dream of—and because of that, they were a threat to us. Still, that war ended almost seventy-five years ago, and it's not like there's been another war since those days. Anabelle never lived in a world where magic users were a threat, and neither did her mother or father. Still, they kept the same vitriol going, just as if they had lived it.

I felt like magic users should be given fair treatment under the law but…I was still scared of them…even though I never had any reason to be frightened. I'd only seen magic a handful of times in my whole life outside the news, and yet I lived in fear that any moment a magic user would incinerate me or drive me mad with just a thought.

*

The school was a little under two miles from the bus stop I'd gotten off at, and the opposite end of Queen Anne Boulevard as the old Prado, which was now the British Art Museum, but everybody called it the Picasso, who'd spent most of his life living in France, opposing the rule of Franco.

Franco was the last of the great magical tyrants to fall. Though the rest of Europe was overtaken in 1945, Franco remained in power until 1975, due to his extraordinary skills with magic, and his relative isolation on the Iberian Peninsula. When he was finally deposed, the hammer fell swiftly and harder on Spanish magic users than anywhere else in Europe.

The British Prime Minister claimed that it was impossible to know which magic users supported the great despot, and thus Britain had to assume the whole country was filled with brainwashed magic users.

In other countries, the justice had been swift. If you wore a uniform and marched against the Allies, you were an enemy. Otherwise, you were a friend, even if you were still treated as a second class citizen.

However, in Spain, the war ended in 1975, which meant many of the men and women who fought against the UK and US after that did so without a uniform. Thus, the RMP assumed every wielder of magic was culpable and thus guilty. Of course, that's just what they force fed us in school. There was surprisingly little information about the war online, at least from any reputable source. I could find nine hundred recipes for brisket, but the only articles about the war were written by kooks and nut jobs.

With each step I moved forward, the school grew in the distance in front of me. I heard the school bell ring signaling the start of classes. I walked as fast as I could toward the school, hoping Anabelle had told our homeroom teacher I was going to be late.

CHAPTER TWO

"Before I hand out tests," Mrs. Lumpkin started, from the front of the classroom. "Are there any questions?"

The groans were palpable in the class as all eyes turned to me. It wasn't my fault that I wanted clarification on things, or that I read the assignment…and in classic me fashion, my hand shot up into the air.

Mrs. Lumpkin picked up the papers, her back turned away from us, and responded before she even turned around. "Yes, Roselyn. What is it?"

I smiled at her. "So am I to understand correctly that Hilter and Mussolini committed suicide within a week of each other. Isn't that a little coincidental?"

"Whether it is or not, that's what happened," Mrs. Lumpkin said with a smile.

"That doesn't make any sense though. I mean, they could have just called a cease-fire, maybe even staved off the firing squad for the rest of their lives. Why would they both commit suicide thousands of miles apart from each other?"

"I'm surprised you haven't looked up that information," Mrs. Lumpkin replied, handing me a test.

"Oh, I did, just for my own reference, but…there wasn't much on it. I mean, lots of sources corroborate that it happened, but nobody says why. And the sources aren't really reliable. Lots of conspiracy theorists and the like. Why isn't there more scholarly data on the war, if it was so important to our history?"

"Ours is not to wonder why, Ms. Light. Ours is just to do or die."

It wasn't a satisfactory answer, but I wasn't going to get anything else out of her. I knew what I needed to know for the test, and the rest of it was my own curiosity, which wasn't really wanted or encouraged in Mrs. Lumpkin's class…or anywhere else. People didn't like talking about the war, even online.

The biggest war in the history of the world, and aside from a few textbooks, nobody had any information about it. I could find a thousand textbooks on the American Civil War or the French Revolution, but for World War II there was nothing except what I learned in school?

Oh well.

I pulled out a #2 pencil from my backpack and flipped open the test. Before I could read the first question, a piece of paper slid onto my desk. I looked up at Tommy, the homely looking boy sitting in front of me. He pointed to the dreamboat at the corner of the class waving in my direction. It was my auburn haired, freckle-faced boyfriend Tyler, flashing a smile with his perfect teeth and pointing at the note.

I opened the frayed paper and read the note inside. *"Meet me in the second-floor janitor's closet after class."*

I giggled under my breath. I wanted so badly to meet him, touch, him, and hold him, but I couldn't just say yes. I had to play the game.

I looked up at him and shook my head, mouthing "no" as I did. He quivered his lip and clasped his hands together as if he was praying, miming "please" back to me. I shook my head more fervently, which caused his lip to quiver more.

"I'm sorry," Mrs. Lumpkin finally cut in. "I thought that I said eyes on your OWN paper. Unless there is something you want to discuss with the class, Roselyn?"

"No, ma'am," I said, turning to my paper, but out of at the corner of my eye I saw Tyler smile, and I gave him the slightest nod.

*

I'd barely pulled open the door to the janitor's closet before Tyler dragged me inside and wrapped his arms around me. It'd been a week since he held me in his arms, and that was too long. Mama didn't allow me to go anywhere after school except straight home, so seeing Tyler was impossible outside of school hours. Still, we made it work, sneaking away into closets and under bleachers…

It was incredibly cliché. It felt like the lovesick schoolgirl from every movie I'd ever seen. Still, those girls were filled with good ideas, and if your mother was strict and you had a deep, aching love for a boy, you did what you had to so you could see him.

After passionately kissing Tyler for a while, I needed air, so I pushed him back. Tyler never resisted when I put on the brakes, and I always respected that about him. We'd dated for over six months, and never once did he even try to reach under my shirt or make me feel bad about wanting to move slow.

"Are you okay?" Tyler asked me, caressing my face.

"Yes," I replied. "Of course. I just…need a second."

"Take all the time you need." He smiled. "Do you think you'll be able to hang out this weekend?"

I shook my head. "Not unless my mother suddenly decides to be cool. The chances of that are nonexistent."

Tyler caressed my cheek. "I get it. I mean I wouldn't want to let you out of the house either."

I smiled. I knew I wasn't much to look at for most people. My hair was flat, my nose was too big for my face, and my dull eyes were hardly spectacular. Still, Tyler didn't care. He just wanted to be around me. All the time. Even when I was in a bad mood. That was real love, there, even though we hadn't said that we loved each other yet.

"Can I ask you a question?" I said to him.

"Of course," he replied.

"What do you think about magic users?"

"You mean Shiners?"

I cringed at the word. It sounded so vile coming from his mouth. "Sure."

"I mean…they're fine. As long as they stay where they are, ya know? They never caused me trouble, so I guess…I mean I don't think about them much at all, come to think of it. Good, they're locked up in ghettos though, cuz if they messed with me, I would ruin their lives."

I sighed. "Well, I guess that's better than hating them."

"Is it?" He asked, scratching his head. "Why are you asking anyway?"

The bell sounded for the next period, and I grabbed my book bag. "No reason. Wait thirty seconds, then come out after me."

I brushed myself off and straightened my hair as best I could. Then, I pulled open the door, only to see Principal Gomez standing in front of me with his arms folded.

"I think you both need to come with me," he said gruffly.

*

We followed Principal Gomez into his office and shut the door. Spaniards weren't punished under the new government established by the British Colonial Society after the fall of Spain. After all, they weren't the problem. Magic users were the problem. When the British took over running Spain, they allowed the Spaniards to maintain their same degree of freedom, as long as they pledged loyalty to the British crown.

Many, like Principal Gomez, did, while the others fled to South America, or were thrown in jail for their insolence. Some called the Spaniards who stayed cowards or turncoats, but I thought of them as survivalists. They had a chance to stay in the city they loved, even if it was called something else, and visit the places they loved, even if they weren't exactly the same as they remembered them.

"I want to forget what I saw," Principal Gomez started. "I very much do."

"That would be so cool of you," Tyler chimed in before I grabbed his hand to calm him down.

"I understand we must have let you down," I said, dipping my eyes to the floor. I was very adept at playing the good girl, and making people think that I was completely innocent. Being caught making out in the janitor's closet…tarnished that image.

"I expect more from you, Roselyn," Principal Gomez said. "This is very disappointing."

"I know, and it was a stupid mistake," I said, listening to the air go out of Tyler's lungs. "It won't happen again."

Principal Gomez smiled. "I am not stupid, Rosie. I know that you have been using that closet for weeks now. I just haven't been able to catch you until today."

"What!" Tyler said. "That's a lie. A bald-faced lie."

Principal Gomez opened a manila folder on his desk and slid a frayed piece of paper over to me. "Would you care to read this?"

I shook my head. I knew what that note was the same one Tyler passed to me during history class. It must have fallen out of my pocket or forgotten when I left class. "No, sir."

"So, you know what this is, then?"

Both Tyler and I nodded. I was starting to think I wasn't going to be able to talk myself out of this one.

"If you could just let me explain—" Tyler said.

"Go ahead," Principal Gomez replied. "I would love to hear this."

"Ummm," Tyler said, looking over at me. "You see…it's just…" He stopped stuttering and took a deep sigh. "It's just that I really like Rosie, and I can't see her anywhere else but school, so yeah… I know it was wrong, but I don't regret it."

I smiled and squeezed Tyler's hand. It was a very brave thing that he did. Plus, I never minded any time he said that he liked me. *I like you, too.*

"And do you feel the same way, Roselyn?" Principal Gomez asked, turning to me.

"Yes, sir," I sighed, looking into Tyler's soft, green eyes. "I know what we did was wrong, but I don't regret it."

"Hrm," Principal Gomez said, curling his upper lip. "This is a suspendable offense. You know that, right?"

"Yes, sir," I replied.

"Still, both of you are good kids, and I suppose if you both promise not to do it again, I will let you off with just a detention."

"I'll take it, for sure, Principal Gomez," Tyler said quickly. "Thank you, sir."

"That's going to be a problem for me," I replied. "I can't be home later than 17:00, like ever, and detention ends at 16:30."

"I understand that, Rosie," Principal Gomez added. "I could suspend you for three days instead. Is that what you want? Of course, that might destroy your ability to become valedictorian. Suspensions count against your grades, and any work you miss can't be made up."

Oh man. I really wanted to be valedictorian; really, really, badly, but did I want to risk drawing the ire of my mom because of it?

"What will it be?" Principal Gomez continued. "Detention or suspension?"

I sighed. "Detention. I'll have to run home."

"Good, good. I suppose we'll see you after school, then."

I looked over at Tyler. "Mama's gonna be so mad."

"Well," Principal Gomez said. "Maybe you should have thought of that before you broke the rules."

*

It's bad enough that I had to sit in a boring classroom every day and listen to a teacher drone on and on, making fascinating subjects boring as piss, but it's even worse when the teacher sits at the front of a classroom and silently made you do your work. I loved to learn, but I hated the school's methods.

I don't know why detention even existed as a punishment since all I did in there was homework. Are they saying that homework is punishment? Are they saying school is punishment?

If that's the case, then they might be right, but I didn't know why they've gotta be so blatant about it. Mama was gonna be pissed when I walked through the door after 5 pm. She wasn't a strict woman, but that was her one rule—always, no matter the circumstances, be home by 5 pm, even on the weekends; even during the summer.

No matter what, we had to be back inside the house by 5 pm. It prevented us from going on vacations, or from me doing any after school activities, or ever having a social life because I always had to be back home by 5 pm.

Once, when I was fourteen, I tried to push the limits. I got home at 16:59 and Mama went ballistic. She screamed and hollered for three hours for having the gall to cut it so close. It was like I wasn't even her kid for a moment, but then she stopped and cocked her head to one side, and she was back to normal again.

As the clock ticked to 16:30, my gut tightened. I clenched my school bag in my hand and stared at the clock at the front of the room, ticking more slowly than I thought possible. Every second was agony, but I had already asked to go early, twice, and was rebuffed, so my only option was to rush out as fast as I could to catch the 16:33 bus home.

Otherwise, I would have to make my way through the dangerous magical ghettos. They were the only way I could hope to get home fast enough. Walking home, even running, would take me at least forty minutes if I didn't take the shortcut through the ghetto.

No matter how much sympathy I had for the magical, I did not want to go through that ghetto. Mama told me that many who wandered into the ghetto never came out. Still, Mama would understand, if it was an emergency.

The clock finally ticked over to 16:30, and I was out of my seat before the teacher dismissed us. I didn't even have a chance to say goodbye to Tyler as I tore out the door and through the desolate hallways of the school. Every classroom was empty, save for teachers trying to get ahead on lesson plans, and only a lonely janitor guarded the halls, sweeping up the garbage left behind by several hundred children throughout the day.

I hopped over his mop and pushed through the heavy metal doors which separated me from the outside. But I was too late by the time I got to the stairs. I saw the 16:33 pull away just as I reached the top of the stairs which led out to the gate onto the street. I had no choice but to take the shortcut through the ghetto.

"Hey!" Tyler shouted at me. "Wait up!"

"I don't have time for this, Tyler," I said back to him.

"I know. You gotta get home, and the bus just left. But if you think I'm gonna let you go through the Shiner ghetto alone, you're crazy."

"I'm not a little girl, Tyler. I can take care of myself."

I don't know why I was so angry at Tyler, but for some reason, the rage at my own mistake spilled over and splashed onto him. However, he didn't retaliate. His face stayed soft and perfect, as it always was when I looked at him.

"I know you aren't," he said, smiling. "But I want to come anyway. Okay? It's not for you. It's for me."

I groaned. "Fine."

I stuck out my hand, and he grabbed it, and we continued down the stairs together, and across the street, to brave the magical ghettos, hoping to come out with our lives.

CHAPTER THREE

Magical ghettos were set up all over Ambrosia after the war. The city couldn't afford to fix up everything at once, so magic users were forced out of their homes and into the worst areas of the city, forced to abandon everything they once had and for most of them, that meant giving up a lot.

Magic users tended to be the upper crust of society. Their powers allowed them to get the best jobs. After all, why would you want to go to a doctor if a healer could fix your broken arm in minutes? And why would you choose a job at all without visiting a seer to make sure that it's the right choice?

That all changed after the war though, when magic users were driven into the shadows. Sure, some people still ventured into the darkness to use their services, but it was a dangerous path, fraught with peril. If a Normal was discovered using magical services, the consequences were severe.

"This is creepy," Tyler said as we passed from the street into the back-alley ghettos. My house was on the other side of the ghetto. If I squinted, I could make it out, past a dozen blocks of ramshackle apartments.

"Why is there no light?" Tyler added.

The minute we passed into the ghetto, it was like all light drained out of the sky. Outside the ghettos, the sun still glowed, but inside the ghetto is was as if the sunset hours ago.

"I don't know," I said, meekly. "I just want to get out of here as fast as possible."

A cold breeze blew through the streets as I bundled myself up in my school jacket. Tyler clenched my hand tighter, and I knew it was more for his own fear than protecting me.

"I don't like this place," Tyler said as we stepped forward.

In the darkness, suns and plus signs glowed ominously through the windows above us. Families, no doubt, using their powers to cook dinner and heal scratches. They could never take that away from magic users. They could take their dignity and their money, but they could never take their powers.

"Let's just get out of here as fast as possible," Tyler said, quickening his gait.

Mama's house was at the other end of the ghetto. I could watch the glowing from the windows of magic users at night if I looked hard enough, but I hadn't taken this way since I was a child – before I knew that magic users were dangerous.

"What we got here, dearie?" I heard from above us.

Out of the shadow, a toothless man floated onto the ground. Three wisps of air glowed on his cheek. He was an Air magic user.

An old woman with frizzy gray hair collapsed the road underneath her as she rose from the ground. A small mountain glowed on her cheek as the earth spat her out in front of us. She was a Mountain user.

"Looks like a little kid and her brat friend," she said, exposing her brown teeth to us.

"We…don't want any trouble…" Tyler said, coyly, trying to feign as much strength as he could muster.

"Then I think you come to the wrong place, haven't ya?" the Air user said.

"Definitely the wrong place," the Earth user added. "Especially with all them nice clothes."

I looked down at my watch. It was 16:43. I only had seventeen minutes to get home, or I would be screwed. "Look, I appreciate what you're doing, but we don't have time for—"

"For what?" Air said. "A little talk."

"Yeah!" Earth replied. "You don't have time for us, cuz what, we are magic users?"

"That's not it at all," I said forcefully. "I have no problem with your kind. I have to get home."

Air walked forward, scrunching his brow. "'Our kind,' love? You know we have a kind?"

"Well," Earth replied, circling around us. "I thought we was humankind or something, but we must not be that, huh? Otherwise, she'd have time for us."

"Please, just let us go," Tyler sputtered.

"Well, you free to leave, aren't ya? I don't see us stopping you."

I took a big step forward, and Earth waved her hand in the air. The cracked asphalt rose up to stop us and coalesced into a wall that blocked our path.

"Now," Air said, turning to us. "I think we can let you go if you just empty your pockets."

"Please," I replied. "We don't have anything."

I turned to Tyler, but he was already tossing his wallet and keys on the ground. "That's all I have. Don't hurt me."

Earth bent down to pick up the wallet from the ground. "Well, that's a good lad. Now, how about you?"

Air leapt forward until I felt his hot, rancid breath on my cheek. "Yeah, dearie. How about you?"

I pressed my back against the wall of earth. My hands pushed hard against the earth. "No! No! No!"

"Rosie! Just let them—"

A flash of light lit up the alley, and the wall behind us exploded into a thousand pieces, raining down on Earth and Air.

"Run!" I shouted, grabbing for Tyler's hand, but he just looked at me stunned for a moment, ignoring my outstretched arm. "Let's go!"

He shook his head as if to snap out of a trance, and together we ran down the alleyway and turned a corner. If we didn't hit any more snags, I could be home on time.

*

"What was that?!" Tyler shouted when we rounded another corner and were out of sight from Air and Earth.

"I know, right?" I replied, breathing heavily. "We almost got assaulted. That was crazy, right?"

"No," Tyler said, shaking his head. "Your cheek. It glowed."

I found my face in a window and checked it out. There was no glowing. There was no mark on my face. I was just as I was before. No different.

"That's crazy," I replied. "I would know if I could use magic. I've been waiting for it all my life!"

I knew what I said was wrong. I knew he would never understand. I hadn't even told my own mother that I wanted to use magic, and here I was spouting off to a boy I wanted to impress; the boy I loved.

"What? You want powers?" he replied. "You want to use magic? What are you? A freak?"

"I'm not a freak," I said, rushing toward him. "I'm a Normal just like you."

Tyler pulled away from my touch. "No. You're nothing like me. You probably brought me here so you could rob me with your freak friends!"

"No! I didn't!" I heard Earth and Air stomping toward us, kicking the ground as they marched. "Please, we have to go. You can be mad at me later."

The shadows of Earth and Air grew larger in the street lamp's illumination. I held out my hand one last time, and Tyler begrudgingly took it.

*

I didn't want to leave the ghetto. I knew when I did, I would have a fight with Tyler, and I didn't want to fight with Tyler…especially because he was so wrong. There was no way that I had magic. Kids only received the gift of magic when they were 13, and I was 16 years old. That was too old to get the Glow.

"We're almost there," I shouted to Tyler.

I could see the end of the alleyway, and I fought to keep running forward, even though I wanted so badly to stop. I was caught between needing to get home and wanting the moment with Tyler to last forever. I feared these were the last moments I was going to have with him, and my stomach tied into knots at the thought.

"Enough!" He finally shouted as we reached the end of the alleyway.

Mama's house was right in front of us, and yet I couldn't get myself to walk toward it. I glanced down at my watch. It was 16:57. I had three whole minutes to watch my life crash down around me.

"Were you ever going to tell me?" Tyler said.

"Tell you what?" I replied. "There's nothing to tell. I'm the same girl you've always known."

"I know," Tyler said, spitting on the ground. "You were always a magic user. I should have known you were a freak."

"I'm not a freak!" I screamed, flailing my arms into the air. "I don't know how to use magic. I've never used magic in my whole life!"

"I watched it happen, Rosie!" Tyler scowled. "Are you saying that I'm a liar?"

I shook my head. "No. Of course not. I think maybe…you just think you saw something you didn't."

Tyler scoffed. "That's just a nice way of calling me a liar."

"Well, I don't know what else to call it," I replied. "Because you're wrong. Maybe somebody else destroyed that wall. Maybe it just wasn't very sturdy to begin with? But I didn't do it."

"I watched you!" Tyler said, pounding his fist into his palm "I watched you do it."

I went to touch him, but he recoiled in disgust. His face scrunched up in horror, and he turned from me. "Don't touch me."

"I thought you were okay with magic users. You said that—"

"I know what I said. That's just a thing…to say…when you wanna look like a caring—the point is…it's not true. I could never—I could never be with somebody like you."

"Please," I said, sobbing. "Just…look at me."

"No," Tyler said before he ran away from me. "Don't ever talk to me again."

I dropped to my knees, sobbing, just as the front door opened. I looked over to Mama's furious and worried look. I could see it in her eyes. She wanted to scream. She wanted to yell, but instead, she just scooped me in her arms and brought me inside.

*

"I told you, nothing good happens after five o' clock," Mama said as she brought me a cup of tea. "Didn't I tell you that?"

I nodded. "Yes, Mama. You told me that."

"And yet, what did you do?"

I sighed. "I stayed out until 5 pm."

"Even after I told you not to?"

I took a sip of tea. Something about Mama's tea brought me back to my childhood, and I smiled slightly, even through my tears. "Can we just not talk about it?"

"We certainly cannot not talk about it, my love," Mama said, sitting across from me with her own glass of tea. "This is a lesson, and lessons need to be learned immediately. You don't smack a dog on the nose three hours after it pees on the carpet, do you?"

I chuckled despite myself. "No, Mama. You don't."

"And you don't learn your lessons days later, either. You need to learn them when your heart breaks and your eyes are wet. That's the only way you'll learn for next time."

"Oh," I said, swirling the tea bag with my finger. "There won't be a next time."

"There will always be a next time," Mama said, taking a big swig of tea. "That's the thing about being a teenager. You always want to push the limits."

I shook my head. "Not me. Not anymore."

"Oh, okay, my love," Mama said with a knowing smile. "We'll see."

"I just don't get it," I said. "He said I was using magic, but I wasn't using magic. I swear I wasn't, Mama. Why would he say I was?"

Mama closed her eyes and calmed her breath. When she opened them again, her eyes were steely and focused. "Tomorrow, we will go down to that school and make sure the principal knows you won't be held late again."

"That's all you have to say, Mama?" I replied, watching her get up and pour her tea down the sink.

"This tea isn't very good, is it?" Mama said, smacking her lips. "I think I got a bum batch. I'll have to tell the Randall on the morrow."

I stood up, furious. "Mama quit changing the subject! Is there any way I could be using magic?"

Mama smiled and grabbed both my hands softly. "Of course not, my love. That's why I don't pay it no mind because it's impossible. Now, go up to bed. Big day tomorrow."

"But it's 17:30."

"I said go to bed."

And with that Mama went about straightening the kitchen. She wouldn't hear one more word about my strange encounter in the ghetto. All I could do was stomp off to bed, hoping tomorrow wasn't a horrible day, even though I knew it would be.

The kids at my school rabidly believed any rumor, no matter how ridiculous, and there was no way Tyler wouldn't spread it the moment he got home.

CHAPTER FOUR

The next morning Mama was standing at the front door by the time I marched downstairs. She was already dressed in her best pink, floral dress, and smiled at me as I walked past her into the kitchen. She hadn't dressed so nicely since we stopped going to church after my confirmation.

"You look…nice," I said, scarfing down the eggs that were my breakfast yet again. *What I wouldn't give for pancakes.*

"If you want people to think you are nice," she replied. "You have to look nice."

Mama never looked nice. She was a cook and a janitor, both in equal measure for different companies around the city. It was as if she couldn't get enough of cleaning…

But that wasn't it. No, it's because we were poor, and didn't have much choice. I told Mama I would go to public school, but she wouldn't hear of it. She would rather us eat ramen every night than forego the best possible education. That was the type of woman she was when it all came down to it. She cared more about my education than anything. Education, she said, was the secret to bettering yourself.

My phone buzzed, but I refused to pick it up. Before I drifted off to bed, there were fifty comments on Tyler's post about my magic use. When I woke up, there were three hundred more. My school only had six hundred students, which meant more than half had commented on Tyler's lies.

I tried to read them all, but they were filled with the vilest and most contemptible words imaginable. I cringed when people threatened to hurt anybody, but these comments were all directed at me. Sure, there were kind people like Anabelle, who tried to moderate, but she was drowned out in the sea of awful.

"I don't want to go to school," I told Mama as I placed my plate in the sink. "Can't I just stay home?"

"It is in times of great trials that we find our character, sweet one. It will be hard, but you will survive."

"And what if I don't survive?" I replied. "What if some crazy person stabs me in the stomach, or shoots me in the face because they think I'm a magic user?"

"That won't happen, my dear," Mama said, stepping into the kitchen. "You have the wildest imagination."

"I'm not imagining it, mom. That is what people said they would do to me next time they saw me. Do you wanna see?"

I went to grab my phone, but Mama placed her hand over mine. My eyes were wet with tears as she stroked my cheek. "I think that's enough of the phone for now, don't you?"

I nodded. "For sure."

"Then let's go."

*

I half expected an angry lynch mob outside my house when I stepped outside. However, all that greeted me when I opened the front door was Anabelle, smiling as ever, as if nothing was wrong.

"Good morning," she said as Mama and I walked down the stairs. "How was your night?"

I followed lockstep with her. "Oh, you know. The usual."

"I watched Gilmore Girls on Netflix all night," Anabelle said. "I know it's old, but it still has something to say. Plus, Rory is my Patronus. I don't so much like the reboot, though."

I grabbed Anabelle by the arm. "So, we're just not going to talk about last night or what really happened, huh?"

"Not unless you want to?" Anabelle replied. "I figured…"

"No…no…" I said, letting her go. "I don't want to…thank you…but just so you know…I'm not…"

Anabelle laughed. "I've been your best friend since we were babies, Rosie. I think I would know if you were a Shine–sorry, magic user."

I couldn't tell if she wasn't using the term because she knew I didn't like it, or because she thought I was lying to her, but either way, I appreciated it. There was usually nothing I hated worse than being pitied, but I didn't hate it in this moment. After all, I was pitiable in that moment. Not only did my boyfriend dump me, but he destroyed my life in the process.

At least Anabelle was on my side. If she turned on me, I didn't know what I would do.

*

When we stepped off the bus outside the school, the normal chatter silenced, and all eyes turned to me. I felt them burning into my soul. My footsteps echoed in my ear as I climbed the stairs to the school's front doors. Principal Gomez waited for us, parting the students with nothing but his presence, arms folded like a bouncer.

"I think we need to talk," Mama said to Principal Gomez.

"Yes," he said. "Let's. Rosie, ma'am. Come with me. Anabelle. I believe you have class soon, yes?"

She nodded. "Yes, sir."

It was brave of Anabelle even to be seen with me for this long, and I didn't want to make it worse. So, I avoided wrapping her in a hug or telling her thanks, but I didn't have to, because she threw her arms around me and pulled me close.

"Be strong, okay?" she said.

"I will," I replied.

Anabelle ran off, into the silence of the halls, as I walked slowly behind Mama and Principal Gomez, who stepped slowly and deliberately with every clomp of his shoes.

"I assume you know why I'm here," Mama started.

"Yes, ma'am. I have heard the rumors. I am an admin on the school's Facebook page. Parents have been messaging us all night, claiming there is a Shiner in our midst."

"Please," Mama said. "Don't use that word."

"I'm sorry, I didn't know you were–"

"Oh, I'm not. It's just a horrible word. I don't like it."

"Hmmm," Principal Gomez hummed, skeptical. "Well, that is good, because you know we have a policy about–"

"I know, Mr. Gomez. I know your policy on integration, and while I don't agree with it, I respect it. I've always respected it. When you kicked those two magical kids out a couple years ago…the ones whose parents lied to you…well, I respected that too…cuz those are the rules."

"Rules are rules, Ms. Light."

"You can call me Greta."

We reached the principal's office, and he sat down behind his thick, wooden desk. Mama and I sat opposite of him.

"Okay, Greta. Then I think you can see my problem, here. A student–"

"I'm sorry, but that's not why I'm here."

"Oh, really," Principal Gomez said, tenting his fingers in front of him. "And why are you here?"

"I'm here because when we signed up for this school, I told you that Rosie had to be home by 5 pm, every day. I told you that, didn't I?"

He nodded. "Yes, ma'am…but she broke the rules. Did she tell you what she did?"

Mama looked over at me. "Being a teenager, no doubt. Probably with that Tyler fellow, right? The one causing all the racket now?"

"How do you know about that?" I asked.

"Please, child," Mama said, laughing. "I have Facebook, too."

"I'm afraid I can't just let Rosie off when she breaks the rules."

"I'm not saying you should, but look what happened when she was late. People spreading lies about her. Kids threatening to kill my poor girl. Is that really the kind of school you want to run here, Mr. Gomez?"

He shook his head. "Of course not, and I promise we are looking into the threats, too, but your daughter—"

"My daughter is a fine upstanding student, is she not?"

The principal nodded. "She is, ma'am."

"And this Tyler fellow?"

"He's also a fine student."

"Then it seems like his word against hers, one fine student to another. And since she claims she's not magic, and I have never seen her use magic, and you have never seen her use magic, and her best friend has never seen her use magic. Are you saying you are going to take a boy's word over my daughter's?"

Principal Gomez sighed. He'd clearly been beaten by my mother's argument. "No, ma'am."

Mama stood up and gathered her purse. "And you will make sure my sweet Rosie gets home on time from now on, yes?"

"I will ma'am."

Mama smiled as she rose from her seat. "Good. I feel like we've made great progress here today." Mama kissed me on the forehead. "See you at home, dear."

*

I kept my head down through the first half of the day. People treated me with equal parts anger, fear, and skepticism. According to Tyler, I could blow people up just by looking at them. So, people kept their distance.

I half wished it was true because I would have loved to blow up Tyler into a million pieces for making my life miserable. It used to be nice having so many classes with him. We could sneak out to the bathroom, and meet after the bell rang for a couple of seconds of making out. However, now it was painful. Gone were the doe-eyed looks exchanged during a boring class, replaced instead with an icy glare.

He wasn't alone, either. Friends I'd known for years treated me as if I didn't exist. They parted for me as I walked past, as if I had leprosy, even though I was the same person they'd always known. I was the same human as I was the day before, but you would've thought that I was an alien with red, demonic eyes and fangs with how they looked at me.

Part of me understood their venom, though. After all, the way Tyler made it sound, I always knew I could use magic, and had hidden it from everyone, like a liar. I wouldn't want to be friends with a liar, and so I understood why they didn't want to stay friends with one either. Still, it hurt that they didn't even ask to hear my side of the story.

Hopefully, it would all settle down, and I would get a chance to explain myself. One thing about kids in my high school, they moved on to the next thing at a lightning pace. By next week, they'll be talking about Christie Shinn's new nose or some other thing, and leave me alone…then I can hopefully win their trust back…and prove somehow that I couldn't use magic.

*

By the time I got to lunch, I was worn out by the constant barrage of silence I received at every turn. I usually sat with a small group of people in the front of the cafeteria. Some said it was the popular table, but all I really cared about were Tyler and Anabelle. Now, I was shunned from it, and ended up at the far back of the lunch tables, in the darkness…not even the dorkiest of the nerdy dared come within two tables of me. I was a social pariah. That was now my lot in life.

Tyler talked and joked with his friends – with our friends – as if he didn't just ruin my life. Anabelle was there, too. I understood that. She'd done me a great favor walking with me this morning. It wasn't like she could risk her status by cavorting with me during school. Before school was one thing, but if she sat with me at lunch, it would be a cardinal sin. She would be shunned, forever, just like me – maybe, worse than me. After all, I was a magic user, but she would be a traitor.

I wanted to look away, but I couldn't stop staring at Tyler. He made a joke, and the rest of the table laughed at it. Everybody except Anabelle. She wasn't pleased at all. In fact, she turned up her lip, disgusted by what she'd just heard, picked up her tray, and walked toward me.

"Hey," she said after traversing the cafeteria. "Can I sit here?"

"Are you sure?" I replied.

She looked back at the group. "There is nobody there I want to sit with, not if they talk about you like that."

I pointed to the chair across from me. "Take a seat then. Welcome to the island."

Anabelle slammed her tray down, hot as a pistol. "I can't believe them, you know?"

I took a bite of my soggy peanut butter sandwich. "What did they say?"

"You…don't want to know," Anabelle said with a sigh.

"Funny," I said with a smile. "I thought I asked."

She sighed. "They were just…acting as if they didn't know. As if they were faking their friendship with you this whole time…as if they always knew you were different…they were calling you a…a…well, you know."

I did know. They were calling me a Shiner. In this school, it was the biggest insult you could call someone. Forget being an outcast, being a magic user could get you hurt…or worse.

"They're planning on hurting you, Rosie. Real bad."

"They aren't going to hurt me," I said. "They were just acting big online last night, and they don't want to look like cowards today. They can talk a good game, but they're too scared to try anything to my face."

Anabelle shook her head. "No. I think they're going to try something, Rosie. They were talking. They were saying they were gonna make you pay for lying to them…they sounded like they were gonna take it out of your hide."

I chuckled. "Let them try. The lot of them couldn't fight their way out of a paper bag."

Tyler turned to me, and I saw the rage behind his perfect green eyes. I hid it from Anabelle, but I was scared. I feared what he and his friends could do to me…if they tried.

CHAPTER FIVE

I wish the rest of the day had disappeared in a blur, but that would have meant something good happening to me. It would mean that I could at least forget about last night for more than a few fleeting moments…it would have meant that time was at least on my side.

But nothing was on my side, and nobody was on my side…except for Mama and Anabelle. The rest of the day was a slow, plodding, disastrous nightmare. I was called down to the nurse's office for an examination, and the police interviewed me about whether I was a magic user. Luckily, in both instances, they turned up nothing. If I could avoid the RMP hunting me down because of a rumor, I felt like I might not be completely screwed for the rest of my life.

Fortunately, even though Tyler caused quite a stir online, he didn't have any proof, and he was too stupid to fake any, so it was my word against his, and since I had no history of being "odd" in any other way, both the medical office and the police let me off with a stern warning about telling the truth.

Of course, they didn't believe me either, and their tone of the voices told me that loud and clear. However, since they couldn't prove anything, there was nothing they could do about it except file it away in their notes that I was a person of interest…one to be watched.

I would likely be watched every day for the rest of my life, just in case I was lying. From now on, I always had to be on my best behavior. It's incredible how easy it was for one lie to ruin a life, and how quickly it changed everything. Now, every day of my life, and every choice I made from here on out, turned on a lie.

The day was so hectic that by the end of it, the last thing I wanted to do was deal with Tyler's crap. I hoped maybe he had moved on, but when Anabelle and I exited the building, we saw a gaggle of them surrounding the gate to the street. It was the first time; I worried that my life might be in danger.

"Hey!" Tyler shouted to me, stepping forward from the sea of angry uniforms. "We've been waiting for you."

"What do you want, Tyler?" I shouted from the top of the stairs. "I have to get home."

"Yeah!" he said. "And do what? Work on your potions?"

"No," I shouted. "Homework. But I really wish I was a witch now, so I could teach you to keep your mouth shut."

"You see that!" Tyler said, spinning around. "She just threatened me! Did you see that?"

"I got it on camera!" One of Tyler's sycophants screamed from the crowd.

"Me too!" screamed another in a high-pitched voice.

"You'll notice then," Anabelle said, moving in front of me. "That she said wish. Not that she would, or could."

"Yeah," Tyler replied. "We can edit that out. I'm taking you down, freak."

Tyler took a rock out of his pocket and chucked it at me. The rest of his lackeys followed suit, and soon enough there was a hail of rocks falling around me.

"Stone the witch!" They all shouted. "Stone the witch! Stone the witch!"

I pulled Anabelle by the arm and ran back inside the building. The rocks peppered the door like rain as the violent group advanced up the stairs.

"Stone the witch! Stone the witch!" They screamed as Anabelle pulled the mop out of a nearby janitor's bucket and barred the door.

"That won't stop them for long," she said. "But at least it's something."

"What are they doing?" I asked. "Are they serious?"

Anabelle peered out the window. "They look serious. Come on."

Anabelle grabbed my hand and pulled me down the hall. The pounding on the door echoed through the halls as the horde slammed up against it.

I wanted to think that somebody would stop them. I wanted to think that maybe, just maybe, they would be punished. But in Ambrosia nobody got arrested for attacking magic users. No, only the magic users got arrested if they fought back.

And that's when it hit me. "They're trying to get me to fight back."

"And use your powers," Anabelle added. "Well, if you had powers. By the way, I really don't care if you do or not."

"I don't have powers!"

"Alright!" Anabelle shouted. "But if you did, this would be a pretty good time to use them."

We turned a corner down another corridor of the school. At the end of the hallway was a door to the back of the school. We rushed toward it and slammed it open. Behind the door was a gate covered in brambles and thatch. The gate connected to a high metal fence which stretched around the campus.

We normally used the back door during fire drills, and only the teachers had a key to the gate behind it. Luckily, everybody had a key if they could climb. It was impossible to climb up the gate from the outside, but craggily rocks from a pre-war stone wall littered the ground on the inside of the gate, which made scaling it easy.

I climbed onto the rocks and hopped over the fence to the other side. In another moment, Anabelle joined me. The back door flung open, and a gaggle of violent jerks I once called my friends streamed outside.

"They must've gone over the fence!" Tyler screamed.

Across the street, a bus pulled up. It would lead us away from the school, but also from my home. I didn't care. I needed to get away from Tyler until calmer heads prevailed if they ever did.

"Come on!" I shouted to Anabelle as I crossed the street.

Cars honked as they screeched to a stop in front of us. A cab nearly ran me over as I slammed on its hood.

"We're walking here!" Anabelle shouted as we sprinted across the street.

I waved my hand to the bus driver as I raced toward the curb. "Wait! Wait!"

The bus driver turned her head just in time to see me flailing at her across the street. The door opened, and I ran inside with Anabelle tight on my heels.

"You're lucky," the driver said as she looked at my school id. "One more second and I would have been gone."

I looked at the gang of my old friends who now wanted to hurt me, and it was hard to feel lucky in any way.

"Thanks," I said as I took a seat a few rows behind the driver.

*

We rode for an hour until the line ended and the driver forced us off. A magic user branded with the Air symbol got off with us and crossed the street, waiting for a return trip.

We were at the edge of Ambrosia. If Anabelle and I wanted to run any further, we would have to climb up onto the A-6 highway bound for Segovia. Even though I wanted nothing more than to keep going, eventually I needed to make my way back home. Mama would be worried. However, that didn't make the idea of turning around any more palatable.

"There should be another a return bus any minute," Anabelle said to me.

I sat on the cool sidewalk and laid my cheek on my knees. "I don't want to go back."

"Yeah?" Anabelle said. "You just want to keep going? We could do that. I hear Avila is very nice this time of year."

"No," I said, shaking my head. "I don't want to do that, either."

Anabelle plopped down next to me. "So, we're just gonna live here now? At this spot, next to the highway, like hobos?"

"I don't know," I replied sullenly. "Maybe."

"We'll need some tents. It seems like hobos have tents, most of them anyway."

"I think that's just the classy hobos," I offered, smiling despite myself.

"And you don't think we can be classy?" Anabelle replied. "I'm super classy."

"Maybe you are," I said, burying my head in my knees. "I'm not though."

Anabelle shook her head. "No. No, you're not. But I'll let you sleep in my tent anyway."

"To get a tent, we'll have to leave this spot, and I don't want to leave this spot. This exact spot right here."

"What about when you have to pee?" Anabelle asked, turning up her nose. "You just gonna sit in a puddle of your urine forever?"

"I'll just…stop peeing, I guess."

"And drinking water, too?"

"If that's what it takes."

"Makes sense. I think you'll die though. Eventually. From dehydration."

"We all die from something, sometime."

"Well, yeah. That is technically correct, so I like the sentiment. But like, I would rather you not die in two days."

"You would be the only one."

"Not true," Anabelle replied. "What about your mother?"

"Fine. Two people."

Anabelle put her hand on my knee. "Your death would suck…for me."

I slowly nodded my head, as I turned to face her. "And this is all about you, isn't it?"

"Well it sure isn't about you," she replied with a smile. "I don't know if you realized this, but I got chased out of school today. I've been on the run for over an hour. I'm scared of going back home. Tyler and his friends might stake out my house, waiting to hurt me or my family."

I let my knees go, and they dropped toward the sidewalk. "I know what you're doing."

"I'm not making a subtle point." Anabelle looked down at her watch. "If we catch the next bus, we'll be home by five, and your mom doesn't even have to know we tried to run away today."

The bus screeched to a stop on the other side of the street. The magic user boarded it. "Fine."

*

On the way back downtown, I noticed that I was being watched by an older, bearded, magic user on the back of the bus, with three red wisps of air branded on his dirty jacket.

He was the same one who had ridden the bus with us on our way out of downtown Ambrosia. I hadn't noticed him until the end of the line when he was the only one left to get off with us. Then, when the new bus came to take us the other direction, he was the only other one to get on, sitting in the back row of the bus, staring right at me.

Admittedly, magic users often rode the bus all day for wont of things to do. Their unemployment rate was astronomical, and the bus was a safer place to spend the day than most ghettos, and if you were homeless then at least it provided you some shelter.

It was illegal, of course, to stay on the bus all day, but most bus drivers didn't care, at least not enough to kick somebody off unless it was really crowded.

I tried to brush off the magic user's gaze. I didn't want to seem paranoid. After all, why would anybody be staring at me? *Was he dangerous?* Probably not. Besides, if he were looking to harm us, then it would have been easy to do as we sat on the edge of town. However, the longer he stared, the more uneasy I felt at his attention.

"Can you stop looking at us?" Anabelle said as if she could read my thoughts.

"Free country," the man replied with a gruff, low, gravelly voice.

"It most certainly is not," Anabelle replied. "It is anything but a free country."

"You're right," he replied in an accent that was distinctly American. "Then, I guess I'll just say, no."

"It's really creepy," I said. "You're creeping us out."

"You look like your father. You know that?" the man replied as he stood up and took a step toward us.

"How do you know my father?" I replied. "I don't even know my father."

"You look a little like your mother, too," the man continued as if I didn't just ask him a direct question. "But you look like the spitting image of your father."

Anabelle stood up as the man stepped down from the area designated for magic users and into the space for Normals.

"You can't be down here," Anabelle said, choking back her fear. "Unless you're getting off at the next stop. Magic users can't be down here."

"She's down here," the man replied.

Anabelle quivered in fear as the man walked toward us. "I don't know what you heard, but she's supposed to be down here."

The man smiled. "It ain't about what I heard. It's about what I saw."

I pulled myself to my feet. "What did you see?"

The man chuckled. "Everything. And you have a world of trouble coming for you, girly. Cuz there are cameras all over the ghettos? And you know what? They saw it, too."

I gulped. "The police already came and interviewed me. Everything is fine."

"The police–" the man said. He tried to take another step forward, but Anabelle pushed him backward.

"You stay where you are, mister," Anabelle said, blocking his path to me.

The man threw up his hands. "Fine, but the police don't know nothing. They wouldn't arrest you unless you were glowing up and down the Plaza de las Cortez."

"We don't call it that anymore, shiner," Anabelle growled.

"I call it that because that's its name. The RMP renamed it, and they are the ones you gotta watch out for. The minute they review that footage of last night, they're coming for you."

The bus jerked to a stop, I grabbed Anabelle and rushed away and down the street, hoping to lose him in the crowd. I didn't want to believe his words, but they struck a deep chord down in my gut.

CHAPTER SIX

"Here's why he can't be right," Anabelle said as we walked down the street between throngs of people working their way in the other direction. "You look nothing like your mom."

"Now, but what about before?" I asked. "When she was younger?"

"I've known you for years, and I've seen pictures of your mom when you were a baby. You look nothing like she did, even back then."

"Maybe he was just being polite," I responded

Anabelle swung me around. "Rosie, he was a homeless Sh–magic user. He doesn't have any reason to be polite."

"Yeah, well he doesn't have any reason to lie, either."

"Nobody ever needs a reason to lie. It's in our blood."

I turned away from her and continued down the street. When I glanced down at my watch, I saw that it was 16:26. We had made it mostly back to the school, but there was a long way to go in the next thirty minutes if I was to be home on time.

"We need to hurry up," I said, pounding my legs faster. "If I'm home late two days in a row, my mom's gonna have an aneurysm."

"With everything that's happened today," Anabelle said, pumping her legs faster. "It's amazing you still care about that."

"About my mom?" I asked, confused. "I made her a promise, Anabelle. You don't break your promises."

Anabelle picked up her pace to catch up to me. "I'm coming. I'm coming."

*

I didn't have to see the RMPs at my door before my gut dropped to the ground. All I had to do was I hear them. I heard them screaming down the alleyway when I was half a block away from the alley. When I turned the corner, a Goliath blocked my path forward. I had never seen one in person. It was larger than I would have ever imagined, scalded with battle scars up and down either side of its chassis. It dominated the alleyway, pointing two gigantic guns down the alley toward my face. Its driver sat inside the cockpit of the mech, steel-faced and dead-eyed.

I just about peed myself right then and there, but I held it together as my knees knocked together. Maybe they weren't there for me. Maybe they were there for somebody else. After all, it wasn't like I was the only person who lived in that alley. Anabelle lived there, too, or maybe they were just looking for a rogue magic user who escaped the ghettos.

"What are you waiting for?" Anabelle said, slamming into my back.

"The Goliath," I said, pointing to the giant mech dominating my vision. "It's pointing really big guns right at me. Don't you see it?"

Anabelle waved it off. "Yeah, but they're not for you. So why are you nervous anyway?"

"Because it's pointing two guns at me, two really big guns."

Anabelle pulled me forward toward the giant suit. I wanted to turn and run, but Anabelle had something I never did…confidence. She had the confidence that only beauty could bring, and the confidence that only innocence could maintain.

Besides, they weren't after her. No, they wanted me. And even though it sounded crazy on the outside, that didn't stop the fact that the military was in my alley.

"Halt!" A distorted voice came from the mech. "State your business."

"Um, I want to go home," Anabelle said. "I live down this alley."

"Are you…Roselyn Light?" the soldier inside the mech asked.

Anabelle's face went wide. "No. I'm Anabelle Donovan. I live five doors from Roselyn. Is she in trouble?"

"That is no concern of—"

Just then the television on the side of our alley flashed with my face. The crawl under the image read *Wanted for Questioning: Roselyn Light.*

The mech driver saw the image and his eyes went wide when he noticed me hiding behind Anabelle's bony shoulder.

"You!" The mech driver shouted.

The Goliath let out a piercing screech throughout the alley, and a half dozen RMPs officers with submachine guns invaded the alley from every direction.

"Halt!" One screamed. "Roselyn Light. You are under arrest for the unauthorized use of magic, concealment of magical powers, falsifying documents, and destruction of city property. Place your hands on your head and come with us."

I looked at Anabelle with fear in my eyes. I didn't know what to do other than follow their instructions, knowing I would never see her again; that I might never see the outside of a jail cell again.

"Do not make me tell you again," the RMP officer shouted. "We will fire if you even try to shine. Make this easy on yourself."

I started to raise my hands. Then, I felt a whoosh of air, and an arm grabs me around the waist. Before I knew what was happening, I was airborne, twenty, thirty, fifty feet into the air. Gunfire broke out below, and I landed at the top of a building. In another moment, I was in the air again, leaping toward another building. And another. And another.

Behind me, the Goliath rose into the air and blasted the jets in its arms and legs toward me. I looked up at my savior, and only saw the grizzled side of a beard. Then, I heard a scream. I looked over and saw Anabelle, held tight under the other arm of the bearded man. I finally recognized my savior as the homeless man from the bus.

"Let me go!" Anabelle shouted, but there was no response from the man, except to fly higher.

We jerked to a stop in midair, and the Goliath flew past us. We dive-bombed toward the ground, and I was sure we would die. We seemed to be aiming for an open sewer grate. It was no bigger than a dog, and we were flying toward it at full speed.

"We're going to diiiie!" I screamed and tucked my head into the homeless man's shoulder.

In a moment, we were through the grate. The man leveled off and flew through the darkness of the sewer, darting left and right until we hovered to a stop, and the homeless man let us go.

"What are you doing?!" Anabelle said. "You have no right!"

"I have every right to help magical people," the man said. "That's my duty!"

"I'm not magical!" I shouted. "If I were, I would know it by now."

The man looked down at his watch. He clicked a button on the side and the time lit up. 17:04.

"Just wait. It won't be long."

"That's stupid—"

Then, I saw the blue glow on the walls of the sewer. All around me, the water rose into the air. My hands flew from my sides to meet it, and then suddenly, my left cheek burned brightly, there was a flash of light, and it was over. Blackness surrounded us again.

"What…what happened," I asked, struggling to see in the darkness after the flash of light.

"I told you," the man said. "You are magical, and I am sworn to protect you."

"Who are you?" Anabelle asked.

"My name is Tibor. I am a pledged member of the Order of the Tuppins. We are sworn to protect the magical, no matter where they are."

"And you just happen to also be homeless?"

"I conceal myself to go better wherever I am needed. Once, we were a storied and noble profession. There were thousands of us, but our numbers have dwindled. So, we go where we are needed most. And I was needed here."

"To protect one little girl?" Anabelle scoffed. "Sorry, Rosie."

"No," I asked. "That's a great question."

"She's not just one little girl. She is a Dual," Tibor replied.

I crossed my arms, still nearly blind in the darkness. "I'm not going anywhere with you until you tell me how you knew that I was magical? And what's a Dual?"

"I swear. I will tell you when we are safe." The ground thundered above us. "But right now, we are about to be found by the Goliaths. Is that what you want?"

In the darkness, Tibor held out his hand. I reached out to take it, but Anabelle grabbed me. "Don't do this. He's crazy."

"Anabelle, I just glowed. I don't know what's going to happen if I go with him, but I know what will happen if I stay here."

I shook off Anabelle's hand and grabbed Tibor's outstretched arm. He turned to the tunnel, ready to take off again.

"Wait!" Anabelle shouted. "Where are you taking her?"

"It's better if you don't know," Tibor said. "If you did, then you would be in danger, and so would everybody that you love."

I felt Anabelle grab onto my other hand. "Well, I love Rosie more than my own family, and she's in danger right now, so I'm coming, too."

"No," I said. "You need to go home and look after my mother."

"Your mother will be fine, but I'm not letting you go off with a random bum, alone."

"If you come with us," Tibor warned, the ground shaking loudly above him. "You will be hunted every day of your life."

Anabelle squeezed my hand tighter. "I made my choice."

It was a touching moment between the two of us that was destroyed when the hot laser of a Goliath blasted through the street and revealed a pair of mechs hovering above us.

"Let's go!" Anabelle shouted.

Tibor grabbed us. In a moment we were speeding through the tunnel faster than I thought possible, and faster than was safe. Behind us RMPs hopped into the sewer, firing their machine guns into the tunnel after us.

"Hold on!" Tibor shouted.

A Goliath crashed through the tunnel in front of us, landing just as Tibor weaved to avoid it. The Goliath fired a laser that cut through the sewer, collapsing the street ahead of us and sending a taxi crashing down into the water.

"Don't destroy the city!" an RMP screamed from behind the Goliath.

Tibor turned upwards into the hole formed by the laser and flew into the sky. Two mechs blasted off into the air behind us, firing lasers that Tibor deftly ducked.

"Fire back!" Tibor shouted.

"I can't!" I replied.

"Yes, you can! That flash means you can control the Light! Breathe, calm yourself, and fire at those mechs, or we're not getting far!"

I closed my eyes and tried to concentrate, but I had no idea what I was doing. I thought about Mama, and home, and how I should have just gone home yesterday and taken the suspension. Now, I would never see home again. Now,

I would never see anybody I loved again. Instead of focusing, I began to cry.

"No crying!" Anabelle said. "Shooting!"

"I can't–" I blubbered as a laser shot across my nose and singed Anabelle's shoulder.

"AHHHH!" She shouted, collapsing on Tibor's shoulder.

"Anabelle!"

And like that, my right cheek began to glow. I flung my arms out, and the tears from my eyes shot out from my face like bullets, turning into ice as they broke through the shield of the approaching mechs.

"OWWW!" Anabelle shouted again, and my left cheek glowed. The heat from it scalded my face. I winced in pain as I raised my arms again. This time, fire appeared in front of me like a flamethrower. One of the mechs dodged to avoid it, inadvertently smashing into its partner.

"Hold on!" Tibor shouted.

I closed my fists, and the fire stopped. He dove down to the street again and weaved through oncoming traffic until he turned into an alley and crashed through a closed window of a condemned building. I tumbled inside and slammed into a dusty wall."

"Are you okay?" I shouted to Anabelle as I brushed myself off.

"I think so," she replied, gingerly raising her arm. "It just burns."

"We need to get you to a healer," Tibor said. "Come."

"How are we going to get out of this city?" I asked. "It's crawling with RMPs, and the sky is full of mechs."

"Madrid had a long and storied history of magical resistance, girlie. This is a stop on the underground, which led fighters into and out of the city after the War. Trust me, and we'll be fine."

It was hard to trust a man who I just met, but he did just save my life a couple of times. So, it was hard not to trust him, as well. Plus, we didn't have many other options.

"I'm with you, whatever you decide," Anabelle said, nursing her burnt arm. "But I think we should ditch the creep and go to a hospital."

"Okay," I replied. "Well, I'm not going back home, and I can't go to a hospital either since they'll be crawling with RMPs looking for me. I guess I'm going with this guy."

"Fabulous," Tibor replied as he led us down the stairs into the basement.

"I wouldn't say that word," Anabelle said. "Ever. Nothing about you, or this, is fabulous."

"You're going to have to watch your friend," Tibor said as the darkness of the basement crept up around us. "The underground doesn't take kindly to Normals."

"Don't worry about us," I said, smiling back at Anabelle. "We have each other's backs."

Tibor went to the corner of the basement and pushed aside an old piano. Underneath, was a latch. When he pulled it, a small wooden panel popped up.

"This tunnel will lead us out of Madrid," he said. "It's very cramped and dark. You'll hate it."

Tibor dropped into the hole and disappeared. Anabelle and I walked up to the entrance of the tunnel.

"After you, I guess," she said to me.

I took one last look at the light. I wondered if I would ever see home again. Then, I descended into the hole and disappeared into darkness.

CHAPTER SEVEN

"When are we gonna be safe?" I asked after several hours spent crawling through the tiny tunnel. "Cuz I have so many questions."

"Just stay calm," Tibor replied. "We'll be there soon."

"I am calm," I replied.

I wasn't calm. I looked calm, but, in reality, I was freaking out. I couldn't see anything in the darkness. My knees ached. My back ached. I felt like screaming with every step we took. Anabelle hyperventilated behind me, so she wasn't doing much better than me. I had to keep it together for her sake, and mine.

"Once we reach the other side of this tunnel," Tibor replied from in front of us. "Then, I will explain everything."

"Will it be worth it?" Anabelle asked from behind me. She'd been wincing in pain from her injured arm since we started through the tunnel.

"Excuse me?" Tibor asked.

"Will all this work and effort be worth it?" Anabelle replied. "Will we actually understand what is going on, or are you just going to fill us with more questions than answers?"

"I don't know if it will be worth it," Tibor replied. "But it will be the truth."

"That's better than I usually get," Anabelle sighed, wincing again at the pain in her arm.

I heard a loud thump in front of me and ran into Tibor as he stopped, and then Anabelle ran into me.

"Ow!" I shouted.

"Sorry," Anabelle replied. "I can't see anything in here."

"We're here," Tibor said. "Be on your best behavior."

"We just crawled through a tunnel for hours," I replied. "I think good behavior is out of the question."

"Yeah," Anabelle added. "We stink, and we're cranky. Get used to it."

Tibor pounded on the door three times. "Just do your best to be polite. Eugenia holds the key to your safety. I hope she's home."

"Or what?" I asked.

"Or we're stuck here…until she gets home."

"Fabulous," Anabelle added.

"Don't use that word," I said, chuckling. "Ever."

After a minute of silence, something moved on the other side of the door. It sounded like a couch scratching across a hardwood floor as a muffled voice called out to us.

Tibor knocked twice, then once, then four times, before slamming his palm on the door and rapping each of his fingers in turn.

"By the Order of the Tuppins, I request entry," he said.

Another moment of silence, and then the wooden latch popped open. Light flooded into the tunnel as Tibor crawled up through the open hole in the floor. He reached his hand back down. I grabbed it and pulled myself up.

At first glance, I was reminded of Bilbo's house in Lord of the Rings. Everything was wooden and meticulously made. All the arches were rounded, and a roaring fire crackled along one wall. Along another sat a long writing desk covered in paper. Nowhere in the room was there a television or modern convenience of any kind.

"Good morrow!" A hunched woman with wild gray hair screeched as she wrapped her arms around Tibor. "You look well, my friend."

"Thank you, Eugenia," Tibor replied. "I wish I came under better circumstances."

"Hush now. There are no good circumstances to use a musty old tunnel. Besides, without strife, we would never see each other."

Tibor gave two more pats to Eugenia's back and then released her. As she let go, puffs of tunnel dirt plumed off Tibor's jacket.

"And who is this?" Eugenia asked, pointing to me.

"This," Tibor replied. "Is Roselyn Light. She was Suppressed. Just found her powers today."

"Tsk tsk tsk," Eugenia said, shaking her head. "A pity that."

"What does Suppressed mean?"

Eugenia placed her hand on the small of my back. "Yes, yes. There is time for an explanation later, but first, a spot of tea and a shower, yes?"

"I don't really want tea," I replied.

"Hey!" Anabelle shouted from inside the cellar. "Can somebody give me a hand?"

Tibor reached inside the hole and pulled Anabelle up by her uninjured arm, while Eugenia pushed me into the other room.

*

"You'll have to excuse the mess," Eugenia said, pouring tea for the three of us. "I haven't had visitors in some time."

Moonlight shone through the small windows on either side of the room. We traveled through the rest of the day and deep into the evening, which explained why I was so tired.

Eugenia's dining room was, for lack of a better word, cozy. The dining room table was barely big enough to fit Tibor, Anabelle, and I without us banging knees under the table. Still, Tibor looked quite content sitting and relaxing, as if this was the most normal thing in the world. Anabelle and I, on the other hand, looked as haggard as Eugenia.

"Okay," I finally said when Eugenia brought over the tea. "We're safe. Now spill it, Tibor. I want to know everything."

Tibor held up his finger. "In a minute. You should always take a moment to enjoy the small victories."

"No!" Anabelle shouted. Her voice boomed through the small room. "No more waiting. Tell us now. Right now. What is going on here!?"

Tibor took a sip of his tea. "Very well. I suppose we should start at the beginning."

"Please no," I said. "Just get to the good stuff."

Tibor and Eugenia shared an eye roll that clearly meant "kids these days."

"How much do you know about what happened to magic users after the war?" Eugenia asked.

"Same as everybody, I guess," I replied. "They were rounded up and placed in ghettos around Europe."

"Hunted is more like it," Tibor replied. "Normals always outnumbered us a thousand to one, but we had the superior power to keep the peace with them. However, the war forced Normals to innovate, and they came up with firepower capable of beating us back."

"Once Normals had the firepower to take us down…they did."

"Hitler, Mussolini, and Franco…they were awful men…and their war was a tragedy…but they saw what would happen if we let the Normals continue to innovate. Their words…they spoke to our pain. Regrettable, of course, in hindsight."

"It should have been regrettable at the time, too,"

"It was," Tibor replied. "Some of us fought against them, you know. That never makes the history books, though."

"It's true. We didn't all agree with them," Eugenia replied. "Not all of us. Most of us just wanted peace. Still, we were all punished for their crimes. What they don't tell you is, there were a lot of Normals fighting alongside magic users, and yet, they were spared."

"And you're bitter about it?" Anabelle said, drinking her tea.

"Not bitter," Eugenia said. "It's just a fact that happened; one nobody talks about. And after the war, suddenly, we lost everything. Our jobs, our status, our money. We were penniless. I'm not saying that Normals used the pretense of war to steal all our wealth, but I'm saying that is what ended up happening."

"That's horrible," Anabelle said. "I never knew that."

"Sure, it's horrible, and this is fascinating. However, I just crawled through a tunnel for hours, and this isn't history class," I said. "Where do I fit into this?"

"We're getting there," Tibor replied. "Haven't you ever heard about constructing a narrative?"

"Haven't you ever heard of…bored to tears?" Anabelle replied, taking another sip of tea.

"Fine," Tibor continued, grumpily. "After the war, those who could flee Europe did. But most of us couldn't; most of us had to figure out how to live in the new world order, with Britain and the US on top, and the rest of us below them."

"Far below them," Eugenia added. "And magic users at the bottom."

"Some people didn't like that," Tibor said. "As you can imagine."

"No," I said. "I imagine not."

"They were determined to get ahead, or at least, have their children get ahead."

"This is where you come in, dearie," Eugenia said. "People will do anything to give their children a normal life. They lied, they cheated, they forged papers…"

Tibor bit his lip in anger. "But the government eventually caught onto all of it, because sooner or later the children got the Glow, and families couldn't hide it anymore."

"The only way they could give their children a normal life, then…" Eugenia said, "was to suppress their powers…for as long as they could."

I looked down at my hands. "And that…is what happened to me?"

Tibor nodded. "Yes. You were suppressed, for your own good, of course. You were given special food, and kept inside a house full of runes and enchantments, to prevent you from realizing your power."

"Those stupid eggs. I knew something was wrong with them."

"Yes," Eugenia said. "Eggs from a magical hen are one of the few things that could suppress your powers."

"Is that why I had to be home by 5 pm every night?" I asked hurriedly.

Tibor nodded. "It gets harder with each passing year to suppress somebody's powers, as they build and build, wanting to burst forth. Soon, you would have needed to be home by 4 pm, and then eventually homeschooled, until your 18th birthday, when you would have learned the truth."

"And by then she would be an adult," Anabelle said. "Fascinating. So, you and Tyler were both right, in a way."

I nodded, taking a sip of my tea. It was sweet and succulent. More importantly, it eased the butterflies floating around in my stomach, which made me want to vomit.

"Yes," I said. "It seems that way."

"That's not all," Tibor said.

"Oh no?" Anabelle said. "Good. This is just getting good."

Tibor turned to me. "Your mother…she wasn't your mother…she was a way nurse. Her job was to look after you until you turned eighteen, then help you control your powers and hide them from society so you could live a normal life."

"She…" I stuttered. "Wasn't my mother?"

"I'm afraid not, dearie," Eugenia chimed in after a big swig of tea. "Your parents, all parents, were placed on the registry after the war. There was no way to raise you without suspicion, so your parents found a surrogate. That is how Suppressing works."

"How many…how many children are being suppressed?" I asked, scared to know the answer.

"Tens of thousands across the world," Tibor said. "We try to help them when we can. Personally, I hate the idea. Hiding from yourself. Trying to fool the government. Lying. But…I am not a parent, and I have no right to criticize."

Anabelle grabbed my hand. "Are you okay? You look a little green."

I nodded. "Yes, is…" I turned to Eugenia. "Is there a shower…and a bed? I need to process this…alone."

Eugenia pushed away from the table. "Of course, dearie. Follow me."

I pulled away from Anabelle and stood up. Everything I knew about my life was a lie, and I didn't know how to parse everything I just learned. All I could do was take a shower and sleep, hoping that when I woke up, this would all be a bad dream.

*

There was no cure for depression like a hot shower. I let the warm water fall over me, and for a moment, I forgot that I had left my home and everything I knew. I forgot that my Mama wasn't my Mama, and whoever she was, she'd drugged me since I was a child to make sure I didn't grow up with powers.

The funny thing was, I'd wanted to have magical powers for my whole life. I thought it would cure all my problems, but instead, it just made them worse. So much worse.

After my shower, I wiped my hand across the mirror and stared at my face in it. My cheeks weren't glowing. For that moment, I was just a normal human and maybe I could go home and see Mama. Maybe I could go back to school…but of course, none of that was true.

I was forever banished from that world; the world I once knew. Worse, everybody thought I'd lied to them, and now the RMP was after me with everything in their arsenal.

Why were they after me though? I was just another magic user, right? They didn't go after any other magic user with this much force. *Why was I different?*

There was a knock on the door. "Are you done?" Anabelle shouted from the other side. "I'm gross, and I want to get clean."

I opened the door. "Sorry. I was just–"

"It's okay," Anabelle said. "I get it. I'm still getting used to it as well."

Anabelle was wrapped in a towel, and I noticed that her bare arm wasn't burned anymore. "They fixed your arm!"

Anabelle nodded, looking down at it. "Yeah, Eugenia glowed and pressed her hands against my arm. After that, the wound just…vanished. It was amazing, actually. I thought I would have a scar. Maybe magic isn't so bad after all?"

"Maybe not," I replied.

"Anyway, time to shower," Anabelle said. "I'll see you in a minute."

"Hey," I said as Anabelle walked into the bathroom. "Thank you."

"For what?"

"I know you don't care for magic users. I know you hate them…thank you for not hating me."

"I could never hate you, Rosie. I love you. You're my best friend. Nothing can change that. Besides, now that I know a couple of magic users…well, let's just say my views are evolving."

I nodded. "Still, I'm sorry about this."

"I made my choice. I don't regret it."

"Yet. But you still might."

She nodded. "Maybe, but I don't right now."

"What about your family?" I said. "Aren't you worried about what will happen to them?"

She shook her head. "They'll be fine. They…aren't even here. They went to Bora Bora or something."

"Without you?"

"Like they always do. And Tara's away at school. Nobody needs me there. They won't even notice I'm gone."

I placed my hand on Anabelle's shaking fingers. "I'm glad you're here."

She smiled. "That's why I am."

"Still, thank you," I said.

Annabelle didn't respond. There was no need. She didn't have to say anything. Her being with me was all that I needed to know about her.

I walked down the hall to a room where Eugenia brought me to change. Inside was a simple pair of jeans and a black t-shirt, along with new socks and a pair of running shoes. She guaranteed me they would fit.

"How do you know?" I asked.

"Magic," she replied, smiling proudly.

I put the pants on and immediately noticed they were three sizes too big. I was a small girl, and the pants were made for somebody much larger than me. I was about to take them off, or at least try to find a belt, when the pants cinched tight on their own, shrinking to fit me perfectly.

I threw on the shirt, and it did the same thing, as did the socks and the shoes. Magic, it seemed, could be used to make clothing fit perfectly. I didn't understand why everybody wouldn't want that, except for clothing designers, of course.

I left the room and walked downstairs. When I was halfway down the steps, I heard yelling from the first floor.

"I won't let a Normal go to Toledo, Tibor!" Eugenia shouted. "It's against everything we stand for."

"If you don't help us, Anabelle's going to die, or worse. They'll torture her for the rest of her life. Then, she'll wish she was dead."

"You shouldn't have brought her here. That's your fault. Who knows what damage you brought onto us all?"

"She insisted!"

"Then you should have insisted harder!"

"She's just a kid," Tibor shouted. "And she risked everything to help her friend."

"Then she risked everything…for nothing, I'm afraid."

I stomped down the stairs, listening to them the whole way, as they bickered with each other.

"Rosie is a Dual, Eugenia," Tibor said. "You know what that means."

"It means she's cursed to hide for the rest of her life."

"What is a Dual, and why is being one so bad?" I interrupted.

Tibor and Eugenia both nearly jumped out of their skins at the sight of me. I think for a moment, they had forgotten I existed, even as they argued about my fate.

"How did you—"

"We can hear you, you know?" I replied. "These floorboards are thin."

"How much did you hear?" Tibor eventually said.

"Everything," I replied. "I'll bet Anabelle did, too. You know she gave up her freedom to come here and help me, right?"

"I didn't ask her to do that," Tibor replied.

"And it is against the rules," Eugenia added. "To bring any non-magical person to Toledo."

"Yeah? And so what about the rules?" I replied. "It seems like the rules never did any of you any good before, and now you're treating Anabelle like Normals treat you. How is that fair?"

"It's just…our way," Eugenia said.

"Then it's time for your way to change, cuz they're stupid."

Eugenia stood. "They'll never let you into the hallowed walls with her."

"Let me worry about that," I said. "Now, tell me what's so hard about being a Dual. I want to know, and know now—"

The house rocked back and forth as an explosion lit up its roof. Another blast sent another part of the roof careening onto the floor.

"What's happening?" Eugenia shouted.

"We know you are harboring a fugitive," A megaphone boomed from outside. "Give us the Shiner, and we will let you live."

"What did you do??" Eugenia screamed, pointing to Anabelle stumbling down the stairs. "What did you tell them?"

"What?" Anabelle shouted. "Nothing. Why are you accusing me?"

"I've helped hundreds of magic users over the years, and this is the first time I've been found out. And it's the first time I let a Normal into my life. Is that a coincidence? No!"

A small mountain lit on Eugenia's cheeks, and the walls of the house rumbled. "I built this house with my bare hands, and I won't lose it today. Not to the likes of you."

"Eugenia!" Tibor shouted. "Give me the coordinates. Let the Tuppins deal with her. You have to save yourself."

"I will not betray the location of Toledo to a Normal."

"Then betray it to me!" Tibor shouted.

Eugenia ambled toward Anabelle, who shrieked as she ran down the stairs, fully dressed with sopping wet hair. Another explosion rocked the wall behind her. She tumbled down onto the floor, and Eugenia loomed over her.

"Enough!" Tibor shouted.

"She will pay!" Eugenia said as the walls rumbled around her.

"That is not your choice," Tibor's voice boomed, stepping in front of her. "I order you as a Knight of the Order of the Tuppins, reveal the location now!"

Eugenia grumbled, and the light on her cheek dimmed. She pulled a notepad out of her back pocket and wrote down coordinates.

"This is a mistake," she said.

"Then it is mine to make," Tibor said. "I will pay for it."

"No," Eugenia corrected him. "We will all pay for it."

Eugenia slapped the piece of paper into Tibor's outstretched palm. He looked it over and stuffed it in his pocket.

"We will try to pull as many troops as possible away from the house," Tibor said. "Will you be okay?"

"Please," Eugenia said, her cheek glowing. "I've lived a hundred and ten years. I've fought much worse than these bozos."

Eugenia raised her arms, and the roof of her house ripped off its hinges. She flung her arms forward, and the roof crashed among a group of soldiers.

"You better go," Eugenia said. "I can't hold them off forever."

Tibor nodded. There was a pain in his eyes as he realized this might be the last time he saw his friend. Then, he gathered Anabelle and I up in his arms and took off. As the bombardment of Eugenia's house thundered below us, we disappeared into the night.

CHAPTER EIGHT

"We'll rest here," Tibor said after we landed in a small clearing in the middle of a dense forest. "We should be safe for a moment."

We had been flying for over an hour, and frankly, I was bored of the wind in my face, and of smelling Tibor's musty armpits. I thought flying would be much cooler, but it was uncomfortable and annoying in equal measure.

"What about Eugenia?" I asked when I stepped foot on the ground again.

"Who cares?" Anabelle replied. "She was about to kill me."

"Hey!" Tibor shouted. "She's my friend, and she risks her life to save magical folks. Forgive her if she doesn't have a lot of sympathy for Normals."

"You know," Anabelle started, "I don't like that word. If you can get offended by people calling you Shiners, I can get offended when you call me a Normal?"

"You're right," Tibor sighed. "I'm sorry. I know you are just trying to help your friend, but being here...complicates things."

I sat on the trunk of a downed tree, covering up my cheeks. "Everything is complicated now. She can't possibly make it much more complicated."

"You have no idea," Tibor said, sitting across from me. "The people of Toledo, well, if you think Eugenia was bad, wait until you see them. They will not like her."

"Everybody likes me," Anabelle replied without an ounce of sarcasm. "I'm adorable."

"What is Toledo?" I asked. "You keep talking about it."

"Of course you've never heard of Toledo. They wouldn't talk about it in any book the government feeds you. Before the war…"

"Oh god. Not another history lesson," Anabelle said, plopping down next to me.

"I'm sorry, but that's what this is," Tibor replied, shrugging. "Do you want to know or not?"

"Not really," Anabelle said. "But Rosie is interested so keep going."

Tibor turned his attention back to me. "Before the war, magical users were scattered across Spain, but as the government turned against us, we retreated to the walled city of Toledo, just south of Madrid. It was our last stronghold. It was the last place we could live openly and freely. Magical users all want to go home to Toledo, but none know where it is."

"Why is that?" Anabelle asked, suddenly intrigued.

"It vanished. In the last days of the war, Toledo vanished from the map, never to be seen again. It has since been talked about in whispers, and secret. Those who make it there never come back. Very few know the truth. People like Eugenia, who have been sending magic users on a quest for Toledo since the beginning, are our last link to the city. Even she knows very little, aside from the coordinates she memorized."

"And we'll be safe there?" I asked.

"No. You'll be free there," Tibor replied.

Free. I didn't think I would ever have a chance to be free again. I thought I would be on the run for the rest of my life.

"But I won't," Anabelle said with a frown.

"I don't know what will happen to you," Tibor said. "Nobody without magic has seen Toledo since before it vanished. You are in grave danger if you continue with us. Perhaps, you can return to Ambrosia and tell them you were kidnapped."

"That would mean that Rosie only has you to protect her," Anabelle said. "I'll take my chances."

Tibor smiled. I liked to think that he saw the bravery in Anabelle's eyes. "Get some rest. We have a long way to go, and I'm drained."

Tibor leaned back, and in a moment, was asleep. Anabelle followed close behind him. I couldn't fall asleep that fast. There was too much adrenaline rushing through my veins. I stared up at the stars for a while, realizing that I hadn't seen so many in all my life. I listened to my heart as its beating slowed, and then, I drifted off as well.

*

I was woken suddenly and violently, as Anabelle shook me forcibly until my eyes popped open. "Get up!"

"What!" I shouted, but I immediately saw the problem.

Both of my cheeks were glowing at once. In front of me, water pooled into an orb that sat hovering in front of my eyes. The trees were dry and wilted, but water kept pooling into the orb. A pulsating light throbbed in the center of it.

"What's happening?" I asked.

"I don't know," Anabelle replied. "But you need to stop it. Just stop it!"

Tibor ran toward me. "Rosie. Rosie. Calm your mind."

But I couldn't calm down. My heart raced at a thousand beats a minute, as my mind flew along with it. I ripped the water from the trees faster and faster, collecting it in the orb floating in front of me. The beacon of light at its center pulsed faster and faster beating in time with my heart as the power thrummed through my body.

"This is very dangerous magic you are playing with right now," Tibor said.

"Who is playing?" I replied. "Make it stop! Make it stop!"

My anger and fear made the orb beat faster and faster. The orb of light doubled in size as we watched it. I started to hyperventilate, as my eyes rolled back in my head.

"Rosie! Rosie!"

I struggled to right my head, but Tibor knew that I couldn't stop what I was doing. He placed a crumpled sheet of paper in my hand and closed my fingers around it.

He gripped the ball of water on either side and flew it into the air. As he did, the water spigots stopped while the heat in the center of the ball grew larger and faster, until it shined like a star in the night sky.

"Tibor!" I shouted

I knew what would happen moments before it did, but I could not stop the ball from exploding in midair. The explosion rocked the valley in every direction and lit up the night sky.

"Tibor!" I screamed again.

But he was gone, and I was responsible for it. I was in the woods, without a guide to Toledo, with only the faintest idea what to do. Only Anabelle remained by my side.

"Come on," Anabelle said, pulling me to my feet. "Somebody will have seen that for sure. We have to keep moving."

I didn't want to move. I wanted to cry. I wanted to stay and mourn the loss of my new friend, a friend who saved my life, and who wasn't coming back. The best I could do was carry on, and save myself. Otherwise, everything he did for me would be for nothing. So, I grabbed Anabelle's hand and followed her into the woods.

*

"Oh my god," I screamed. "Oh my god. What do we do now?"

"Breathe," Anabelle replied. "Breathe. Alright. We'll figure it out."

"I just blew up Tibor!" I shouted. "How do I relax after that?"

"I don't know!" Anabelle screamed. "Just do it, okay? You're freaking me out."

"They're going to be on us any minute. And where do we go? What do we do?"

Hey!" Anabelle shouted. "I need you not to freak out, because if you freak out, then I'm going to freak out, and we can't both be freaking out, okay?"

I nodded. "Okay. Okay. You're right."

"Now, think."

I rubbed my temples, trying to calm myself down, and that's when I heard the paper crinkle in my ear. Then, I felt it in my hand. Of course. Of course.

"I got it." I unwrinkled the paper. "It's the coordinates. Do you still have your phone?"

Anabelle nodded. She pulled open Google maps. "Alright. We're in Crying Onion National Park, about 275 kilometers north of Ambrosia."

"Isn't Toledo south of Ambrosia?"

"I guess not anymore," Anabelle replied, as confused as me. "I don't know. I'm just reading the map."

"Whatever," I sighed. "Where are we going?"

"43.2493141, -1.9137893."

Anabelle typed the numbers into her phone, then sighed loudly. "That's over 200 kilometers north of here."

"We're screwed," I said, grinding my teeth.

"You know how we get there?" Anabelle asked.

"How?"

"One step at a time," Anabelle said, smiling.

"Fine," I replied. "Let's go. But I'm not going to like it."

"Me either," Anabelle said, starting up a steep hill in front of us.

I both marveled at and hated her ability to make anything positive. I was quite sure we would be captured, but Anabelle's cheeriness made me think, for a moment at least, that we might be alright, as long as we kept moving forward.

As I took a step up the muddy incline, I heard two Goliaths land in the distance behind us. Soon, they would be on top of us, unless we hurried along.

*

"It should be just up ahead," Anabelle said, after a full night of walking, uphill, toward a mountain pass that would take us down the mountain, where we could hopefully find a road or at least a ranger cabin.

"I'm so tired," I said through gritted teeth. The sun peeked out over the horizon as we marched up the hill.

"Yeah," Anabelle replied. "But we put some good distance between the Goliaths and us during the night. Hopefully, they'll turn back before long if they don't find anything."

"What do you think the chances are of that?" I asked.

"I prefer not to think about the odds. They'll bum you out."

As the trees parted in front of me, the entirety of the Iberian Mountain Range spread before me and disappeared deep into the horizon. We learned about the mountain range in geology class last fall, but all I remembered was that it was big…and long…and people died hiking it every year, people with way more gear than us.

"This is nice, right?" Anabelle said. "I mean, we don't have water or food, but besides that, it's a great view."

She wasn't wrong. The view was lovely. The whole valley lay in front of us, and the sun glistened down on it majestically. After staring out at the countryside for a long while, my eyes tracked down, and I saw the most beautiful site in the whole valley. Towns speckled the forest. Towns which would have people in them, who could help us.

"There!" I shouted. "If we can make it down the mountain, they'll have food, water, maybe a bed."

"And they'll have people," Anabelle said skeptically. "I don't know if that's a good idea."

"Maybe you're right," I replied, sucking in the fresh mountain air. "How much further again?"

Anabelle looked down at her phone. "200 kilometers."

I laughed. "I'm not going to wait 200 kilometers to eat…or drink."

"We can find a stream," Anabelle replied.

"Are you kidding?" I scoffed. "Bears pee in streams."

"I dunno about that," Anabelle crossed her arms and arched her eyebrow. "State your evidence."

I nodded. "Okay. We are in the woods, right?"

"Yes?" Anabelle said, confused.

"And streams are in the woods, right?"

"Sure. I don't think–"

"Then I have one question for you? Does the wild bear pee in the woods? Boom. Logic."

Anabelle sighed. "I am too tired to argue with you. That was stupid though."

"Noted," I said, starting down the mountain. "Now, let's go."

CHAPTER NINE

Walking downhill was much easier than going uphill. We made it to a road in less than an hour. From there, we followed the sinewy path until we saw the outline of a tall, rocky building with a white-washed second floor, and a brown roof which beckoned us toward a little town. As we walked into the village, we passed a sign that read Villanueva de Cameros.

"I'm surprised it still has a Spanish name," I mumbled as we continued past the sign.

"It's probably too small for the RMP to care about. Look, the City Hall sign is in English."

I looked up at the building I saw at the entrance of the town—the one with the white-washed second floor. The side of the builder had a sign that read "City Hall." Next to it sat a little cobblestone police station, with three police cars parked in front. It was kinda cute how few people it took to police such a small town. In Ambrosia, even the smallest police station had dozens of cruisers. Still, no matter how small they were, if even one of the officers recognized us our journey would be short-lived.

Anabelle looked down at her phone. "There's a hostel a couple of blocks north. Looks like it has a restaurant inside. Not very highly rated, but at least it's cheap."

"As long as it's food, I'll be fine."

"Just be careful," Anabelle said as we continued to walk. "It doesn't take a genius to figure out we might end up here. It's not like there are a lot of towns around. So, I'll bet the RMPs will be down here eventually searching for clues about the explosion."

"You worry too much," I said.

"That means a lot, coming from you," she replied.

*

The moment my butt hit the chair of the little restaurant's table, my feet started to ache. I hadn't sat in at least a dozen hours, and during that time we walked over forty kilometers. I was used to walking, or at least I thought so, but the burning in my thighs told me otherwise.

Anabelle pulled out a wad of money from her jeans and placed it on the table in front of us. She started counting it slowly, mumbling under her breath, as if it was normal to walk around with a big wad of cash.

"Where did you get all that money?" I asked.

"Don't get too excited. They're mostly one-pound notes. So, try to eat light."

"I'm sorry," I replied. "I just…can't do that. I haven't eaten since last night. I'm starving."

"I'm not saying to do it," Anabelle said. "I'm just saying try, okay?"

A teenage waiter in a wrinkled shirt sauntered over to us. He was dark and cute, even though his head was too big for his body. His face was covered in patches of stubble, and his curly hair held tight against his head in an afro. "English or Español?"

"English, please," I said, smiling. "Two waters, please."

"Sparkling or still?"

"Still."

"Very good. I'll give you a minute to look over the menus," the waiter said, before walking away.

My throat felt scratched and worn. My bones were weary. I just didn't realize how much until I sat down and had time to relax.

"It's been a while since I've been asked if I spoke Spanish," Anabelle said. "I kind of like it."

"We're not on vacation," I replied, recognizing the giddiness in her eyes. "This isn't a fun adventure."

Anabelle took the napkin in front of her and placed it on her lap. "No, but it is an adventure, and I love a good adventure, you know? I've been so worried about our survival, I haven't enjoyed it for even a minute yet, and that's a pity."

"You really do, don't you? Enjoy it, I mean."

"I can't help it. It's a flaw, and I know it. But I love my flaws."

The waiter came back over with the waters, and I downed mine in one gulp. I went to reach for Anabelle's, but it was already gone.

"Another please," I said.

"Me too," she said.

The waiter placed a basket of bread between us, and I reached for it like a rabid wolf. I stuffed as much bread in my mouth as I could handle, and ordered a platter of meats and cheeses for us to share. When we were done, Anabelle ordered two sandwiches for us to split.

The only other person in the restaurant besides us and the waiter was an old, wrinkled woman with a red eye embroidered on her shirt. It meant she was a Seer. She knew the future and the past. She didn't speak, only looked out at the horizon, as if it held the answers to all of life's questions.

"Is that all?" The waiter asked us, walking back up to the table. "Will there be anything else?

"Maybe," I replied. "Do you have a room available?"

"Let me check," the waiter replied.

"What are you doing?" Anabelle said. "We have to keep moving."

"And we will," I replied. "But right now, we look like two junkies. Nobody is going to pick us up or help us out. We need to clean up, and then we can figure out a ride, okay?"

"Okay," Annabelle replied.

"Good news," the waiter said. "We have a room available."

"We'll take it," Anabelle and I said in unison.

*

I flopped on the bed after my shower, covered in a coarse robe which grated against my skin. The towels were thin, and the water was cold. Still, it felt good to be clean.

"Can I just sleep here forever?" I said, sighing contentedly.

"I think that would not be a good idea if we ever want to get to Toledo," Anabelle replied. She was already dressed and ready to move on, sitting cross-legged on the bed, waiting for me.

"Yeah, but like, do we really have to get there?" I asked. "I mean, this town looks nice."

"I am NOT spending the rest of my life in this town," Anabelle said, holding her phone in the air. "They don't even have good reception here. I got a better signal in the bloody mountains."

A loud banging on the door jolted me to my feet. I scrambled to the bathroom and quickly threw on my clothes, as the rapping on the door continued in earnest.

"Who is it?" Anabelle asked.

"Abierto," a woman's voice said from the other side of the door. "Open."

The voice didn't sound hostile, so when I finished changing Anabelle opened the door. On the other side was the small woman from the restaurant. She beckoned us forward.

"Come," she said.

"We don't really–"

"Come!" the woman said forcibly.

Anabelle and I looked at each other and shrugged. I grabbed the key to the room as we marched forward and down the narrow staircase, behind the old woman. When we got to the bottom of the stars, our waiter stopped us.

"Mama, no!" he shouted.

She just smiled at him, and kept walking, beckoning us forward. She ambled into the restaurant as the waiter held his hands in apology.

"I'm so sorry about this," he continued. "My Mama sometimes doesn't understand that guests want to be left alone."

"It's okay," I said, holding up my hand. "We all have mothers."

Except, I realized, I didn't have a mother. I had a woman who lied about being my mother for years, but I didn't have an actual mother. Suddenly, I was sad. Sadder than I had been since I left home. Since we fled, I'd been angry, scared, lonely, and frightened; but I hadn't been truly sad. Anabelle must have felt my sadness because she put her hand on my shoulder.

"Come on," she said. "Let's see what the old lady wants."

I nodded and moved toward the window, where the old lady once again looked out off into the horizon, in silence. We ambled over and stood next to her.

"What are we looking for?" I asked.

"Wait," she replied.

"How long?" Anabelle asked.

"Wait," she replied, softly.

I turned toward the waiter as if to ask what we were doing, but he just shrugged his shoulders. "This is how she gets. She'll stare off into space for hours sometimes. I try to ignore her when she's like this."

"She's a seer, right?" I asked.

"Yes. She used to be a really good one, too. People would come from miles around to get a reading from her. Her mind, though, isn't what it used to be—"

"Hijo!" The woman screamed.

"Lo siento, Mama," he said contritely to his mother, then he took a step toward me. "Still, it's true."

The woman rose a shaky finger into the sky and pointed it down the road. "Alla. There."

As she pointed toward the road that led back up the mountain, four Humvees barreled down the street toward us. They were black, loud, and topped with machine guns. Two Goliaths flanked them on either side as they pulled into the police station next to city hall.

"Oh my god," I said, as my throat dropped into my stomach. "They're coming for us."

"Watch," she said, staring intently at the trucks. "Watch."

A dozen men piled out of the trucks. Most of them marched inside, but two ran around to the back of the last Humvee and slid a stretcher out of the trunk. The man on it was badly bruised, but I would know him anywhere. It was Tibor. He screamed out as the two men carried his stretcher into the police station.

"It's Tibor!" I shouted, shaking Anabelle's arm. "And he's alive."

"Well that sucks for him," she replied.

"What do you mean? It's great. It means I didn't kill him."

"Yeah, sure, but the government has him now. He'll be lucky if he ever sees the light of day."

"You're right," I replied. "We have to save him!"

"Are you crazy!?" Anabelle squealed. "Those are the same people that are trying to capture us."

"Yeah? And he was trying to save us from them. We owe it to him to do the same."

"We don't owe him anything," Anabelle said, waving her arms in the air. "He told us to save ourselves, and that's what we're doing."

I turned to her. "How Anabelle? We're almost two hundred kilometers from the coordinates he gave us, and we don't know what we'll find there. We have almost no money. We have no skills. The odds we make it to Toledo alone are very slim."

"Toledo!" The old woman said, her eyes wide. "Toledo!"

"That's right," I said. "Do you know it?"

The old woman smiled and disappeared into the store. Her son rubbed his head. "I'm sorry. She…is very old. She hasn't talked to another magic user in a long time."

"I don't know if I would call myself a magic user," I replied.

"She's more like a magic…accident waiting to happen," Anabelle added with a chuckle.

I sighed. "Unfortunately, she's not wrong."

The old woman smacked her lips as she came back with a picture. She held it up to us. It was a picture of a young woman and a young man. They looked to be about sixteen years old, the same age I was now. They were smiling at each other. A walled city, sitting on the edge of a mountain, rose behind them. Behind the wall, rising from a river at the base of the hill, buildings of all sizes and shapes lined jagged, narrow streets carved into the hillside.

"Toledo!" the woman said. "Toledo!"

"This is Toledo?" I asked. "You've been there?"

The woman nodded sweetly. She pointed to the young women. "Es me." She then pointed to the man in the picture, then the waiter. "Y su abuelito."

"That's where we're going," I said. "Do you know where it is?"

The woman shook her head, sadly. "No. Is gone."

"No," Anabelle replied. "It still exists, and that man knows how to get there."

Anabelle pointed back to the police station, surrounded by Goliaths and soldiers. Inside, laid our best hope of getting to Toledo. All we had to do was save him…from the best-equipped military on the planet.

"You're saying that man, in there, knows how to get to Toledo?" The waiter said. "I always thought Mama was just crazy."

"She's not crazy," I replied. "At least not any crazier than us. Our friend's name is Tibor, and he is from the Order of the Tuppins. He is sworn to help me get to Toledo. Can you help me save him?"

The old woman smacked her lips. "Si. Si. Ayundese."

"Well," the waiter said. "I guess we're helping, then. My name is Eduardo. This is my mother, Charro. I suppose since we're all gonna die today, you should at least know our names."

"No dying!" Charro said. "Not today."

And then she sat down, staring at the police station, lost in thought as if the rest of the world ceased to exist.

"Come on," Eduardo said. "She could be like that for a while."

"Where are we going?" Anabelle asked.

"To prepare," Eduardo replied. "When she comes to, she'll have looked at a thousand different options, and I hope one of them will work. We need to be ready when she tells us her plan."

"We'll be ready," I replied.

"One more thing," Eduardo said. "If we are going to help you, I want to know where Toledo is…"

I gulped. "That's not really my information to give."

He nodded. "Well, if you don't give it, then I won't let her help you."

Did it really matter if one more person knew the location of Toledo? Did it matter if I gave it to everybody? After all, right now it was only the stuff of legend.

"Fine," I replied. "What do I care? It's not like I even know this place exists or not. You help me; you can have the coordinates."

Eduardo smiled. "Then you have a deal."

CHAPTER TEN

Charro spent three hours staring out into space, not saying a word before she snapped out of her daze and wrote down an action plan, which Eduardo then translated into English.

"I want you to remember something," he said when he handed the paper to me. "If you follow this, it doesn't mean that the plan will succeed. It just means this plan is the highest likelihood of success. There is no accounting for the free will of people…or their stupidity."

"How many scenarios did she run?" I asked.

I'd found out that Seers don't predict the future. They envisioned thousands of possibilities and could relay the most likely path for success…but that didn't mean you were guaranteed success if you followed their advice. It was still only a guess, but one with a high likelihood to work.

"Enough," he replied. "She could have run more, stayed in there for days if she wanted, but if we wait much longer, your friend won't be around."

It was true. It seemed the RMPs were planning to ship out soon. Two of the Humvees were already gone, along with three of the Goliaths. All that remained were a small detail of four men, and one Goliath. It could have been so much worse, but it was still a massive force, especially for a couple of girls who had rarely been in trouble up until a few days ago.

After getting the plan from Eduardo, I walked up to my room. The first phase of the plan was set to begin in fifteen minutes. Anabelle bought us new, dark clothes, to prepare for our mission with the money she had left. If this didn't work, we would be screwed without any money to reach

Toledo. Of course, if this didn't work, we would likely be arrested and jailed, too.

"I hope we don't die," Anabelle said as we sat on the bed after changing into our new clothes. "It would suck if we died."

"We're not gonna die," I replied. "We'll probably be captured, though."

"Is that better or worse than dying?" Anabelle asked.

"I guess it depends on what happens after you die, huh?" I said, placing my head in my hands.

Anabelle stood. "I guess so. Still, I would rather we did neither."

"Me too," I said, standing with her. "But, it's good to prepare for the worst."

We both took a long sigh and then looked deeply into each other's eyes. There wasn't a lot that needed to be said between us. We had been through so much and a lifetime of friendship flowed between us. She wrapped her arms around me, and I squeezed her tight.

"Love you," she said.

"Love you, too."

My eyes wanted to cry, but I forced them to remain dry. I felt Anabelle tighten her lip, trying to remain strong for me. We tried to bolster each other's confidence and tried to ignore the reality that we probably wouldn't see each other again.

*

For the first phase of our plan, Anabelle and I had to split up. If we both succeeded, then we would see each other again at the end. If not, then whoever remained needed to make their way to safety. If it were only me, then Anabelle would make her way back to Madrid and somehow convince the RMPs she was kidnapped. Whereas, I would carry on to Toledo if she were captured. We promised each other that we wouldn't try to rescue each other, no matter what. We couldn't live with ourselves if one of us died saving the other.

For my part, I was to queue up in the back of the police station behind an old green dumpster and wait for Anabelle to make her move. At exactly 14:47, the Goliath driver would get out of his mech to use the bathroom. His bladder had been full for hours. He'd been promised relief, but nobody ever came to help him. Now, pissed, he couldn't wait anymore without peeing himself.

I looked down at my watch. It was 14:47. Sure enough, the man in the mech suit pushed open his protective bubble and hopped down, grumbling furiously to himself. Now, Anabelle had three minutes to hop into the suit and take off with it. Anabelle found some basic Goliath driving instructions on a very shady website and spent a long time memorizing them to prepare, but we didn't know if it would be enough.

There were no other guards outside the police station, as one Goliath was usually enough to deter any rabble-rousers. So, when Anabelle ran across the street and hopped into the suit, there was nobody to stop her, except a nosy neighbor that was hanging her clothes above me.

"Hey!" I said, pulling a white sock out of my pocket and waving it up at the woman. "I think you dropped this!"

She looked down at me and the sock that was in my hand as Anabelle pulled down the bubble.

"That doesn't look like one of mine," the woman said.

"Oh, well it just fell, and I figured there are no other lines up there, so it must be yours. I guess I'll just throw it away."

"No!" the woman said. "I'll come down. Can you meet me?"

I heard the boosters thrust upwards and turned to see Anabelle shakily pilot the Goliath into the air. I was impressed. Of all the parts of the plan, her flying was the one I worried about the most. After all, it's not like we were trained pilots, and Anabelle only had a limited time to figure out how to fly a complicated mech.

"Oh my god!" I shouted. "That woman just stole that Goliath!"

"Help!!!" The woman shouted from her window, screaming. "Thief!!!"

I ducked back behind the dumpster as the woman focused her attention on the mech. The Goliath driver and all four RMP soldiers left inside ran out of the building.

"Stop!" One of them shouted as they sprinted to their Humvee.

As they did, the door to the police station swung closed, and I slid inside just before it did. Now, I was in the cell block in the back of the police station. Usually, only authorized personnel was allowed with the prisoners, but Charro's plan put me here without any need to see the guards…yet. I couldn't avoid interacting with the guards for the next part of the plan.

There was a commotion in the front of the building, as the RMPs screamed at the police officers to get off their butts and help them. That was part of the plan. The police held the keys to the cells, and I needed them to open the door to Tibor's cage.

All the cages were empty, except for the one at the end of the hallway. Tibor, burned and scarred, laid in the cage, writhing in pain.

"Tibor!" I whispered, walking up to his cage.

He flinched when he saw me. "You aren't here. You aren't real."

"Yes, I am. I'm here to save you."

"Rosie?" He came out of his daze and rose to his feet. "What are you doing here?"

"I told you," I replied. "I'm here to save you. I need you to cause a distraction, so I can get the keys from the guard."

"You're going to get yourself caught. Get out of here."

I shook my head. "Not without you. Cause a scene. Do it now!"

Tibor squinted at me for a moment. Then, he sneered and dropped to the ground, convulsing.

"Help!" he shouted. "Help! Help!"

In the commotion, one of the officers ran into the back room. He saw Tibor convulsing and mumbled worriedly to himself. In his panic, he fumbled with his keys and opened the door to the cage and ran inside.

"Sir!" The officer shouted, screaming at Tibor. "Are you okay?"

I walked forward and tied my sock around the lock to the cell door. Meanwhile, Tibor convulsed more fervently on the floor, arching his back and rolling his eyes back in his head.

By the time I slinked back into the shadows, the officer was on his feet, flustered and scared. He ran out of the cage and slammed it behind him. However, the cage didn't lock, because my sock blocked it. Instead, the cell door slammed back open, and I ran inside.

"Come on," I said to Tibor. "There's not much time."

Tibor wrapped himself around me, and we ambled out of the cell, slowly. Too slowly for my liking, but every step was agony for him. I looked down at my watch. 14:49. We had less than a minute to make it back outside.

"I need you to hurry," I said.

"I can't," he said, wincing in pain.

"I know it hurts, but it's better than being in the cage the rest of your life."

Tibor nodded. He knew the cost if we failed. Not only would he be arrested, but I would be as well. We ambled down the hallway, and I pushed open the door just as the officer came back with a first aid kit. As the door closed behind me, I watched his eyes go wide as he noticed Tibor was gone.

14:51. It would all be over in a few seconds. The RMP's Humvee was gone from the front of the station, as were all but one of the police cars. Eduardo and Charro pulled up in a beat-up, blue Peugeot spouting black smoke from its muffler. They wore bandanas over their faces to hide from the watchful cameras which dotted every corner.

"Let's go!" Eduardo shouted. "We don't have much time!"

I swung open the back seat and threw Tibor inside. He winced as I laid him down roughly. I didn't want to hurt him, but we were on a tight schedule here.

"What are we–" Tibor asked.

"Don't ask questions," I replied, hopping inside. "Go!"

Eduardo peeled out as fast as the little car could handle, just as the officer ran out of the back door and watched us drive away.

"Thank you," I replied.

"Don't mention it," Eduardo replied. "This is the most excitement we've had in years."

Eduardo spun the car around and hopped a curb. Then, he veered down a shallow embankment into the forest.

"We used to go off-roading with my dad; God rest his soul. Hold on."

The car rattled and rocked as it made its way down the small cliff. Eduardo swerved through the trees as we made our way to the bottom. Once at the bottom, Eduardo cut across a short field, before we disappeared into the forest on the other side.

Altogether, it took less than five minutes to free Tibor, but it felt like an eternity.

*

Eduardo finally brought the car to a stop in the middle of a large clearing. We had driven for over an hour through the forest, and I could barely believe that the little car didn't break down yet.

"Now we wait for your friend," Eduardo said. "If she made it."

"She made it," I said, getting out of the car's back seat.

In truth, I said it with more confidence than I felt. Anabelle was resourceful and full of surprises, but to the best of my knowledge, she didn't know how to drive a mech, fly a mech, or evade RMPs for any length of time. God bless her, though, for trying.

She really was a criminal now. Before stealing that Goliath, she was at worst an accomplice. She could claim she was kidnapped and feared for her life. She could claim a lot of things, but after she stole that mech, that all changed. She couldn't go back home. She couldn't have her old life back. She had to come with me, and we had to hope we could start a new life in Toledo.

Eduardo stepped out of the car to wait with me. "What do you think the odds are of her coming back? Seriously, don't lie to me, or yourself."

"If it were anybody but Anabelle, I would say they aren't good, but she has an incredible capacity to surprise me."

"My dad was like that. Sometimes, I still think he's going to walk through the door."

"What happened to him?"

"He…wanted a better life for me. So, he forged all of my papers. When they found out, they arrested him. Mom and I fled Barcelona…ended up here. I never saw him again."

"Is that why you helped us?"

Eduardo nodded. "Least I could do was try to stick it to the RMPs who stole my father from me."

"Plus, you get the coordinates for Toledo," I replied.

"I don't care about that," Eduardo replied, pressing his back against the door of the car. "Mama has been talking about Toledo for most of my life. I want her to see it again, one last time. Personally, I think you are on a wild goose chase, and you've been on it since way before you saved that jacked up dude bleeding all over my back seat. Why did you do it anyway?"

I looked into the back seat of the car. Tibor was asleep, curled up against the door. The side of his face was burnt to a crisp. Dark scars speckled his neck and left arm. I did that to him. I knew I did that to him, and he was arrested because of me, too.

"I owed him," I replied.

"I think you repaid your debt in full, then."

I shook my head. "No. I need to get him to a healer first. Maybe, if they can fix him, we'll be even."

The sound of grinding gears echoed through the forest. The stomping sound of the mech crashing through trees followed it. A spotlight shone through the woods, wobbling as it inched toward us.

With a stumble forward, the mech crashed into the clearing. The bubble surrounding the cockpit illuminated as the mech stood upright. Inside, Anabelle smiled at me. I rushed over to her as the bubble popped open, and Anabelle jumped down from it.

"You're alive!" I shouted. "How can you be alive?"

Anabelle laughed. "You know, it's not that hard to pilot that thing, at least the basics. It probably gets harder to master it, but meatheads can get it, so I figure I can learn, too."

"How did you escape from the Humvees chasing you?"

"I just…flew…They can't fly, Rosie. They're just trucks."

"Fair enough," I laughed. "Well, I'm happy to see you."

She nodded. "It's good to see you, too. How is our boy?"

My smile turned downward. "He doesn't look good. He needs a healer, and quick."

"I know where you can find one," Eduardo said. "For a price."

Anabelle sighed. "What is it? You already have everything we have."

Eduardo pointed to the mech. "I want a ride in that thing."

"You can ride as much as you want," I grumbled. "Once you take us to a healer. Tibor's about to die. We don't have time for fun."

Eduardo nodded. "Fine, but I'm taking a raincheck."

CHAPTER ELEVEN

"You brought him to me just in time," Tibor's healer said from his bedside. Her name was Galena, and she was a third-generation healer. She was short and thin, with strong hands that had cracked skin at the knuckles from dryness and overuse. She was younger than somebody with so much power should be, not much older than Anabelle or me, if at all. "Much longer and he would have been a goner."

Galena rubbed her hands together and placed them on Tibor's face. The plus sign on her cheek glowed, pulsating faster as her hands glowed a deeper yellow, then turned orange, before becoming white. She closed her eyes, and I watched as the crust of scar tissue faded away, slowly.

"This will not be quick," Galena said. "He is very hurt. I must be alone with him to focus."

Eduardo pulled my arm, but I fought to stay. He leaned into my cheek. "Come on. Let her work."

Eduardo pushed open the door to Galena's hut, and I followed him outside. In front of us, the giant Goliath stood guard. Anabelle sat inside the mech, using the controls to turn it side to side with glee.

"I never much cared for science in school," she said. "But this is pretty cool, huh?"

"Pretty cool," I replied. "I've known you too long, so the thought of you with a mech is frightening in oh so many ways."

"I think I figured out how to make it shoot," she said. "Wanna see?"

I smiled. "Yeah, that I want to see."

"Alright," Anabelle replied. "If I pull this lever, the mech arm should go up." Sure enough, with her words, the mech arm rose into the ground. "And if I flip this button," she continued, "The hand should turn into a gun."

I heard a click from the cockpit. With it, the mech's hand retreated into its arm, and a large laser cannon came out of it.

"Looks like it's working," I said.

"This is gonna be awesome," Anabelle said. "See that pile of rocks over there?"

I followed my line of sight from the robot's arm to a pile of boulders a couple of hundred feet away. "I see them."

"I'm going to blow them up now!"

Anabelle flicked a switch and a blue laser shot from the end of her arm, pushing the mech backwards. The laser sliced through the air, through the rocks–which did explode by the way–and up into the air, as Anabelle's Goliath fell backward onto the ground.

"Ow!"

The Goliath's arm flipped from gun to hand, and it pushed itself to its feet with the help of the rockets in its back.

"That has more kick than I thought," Anabelle said, flipping open the cockpit.

"Maybe leave the toy alone for a minute," Eduardo said. "Before we get found out."

"Are you kidding me?" Anabelle said. "I'm doing that again! But next time, less power. Or maybe reverse thrusters to combat the kickback. Or both!"

Eduardo rolled his eyes as he sat down next to the hut in a rickety old lounge chair. I sat across from him in a worn dining room chair. As I pressed my weight down upon it, the cushion sounded as if it would fray and pop out.

"They aren't going to let your friend into Toledo with that thing," Eduardo said. "Not if Mama's stories are even close to being accurate."

"We'll see," I replied. "Anabelle is very persuasive."

Eduardo nodded slowly. "I see that. Stupid too. Getting caught up with this, as a Normal."

"She doesn't like that word."

"Sorry," he said. "I didn't know."

"It's okay," I replied. "I could say the same of you, though. You don't have to be here."

Eduardo snapped his fingers, and a butterfly appeared out of nowhere. On his cheek, a bright square illuminated. He was an illusionist. "Yes, I do."

"Oh, I didn't know."

He looked down at the butterfly, whose wings flapped faster and faster. "I don't use it much, not anymore. There are much more important things to worry about."

Eduardo circled his hands in the air, and the butterfly turned into a cat. It leapt at me. I almost fell out of my seat as the cat jumped through me. It ran toward the woods behind me, disintegrating slowly as it moved further from Eduardo.

"That's amazing," I replied. "Seriously, amazing."

"It's just parlor tricks," Eduardo replied. "I hate it. At least if I was Light or Ground, I could do something useful.

Illusions…they are just for show. I am cursed with useless magic, which can be used for nothing."

I placed my hand on top of his. "It's not nothing. You'll see."

I enjoyed the touch of Eduardo's hand under my own. I almost didn't want to pull it away, but when Galena slid out of her hut, I slid back in my chair toward her.

"How is he?" I said, standing.

"It is hard to say," Galena replied. "He is a fighter, but the damage…it is bad. There is still much work to be done. I will know more later."

"Can I see him?" I replied.

"I still have a lot of work to do before he is ready for visitors," Galena replied. Then, she turned into the hut, disappearing behind the door.

I bit my lip to prevent it from quivering. I was sick of being strong. I hated every minute of being out in the wilderness. More than anything else, I loathed camping. My idea of roughing it was staying at a hotel that didn't have room service

"Come on," Eduardo said, rising from his chair. "Let's go get dinner."

"How are we going to do that?"

Eduardo walked down toward the car where Charro busied herself picking up kindling. They mumbled to each other for a moment, and then Eduardo beckoned me over. I looked up at Anabelle and furrowed my brow, but she only gave me a passing nod, intent on learning her new toy.

*

"You're not going to kill me, right?" I asked as Eduardo led me deeper into the dark woods.

Eduardo hopped down a small ledge. "If I were going to kill you, I would have let the RMPs capture you."

"Sure, sure," I replied, crawling down an embankment. "Unless you get your jollies from doing it yourself."

"That would be quite a story," Eduardo said, pulling a branch from his hair. "But I think there would be easier ways than this."

"Possibly," I replied, ducking under a branch. "But I don't know you very well."

"Relax," Eduardo said. "As long as your best friend has a thousand-ton mech by her side, you're safe around me."

"That's only slightly more reassuring," I said, pushing through a clump of tree branches.

As I did, the forest opened onto a creek which ran off into the horizon. Inside the river, salmon flapped their tails against the current, trying to make their way upstream like idiots.

"Watch out for bears," Eduardo said.

"Bears?" I said, nervously.

Eduardo stepped into the creek. "Yeah, it's salmon season, and bears know it as well as me. They wander along the river and creeks on this mountain all season, looking for a stream with salmon in it. If they catch our scent, they'll come running. You don't want to be here if they do."

Eduardo took off his shirt and threw it to me. Underneath, his muscles rippled and glistened in the evening sun. I thought he was a bit goofy when I first met him, but as he crouched into the stream, I couldn't help but think that Eduardo was kinda hot.

"What am I doing with this?" I asked, holding up his shirt.

"Catching," he replied.

"Excuse me?"

"I'm going to throw you the fish, and you're going to catch them."

"I don't think so."

Eduardo stood upright, hands on his hips. "Do you want to eat, or not?"

I felt my grumbling stomach. I was hungry. Very hungry. "Fine, but be careful. I don't wanna get hit in the face with a fish."

Eduardo laughed, bending down over the rushing creek. "That would be a you problem."

"Until it happens," I replied. "Then it's a *you* problem."

Eduardo shifted his weight from one side of his body to the other. His fingers wiggled as he stood deep in concentration. "The secret to catching fish with your bare hands is that you have to be quick."

Eduardo slammed his hand into the water but came up with nothing. He tried it again, and again. Each time, he caught nothing. The longer it went on, the more I laughed.

"This isn't as easy as it looks!" He said.

I snickered. "No, nor is it anywhere near as impressive."

"Do you have a better idea?"

I thought about it for a minute. I was scared to use my powers again, but I was also stupid hungry. "Get out of the water. I have an idea."

Eduardo stepped out of the water. "Fine. This I gotta see."

I closed my eyes and imagined the water flowing through me. I imagined picking up the current of the river and holding it in my hands, and along with it, a gaggle of fish. I opened my eyes and tossed Eduardo's shirt to him.

"Catch them."

I raised my hands over my head, fresh with the vision of lifting the water in my mind. I felt the cool glow on my right cheek refresh me. My hands rose into the air, and with them, the water rose out of the creek. Underneath the river, salmon flopped around, trying to swim forward unsuccessfully.

"Incredible," Eduardo said, breathlessly.

"Hurry up," I replied. "I can't do this forever."

Eduardo dipped down and scooped the flopping fish into his shirt. As he did, I felt the heat from my left cheek scalding me. I looked up at my hands and saw the fire burning inside of my palms.

"Eduardo!" I shouted. "Move!"

Eduardo turned to me and saw the fire in my hands. His eyes went wide, and he dove out of the way, just as a firebolt shot out of my hands and exploded into the empty creek where he just stood. The water came crashing down, and I fell to the ground.

"I'm so sorry," I said, unable to hold in my tears any more. "I'm so, so sorry."

"You're a Dual," he shouted, scrambling over to me. "I've never met a Dual before."

"I don't even know what that means," I replied. "People keep saying it, but I don't know what I am. Every time I think I have a clue, everything changes."

"I think that's just life," Eduardo said. "But that sounds like it sucks."

"It does," I replied, trying to hold in my tears. "It really does."

I collapsed into his arms and cried. I cried for everything in my life that had gone wrong. I cried for my mother, and Anabelle, and I cried for my powers. The powers that should be a great gift, and were instead an incredible curse.

*

We sat next to the creek for another hour as Eduardo held me in his arms, and I sobbed until I had no tears left in me. Then, I disappeared into his chest until day turned to night. Finally, I pushed away from Eduardo.

"Feel better now?" Eduardo asked.

I shook my head. "No, but at least it's all out there now."

"I have a feeling you have a lot more inside," he replied. "Are you ready to go?"

I nodded. "Yes. That, I'm ready to do."

I was hungry before, but I was starving now. Eduardo led the way back to Galena's hut, lugging the fish we caught behind him. By the time we got back, Charro had started a fire for the fish.

"There you are!" Anabelle said. "We were about to send out a search party for you."

Eduardo continued to the campfire and handed the fish to Charro. Meanwhile, Anabelle rushed over to me, giddy like a little schoolgirl.

"So, what kept you so long?" She asked. "Did you – you know – with Eduardo?"

I laughed through my sadness. "Oh god no. We just…fished."

"Sure," Anabelle said. "I'm sure you just fished."

"Tibor, is he…?"

"I don't know," Anabelle replied.

I walked toward the hut. "I need to see him."

"What's wrong?" Anabelle asked.

"Everything," I replied, pushing open the door to the hut. "It's time we get going."

Inside the hut, everything was dark except for Galena's glowing hands. She knelt bedside Tibor, pressing her hands to his chest. Tibor's callused and scarred arms were now almost fully healed, and his face looked as if it had never taken the heat of a bomb.

"Sit," Galena said with a whisper.

"I envy you," I replied.

"Why?" Galena asked.

"You heal people. I only seem to be able to hurt people."

The light from her hands illuminated her face, and I saw her smile. "Hurt, help. These are things all magic can do. I could spend my life healing the evil and the wicked, or I could refuse to help those who cannot pay. Magic is a gift, but it is a responsibility which can be used for the light or the dark."

"Maybe, but I did this to him," I said, looking at Tibor's face. "And you fixed it."

"Yes, but you also brought him here. That was also you. The magic is a part of you, but it is not the only part of you."

I smiled at Galena. "Thank you."

She raised her hands and stood. "Stay with him if you would like. He could use the company now."

She walked out of the hut, and I took Tibor's hand in mine. His eyes flickered, and he flopped his head toward me.

"You," he said. "It's good to see you."

"I'm sorry," I said. "I didn't mean for this to happen to you."

A deep sigh left Tibor's lips. "I know."

"No, you don't. I don't even know what I'm doing. I almost killed Eduardo. I just…I'm dangerous."

"Hey," Tibor said, cupping my hand in his and squeezing it tightly. "You'll figure it out. It's not easy, this. Especially when you are a Dual."

"What is a Dual?" I asked. "And don't use any flowery language this time, alright. Just tell me straight."

"Somebody who can wield the power of two magic castes. They are powerful. The most powerful among us, some would say. The Great War was started by duals. Hitler, Mussolini, and Franco were all Duals. Magic users bestow great reverence onto Duals. They are feared as much as they are worshipped. It is said that wielding one power is the second hardest thing to do in the universe. The first is wielding two."

"Like Eugenia?"

"Yes. She is a healer, but she also can control the Earth."

"Is that why they are after me?"

Tibor nodded slowly. "You are dangerous to them."

"I'm scared," I said. "What if I can't figure out how to use my power? What if they are right? What if I am dangerous?"

"Hey!" Tibor said. "When we get to Toledo, you'll be put into the best magic schools in the world. They will help you."

"And what if I blow everything up before then?" I asked.

"Don't do that," Tibor replied. "Now help me stand. I smell fish, and I'm starving."

"I don't know if Galena would like that."

"She'll get over it. Come on. I don't have all night."

"Fine."

Tibor leaned his hand on my shoulder. I lifted him to his feet. He didn't groan or wince, and he walked without any help at all. The work Galena had done in such a short time to bring Tibor back from the brink of death was a miracle.

Tibor opened the door to the hut and came face to face with Anabelle's enormous Goliath.

"Duck!" he shouted, rising into the air.

"Wait!" I said. "Don't freak out. That's ours. We stole it."

"You brought this thing here…on purpose?" Tibor asked.

"Of course," Anabelle said. "Pretty sweet, right?"

"No!" Tibor said. "It's not sweet. Don't you know those things have GPS trackers on them?! We have to go now!"

But it was too late. The sounds of Goliath thrusters blared in the distance. The trees snapped from the Humvees barreling toward us. Suddenly, the whole woods lit up with headlights.

It was the RMPs, and they had found us.

CHAPTER TWELVE

"What are you doing to my ship?" Anabelle asked as Tibor crawled up into the cockpit of the Goliath and starting fiddling with the buttons.

"Fixing it," he replied, pulling open the wire casing under the dashboard.

Twenty-four different Humvees. That's how many I counted, and fifteen Goliaths in the sky. They had sent an entire battalion after us. No, after me. I couldn't believe they would take me alive, not with so much firepower at their disposal.

"Isn't this overkill?" I asked as Tibor pulled wires out from under the chassis. "I mean, I think there is a better use of military resources than tracking me down, right?"

"Not if you're a Dual there's not," Tibor replied. "If she's a Dual, then it's under kill, probably."

"What does Rosie being a Dual have to do with anything?" Anabelle asked as Tibor hopped down and ran around the back of the Goliath, pulling out wires as he went.

"One percent of magic users can use multiple castes of magic, and magic users are only one-tenth of 1 percent of the population, so you do the math. There aren't very many of Rosie, and they aren't many magic users as powerful as her either."

"Less than a hundred in the whole world," Galena said.

"That's impossible," Anabelle continued. "Hitler. Mussolini. Franco. They could all use multiple forms of magic."

"Yes," Tibor said. "And that's why the UK thinks all Duals are evil."

The wind went out of me like I was kicked in the stomach. "They think I'm evil?"

"Hey!" Anabelle shouted. "You're not evil."

"Thanks," I said, with very little comfort.

"She's not evil, right?" Anabelle asked Tibor.

"No," Tibor said, struggling to get around the side of the mech. "She's not evil just because she's a Dual. That's crazy. If she's evil, it's for other reasons, but don't worry. I don't think you're evil."

"Attention Shiners!" A loudspeaker blared out. "You are harboring known fugitives and need to turn them over to the government right now. If you do not, we will be forced to open fire on you."

Tibor turned to Charro and Eduardo. "Get in your car. Wait for me."

Charro and Eduardo ran off. Galena grabbed onto Tibor's arm. "And what about me? Everything I own is inside."

"You can rebuild again, as long as you're alive," Tibor said. "Go with them."

With one last look at her home, Galena ran off with Eduardo and Charro. Anabelle stepped forward because of course, she did. "And what about me? You've gotta be crazy if you think I'm driving away like a coward."

"No," Tibor said, shaking his head. "You're flying away, like a hero."

"Excuse me?"

"I disabled the tracking beacon on this Goliath," he said. "Pick them up and fly them away. Rosie and I will distract them."

"Ummm…" Anabelle muttered. "No. you need me here."

He shook his head. "Maybe, but they need you more. They didn't sign up for this, and you have to make sure they are safe, okay?"

"Okay."

"You do know how to fly it, right?"

Anabelle bobbed her head. "Kinda."

"That had to be enough because you're all we got. I can't do it myself. I have to lead them away from here to give you a chance to escape. So, it's up to you. Their lives are in your hands."

"Where do I meet you?"

Tibor pulled out a piece of paper and scrawled something down. Then, he handed it to Anabelle. "If we aren't there in an hour, go on without us."

Anabelle nodded. "I got this."

Tibor placed his hand on her shoulder. "I know you do."

Anabelle gave me one last hug. "One day, we'll get to stop doing this."

I hugged her back. "Unfortunately, that day isn't today."

Anabelle squeezed me once more and then ran into the cockpit of the mech. She closed the cockpit bubble and gave a thumbs up to me.

"So, what are we going to do?" I asked.

"We're going to give them exactly what they want," Tibor replied. "They want to believe you're dangerous. We're going to show them danger."

"But I'm not dangerous, right?"

"Only as dangerous as you want to be, and right now I need you to be really dangerous. You know all that destruction you've been scared about?"

I nodded. "Yes. It's all I think about."

"I need you to unleash it. All of it."

I gulped. "I…can't…I can't do that. What if I hurt people? What if I hurt you?"

"These people are going to kill you, Rosie. Make no mistake. They are going to imprison you, torture you, kill you and dissect your brain to see what makes you tick because, that's what they do. And as for me, you've already hurt me remember, and I turned out fine."

"Yeah…I guess…but—"

"We don't have time to argue. Just close your eyes and think of fire," Tibor said. "I'll do the rest."

I took a deep breath and closed my eyes. I thought of a burning fire in front of me, and my left cheek started to glow. The heat felt nice at first, but it wasn't long before it started to burn brightly.

"It hurts!" I shouted.

"Then let it out!" Tibor replied.

I opened my eyes, and my hands were on fire. I extended them, and the fire shot out onto the trees in front of me. The trees immediately went up in a blaze, and the fire extended up into the branches after a few seconds.

"Go!" Tibor shouted to Anabelle.

Her mech lurched forward and picked up the car in front of it, as the people inside looked on in horror.

"Don't stop," Tibor said, grabbing me under my arms. "Whatever you do."

Tibor lifted me into the air, and the cool breeze felt good against my burning cheek. I looked down at the soldiers staring up at us, and the fire in my hands grew in intensity. It burned red, and then intensified to a bright yellow.

"Shoot her down!" One of the men shouted into his megaphone, and a hail of bullets flew up at us. Tibor dodged them as I laid down cover fire. Soon, the Humvees were engulfed in flames. The men started to cough and had no choice but to bail out of their Humvees to escape.

"We're not done yet!" Tibor said.

In front of us, a squad of Goliaths lined the sky. I turned my hands into the air and fire spat at them. The smoke from the trees rose into the air, and the fire helped cover Anabelle's escape. None of the mechs went after them, instead choosing to chase after me.

"This is going perfectly!" Tibor shouted.

"It is? Last time mechs chased us, we almost died."

"Yeah, but I didn't have a Light breather with me then. Go hotter!"

I closed my eyes and imagined my flames moving from red, to orange, to blue, and eventually to white. As I thought it, my hands did it. I fired at the Goliaths. The first of the mechs cracked its windshield and had to make an emergency landing.

"The trees!" Tibor said.

I pushed my hands down and lit the trees behind me. They went up in flames quickly, and the smoke obscured us from the mechs following close on our tails. I turned back to the front of us and saw a raging river in front of us.

"There!" Tibor said. "The river! "Think of a bubble!"

"What?"

"Just do it!"

Tibor dive-bombed for the river, and with a splash, we were underneath the water. My hands stopped burning, and the glow from my left cheek stopped. I looked over at Tibor as we drifted down the river. I wanted to surface, but Tibor held me down. He blew out his cheeks like a puffer fish, and I knew what he meant for me to do.

I closed my eyes and imagined a bubble around us, protecting us from the water. My right cheek glowed. This one didn't burn but felt cool and relaxing. I held my arms wide, and a bubble appeared around us, with fresh air inside.

Above us, the mechs searched through the forest, but they had lost us. We were invisible to them.

*

The river washed us ashore five miles downstream. I could see the fire raging in the distance, but it was far enough away that I didn't feel its heat.

"Should I feel bad about that?" I asked, wringing out my hair.

"Rosie, when you get older, you'll realize you feel bad about everything. Sometimes, you'll be walking, and some random thing you did when you were eight will rush through your mind, and you'll feel bad. So, yeah. You should feel bad for that, but you'll feel bad for a lot more than that, trust me."

I didn't like the answer to the question, but at least it was real, and because it was real it felt like the truth, even if I hated it.

"Is everybody that helps me going to get hurt?" I asked another hard question I really didn't want the answer to.

Tibor wrung out his shirt in the tall grass. "First off, Galena was helping me, not you."

"She was helping both of us."

"And second…maybe that will happen. Maybe everybody you know will be hurt. It's possible."

"You're not very reassuring."

"Life isn't very reassuring, kiddo. All we can do is hope that people's sacrifices were worth it, when they give it and know it is their sacrifice to give."

"What if they don't understand the sacrifice they are making?" I asked.

"I don't know, then," Tibor sighed. "I wish there were easy answers, kid. I really do, but life is messy and gross, and sometimes there's not an easy thing to say. Maybe my life would have been better if I had never met you, or maybe yours would have been better if you'd never found out you had powers."

"That's a good possibility. Then I would have a boyfriend, and a mother, and a life."

"Yeah? Well, the thing is you would've found out eventually, so why not now? And I would have gotten in trouble for helping somebody, so why not you?"

"You're not very good at this," I replied, whipping my hair back.

"I never claimed to be," he replied. "I'm just trying to get you to Toledo. I don't have some grand plan after that. And I didn't have one up until now, except to survive. Sorry, if you wanted a Yoda, but I'm just a regular Padawan."

"Alright, Obi-Wan," I said with a chuckle. "Let's find the others."

*

By the time we got to the meeting point, Anabelle's Goliath and Eduardo's car were already there waiting for us. Eduardo, Galena, Charro, and Anabelle stood in the middle of the field, excitedly waving as we landed.

"Did you do that?" Anabelle asked, pointing to the fire raging in the distance.

"Yeah," I replied. "Maybe I should have pulled back a little."

"Dang, girl," Anabelle said, giving me a high five. "You are powerful."

"That fire will rage for days," Galena said, "and destroy everything I held dear."

"I'm sorry," I said, walking over to her. "This was my fault. I should never have involved you."

Galena nodded. "You did not put a gun to my head, but yes. I wish I were not involved."

"Alright," Tibor said, slapping his hands together. "Let's go to Toledo."

Eduardo shook his head. "We won't be going with you. I've seen what it's like to be near you, and I don't like it. I hope to see you again, but we will make it to Toledo on our own. Annabelle gave us directions already."

"Are you sure?" I asked. "Like, we can fly you there. It's so much faster."

Eduardo shook his head. "I've had enough flying for one day."

"We can drop you off at the highway, at least," Anabelle said.

"Thank you, but we will be fine" Eduardo replied. "And thank you, Rosie, for saving us."

"You're welcome," I said, turning to Galena. "How about you?"

Galena shrugged. "I don't know where to go now, but Toledo sounds as good a place as any to rebuild. I will travel with Eduardo if they will have me. You bring danger at every turn."

I smiled. "I can't argue with that."

"Come on," Eduardo said. "You're welcome with us. It's a longer drive, but a safer one."

Galena happily jumped into the back of the car. "Goodbye!"

"I already punched directions to Toledo into the Mech," Anabelle said. "We're more than halfway there. We should be able to make it by daybreak if we don't stop too often."

Tibor nodded. "We'll follow you, then."

Anabelle jumped into her Goliath and dragged down the glass of the cockpit. I was amazed at how confident she looked after just a couple hours of flight time.

"Next stop Toledo," I said to her.

She nodded. "Next stop, Toledo!"

Anabelle fired her blasters and boosted off the ground. Tibor grabbed me around the shoulders. "I hope this is the last time I have to carry you."

I nodded. "I hope so, too."

He lifted us into the air, and we started off to our destination. *Toledo.* It brought a sense of wonder just thinking about what could be waiting for me there. The word brought the prospect of a new life. The word brought me hope.

CHAPTER THIRTEEN

After two hours of non-stop flying, I forced Tibor to land and take a break. The skin under my armpits was rubbed raw, and he'd nearly dropped me a half dozen times as he struggled to stay awake or when I squirmed to find a more comfortable position that didn't exist.

"I'm not flying with you anymore," I said to Tibor as we sat on the side of a mountain.

"Good. You're heavy."

"Well, I'm not going to carry you," Anabelle said. "Just kidding I will totally carry you."

"I've been thinking about it for a while," I replied with a smile. "And I don't think I need either of you to carry me. Check it out."

I closed my eyes and thought of the fire emanating out of my fingers. My left cheek started to glow, and burn slightly. I opened my eyes and placed my hands on the ground. Jets of fire came out of my fingers and created little booster rockets that pushed me off the ground.

"Pretty cool, huh?" I said.

"Sure," Tibor replied. "Until you lose focus, which I predict will happen in about twenty seconds."

"I'll take that bet," Anabelle chimed in. "I don't think she'll even last that long."

"Hey!" I shouted. "Not cool!"

"Sorry, my friend," Anabelle said. "I've known you too long and too well to bet on the over in a situation like this."

I'll show them. I closed my eyes and used every ounce of concentration to power my hands. It was hot on the ground, and on my cheek, and I didn't like it. I wondered how long people could go without–

–and bam I hit the ground.

"Pay up," Anabelle said, sticking out her hand.

"With what?" Tibor asked. "We didn't bet anything."

"I'll think of something," Anabelle said, slapping me on the back. "I guess that means you're riding with me."

I sighed. "I guess so."

*

We arrived at the coordinates for Toledo right as the sun readied itself to break over the horizon. Anabelle swooped down first. She was becoming quite adept at flying her mech. I would have never known she only took over ownership of it a day ago.

"We're here," Anabelle said through the microphone of her mech. "I don't see anything."

I hopped down from the robot's mechanical arm and felt the dewy ground. It certainly didn't feel like the lost city of Toledo. It felt like a forest, like any forest in the world. All around us were trees and grass, but no lost cities. Not even a model of one.

"I don't know. It doesn't look very impressive, though."

"I feel like if there were a city here, we would know about it, right?" Annabelle said. "I mean, this looks like a forest."

"Stop right there!" An old man screeched, stepping calmly out of the woods.

His hands laid against a large walking stick, and his beard rested at his knees. His bald head glistened in the sunlight, and his haunting yellow eyes stared menacingly at us.

"We don't want any trouble with you, mech," the man continued. "Leave now, and we shall not harm you."

"Whoa!" I said, standing up. "What are you doing? That mech is my friend."

"You befriend the RMPs; then you are an enemy of the Tuppins! An enemy of the Tuppins will be destroyed by the Tuppins!"

"What are you talking about, dude?" Anabelle replied. "We hate the RMP. That's why we stole this Goliath from them."

"You dare lie to a Knight of the Tuppins!" The man screamed, waving his stick high in the air. His cheek glowed with a blue mountain. His eyes turned a crisp blue, and yellow lightning crept up the side of the stick. "You leave me no choice!"

The man slammed his stick on the grass below him. A flash of thunder echoed across the field. The ground quaked under us, as it formed into a hand that grabbed us tight. The Goliath crunched and cracked underneath the fingers of the great, rock hand that the old man controlled.

"Stop!" Tibor said, flying down from the sky. "Let these children go!"

Tibor's cheek glowed brightly, and a gust of wind blew us out of the rock's fingers. Anabelle turned on her thrusters and grabbed me before I hit the ground.

"You work with the enemy of the Tuppins!" The old man said.

"Eustace!" Tibor shouted. "Stop."

The old man cringed at the name that escaped Tibor's lips. "How do you know my name?"

Tibor pulled back his shirt to reveal a tattoo on the left side of his chest. I squinted closer to see it more clearly. In the center was a teacup, surrounded by a sun, which radiated out in every direction. "I am Tibor, Knight of the Order Tuppins."

"Impossible. To be a Tuppins, you must be born a Tuppins!"

"Or marry a Tuppins. Or save the life of a Tuppins. I fall into the latter two categories. The gods rest my wife's soul."

Eustace's stick glowed blue as he spun it in the air. "You taint the line of the Tuppins by fraternizing with the enemy."

"These are not your enemies." Tibor gestured toward me with his outstretched arm. "This one is a Dual."

"Impossible! There hasn't been a Dual in forty years."

Tibor wrapped his fingers around my shoulders. "I know, but she is one. Show him."

I turned to him. "I'm scared."

Tibor whispered in my ear. "I know, but I'm here. You can do this."

I closed my eyes and thought of a flame. When I opened my eyes, a small flame emanated from my fingers, and my left cheek grew hot against my face.

"That proves nothing," Eustace scoffed.

I closed my eyes again and thought of dew drops. When I opened my eyes, I swirled my hand around until I pulled the moisture from the grass into my palm.

"Impossible," Eustace said, dropping to his knees. "I never thought I would see another Dual. Not in this life."

"We must enter Toledo," Tibor said. "These children need protection. Where is it?"

Eustace held up his finger. "The place will reveal itself when the will is ready." Eustace pointed his finger at Anabelle. "And what of she? What powers does she possess?"

"Me?" Anabelle said. "I don't have any powers. I'm just a girl."

"A girl!" Eustace shouted. "No powers! You blaspheme the Tuppins!"

"Calm down–" Tibor started, but Eustace wouldn't calm down. He took a mighty step forward, and the earth quaked again.

"You dare defile the holy city with your blasphemous ways. You have been judged by the Tuppins, and the Tuppins have found you wanting!"

Anabelle leveled the metal arms of the broken Goliath at the knight. "Don't make me–"

With the flick of his wrist, the knight pulled a tree out of the ground and flung at her. Anabelle jumped out of the mech, and the tree smashed through it and embedded itself deep in the metal suit.

"Why did you do that?" Anabelle shouted.

With another flick of his wrist, Eustace pulled up the earth to surround Anabelle up to her ears with mud. With one last flick, he did the same with both Tibor and me.

"Poor Tuppins," Eustace said to Tibor. "You have been away for too long. Now, you will be judged by the Council of Toledo, and you will be judged wanting and stripped of your rank forthwith."

Eustace raised his staff into the air, and the mud surrounding us cracked loose from the earth. We floated into the air, unable to move.

"How is he doing this?" I asked. "How is he so powerful?"

"The staff. It magnifies his power. We cannot defeat him while he holds it."

"You could not defeat me without it, either, Tuppins," Eustace replied, quite proud of himself.

Eustace clacked his feet together and turned away from us. He waved his free hand. In front of him, the forest parted, and he stepped forward onto a stone path surrounded by sky.

The stone path wasn't one that had previously been there or one that Eustace made. No, it was as if the path was cloaked in Mirror magic, and he revealed it. As he moved forward, he dragged us along behind him.

"It is sad, for all of you, but especially for you, Normal. We can never let you go again, now that you know the secret to this place. It is a pity."

"Sure you can," Anabelle replied. "I'm not going to say anything."

"Yes, a pity," Eustace snapped his fingers, and a piece of stone slammed tight around Anabelle's mouth. "We do not take kindly to Normals here or magical folks who fraternize with Normals."

Eustace pulled us forward, and a path opened to us that wasn't there a second ago—except it wasn't a path at all, it was a bridge.

On the far side of the bridge, a huge stone gate stood a hundred feet tall. Small roads jutted up and down the hillside in front of us. On either side of the bridge, a hundred-foot drop led to a river below. A river. A real bloody river, right below us, which was hidden from sight. *How did it get water? How did it flow?*

"What's happening?" I shouted to Tibor.

"Welcome to Toledo," Eustace said. "I hope your stay is brief."

It was a magical, transfixing sight. High above us, wizards' and witches' cheeks glowed without fear of reprisal as they flew high into the air. At the top of the city, a large cathedral bell rang across the hilltop.

I turned back to see the path behind us close. Around us, the sky glowed bright pink and throbbed with deep power that resonated through my soul.

"We have not had a visitor here in some time," Eustace continued.

"What about all the people Eugenia sent here from Madrid?"

"Ah yes, Eugenia. A poor, misguided woman. Well those are not visitors at all, are they? Those are trespassers, sent to deceive us, like you, and have been dealt with in the way all trespassers are dealt with, yes? As a Knight of the Tuppins, I relinquished them to the Council, and they were judged."

"You can't do that!" Tibor screamed. "They were innocent!"

"Nobody is innocent in the eyes of the Tuppins! Neither are you, deceivers."

"We're not here to deceive you!" I shouted, and with another snap, my mouth was covered with clay.

"I demand to speak to the Order!" Tibor shouted.

"Oh, the only reason you are still alive is that you wear that tattoo, blasphemer though you are. Don't you worry, the order will deal with you? They will deal with all of you."

I finally made it to Toledo and was as much a prisoner here as I would have been on the outside. Maybe more so.

BOOK TWO

"Chosen"

PROLOGUE

Bang! Bang! Bang!

The door slammed hard each time I pounded my fist against it. I had been shouting into the night for five minutes; I was getting worried that nobody was coming, and I just lost my wife to the Royal Military Police for nothing. *Please open the door. Please open the door.*

"Hello!" I shouted, rapping my knuckles against the door yet again.

The baby in my arms cried out for something. She wanted her bottle. Or her blanket. Or her mommy. She probably wanted her mommy. I wanted her mommy, too, more than anything. However, the Royal Military Police had her now. They'd have us, too, if I didn't get inside soon. They were after us. A crying baby and shouting father weren't exactly inconspicuous.

"Shh, shh, shh," I said, softly. "Mommy will be back soon."

I lied to her. It might have been wrong, lying to a baby, but I didn't care. It wasn't like I would see her again, not for many years at least. *Do you want your last words to your baby to be lies, Tom? Do you really?*

"Open up!" I shouted one more time. The tears came stronger with each passing minute.

I tried to hide the pain at seeing my beautiful wife fighting against the monstrous Goliath mechs that hunted magic users everywhere. I suppressed my feelings for the sake of the baby, but I couldn't fight them back much longer. They bubbled up as my adrenaline wore off, and the hurt was too much to bear.

"I'm coming!" I heard a sweet voice bellow from inside. "Who's causing such a racket at this hour?"

"Please!" I shouted back. "Hurry."

The lock clicked open from the other side of the door, and the knob creaked as it turned to the left. I didn't wait for the door to swing open before I pushed my way inside.

"I'm sorry," I said, spinning around toward the door as an old woman with white hair and glasses, dressed in a tattered, white, nightgown quickly pushed the door closed. "I'm being chased and I couldn't—"

The woman held up her hand. "It's okay, dearie. You're not the first person to shove open a door in my face…not even the first one this week."

The baby wailed in my arms. I didn't know how to fix her. That was Susie's job. She was the one who wanted to be a parent. She was born for it. I was all thumbs, most of the time. I could barely change a diaper.

"What's her name?" the old woman asked.

"The baby?" I replied. "We…we didn't give her a name. We thought it would be harder to let go that way."

"That's smart," the old woman said, nodding. "My name is Matilda."

"Nice to meet you," I replied.

"And you are?" she asked, holding out her hand for me to shake.

"Is that wise?" I asked, refusing her outstretched palm. "That you know my name? I thought that we were trying to be secretive. Are we not trying to be secretive?"

The old woman smiled. "I don't think I can glean much from you telling me your first name, can I? It's a simple pleasantry. You can lie to me if you want."

"No," I replied, bouncing the baby up and down. "I'll tell you. I…it's Tom. My name is Tom."

"Well Tom," Matilda said. "May I hold her?"

I looked down at my baby. Matilda had made a reasonable request, but for some reason, I didn't have the will to let her go. She was crying and scratching at my arm, trying to break free, and yet all I wanted to do was hold her for one second longer.

"I can't seem to give her up, but if you can get her, then go for it."

Matilda scooped her arms around the baby and brought her to her shoulder, as I unlatched my fingers. "This is very traumatic for everybody, Tom. I know that. Babies should not be separated from their families, but these are dark times, Tom, there is no denying that."

I wanted to reply that I knew exactly how dark the times were, but all I could do was cry big, sloppy tears as I collapsed on the floor. Matilda squeeze my shoulder as she walked past me. "When you're ready, come into the kitchen. I'll make tea."

As she walked out of the room, I realized my baby wasn't crying anymore. Maybe she would be fine here. Maybe she would be fine without me. *Would I be fine without her though?*

*

"My wife's name was Susie," I said without any provocation.

Matilda sat across from me, slowly rocking a wooden crib which held my daughter. My daughter looked happy, looking up at Matilda, and giggling. She had no idea I would soon leave her forever, just like her mother had, except my abandonment wouldn't be filled with heroics, only shame.

"That is a pretty name," Matilda said. "Was she a good mother?"

I nodded. "The best mother. She loved that child more than I ever thought possible. I think she loved her more than me to be honest."

Matilda cocked her head toward me. "But this baby is you, Tom. She's the best part of you, and the best part of her. So that makes sense."

I sipped my tea slowly. It was still very hot. "I don't know about that. Susie was pretty wonderful. I'm just the putz that didn't deserve her."

Matilda chuckled. "Genetically, this little one is made up of the strongest DNA from both you and Susie. The DNA that survived, struggled, and fought to thrive. It is the best that remains from the both of you, just like you are the best of your parents, and this sweet girl's children will be the best of her."

"Do you think she'll live long enough to have children? To have any kind of life in a place like this?"

Matilda shrugged. "I don't know. I know you are doing the right thing though, the best thing for her."

I took another sip of tea. "Do you think so, really?"

"You and your wife are both magic users, yes?"

I nodded. "Both. She is of the Moon, and I the Light."

Matilda took a swig of her tea. "The Seers say those two don't get along well."

"Well, we must be the exception then, because we got along like two peas in a pod."

"Good, good," Matilda said, rocking the baby gently. "Well, since you are both magic users there is an 80 percent chance that your child will be cursed with magic as well. If you take care of her, she will be watched her whole life. If my nursemaids take care of her, though, she has a real shot to grow up normal."

"Normal," I scoffed. "As if there is such a thing."

"As much as there is, we will give it to her." Matilda placed her hand on mine. "It really is the best thing for her."

A bang at the door startled me. Then, another tightened my stomach. A third sent it into my throat.

"Who is it?" Matilda asked sweetly.

"RMP, ma'am!" A gruff voice responded from the other side of the door. "We need to speak with you immediately!"

Matilda stood up and brushed herself off. "Don't move a muscle."

Matilda snapped her fingers, and a square on her cheek glowed. She was a Mirror, which meant she could create illusions with her mind, and with her command to remain still, I immediately knew that she had cloaked me in invisibility.

"Hang on! Hang on!" Matilda shouted as she moved toward the door. "I'm an old woman, and I can't move very fast."

Matilda took a deep breath and waved her hand over her face. Her cheek stopped glowing as she masked her magic. Then, she opened the door. A tall, slender man with a perfectly manicured RMP uniform stood on the other side. He wore a blue coat with crisp lapels. He wasn't a grunt soldier, the tri-corner hat he wore indicated his rank, but he was flanked by two soldiers, wearing hard stares and carrying M-16s.

"Ma'am," the officer said, crinkling his bushy mustache. "We are looking for a man and a baby that came this way. Have you seen them?"

Matilda shook her head. "No officer. I have been in bed since half-past eight, reading. I just came downstairs a couple of minutes ago."

The baby screamed out for comfort, and the soldiers peered inside. "Whose baby is that?"

"My neighbors. They're on holiday and asked me to watch her for them."

"On holiday?" The officer screeched. "And they didn't take their baby with them?"

"They just needed a night alone, sir, if you know what I mean. They'll be back on the morrow to pick her up."

The officer flipped open his notebook. "I see. And who are these neighbors so we might corroborate your story?"

"Oh dear," Matilda said. "I'm not in some sort of trouble, am I?"

"No ma'am," the officer said, shivering in the cold night air. "We just have to follow up on every lead."

Of course, of course," Matilda said. "Oh, I'm sorry. Are you chilly, officer?"

He shook his head. "I am comfortable, ma'am. Please, just answer the question so we can be on our way."

"It seems dreadfully chilly out there. And you without a long coat. What did they do, rustle you out of bed?"

He nodded. "They did at that, ma'am. Urgent matters, you see, demand immediate attention."

"Dreadful. Just dreadful that they would send you out without a coat. I'm sorry for you, my boy. I truly am. Where are my manners? Would you like to come in for tea?"

What was she doing? Offering tea to our enemies? She was going to rat me out. I was doomed, and if I was doomed than so was my baby.

I looked up toward the back door of Matilda's house. If I got a running leap, I could steal the baby and disappear into the night. I don't know where we would go, but we would be safe, at least for the moment. That's what my wife wanted, for our baby to be safe, no matter the cost.

The officer took a deep sigh and placed his pad away. "Never mind, ma'am. You have a good night."

"You do the same, dearie."

Matilda smiled as she shut the door. Once she locked the door, her smile turned into a sneer. She peeked through the window blinds next to her, and when she was satisfied, she walked back toward me.

"My, my, my," Matilda said, snapping her fingers again and breaking her charm. "You really are in desperate need of my help, aren't you?"

"What are you talking about? You almost got us caught!"

Matilda sat down cordially, completely ignoring my accusation. "No, no, no. Those officers just need to take notes for the sake of recording things, even if they hate it. It's not important what they write, just that they write. He knew that if I told him about the baby, he would have to search another house, or worse, come back here tomorrow to talk to the neighbors. Nobody wants that, least of all him. I could tell just by looking at him that he hasn't left his desk in a month. That kind of person doesn't want to be on door duty."

"Fine," I said, snarling into my tea. "So, what do we do now?"

"Now, you go. Wait until the coast is clear, and you vanish. Live your life. Forget your daughter. She will be safe in my care until she turns eighteen. Then we will tell her the truth, and help her live with her powers in secret, just as I have. Perhaps, we'll get lucky, and she won't have any powers at all."

"Don't get my hopes up," I said. "There's no hope of that, is there?"

"There's always hope," Matilda replied.

I nodded. "Thank you."

"It's my pleasure," Matilda replied, rocking the baby to sleep.

I stood up and caressed my baby's face one last time. She looked so much like Susie. I hoped one day I would be able to tell her that to her face.

"You know," I said. "I always liked the name, Roselyn."

CHAPTER ONE

I didn't like Toledo much, at first glance. However, I probably would have found it much more appealing if I wasn't hovering over it in a ball of mud, the prisoner of a crazy city guard named Eustace. He'd captured Tibor, Anabelle, and I before we'd even gotten past the protective barrier cloaking the city.

"It wasn't always like this, you know," Eustace said, leading us up the narrow main street of Toledo.

I was told that Toledo would be a welcoming place, where I would find shelter and refuge. Tibor, the man who led me here, promised that to us. However, when we arrived, I was arrested by a Knight of the Tuppins, encased in mud, and hoisted into the air for all the citizens of the city to gawk at as we passed.

"Come see!" Eustace shouted. "These three heretics tried to enter the walled city of Toledo. They are liars and blasphemers. Now the Tuppins will bring them to justice."

Three of us. One of them was me. Hovering in front of me, floating in the air for the whole city to see, was Tibor. He was the one who told me that I would be safe here. He's the one that convinced me to come here in the first place, so I blamed him most for our current predicament. Sure, he saved me from being arrested by the Royal Military Police back in Ambrosia, but he also got me arrested by the military police of Toledo, so…at best I exchanged one jailer for another.

In front of our airborne pack, also hoisted into the air in a ball of thick mud, was my best friend, Anabelle. She was the only one of us that didn't have any magic at all…and she was the reason we were arrested. To his credit, Tibor tried to tell us that Anabelle wouldn't be treated well when we got to Toledo, but we didn't listen. I didn't listen. I didn't want to listen because I didn't want to leave her. It was selfish, but then, I was selfish.

"The city used to be closer to the ground, on a much smaller hill," Eustace commented. "But once we moved the city, our beloved city council improved it, pulling the hill higher so our Cathedral could be closer to the Heavens."

The city of Toledo sat on a steep incline. I was almost glad that we didn't have to walk up it because the streets tilted toward the sky at a nearly unwalkable angle. Cars passed us with tiny propellers against their tailpipes to help push them up the steep incline. Bubbles floated out of their mufflers.

"Powered by bubble bath," Eustace said with pride, stroking his long, ratty, mud-caked beard. "Very environmentally conscious, we are."

Of course, not everybody used cars. Broomsticks zipped past us right and left as Eustace climbed the steep incline toward the city.

"Enjoying the tour?" Eustace said. "It's the last you'll get. It's either prison or the hangman for you all. Either way, I am glad I am not you."

I wanted to speak. I wanted to scream, but I couldn't. Eustace had covered my mouth with sticky mud which prevented me from doing anything but mumble. It prevented any of us from talking. Eustace bested us in combat one at a time with ease, as if we weren't even trying, with the help of his power amplifying walking stick. Apparently, sorcerers can use objects to enhance their powers. I didn't know that.

Of course, there wasn't much I did know about magic until I realized I could wield it. Most magic users – all magic users – were supposed to get magic when they turn

13. However, I didn't receive the gift of magic until I was 16, and joy of joys I was given two different types of magic; the Light and the Moon, which mean I could control fire and water.

"Yes, yes. Look at them in horror," Eustace said as we passed a group of school children hovering in the air on a magic carpet with their teacher. "This is what happens when you battle the Tuppins. None are a match for our might."

Having two powers made me a Dual, which was very dangerous to the government of Ambrosia for some reason. Probably because there were very few Duals in the whole world, and the magic world rallied around them. It didn't help that some of the worst humans in history were Duals…Hitler, Mussolini, and Franco, the three Fathers who set out to destroy all Normals in the 30s and 40s.

They failed, of course. Their defeat at the hands of the Allies led to the UK taking over all of Europe and laying down a strict anti-magic policy across the whole continent. Since then, magic users have been second-class citizens at best, and prisoners at worst.

"Look here, everyone!" Eustace shouted as we rose higher into the air. "These infidels will be dealt with quickly. Your Tuppins look out for all of you."

Eustace enjoyed the theatrics. The Tuppins were, apparently, the guardians of Toledo. Tibor was a Tuppins, but he did not know just how much they hated outsiders, or at the very least, he didn't want to tell me.

The funny thing was that Toledo didn't look much different from Ambrosia, which used to be Madrid before the war. Sure, it was hillier than Madrid, well, really one big hill, and there was a wall around the city which rose a hundred feet in the air, but other than that, the cramped cobblestone streets reminded me of the old areas of Ambrosia, like the Gothic Quarter, where our beautiful Cathedral looked out over the city.

The only thing that was different were the shops. Sure, there were wig shops, and bookshops, and candy shops, like in Ambrosia, but Toledo's shops were like nothing I'd seen before back home.

For instance, the wigs sitting in one window changed colors, lengths, and styles by themselves every couple of seconds. Inside the window, a bald woman placed a wig on her head and it immediately melded into a short bob to perfectly match her outfit.

In the window of a bookstore, the text of magazines and novels moved across the page and turned into images that played out in grand detail. A wordy knight fought a letter-breathing dragon in one; a man professed his love for a woman in another.

The candy inside the sweets shop floated above their boxes, lighter than a feather. A plump girl with pigtails popped a cupcake with a stick and sent it flying into her mouth, swallowing it in one gulp without chewing.

The people of Toledo used their magic without any fear of repercussion. Every cheek glowed with one of the seven signs. There was the sun that represented the Light and fire, the moon which represented Moon and water, a mountain represented Ground and the earth, three wisps of wind represented Air and the sky, an eye represented Seers who could see the future and the past, a plus sign represented Health and healing, and finally a square represented Mirror and illusion.

Every magic person was branded with an invisible mark under their cheek that only glowed when they used magic.

Eustace had the Ground or earth. Tibor could control the Air. I, as a Dual, could control both fire and water.

"Be strong," a young woman whispered to me as we passed her. She carried a basket of buns down the street. An all-seeing eye glowed on her left cheek, meaning she was a Seer. "This too will pass."

What did she know that I didn't? A lot, I'm sure, since she was a seer. Or was she just trying to comfort me for a moment and take my mind off my situation?

What a stupid mistake, coming here. All I wanted to do was go back to Ambrosia and lay in my warm bed one last time. I would give all I had for one more cup of Mama's tea. Of course, all I had was nothing, and Mama wasn't really Mama, was she? She was just somebody paid to bring me up and suppress my powers.

"We are almost there," Eustace shouted back toward us. "Don't fret. You will soon be judged for your crimes. The Tuppins are strict, but they are fair."

I turned my eyes to Tibor for confirmation. Flecks of mud stained his scraggly beard. I hoped he would give some hope in his eyes, indicating that we would at least get a fair trial. Unfortunately, he solemnly dropped his eyes, and in that moment I knew…the Tuppins would not be fair.

"Ah yes," Eustace said, shimmying up the hill, his left leg dragging behind him. "We are almost there."

The incline leveled off into a bustling square. In the center of the square, a statue of an angel slashing at an evil demon rose into the sky. Water poured out of a dragon into a fountain below, and then danced along the rim of the stone fountain in a zig-zag pattern, the work of a powerful Moon, no doubt.

To our left, dozens of wizards and witches dressed in long black coats flung open their orange shutters and stared mouth agape at us. In front of us, a dozen younger witches sat in front of a McDonald's, eating hamburgers with rapturous glee. When they saw us, their joyous expressions turned to scowls.

"People of Toledo," Eustace blared from in front of a statue in the center of the square. "I have defeated three more usurpers who came here to upend our way of life and destroy everything we hold dear. Luckily, your Tuppins are here to protect you, as we have always protected you, and will always protect you."

The crowd in the square cheered for Eustace, and he loved every second of it. He waved his hands up and down begging and pleading for more so that he could satiate his love of attention.

"Now," he continues, quieting the crowd. "These spies will be judged for their crimes against us."

Which was it, I thought, *were we traitors, usurpers, or spies?* I guess at the end of the day it didn't matter. It's not like the trial would be fair anyway. We were a spectacle, a show of strength that the Tuppins could use to show their power.

Eustace slammed his walking stick on the ground, and we fell to the earth. My mud enclosure burst into a thousand pieces, as did Tibor's and Anabelle's. Before we could right ourselves, Eustace spun his walking stick. He cheek glowed along with the jewel at the center of his staff, and the mud around us turned into a linked chain. It bound our hands and shackled our feet.

"You will behave inside the city hall," Eustace said to us. "Otherwise, there are thousands of magic users around should you choose to disobey the will of the Tuppins."

Eustace grabbed his stick tightly, twirling it in his hands as he turned toward the large building to our right. It didn't look like the other building in the square. Those, and all the ones we passed looked like they were built by the hands of people centuries ago, but this building rose from the ground with the intricate detail it would take a million people to replicate.

The columns on either side of the building were made from wood, and carved with screaming faces up both sides of its length. Atop the building, a black awning hung to block the light. Painted on its roof was a depiction of a golden-haired angel in a fight with a thousand humans, slaying them as easily as I would order a pizza.

It didn't look like the place one would go to seek justice, and as Tibor held his head low when we passed under its arches, I knew we wouldn't find any.

CHAPTER TWO

Walking into the city hall felt like I was stepping back in time a few decades, if not a few centuries. There weren't any computers, metal detectors, or even televisions mounted on the walls feeding us commercials.

Instead, desks on either side of a checkered walkway were filled with secretaries and clerks using large typewriters. Finished paperwork floated through the air toward file cabinets that lined the walls behind them. Wisps of air glowed on the cheeks of the workers as they cheerily typed away as if they weren't years behind the times.

It seemed a criminally inefficient way of doing things. That kind of whimsy was cool to look at, but I couldn't imagine the painstaking tedium of searching through rows of file cabinets whenever I needed anything or writing a document without the convenience of spell check, which has saved my life more times than I care to admit.

Each clerk sat behind a high, mahogany podium, carved with different depictions of the same beautiful angel from the square fighting and beating back hordes of human soldiers.

The podiums seemed to tell the story of an angel, sent from Heaven, who slew an army of humans and was exalted for her bravery in combat by magicians who shot fireworks out of their wands to celebrate her victory in battle. Considering Toledo was hidden from the world for failing to win a war against Normals, the carvings seemed a little out of place. Still, they were pretty nice and quite intricate.

Had they carved the grooves by hand or used magic to do it? I realized it was a stupid question the moment I thought it. Of course, they used magic. They seemed to use magic for everything.

All the clerks wore pointed black hats and matching robes. Their robes were emblazoned with one of the seven marks, but I only saw two in the hallway as we walked toward a tall podium at the far end. The Airs typed the documents and breezed the finished papers into their correct cabinets, while the Eyes shuffled through cabinets looking for files.

There weren't any other marks in the entry hallway to the City Hall, but that didn't mean their presence wasn't felt. The heat from the air ducts must have come from the Light, blowing fire into the embers under the building to power the heaters, while the Moons filled the cherub fountains which danced in the center of the hall.

"Brutus!" Eustace shouted, the exaggerated Rs rolled off his tongue playfully toward an impish little man sitting behind a comically large desk which he could barely see over.

"What do you want?" Brutus asked in a gruff, exasperated manner, sighing behind the tallest desk at the end of the hall.

"I have prisoners which the council must deal with post haste," Eustace replied, elegantly…the kind of elegance only somebody without any culture would try to embody, clumsy and oafish, nearly comical in its hyperbole.

"They are in a meeting," Brutus replied, unimpressed, maintaining perfect posture as he looked down at Eustace both figuratively and literally, over his very thin, circular glasses.

"Of course they are, and I'm sure it is with very important business, but I contend this is pressing enough to warrant their attention, perhaps the most pressing business of the day."

"I'm sure it can wait until they are free, which should be an hour or so from now."

"Brutus," Eustace said, slamming his walking stick on the ground. "There is a Normal amongst them. Are you not aghast? Does that not offend your erudite sensibilities?"

The room gasped at the word Normal. All eyes turned to us. The papers fell to the floor, and the thump of the file cabinets stopped. The room fell silent, and Brutus nearly fainted as he fell back in his chair.

"A Normal. Here? But how?" Brutus stuttered, stumbling over his words as if he had forgotten how to speak.

"I'm sure I don't know," Eustace replied. "That is a matter for the Council. I am only the messenger, I'm afraid. This sort of thing is far above my level. I find and subdue those that would do us harm. It is up to the Council to deal with them as they see fit."

"Of course," Brutus said, dabbing himself with a wet rag. "Maribel!"

A short, squat woman with a bright smile pushed through a door that appeared on the left-hand side of Brutus. Her cloak drifted down to the ground, and it looked as though she hovered as she moved toward us, except her cheek didn't glow with the three wisps of Air that would have allowed her to control the wind.

"Yes, Brutus," Maribel asked, happily, with a smile so wide it made my cheeks ache. "How many I be of service?"

"Take these four inside the chambers," Brutus said with a curt wave of his hand. "Tell the council that it is an urgent matter that must be handled immediately."

"But sir," she stammered. "We have orders never to interrupt them for any reason."

"I know what we were told, woman!" Brutus shouted, slamming his palms on the desk. "Now, I am telling you something different." Brutus lowered the timbre of his voice, and he let out a low growl. "Is there a problem with that?"

Maribel scrunched up her nose and shook her head rapidly from side to side. "No, sir. No problem with me. I can't say the same for the council, and I won't take the blame if they are miffed at my intrusion."

"If they have a problem," Brutus said, dipping a quill pen into an inkpot and scribbling on a large ledger. "They can take it up with me."

Seriously? They used quill pens and inkpots? Still, in this day and age? I know they've been in hiding for seventy-five years, but at least use a fountain pen or something.

Maribel beckoned Eustace forward to the door. "Come now. We must be quick like bunnies."

Eustace yanked our chains forward, and I lurched toward the door, slamming into Tibor and Anabelle as I fell on the ground.

"Quit your dawdling," Eustace said. "This is no time to lay on the ground."

Eustace slammed his stick on the ground. His cheek glowed with the outline of a mountain, and the floor leapt up below me, pushing me to my feet with an awkward shove.

"No ground magic!" Brutus shouted, disgusted. "Really, such a brutish form of magic. It's a wonder you can bathe yourself in the morning."

"Bathe better than you," Eustace said, grumbling. "Better than you at a lot of things."

"What was that?" Brutus said to Eustace, nearly overpowering him with his voice alone. "Say something?"

Eustace opened his mouth to speak, but he thought better of himself and slung his head to the ground. "No, sir."

"That's what I thought," Brutus said, smugly. "Now, get out of my sight, before I have the janitors sweep you away with the disgusting mud you dragged inside."

I found it hard not to chuckle as Eustace disappeared behind the door after being put in his place. I didn't know who this Brutus was, but I liked him the most of anybody I met so far in this awful city, and I still didn't like him at all.

*

On the other side of the door, Maribel led us through a maze of twists and turns through sinewy and curved hallways that must have been crafted with powerful magic in order to exist. Doors laid at forty-five-degree angles and corridors spun like a corkscrew. We passed witches and warlocks that glowed with squares on their cheeks indicating that they were all illusionists.

Maribel's cheek glowed with a Square as well, and I realized that Mirrors were likely the only ones able to navigate the twists and turns of the hallways without becoming lost in the confusing labyrinth. If Eustace weren't pulling me, I would have gotten lost for sure, as Maribel stepped too quickly for me to follow.

"Let's get a move on," Maribel said. Her voice cracked with command. She was nervous, even if she hid it well. "There will be enough time for dilly-dallying later when the council has dealt with you."

It was easy to see how out of place Eustace was in the City Hall. Every mage we passed was meticulously coiffed and styled. Not a single hair was out of place on their head, and their clothes were ironed with a perfect crease that only came with delicate care. The people inside the city stood up straight as an arrow and moved with purpose.

Eustace on the other hand, hunched when he walked and dragged his left leg behind his right. His clothing was riddled with holes and stains. His green cloak was dirty enough that I would have easily believed he rolled in mud for pleasure. He seemed almost feral in his appearance, as if he lived in the woods for too long, compared to the refined sophistication of those who worked in City Hall.

As we moved, the mud chains that held our arms and legs flecked off onto the ground, and on either side of me, vents opened to suck up any excess dirt. They were serious neat freaks in City Hall, like none I had never seen before, and my Mama…well, the woman I thought was my Mama until a couple of days ago, was a maid, so I knew something about clean.

"It's right up this way," Maribel squeezed out as I turned a twisted hallway with a door turned on its side at a ninety-degree angle, and only large enough for a mouse to fit through.

Maribel skittered down the hall and up one of the walls until she was aligned with the door. Then, she snapped her fingers and the hallway expanded in front of us, tilting and spinning until finally it was straight as an arrow and the door was upright. She pushed open the door and walked inside.

"Follow me," she said as if all this perfectly normal. Of course, to her, it was, which fascinated me to no end. "Be quiet in the council chambers."

The council chambers looked like the courtroom in a very old movie, except that instead of a single bench for one judge there were undulating benches for three. In the center, in the highest chair, a man with a long beard and deep wrinkles blustered away. His deep emerald eyes sunk into his head behind thick reading glasses. On one side of him, a bald man with a white handlebar mustache stared up at him. On the other side, a red-haired woman with a bitter face and cold eyes rapped her fingers on her cheek.

"And pursuant to bylaw 15.091," the blustery man at the center said. "It would behoove us to move forward with our plans to radicalize…"

The old, blustery man took notice of us as Maribel closed the door to the room and stood behind a wooden bench at the back of the room.

"What is the meaning of this?" The old man tutted. "This is a very private affair. We demand the highest confidentiality."

"Yes, sir, Chief Justice Abalos," Maribel said, her head dropped low. "But Mister Eustace here has an urgent matter to put before you."

"More urgent than our continued safety?" Abalos blustered. "For we are discussing nothing less than the continued existence of all magical folks the world over."

"And you debated it last week, and you'll debate it next week," Eustace said. "Just like you've debated the same thing for seventy-five years without taking any action."

"How dare you!" The red-headed woman, scolded, removing her hand from her face to reveal an amber brooch. "You insolent cur. We could banish you—"

"Yes," Eustace said. "You could…except nobody wants to do my job. I know, you tried to get somebody else to do your dirty work outside the walls, and nobody volunteered, because they are too chicken to deal with the real world and get their hands dirty."

"Now see here," The shiny, bald man with a bushy mustache said. "You cannot talk to the council in this manner. We could find you in contempt."

"You already find me contemptible," Eustace groaned. "It's not too much to hold me in contempt, too. But what I have to say is too important to stand on ceremony."

Chief Justice Abalos held up his hand. "Enough. We could continue in this manner for hours. It is both tedious and unnecessary. Let us hear him out and get back to the business at hand."

"Thank you," Eustace said, scowling at the bushy-mustached man before he turned his ire toward the woman. "As I said, I have business you need to hear right now."

"Then get on with it!" The woman with the brooch said, exhausted.

"That little girl right there," Eustace said, pointing to Anabelle. "Is no less than a Normal! I found her roaming around outside the gates of our fair city."

A collective gasp came from the council chamber. Chief Justice Abalos nearly fainted in his chair, but he hung onto the bench. "A Normal! Here!"

I wanted to scream. I wanted to shout, but my mouth was still bound by the mud that Eustace used to silence the three of us.

"As I told you, there is a war still out there, and we need men to fight it!" Eustace shouted. "We cannot hold off any longer!"

A blue light shone from behind me. Three wisps of air shimmered brightly on Tibor's cheek. With a deep gust of wind from his nose, Tibor blew through the mud that bound his face. *Could he have done that the whole time?*

"She is not the problem!" Tibor screamed. "By Order of the Tuppins, I demand to be heard."

Chief Justice Abalos leaned in closer to get a better look at Tibor. "And who are you to make such a claim?"

Tibor pulled back his shirt to reveal a tattoo on his chest. It was a teacup with a sun radiating out from every angle.

"This mark proves I am a Tuppins. I am kin to you, and the order, though I have never been here until today."

"And how do we know you are not lying?" The woman with the brooch asked.

"Yes, yes," the man with the bushy mustache added. "It is easy to get a tattoo on any street corner, from any wandering hobo."

"Perhaps, but only a true tattoo of the Tuppins, bound with magic," Tibor replied, "can do this."

Tibor closed his eyes. His cheek glowed softly. Then, a moment later the tattoo on his chest glowed as well.

"My god, man," Chief Justice Abalos said. "You truly are part of the order."

"That I am," Tibor said. He took in another gust of wind, and on the exhale his chains broke. "And I demand to be heard."

"Don't listen to him! He's a liar!"

"I do not lie!" Tibor's voice boomed. "I came here – we came here – to make sure Roselyn Light made it safely to Toledo."

Tibor pointed to me with pride, smiling, but he was the only one grinning. The rest of the council, Eustace, and Maribel looked confused. Even Anabelle looked at him with contempt.

"Why is she so important, then?" Chief Justice Abalos asked.

"Because, she is a Dual," Tibor replied. "And, more importantly, your granddaughter."

CHAPTER THREE

We were led into Chief Justice Abalos's private chambers after Tibor dropped his bombshell revelation about me being Abalos's granddaughter. Our mud chains flaked dirt onto the thick ornamental rugs covering the deep wood floor.

"What do you mean, she's my granddaughter?" Chief Justice Abalos asked, leaning against the rich, deep oak bookcases that lined walls on either side of his office with leather-bound books. "She can't be my granddaughter."

I tried to scream in agreement, but I could only wave my hands and mumble loudly since my mouth was still covered in mud. Anabelle joined me in flailing her arms until we looked…well, we looked just ridiculous.

"Would you get that stupid mud off their mouths?" Chief Justice Abalos shouted.

"But, sir," Eustace started. "They are prisoners."

Chief Justice Abalos scowled at him, moving from the bookcase to the mahogany desk stacked with notebooks; a typewriter sat in the center, gleaming brightly as if it had never been used. "I have long ago accepted that you are useless, but don't make me ask again."

"Fine," Eustace said, grumbling.

Eustace snapped his fingers, and the mud from our mouths fell away. I was free, finally, and I had a lot to say.

"Thank the lord!" I shouted.

"Praise Jesus," Anabelle added, pulling chapstick out of her pocket. "My lips have been chapped for the longest time."

"Now," I replied, turning to Tibor. "What do you mean I'm his granddaughter? I wasn't born here."

"I'm saying," Tibor said, pointing to Chief Justice Abalos. "That your son, Thomas Abalos and his wife, Susan Marie Abalos, fled Toledo when Susan was six months pregnant, and when the baby was born, she was surrendered to the nursemaids to be brought up like a Normal."

"Blasphemy," Eustace crowed. "It just isn't true. No one ever leaves Toledo."

"You're only lying to yourself if you believe that," Tibor said. "Toledo isn't a prison. People are free to come and go as they please, if they wish, just like any other city. Isn't that right, your honor?"

"My son died," Chief Justice Abalos growled. "This is a well-known fact, and that you would come here spouting such lies is an insult to our way of life and your oath as a Tuppins."

"That's what I've been trying to tell you," Eustace growled. "They are heretics of the highest order and should be dealt with swiftly before their blasphemy spreads."

"What does swift justice mean, exactly?" Anabelle asked.

I assume she knew the answer because I read between the lines of Eustace's menacing tone without him saying a word.

"To kill you all," Eustace said, predictably, "As an example to the others who would dare fight against us."

"I hate that plan," Anabelle said. "I'm just gonna come out and say it. Not a fan."

"Seconded," I replied. "Besides, it's easy to see if Tibor's telling the truth."

"How?" Chief Justice Abalos asked.

"Use a seer. Have them look into the past. They can tell if we're telling the truth, easily, right?"

"I suppose," Chief Justice Abalos said. "That is possible."

"Oh my god," I replied. "Have you really never thought of that before? I can't be the first person to suggest that, right? It's so obvious."

"Regardless, it is a good idea that we should try."

"Good," I replied, sitting down in the plush chair in the corner of the room. "We can wait. This is the nicest place I've been in a long time. No rush."

Chief Justice Abalos sneered. "You certainly have my son's cockiness. Eustace, bring me a seer…and take these other two to the dungeon."

"My pleasure!" Eustace replied, pulling on Anabelle and Tibor's chains. "And what about her?"

"You can leave her with me," he replied, turning to me with a smile. "I think I can handle one little girl. Besides, she might just be family."

The mountain on Eustace's cheek glowed, and the mud chains binding my hands crumbled. "As you wish."

"No!" Anabelle said as Eustace dragged Tibor and Anabelle out of the room. "Stop! I don't wanna go! Don't make me go!"

"Please," I said turning to Chief Justice Abalos. "Please let them stay."

"Take them away," Chief Justice Abalos said, emotionless.

"No!" I replied, tugging on Anabelle's arm. "Come back!"

I pulled Anabelle's arms with all my might until a square glowed on Chief Justice Abalos's cheek. The room stretched to triple its size until I couldn't reach Anabelle anymore. She swirled into a dark hole in front of me, and then she was gone, leaving only a closed door behind her.

"What are you going to do to them?" I snarled. "Bring them back."

"They will be fine," Chief Justice Abalos replied. "If the Tuppins told the truth, you will see them again very soon."

"And if he didn't?"

Chief Justice Abalos walked behind his desk and poured himself a glass of scotch from the bar under the window, light streaming through it into the room, blinding me to everything except his ominous shadow. "Then you will join them, soon."

I plopped down on the chair again and folded my arms. "I guess we wait then."

*

"Look into my eyes," a middle-aged woman with dark gray eyes whispered to me. She was a Seer. As I stared into her eyes, her pupils dilated, and her cheek started to glow with the mark of an all-seeing eye.

"What are you doing to me?" I asked. "Can't you just look into a crystal ball or something?"

"No child. That is a fallacy," the seer said with a wry smile. "Most people think a Seer can journey wherever they want and see whatever they want, but our power doesn't work that way."

Chief Justice Abalos shook his head. "Not if you want to be effective, at least. For a seer to be effective, they have to know where to look."

"I will be looking deep into your past," the seer said, placing her hands above mine.

"They say the eyes are the gateway into the soul," Chief Justice Abalos said, swirling the scotch in his hand. "I don't know about that, but they are certainly the window into the past."

"Quiet now," the Seer said. "I need complete concentration."

Chief Justice Abalos took a sip of his drink and quieted his mouth. The ice swirling in his glass was all I heard. The smell of fine tobacco filled the room. Then, a whoosh of air came from the fan. The curtains hanging against the window swished back and forth.

The Seer hummed under her breath as her pupils continued to dilate until there was no color in them, only blackness. Then, the blackness of her pupils expanded outside of just her eyeball and across her face. It wrapped around my head and engulfed my vision. I fell and fell until I slammed into a cobblestone street.

I pushed myself to my hands and knees. I was in the Plaza Mayor, back in Ambrosia. I recognized the statue of Charles III on horseback at its center. As I spun around, Three Goliaths loomed over me. I screamed out and turned away from them, fearful I would be caught. However, they looked through me as if I didn't exist.

"Don't let her get away!" A soldier shouted as the Goliaths rushed forward.

I tried to run, but my legs were glued in place. A squad of soldiers ran toward me, and I couldn't do anything but watch as the sprinted through me as if I was a ghost.

"What is happening?" I shouted, scared and confused.

"Calm your mind," the Seer's voice said. "You are seeing the past now."

A wall of water sprung forth from a young woman standing in an alley. She was beautiful and scared. Her lip trembled as she looked back at a man holding a baby.

Then, the woman disappeared behind a wall of water. A stream of water shot through the alleyway and toward the Goliaths, who struggled to move forward. The water shot at me in a rush, and I braced myself against it, but as the stream splashed against me, I was suddenly in blackness again.

When the blackness faded, I was inside a hospital room. The same young woman laid on a bed in stirrups. She was panting and screaming as the man from the alleyway held her hand tightly. A doctor sat at the woman's feet as the woman pushed and pushed, while nurses crowded around her.

"One more good push!" The doctor said. "The baby is crowning."

"You're doing great, Susie," The young man said, kissing her hand.

"I hate you, Tom!" Susie shouted. "I hate you! I hate you! I hate you!"

"Is that my father?" I asked. "And my mother?"

"Yes," the seer's voice replied. "Quiet your mind and your voice. Experience the moment."

A baby's voice screamed in the ether. The doctor stood up, and a tiny baby, a little me, screamed bloody murder into the room. As mom and dad collapsed into each other's arms in tears, the scene faded.

When it reappeared, Tom, my dad, was inside this very room, screaming at Chief Justice Abalos. Mom stood behind him, very pregnant.

"I don't want to live your life!" Tom screamed. "There is a great world out there, and I wanna see it. I want my baby to see it."

"You, all of you, have everything you need right here in Toledo!" Chief Justice Abalos said.

"No," Tom shouted. "You might, but I don't."

"Please," Susie chimed in. "Give us your blessing. It doesn't have to be like this."

"Yes," Chief Justice Abalos said. "It does."

"We want you in our child's life," Susie replied. "She needs her grandfather."

"If that were true, you wouldn't leave."

Tom turned to the door. He grabbed Susie's hand and walked toward it to leave. Abalos' cheek glowed, and the door turned into a wall.

"If you leave this place, you will be dead to me. Never come back. Your life is forfeit."

Tom looked back, a tear in his eye. "Then it is forfeit."

I slammed back in my chair as the room came back into focus. It spun for a minute, and then it stopped with a jerk. The Seer's eyes returned to normal as she smiled at me.

"That was intense," she said. "Are you okay? Sometimes people freak out their first time."

"That was…" I replied. "Freaking awesome!"

The Seer laughed. "You really are one of us, then."

"Well?" Chief Justice Abalos said. "What did you see?"

The Seer stood. "Everything that man told you is the truth. She truly is your kin. A miracle come back from the dead."

"Well," Chief Justice Abalos said, finishing the last of his scotch. "That is interesting. Very Interesting"

*

After finding out that I was his granddaughter, Abalos warmed to me almost immediately. He poured himself another glass of scotch and spent a long time studying my face as I sat across from him, in an uncomfortable chair with rivets digging into my back.

"You do look remarkably like my Thomas, now that I look closer," he said. "And he looked remarkably like my wife."

I nodded. "I always thought I looked nothing like my mother, but then my mother turned out to not be my mother, so I don't know who I look like."

"You poor child," he said. "It must have been hard for you, growing up so far from your people."

I shook my head. "I never knew you were my people. I always thought I was just a Normal. So, it was fine."

"That is the worst part about it!" he said. "What kind of world do we live in where a magical child can't embrace her gifts? Especially if you truly are a Dual."

"You haven't been outside Toledo in a long time, have you?"

Abalos shook his head. "Not in decades. I don't see the point. However, I have spies everywhere, who report back to me, and keep me abreast on the outside world."

"You need to fire them, then. It's a bad world out there for magic users; grand …pa…what do I call you?"

"Hmm…interesting question. I always liked…Abu personally, but I'm pretty agnostic to the whole thing. This is all very new to me."

"I hate that," I replied. "What do your other grandkids call you?"

Abalos sighed. "Tom was my only child. His mother, my wife, died in childbirth and I never remarried. You were my son's only child. Which makes us, the last of my line, and you, my only kin. I thought my line would die with me, but now I know it can continue. That makes me happy."

I smiled at him. It was weird to witness the stoic facade come off a man I'd initially judged to be hard and watch him become just another human.

"How about Pop? Simple. Classic."

"No," he said, disgusted. "Not that."

"Hrm," I uttered, thinking hard. "What about Lito? Like abuelito, but also, not."

"Appropriate," he said, smiled. "That would be fine. Now come, there is much to do."

"What about my friends?" I replied.

"They will be fine," Lito said. "You have my word. You will see them soon."

I didn't have any reason to trust him, but for some reason I did. After all, we were family, and even though I had been lied to by my family for my entire life, they weren't my biological family. This was a new start. My grandfather wouldn't be like all the rest. I could tell. Things were about to turn around for me. I felt it deep in my bones.

CHAPTER FOUR

Lito navigated us masterfully through the deep, dark labyrinth of City Hall. "These twists," he said. "Are meant to drive intruders mad."

I believed it, too. I would have been lost a hundred times if I hadn't clung tightly to his robe. His cheek glowed with the distinctive square mark of an illusionist until we reached a tropical forest replete with torrential rainfall. Lito walked through the downfall, bone-dry as the droplets careened off him.

Lito wiped his hand across the palm fronds of a downed tree, and a door appeared in front of us. He pulled it open, and the brightness of the midday sun shone on us. We walked out into an alleyway on the side of the building, and down the street toward the square.

"It's not the real sun of course," Lito said as he placed a pair of sunglasses on his face. "But it is bright none the less."

"Is anything true about this place?" I asked. "Why fake the sun?"

"These people, my people, do not want to feel trapped. When we first isolated ourselves, all we had was a dome surrounding the city which looked out into the world beyond us. We thought that it would give people a sense of belonging to the world, even though they weren't part of it anymore."

"Didn't work?" I asked.

Lito shook his head. "It is unfortunate, but the citizens of Toledo felt like they were caged animals. They fought against us, even though we were trying to help them. So, we created this illusion, to help ease their minds about the transition."

"And it worked?"

Lito sighed. "For the most part. Still, there are some that want to leave, and we can't stop them."

"People like my dad," I said.

"We don't talk about them after they leave. They are dead to us." Lito stopped for a moment. "Let's get something to eat."

My stomach growled at his words as if it had forgotten that food existed. I nodded my head ferociously. "Yes, please."

*

Honestly, I was a little disappointed in the food that Lito chose for us. There weren't floating salads, or hopping frogs, or singing fish at the place he chose. In fact, it was a place I knew well, and actively avoided. He took us to a McDonald's, where he ordered us both Big Macs.

"How do you get McDonald's here?" I asked as we sat down with our trays, trying to mask my disappointment.

"One of my scouts found it on her travels. It's delightful, I think."

"And they just deliver ingredients to a forest in the middle of nowhere?"

Lito laughed. "Of course not."

"So how do you get it here, then?"

"We don't," he admitted. "It's all a ruse to make citizens feel like part of the world at large."

"Isn't that…illegalish? I mean there must be some sort of trademark laws or something."

"A bit," he nodded, poking at his burger. "However, I figured that if the Spanish government couldn't find us, then McDonald's couldn't either. It's a simple reminder that we are still part of the world, even if we are separated from it. It's almost as if everything is normal, at least in their minds."

"Everything isn't normal, though, is it?" I asked, biting into my sandwich. I never liked McDonald's, and this time wasn't any different. Still, it was food, and I was starving.

"No," Lito said. "It isn't."

Lito didn't pick up his food at all. Instead, he watched me eat, smiling as I downed the burger. When I finished, he pushed his tray over to me.

"Eat more. You're skin and bones."

"Aren't you going to have any?" I asked.

He shook his head. "No. I was never a big fan of this food. I just wanted you to feel like home, at least for a moment."

"You think I eat McDonald's at home?"

"My son loved it, so I just assumed."

I swallowed another bite of Lito's burger almost despite myself. "I'm only eating this because I'm starving. I haven't had fast food in years. Mama made all our meals from scratch."

"Are you even old enough to not have done anything for years?" He asked, smiling.

I swallowed another bite of food. "I'm old enough to get chased by the RMP and barely escape with my life, so I'm going to say 'yes.'"

"Fair enough," Lito replied. "Does that mean you aren't enjoying your food?"

I shook my head. "It's fine, but on the way into town, there were so many magical food shops, with floating things and weirdly colored fruits. I was kinda hoping for that."

"Why didn't you say so?" Lito replied.

He closed his eyes. The square on his cheek pulsated a deep blue. As it did, the Big Mac in my hand grew three sizes and ballooned into a beach ball that swirled with a thousand colors that exploded before my eyes, including some I had never seen before.

Lito opened his eyes and smiled. "All of that is just an illusion, you know. Just a lot of special baking powder and a well-designed oven. The magic makes the food taste kind of…awful if you ask me, like they are trying too hard."

"It's cool, though." I watched the balloon, which had been my hamburger, float into the air, bobbing up and down. "So I can eat it?"

"Of course."

I hungrily ripped off a piece of the balloon. The rest of the patrons in the diner scoffed at me. I must have looked like a true tourist, but I didn't care. It was amazing, and no matter what Lito said, it was the best burger I'd ever tasted.

"I always found it annoying to eat like that," Lito laughed. "But my son, he got a kick out of it when he was your age."

I took another bite, and his words processed as I swallowed. "Can you tell me about him?"

The light from Lito's cheek dimmed and faded into nothingness. As it did, my balloon turned back into a sandwich, and floated back down to my tray, no longer filled with magic.

"I'm sorry, I didn't mean to…"

"It's fine," Lito said, holding up his hand. "I haven't thought about him…I try not to think about him…and when I do…it is difficult."

I placed my hand over Lito's as it strummed the table. "I understand. It must be hard to lose someone you love. I thought I loved people once…my mother…fake mother…she's lied to me my whole life, about everything."

"Yes, the ones you love always hurt you."

I dropped my head and started to cry. I had been working so hard to be free, to forget my past, that I never took any time to grieve for my mother, or whatever she was to me. Even if she didn't birth me, she took care of me and nurtured me. What happened to her once I was gone?

Lito reached into his pocket for a handkerchief. "Perhaps we should talk about this later. After all, this is a happy day. We should celebrate finding each other. Besides, we have much to do."

I grabbed the handkerchief from Lito's outstretched arm and rubbed my eyes. "Yes. We should be celebrating. You're right. It's just, sad, you know?"

"I do at that." Lito looked down at a gold banded watch on his wrist. "My, my, my. Look at the time. I have a very big surprise for you." He held out his hand. "Shall we?"

I looked up at him. "I know I should be happy but…can I cry…just a little more? Or are you in a rush?"

He nodded. "I'm in no rush, my dear. You can do anything you want. My surprise can wait a little while longer."

*

Eventually, I ran out of tears, and we left the restaurant. I would be lying if I said it was the first time I openly wept in a McDonald's, or that I was ashamed of it. Sometimes, we all need a good cry.

Lito held his arms behind his back as we walked up the street toward a towering church at the top of the hill.

"This is the Primate Cathedral of Saint Mary of Toledo. It has stood since the twelfth century, watching over us. Truly a masterpiece."

The cathedral was a sight to behold. It stood out like a beacon above the worldly concerns of the city, a site where all the city's spiritual energy emanated from and toward. My eye tracked up the intricately designed facade and up the steeple at the top of the cathedral, where a faint beam of blue light pulsed into the sky.

"What is that?" I asked.

"That is where all the power generated to run our barrier comes from, along with most of the city's power. Without that spire, and the light that emanates from it, we would not be able to remain hidden from the world, and we would invite attack from all those who seek to destroy us."

"Wow," I said. I wanted to say more, but I was in awe of the Cathedral, and what it meant to the city.

"You know," Lito said, his dark robe scraping along the ground, "you are very special."

"Am I?" I asked. "I never thought I was special."

I had lived for sixteen years, and until last week, I was completely average and perfectly unspectacular in every way.

"Very much so," Lito replied. "Duals are very uncommon."

"That I know," I replied. "There's less than a hundred in the entire world, right?"

"Seventy-three actually, but who's counting?"

"You are, clearly," I replied.

Lito chuckled. "It is my job to keep tabs on everything magical that happens both inside and outside the city walls. Though, as you mentioned, I often do not do as good a job as I would like. My spy network can feed me information, but we are still blocked off from the world."

"You got a McDonald's. I guess that's something," I said, climbing the hill toward the cathedral.

Lito sighed, following slowly behind me. "A dreadful place, I admit, but I suppose it is something that ties us to the world."

"Maybe look into KFC. They're pretty good. Or just…like, abandon all fast food. That would probably be better."

"That is a good point," he said. "I always feel terrible after eating there."

The road narrowed at the top of the hill as the pavement turned to cobblestone, and the Cathedral grew until it dwarfed everything else in the town. Looking down from the top of the hill, I saw the roofs of every house in the city, and out to the great stone walls that protected it. Beyond the wall, the bubble surrounding the city pulsated with colors from orange to pink that swirled together and mixed into the sky. At the apex of it all, right above us, the cathedral shot a blue light into the sky which made everything possible.

"You are about to see one of the wonders of the world," Lito said. "Have you ever seen a great wonder before?"

"I have seen pictures of the Grand Canyon."

Lito chuckled. "You are funny, Rosie, and strong, but nothing you've seen can prepare you for what you're about to see in this cathedral."

"I've been in churches before, abuelito. Lots of them. When you've seen one church, you've seen them all."

Lito shook his head. "No. When you see what is beyond these walls, everything will change."

I stepped toward the massive oaken doors that towered above me. When I pushed open the door, it creaked at me, as if bidding me to enter. Angels carved into the door started to glow blue, and cracks of aqua light splintered through the wood as it gave way to my touch, and the great door swung open.

"There is old magic inside these doors," Lito said. "And it welcomes you to enter."

I stepped into the cathedral. Inside, every pillar was lit by a dull blue light, just like the one that glowed in the door. A low chorus of voices hummed through the church, echoing off every marble wall, and giving an ethereal, haunting beauty to the carved stonework along every surface.

"Come," Lito whispered, leading me toward the back of the church, around the front of a wrought iron cage with golden tipped spikes on the top of it.

My feet clomped across the marble floor, but Lito's stayed silent as if he glided above the ground. I knew that was impossible. He was an illusionist and couldn't fly, but he moved gracefully enough that I almost believed he could walk on air.

"This church was destroyed in the seventh century when the Moors invaded. They built a mosque on this ground. Then, when they finally reconquered Toledo, the

Catholics destroyed that mosque and built this church to be the envy of the world."

Whoever built the cathedral clearly wanted to make a statement about opulent wealth, namely that they had it. Every surface in the church was accented with gold. On either side of the church wall, high above the ground, enormous, gilded organ pipes shot into the sky. In front of us, in the center of the church, sat an open cage with a hundred wooden chairs. A chorus of men and woman, dressed in burgundy robes, sang into the heavens providing the hauntingly beautiful music I heard reverberating through the halls of the church.

"Each of those chairs is carved with a part of the magical struggle we faced against the Normals, from our creation to the rise of magic, and eventually our downfall."

"Our creation?" I asked.

"There are those that say we were descended from the angels themselves, Rosie," Lito said. "Or the Valkyries as the case may be."

"But that's crazy," I said. "That's crazy, right?"

"Possibly," he said, but I got the sense he was holding something back.

Lito led us around the chorus cage, toward the back of the church. Behind the cage was a statue carved in marble that stood a hundred feet high. At its base, rising through the sculpture, a thousand men and women screamed toward the heavens, grasping at the angels for help. The angel rose above the men and women, seemingly breaking free of the sculpture and rising into the sky. A beam of light shone through from a light in the ceiling, illuminating the face of the smiling angel, arms outstretched, floating up to Heaven.

My eyes tracked the light toward the crack in the ceiling where the calm, blue light originated. Surrounding a skylight which let in the light, a dozen angels and demons beckoned the angel from a bed of clouds, as if her work on Earth was complete and it was time to come home.

Lito's fingers drew a line from the humans suffering to the sky above. "This depicts the final battle between Normals and magic folk, guided by the light of the Valkyrie, which will lead us to victory, and the promise of everlasting life."

"Brutal," I said. "You really believe this will happen?"

"There are a great many things that I believe, and soon you will learn the reason why. I am very excited for you."

All of the lights dimmed as we reached a small alcove in the back of the church. My stomach tightened as I followed him from the light into the darkness of a small hallway which eventually ended at a set of stairs that led down into the dark abyss.

"This is as far as I can take you, little one," Lito said. "You must do the rest on your own."

"Excuse me?" I replied. "You want me to go into the creepy darkness alone? I don't think so. That's how people get murdered."

"Trust me," he replied. "You will be fine. Just remember to be humble and polite when you meet her. She can spell fear and hates bravado."

"Her?" I replied, frantically. "Who is her?"

"You will see." Lito smiled calmly at me. "Just remember, you are special. There is not one other like you in the whole world."

"Well, there are seventy-three others."

"Yes," he replied. "But there is not one other like you."

He gently nudged me forward without another word. I took a step down the ominous, marble steps, listening to my feet to clomp with every step I took deeper into the darkness.

CHAPTER FIVE

At the bottom of the stairs, thin cobblestone passageway trailed off into the darkness. There was no light in the hallway. I had to take it on faith that the way forward was safe. A test no doubt, but one I had no interest in taking. I'd only met Lito a few hours ago, and people had a history of abusing my trust. I wanted to believe he had my best interests at heart, but it was hard.

Then, I remembered that I was a Dual. One of my powers was Light and the fire it controlled. I hadn't thought about my powers much since entering Toledo. I was so concerned with the magic around me that I forgot the magic within me.

I closed my eyes and imagined a small flame shooting out from the end of my fingertips. I opened my eyes and felt my left cheek glow with the Sun, the symbol of the Light…except, nothing happened. I closed my eyes again and imagined an orb of water forming in my hands. This time, my right cheek glowed with a moon, the symbol of Water. I opened my eyes, and again nothing happened.

A thin crack in the ceiling pulsated with a deep blue hue in tune with my own magic, but aside from that, I was powerless here. Still, at least my cheek gave me some light, and the blue hue from above amplified it.

I stepped forward slowly and carefully. Every time my foot touched a cobblestone block, I pressed it down gently to test for a trap. I placed my hands on the damp walls, and its slime rubbed off on my palms. It smelt like stale water, the kind that stagnates on the tops of a still lake. My stomach rose in my throat.

Still, I pressed forward and caught the breath trying to escape my mouth. I held it in my lungs as I took another step and only let it out when my foot touched the ground again. Then, my other foot raised, and I held my breath until once more my foot landed on solid ground.

Finally, after a hundred or so careful steps, my foot kicked against a wood door. My hands shifted from the dewy walls and slid down the splintered wood to find a latch.

"There's a door down here," I yelled back up, expecting a response from Lito. However, all that returned was silence.

He must have known there was a door in the basement, or he wouldn't have sent me down. He must have expected me to open it, and go inside. *Why else would I be here?*

I pressed down on the latch and heard a click from the other side of the door. I slowly pushed open the door, and it let out a creaking noise.

"Hello?" I said meekly. My voice filled the small room and bounced back at me.

A blue glow, the same color I had seen in the hallway, but richer and fuller, emanated from the middle of the room.

A large tank of blue liquid. A dim blue light pulsated through a large glass cylinder in the center of the room. Tubs connected it to the ceiling. In front of the container sat a white chair with its back turned towards me.

It was unlike anything that I had seen before in Toledo. The rest of the town was ancient and old. The chair was sleek and modern as if somebody had fashioned it from the accessories in an Apple store. Dozens of small tubes connected the chair to the cylinder at the center of the room. It was as if the twenty-fifth century collided with the twelfth

A low moan originated from the chair and grew into a prolonged groan in the center of the room. Something moved on the armchair. The next instant, the chair spun around to reveal a woman, blue shimmering through every vein in her body. On her head sat a silver helmet with tubes that sent blue liquid into the cylinder behind it. When her eyes opened, they shimmered blue as well.

"Hello," the woman uttered in a quiet voice. "You must be Roselyn. I'm so happy to meet you."

"W-w-w-w-" I couldn't speak. I was too scared to move. My grandfather had sent me to get my brain sucked out by an alien, and that wasn't very cool. If I lived, I would never trust an adult again, ever.

"I'm sorry," the voice moaned. "I must look a fright."

The glittery blue body pulled the helmet from its head, and the blue light throbbing through its veins stopped pulsating. The being clapped its hands together, and lights turned on throughout the room. No longer did the body look a scary blue mess, but instead like a smiling woman with blonde hair and perfect teeth. Her ruby lips made her teeth shine even more, and when she stood, it was with the grace of a model walking a runway.

"Where are my manners?" she said. "My name is Fiona."

But I still couldn't talk, because at that moment her wings extend behind her, and filled the room. She was an angel – an honest to god angel.

"I'm not an angel, actually," Fiona said. "Sorry, I should have let you ask your question. Sometimes, I live in the future."

"W-w-w-what are you then?" I replied.

"I'm a Valkyrie."

"Oh," I replied. "That's way more normal. What's a Valkyrie?"

"Like from Valhalla?" she said. "Don't you know of Valhalla?"

"Where I'm from, if you have wings and live in a church, you're an angel."

Fiona sighed. "That would be a very human thing for you to say. I suppose I can't blame you. It's not like we do a very good job of publicity, after all."

"What is a Valkyrie then?"

Fiona was silent for a moment, a long moment, as she thought of the right words to explain herself. "It's like an angel, but we fight a lot more, and we're not from Heaven. We're from Valhalla, where the Norse gods wait to welcome warriors of great strength to their everlasting life."

"It sounds like you're an angel from Heaven," I replied, but then I thought better of myself. "But I'm clearly wrong, or something."

Fiona scratched her perfect head. Even as she ran her hands through her hair, not a single strand fell out of place. "It's not that important, in the grand scheme, is it? I suppose you can call me an angel if you want. Odin knows the rest of them do. I stopped trying to explain myself to them years ago."

"Years ago? You've been here for years?"

Fiona nodded. "Since before the great war, by a couple of centuries. I was here when this place was built, actually. Crafted some of the columns myself."

"And nobody knew about it!" I replied. "How is that possible?"

"Lots of people knew about it. You're only just now learning about it now. There's a difference."

"I've read a lot of history," I replied. "And nobody's ever mentioned an angel…Valkyrie. Or whatever. I would have remembered that."

"What people don't know about the world can just about fill the sun a million times over. Just because you have never read about it, my dear, does not mean it does not exist, or it did not happen. I have lived in this body my whole life. I am very sure when I came to earth."

"Of course," I replied, detecting some frustration in her voice. "I'm sorry. This is just…a lot to take in, you know?"

She nodded. "Yes, this has been quite an ordeal for you, and now, I have only complicated things. I am afraid I still have one very important question for you, however. It is of dire importance."

"What is it?" I asked, hurriedly.

"Would you like some tea?"

I couldn't help but chuckle, and for a moment the tension was lifted. "You know, I would, I really would."

*

I didn't know if Fiona was an angel or a Valkyrie, but her tea was heavenly. Not only did it have the perfect ratio of tea, milk, and lemon, but it smelt like a field of lemongrass right after a morning dew.

We sat in her kitchen, offset from the main chamber. It was a quaint room, small but meticulous. Her kitchen doubled as a living room, full of bookcases along both walls and a small cot in a dark, black corner. Nothing was out of place, and no space was wasted.

"Can I ask you something?" I said as I took a delicious sip of lemon tea.

"Of course," Fiona replied from the other side of the table, her cool blue eyes staring intently at me.

"I know that I'm a big muckety-muck's granddaughter," I replied. "And a Dual…but…why are you all being so nice to me?"

Fiona laughed so hard tea almost came squirting out of her nose…and then it did. "You…you truly don't know how special you are, do you?"

I shook my head. "I know I'm one of seventy-ish Duals in the world, but everybody here is special, so I don't get it. So I can use two types of magic, so what? That doesn't make me special."

"No," she said. "That's not what makes you special. What makes you special is that you are the only Dual who is under forty years old."

"Huh?" I replied. "That can't be."

She nodded. "I'm afraid so. You are the first Dual born in a long time, which makes you extra special. So special, you could be the key to our future."

"The key?" I asked, confused. "What key?"

"The key to bringing Toledo out of the shadows and saving magical folks everywhere."

Fiona stood and walked over to her bookcase. She pulled down a thick leather book from one of the shelves. She brushed the dust off its cover as she sat back down.

"Come on, now," I scoffed.

"It's true," she said, flipping through the book. "This was all prophesied eons ago. The rise. The war. The fall.

Even the invisible city which was magic's last hope for survival."

Fiona placed the book in front of me. The left page was an illustration of an angel flying up to heaven as dozens of men fell into the flaming abyss.

"I believe you," I said, closing the book and sliding it back over to her.

"You should never believe anyone," Fiona replied, sitting back down. "But I'll summarize for you since you've had a tough couple of days. The story I showed you tells of a prophet, a chosen one, who will lead us back from the brink into a new golden age."

"And you think it's me?" I asked with a smile.

"I know it is," Fiona replied.

"I'm no prophet, and I'm definitely not a chosen one."

"And yet," Fiona replied, sipping on her tea. "I have chosen you. Funny, that, isn't it?"

What kind of chosen one was I? I couldn't even get my friends out of prison. I couldn't even help those closest to me.

"Don't worry," Fiona said, placing her tea on the table. "I will see to it that your friends are released as soon as possible. I have foreseen it."

"Oh," I replied. "Thank you. I suppose that means you are a seer."

"No," she replied. "I have the power of all seven of the signs…and I will show you how to unlock them, too, if you will let me."

CHAPTER SIX

I spat out my tea across the table after Fiona's ridiculous comment. "What do you mean, you'll show me how to use all my powers. I only have two. That's why they call it Dual, and not Tri, or Seven."

Fiona shook her head. "You humans and your primitive understanding of the world. Just because nobody has been able to wield more than two powers, doesn't mean it can't be done. The power is inside you. Inside all of you."

"They why are there less than a hundred Duals in the world if all magic users can access multiple powers?"

"Not just them," Fiona replied. "Inside all humans, magic or no."

"That's crazy," I said. "I haven't met a ton of magic users, but I've met a lot of Normals, and they don't have a magic bone in their bodies."

Fiona sat down her tea onto the table. "That's what you thought about yourself as well before you found your powers. And yet, just a couple of days ago, you discovered multiple."

"But that's because I was Suppressed. What are you saying? That everybody in the entire world is suppressed?"

She nodded. "That's what I'm saying. After all, magic folks can Suppress their kin specifically because they studied the brains of Normals and found out how to manipulate your neurons to inhibit your innate abilities…or I should say, I have studied the brains of Normals. The rest of you just implemented my findings."

"So, you are the reason I was Suppressed?"

She shook her head. "No, I just planted the seed and gave the council the tools. They are the ones who allowed it to happen."

"Do they know that it's because of Normals that we can be suppressed?"

She shook her head, taking another sip of tea, casually, as if we were talking about the weather. "They know what they need to know, as do you."

"So that's all I need to know, huh?" I replied snidely. "If that's so, why tell me anything?"

"Because we are a team," Fiona said. "I can't save the world without you, and you can't unlock your true potential without me."

"And what if I don't want to unlock my true potential? What if I am fine being a Dual?"

Fiona shrugged. "Then, I will kill you."

"Excuse me?" I said, sure that I heard her wrong. "Did you say you'll kill me?"

Fiona nodded. "Yes, I will kill you and examine your brain for clues as to why you exist, just as I have several dozen times before."

"Before?" I replied, exasperated. "Several dozen times."

"That's right," she said matter of factly.

"But I'm the savior, aren't I? Didn't you just say that? How can you kill me if I'm the savior?"

"The prophecy never said how you saved the world, just that you did. You can be as useful dead as you are alive."

"And what? Those others were the savior, too."

"Obviously not," she replied. "Though we thought so at the time. Still, we only need to be right once, no matter how many times we are wrong."

"You're crazy," I said, slamming my hand on the table so hard my teacup tipped over. "I'm a human being. You can't just dissect me like a lab animal."

Fiona held up a single finger, and her eyes turned steely. "Sure, I can," she scoffed. "I see everything clearly because I am not part of humanity. You humans have a misplaced duty to each other, but I have no such qualms. My duty is to see humanity unlocks their true potential. Now, I would love it if you helped me in that aim willingly, but I can get almost as much information from a dead body as a live one."

"Is that a threat?" I asked. "Because I want to make sure I'm hearing you right. Are you threatening me?"

"No," Fiona stated flatly, with a broad smile across her face. "It's a fact. I'm telling you what will happen. If you perceive it as a threat, then so be it. I hope it doesn't come to that though. I very much want us to be friends."

I was angrier than I had ever been in my entire life, but I feared Fiona and her powers as a Valkyrie. She could destroy me in a single instant, and while my life had become complicated, I was very much attached to it. That being said, I didn't have to help her for free.

"If I'm going to help you, I want my friends released now," I said.

"As I said," she replied. "They will be released soon."

"Fine," I replied, confidently. "I will help you the minute my friends are free and safe."

"Very well," Fiona replied. "I shall make it happen. However, do not take my help as a sign of weakness. It is a sign of good will. I want you to help me freely, but I do not need you to help me freely. Understood?"

I nodded. "Understood."

I turned to leave, but Fiona cleared her throat one more time. "I would also appreciate if this conversation stayed between you and me. There is no need to bother the council, or your friends, with what we spoke about here today."

"Is that a request, or an order?" I replied under my breath.

She shrugged. "You can take it any way you would like. However, if I should hear that you spoke to anybody else about it… Well, things will get very bad for those you love, very quickly. Understood?"

I took a step toward the door. "Understood. I will keep my mouth shut."

"Good girl. I knew you would see things my way."

*

I climbed back up the dark stairs from Fiona's chambers where I saw my grandfather's smiling face. I wondered if he was aware of Fiona's brutal nature. *Did Lito know how horrible his Valkryie was, or was he blind to her true nature?*

Her flawless visage belied her intentions, and I knew how often a beautiful face tricked people, men especially. I had seen it time and time again – beautiful beings getting away with horrible acts because of their looks, and Fiona was the most beautiful of them all.

"Pretty amazing, wasn't she?" Lito said.

She wasn't, but I couldn't say that to him. After her veiled threats (and her outright ones) I didn't know what would happen if I spoke ill of her. I also didn't know if I could trust Lito. I had only known him a single day, and in that time he'd locked up my friends and brought me to meet a sociopath.

"Fine," I replied. "She was fine. Can you take me to see my friends now?"

"I'm not sure if that is a good idea," Lito replied as I reached the top of the stairs.

"Fiona said I could, and that she would have them released."

"Are you sure?" Lito asked, confused. "That doesn't sound like her."

I nodded, solemnly. "Yes, I'm sure. Can we go now, please?"

Lito looked puzzled. He clearly expected me to be enamored with Fiona, but I couldn't hide my disappointment in meeting her. He wanted to probe deeper, but he stopped himself. Instead, he walked me out of the church without saying another word.

*

My heart fluttered, and stomach churned as we walked through the main plaza of Toledo, where city hall rested on one side. We didn't walk toward the ornately decorated building though. Instead, we crossed to a plain, black building which sat kitty-corner to it. Unlike City Hall, this building didn't have carved wood accenting every surface. Instead, it was stark with black tile that made up the majority of the facade.

"This is the courthouse," Lito said to me, walking through the thirty-foot-high black door. People in black suits and pointed hats shuffled around with gloomy looks on their faces. I half-expected to see a placard above the door that read "All hope abandon, ye who enter here," but that would have added much-needed decoration and charm to a building that had none.

The black tile motif from the exterior continued into the long hallway connected to the entrance. Two guards dressed in long black robed nodded at Lito and allowed him to pass. Everybody seemed to know my grandfather by reputation alone, if nothing else, and gave him a wide berth to walk out of a combination of fear and respect.

We passed the entrance guards and hopped onto an elevator. A flock of eagles flapped their wings above us, grasping onto the cables that held the elevator afloat.

"Sub-basement three, please," Lito said, looking up into the grate above us.

The eagles cawed in acknowledgment at Lito's request, and the elevator jerkily lowered toward the ground.

"Your elevators are run by eagles?" I asked.

He nodded. "Of course. Why do you ask?"

"It just seems like there would be eagle poop everywhere. Don't you use electricity?"

"Sometimes, but not unless we need it. We like the old ways here," Lito responded, glancing up at the cage as if he never considered a bird would poop on him.

"That's crazy," I replied, but I didn't say another word. *Why do they do things the hard way at every turn?*

As much as I appreciated the whimsy of the magical folk, they chose to make their lives harder seemingly because of willful ignorance. Normals might not be perfect, but they used the technology available to them. Living here, for any length of time, at least, would be frustratingly maddening. I could see why my father wanted to leave.

A couple of minutes later, the shaky elevator came to a stop, and the eagles chirped at us. The elevator opened and the square on Lito's cheek glowed brightly.

"Follow me closely. This is a dangerous place, and it's easy to get lost."

Lito hurried out of the elevator and made a quick left down the dark hallway. The way forward opened in front of him. Guided by a white light, I ran forward to keep up. The darkness enveloped the hallway behind me as Lito turned left, then right. He turned more quickly than I could follow with my much shorter legs.

"Here!" Lito shouted, and he reached out his hand as the darkness fell around me. With a hard yank, Lito ripped me from the darkness and into a row of cells lit with overhead hanging lights.

"When I say to stay close, I meant it," Lito scolded. "I almost lost you."

"You were..." I said through gasping breaths. "Just so fast."

"You must go fast down here, and listen closely," he replied. "We designed it for those that knew where they were going. You cannot find your way out if you do not know the way. Many have died wandering its paths."

"Sounds harsh," I replied.

"It is our way," he said, walking forward. "Now come, your friends are just ahead."

I didn't like their magical ways very much. They were brutish and unnecessarily cruel. It lacked empathy for anybody except those endowed with the knowledge needed to get ahead in their world and destroyed everybody else in the process.

CHAPTER SEVEN

I heard Anabelle talking from her cell before I saw her. Her voice boomed down the narrow prison hallway made of dark, dank stone. There wasn't an ounce of fear in her voice, and it sounded like she was talking to an old friend.

"Would you say you're a cat person or a dog person?" She asked, her thin arms sticking out of the cell, waving in the air.

"I don't care!" Tibor shouted from the other side of the hall. I couldn't see him, but I felt his frustration. He wasn't much of a talker, and that's all Anabelle wanted to do. You couldn't shut her up. I usually acted as her sponge, soaking up her chattiness so nobody else had to deal with it, but alone in a dark cell, there was nothing to hold her back from laying her gift of gab on Tibor.

"You have to pick!" Anabelle said. "That's part of the game!"

"What game? You've just been asking me questions for hours."

"That's the game!" Anabelle said, exasperated. "It's called questions. Don't you know anything?"

"You're ridiculous," Tibor sighed.

"She is," I said, walking down the hallway. "I love it though."

Tibor let out a relieved sigh. "Oh, thank the gods. Please, get me out of here. Let me out, move me, torture me. Anything, please. I can't deal with this anymore."

"I'm not going to torture you, Tibor," I said, walking between their cells. "I think Anabelle is doing a fine job of that."

Anabelle's arms flailed in the air. "Rosie!!! You're here!!!"

She reached through the cell and pulled me close for a hug. I felt the tip of her nose as she squeezed my face against the rusty bars.

"It's good to see you," I said.

"And it's good to see you, girl!" Anabelle replied. "Tibor is not a talker or a listener. He's kind of a wet blanket."

"I'm right here!" Tibor said with a sigh. "You don't have to insult me."

"It's not an insult. It's just a fact."

I pushed off the bars and out of Rosie's grasp. I turned to Tibor, who nodded at me. I nodded back and gave him a brief smile, which he did not return.

"It's good to see you," I said to him. "Both of you."

"Does this mean we're getting out of here?" Tibor said.

"Wow, cutting to the chase, huh?" I replied. "I'm fine, by the way."

"Once you've been locked in a cage for days, you can talk to me about quick."

"One day," Lito replied. "It hasn't even been one day."

"Really?" Anabelle squeaked. "It feels like forever. Can we please leave now, though?"

"We are waiting for the final word," Lito said.

"Aren't you the final word, sir?" Tibor said. "You are the Chief Justice."

"Even I have bosses," Lito replied. "Hopefully, we will get you out soon."

"I hope so," Anabelle said with a huff. "This place is seriously grimy. Like gross squared to the fifth power."

"Just hang tight a little while longer," I said. "I'm working on it, and I miss you."

Anabelle grabbed for my hand, and I gave it to her. "I miss you too, girl. Please, for the love of god, let me out soon. I can't believe I'm saying this, but I'm running out of things to talk about."

"I promise," I said. "I have so much to tell you, and so much I can't tell you that I want to tell you. Dude, just know, it got real weird really quick for me."

"Good weird?" Anabelle asked.

I shook my head. "Just weird weird."

"That's enough," Lito said. "Normals cannot know what we know."

"Alright," I said throwing up my hands. "You won't know, but you'll know when you know, you know?"

"Totally," Anabelle replied with a smile.

The darkness in front of us parted. Two guards in thick dark cloaks stomped forward in lockstep. Their cheeks glowed with the sign of the square. Their jaws clenched tight with cold, dead eyes that looked through us as they walked past.

"Oh, good," Lito said. "Just in time. You can come home for supper."

"Anabelle Torres and Tiberius Goodsen," the shorter guard said. "You are hereby ordered to appear before the council on the matter of your treason."

"Preposterous," Lito said. "I would have been informed of this. I'm the Chief Justice of the City Council."

"That's not the council he's talking about, sir," Tibor said. "He's talking about the Council of the Tuppins, right?"

The taller, fatter guard nodded. "Correct. They will decide your fate."

Lito scoffed loudly. "They have no right to usurp my authority."

"I'm afraid they do, sir," Tibor said with a knowing sadness. "As a Knight of the Order, they are the only ones who can judge me."

"And what about me?" Anabelle said with a whimper. "I'm not a Tuppins."

"No," Tiber said. "But since I brought you here, you are my responsibility. Thus, the Tuppins will decide your fate with mine."

The guards stepped forward, and both of my cheeks started to glow, one with the Light and one with the Moon. "I won't let you take them."

Lito put his hand on my shoulder. "No, child. This is not a fight you can win."

I turned to Tibor, tears streaming down my face, and he nodded to me. It was true. I couldn't win this fight, and I knew it. I turned over to Anabelle, who cried with me.

"I really thought you were gonna save me, Rosie," She said with a whimper. "Please, don't let them take me. Please get me out of this."

"I will," I replied. "I swear it. Both of you."

The guards unlocked Anabelle and Tibor's cages and led them into the darkness. Lito held me by the shoulders as they disappeared from sight.

"Don't make promises you can't keep," Tibor said in a low whisper.

"But we will be able to save them, right?" I asked.

"I don't know," he replied. "The Tuppins is a strange order. Their ways are lost on me."

"You have to save them," I said pointedly. "You have to stop them."

"There's nothing I can do," Lito replied. "I'm going to work my contacts. I promise I'll do everything I can."

A half-hearted promise wasn't good enough for me. However, I knew someone that could fulfill a promise. She owed me my friend's safety, and I would make sure she fulfilled her promise.

*

By the time I reached the Cathedral, I was madder than I had ever been in my life. Fiona promised my friends would be safe, and in return, I would help her.

"Fiona," I shouted through the hall of the church. My voice bounced off every wall and back to my ears. "Fiona!"

A chorus of shushes boomed from the middle of the church as the chorus hummed away in somber relief.

I didn't care about them. I was on a mission. "Fiona!" I shouted even louder.

I found her standing under a wide-brimmed hat which floated untethered over a red square slab of marble which stood out among the muted stone around it. A dozen more surrounded her above their own slabs of marble.

She looked down at the stone mournfully, with her eyes closed. "This is the grave of the first friend I ever made on Earth almost a thousand years ago."

"Fiona, the Tuppins took my friends. They took them to trial. We have to help them."

"Did you know that each of these hats hanging in space represents the cardinals of Toledo, dating back to the thirteenth century. They hang above these tombs as a symbol of their ascent into Heaven. Isn't that nice? I like to think my friend is in Valhalla now, sipping mead with Odin."

I wish I had more than a moment to consider the history behind her words, but they simply angered me more. "Didn't you hear me? We have to go."

She nodded. "I heard you, but time is as long as it is short. There is always time until there isn't any."

"Well," I snarled, "There isn't any more time now. If we don't do something Anabelle and Tibor be found guilty, and who knows what will happen then."

"They'll be killed," she replied. "That's what will happen. And life will move on, just like it did for those who lost these cardinals. Just like it did for my friend. This place moved on without them, and so will you."

"I don't want to move on without them. I want my friends back."

Fiona's eyes glared into my soul. "I understand what you want, but I know what you need. You need to unlock your powers, and to do that, you need complete focus. I'm not sure those two are good for you. I mean look at you now, shouting through a church like an animal. Seriously, what has gotten into you?"

"We had a deal," I said, staring back into her ice blue eyes, tamping down my bubbling fear with every ounce of courage I could muster.

"I know," she replied. "And I think it's time we renegotiated. There must be something else you want.

Perhaps a nice hat, or a beautiful castle overlooking the city. All that is open to you right now."

My voice boomed through the columns of the cathedral and rattled the organ pipes above. "I only want my friends, and if you want my help, get them freed right now! Otherwise, I'll do it myself."

"You don't need to do that," she replied. "I will help you. If this is truly what you want, then I will help you."

"Don't mess with me," I replied.

"My dear," she scoffed. "I am only helping you as a courtesy. I would rather you help me willingly, but please remember, I do not need you alive. I would only like you alive. However, soon your annoyance will grate on me, and you will not be worth the trouble."

Her words took the wind out of my sails. I truly had no power in this relationship. I could feign it for a time, but at the end of the day, it was her that wielded it over me.

Fiona hovered toward the other side of the church. I hurried behind her, confused as to why we weren't going out the door.

"Where are we going? We need to find the Tuppins, now!"

"My dear," she replied. "The Tuppins work inside the church. They are the personal guard of the Cathedral. Rest assured though, they do not work for me. They do work with me on occasion though, so I should have some pull with them to save your loved ones."

Fiona dipped into an alcove surrounded by mighty stone pillars on the other side of the church and landed gracefully on the marble floor. She placed her hand on a stone statue of the Virgin Mary holding the baby Jesus with reverence. The statue bent to her will and moved backward, revealing a stairwell underneath with a pale orange glow emanating from it.

Angry voices shouted over each other as we descended the stairs and walked through a stone passageway, like the one that led to Fiona's room. On either wall of the hallway were tapestries that depicted men with great valor, clad in gold, shooting blue lightning out of their eyes as they defeated a robed, bearded army wielding primitive sticks in the battle against them.

"We mustn't dawdle," Fiona said from ahead of me. "The Tuppins's justice is as quick as it is brutal."

The angry voices grew louder as we neared the other side of the corridor and the hallway opened into a circular room. A hundred men with long, white beards screamed across at each other. In front of them, a strong-jawed man with a kingly robe and crown stroked his salt and pepper beard from a high chair above them.

In front of the man, kneeling on the floor, Anabelle and Tibor held their hands in front of them, bound with earthen chains, pleading for justice. However, from the icy glare of the man above them, their pleas would go unheeded.

"Very well," the bearded man said, a grim timber ran through his gravelly voice.

"That is Miguel III," Fiona told me. "He presides over the Order of the Tuppins."

"Okay," I replied.

"Miguel, my love," Fiona said, smiling. "I know you are busy with important matters, but before you pass judgment on these two, may I say a few words in their defense?"

Miguel stared at Fiona, smitten as a lovesick schoolboy. He was enamored with her, and she played it for all it was worth. Her body glowed the faintest blue as she rose into the air to address Miguel at eye level.

"Why Fiona," Miguel said with a big smile. "You are looking lovely, as always."

"Thank you, my dear, but I come not for pleasantries. I come on urgent business. I come to speak on behalf of these two condemned souls."

"You wish…to speak for these two? Surely, they are below your regard, my lady. Insolent curs not worthy of your breath, and it angers me that they take a moment of your thoughts."

"And yet, they have taken much of it on this day, and I ask you to take pity on them, and allow them to leave this place of honor as free people, for my sake."

Miguel smiled. "You know, My Lady, that can never happen. This Knight of the Tuppins brought a Normal to our door. He could, for all we know, be plotting against us."

"I'm not!" Tibor screamed, rising from his knees. "I would never…"

A plump guard smashed him over the head with the butt of his broadsword. "Quiet!"

"I understand, your Grace," Fiona said. "However, he also brought a gift for us, the first Dual born in eighty years!"

The crowd gasped as Fiona pointed to me. Every eye turned to stare at me, mouth agape and eyes agog.

"Can it be?" Miguel replied. "And you think…"

"She might be the one to fulfill the prophecy, and these are her friends. She has asked for leniency, and for us to do the hard work of fulfilling her chosen role, these two must be forgiven, for the sake of all magic people the world over."

Miguel thought for a moment, a long moment before his nose crinkled up in disgust. "I'm sorry my lady. My aims are often aligned with yours, but the Tuppins cannot abide by such blasphemy as this traitor. I have made my decision. They are sentenced to death. To be carried out immediately!"

"No!" Fiona screamed. "You mustn't. Be reasonable."

"Begone, my lady. This is no place for a woman!"

My eyes glowed blue, as did both my cheeks, I felt the fire grow in my belly, and yet, when I opened my mouth to breath flame, none came, nor did water spout from the ground.

Instead, the Earth quaked under me and rippled up to the ceiling. Cobblestones shook free of the roof, and the Knights that filled the room rushed for the passageway to the Cathedral. The last thing I saw before I passed out was Fiona staring at me wide-eyed as if she just witnessed a miracle.

Before I passed out, I thought I heard her mumble, "Well, now we have a triple…"

CHAPTER EIGHT

I slipped and fell through the darkness of my mind for I didn't know how long, but eventually my eyes blearily fluttered open, and I woke. It took me a moment, but when my eyes focused again, I saw Lito's smiling face looking over at me from a chair in the corner of a small room filled with antique furniture.

"Hi," Lito said. "Welcome back. You gave us quite a scare."

I laid on a large four-poster bed, with a lace canopy drooping down from the wooden posts around me. Along every wall were beautiful paintings of old men, encased in elaborately carved picture frames. A wooden cabinet sat against the far window, and an oaken night table was beside me.

"Where am I?" I asked, groggily.

"My house. Once the house of the famous painter Francisco Goya, though I have spruced up the place a bit."

"What happened?" I asked, barely registering what he told me.

"Something amazing," Fiona said, walking into the room through a small wooden door next to me. "You are the first person ever to use a third power; that of the Ground."

"That's impossible," I replied. "Nobody can use more than two powers."

"I thought so too, at first," Lito said, standing up. Either the room was too small, or he was larger than I realized because he nearly hit the white plaster ceiling. "But the Tuppins confirmed it with a dozen eyewitness accounts of your cheeks glowing with a mountain and the ground quaking beneath you."

I shot up in bed, remembering the quake that sent the roof of the Tuppins building crumbling down. "That was me?"

Fiona nodded. "Yes, you have demonstrated something amazing, Rosie. There is no doubt you are the one to fulfill the prophecy."

I didn't care about that, or anything else. "Tibor and Anabelle, are they okay?"

"Everybody is fine," Fiona said. "I convinced the Tuppins to hold off their sentencing until we could examine you more fully. After all, it seemed as though your friend's verdict set off your powers, but we will know more with testing."

I shook my head vigorously. "No deal. I will never help you while my friends are imprisoned."

"You are in no position to demand anything from me," she scoffed. "As I said, I would like you alive, but it's not a requirement."

In the light from the window, I noticed a twitch in Fiona's eye. She was lying. I knew it in the cockles of my soul, and even if she wasn't, I was willing to call her bluff.

"You're lying, Fiona," I said, steely-eyed. "If you are willing to kill me, then do it."

"Please, ladies," Lito said. "There is no need to kill anyone."

"Shut up, Charles," Fiona grumbled, looking straight through me, deep into the recesses of my soul. A sudden chill went through my body, and I felt her trying to force her will upon me. However, I was not the meek child I was when I left home. I had been forged in the depth of loss and pain, which made me strong.

"Free my friends," I snarled. "Now, or I will never help you."

In another second, her eyes broke from mine, and she looked down at the ground. "Fine. It will be done. Then, you will unlock all your power under my guidance and the mages with once again take their rightful place in the world."

"You do whatever you have to do," I replied. "But do not come back unless you have my friends, understood?"

Fiona turned toward the door. "Watch yourself, child. You don't know your place."

"Yes, I do," I replied, as Fiona walked through the door. "My place is with my friends."

When Fiona was out of sight, Lito turned to me. His eyes were big as saucers as he tried to cover his trembling lip. "You are playing a dangerous game."

I nodded. "So is she."

Lito wanted to say more, I could see it in his eyes, but he didn't want a fight. Instead, he forced a smile. "Come, my child, let us take a walk and forget this unpleasantness."

I didn't want to move anywhere until I saw my friends, but I knew Fiona wouldn't be back for a while, and instead of fretting in bed, taking a walk to clear my head sounded like a good idea.

*

We walked down a long hallway lined with paintings of old, white men stoically staring off into space. We turned left into a room where even more paintings lined the hallways, all lit to accentuate their beauty. I didn't see it though. To me, each painting was as boring as the one before it. I mean, how many old white dudes could you see in one day before they all looked the same?

"And this is one of my favorite rooms of the house," Lito said. "Every one of these painting was drawn by the Spanish masters, including Goya himself. Sometimes, I come here to think, surrounded by geniuses from generations past."

Lito pointed to a painting of Jesus with a red toga. It was painted with brighter colors than the others, and for some reason, Lito thought this was special. "Goya was famous for his use of light. Do you see how his use of red sets this painting apart from the others in this room?"

"No," I replied. "It just looks like another painting of Jesus carrying a cross. Do you know how many of these I've seen in my life?"

"Unfortunately, in this period, the only people who could afford to hire painters were noblemen and churches. That's why there's so much of it."

"No, I get it. Old white men with money paying old white men without money to paint them. It's just, how many of them can you see before you just get numb to it. I remember there was one cool one where this old guy was eating a baby. Do you have that one?"

Lito shook his head. "Saturn devouring his child. No, unfortunately, that was in the Prado…when it was called the Prado before the British took control of it."

The contempt in Lito's voice was palpable. Venom punctuated every word that came out of his mouth and dribbled into my ears.

"Is that why you hate them? Normals?" I asked. "Because they took your culture from you?"

"They took everything from me," Lito grumbled. "There are so many reasons to hate them, child. That is one of the thousands. Low on the list, but still on it."

"I don't get it, though. It seems like magic folk all started the war. I mean, Hitler, Mussolini, Franco. These were all awful men, who wanted to exterminate Normals. You were on the wrong side of history, weren't you?"

Lito sat down on a bench at the middle of the room. "That is one way to look at it."

"No," I said, sitting next to him. "That is the only way to look at it."

"Careful," Lito growled. "Remember that history is written by the winners. There is always another side."

"Magical folk exterminated thirty million regular people, unprovoked. What other side of history is there?"

"That's not what we wanted, not at the beginning, and it's not what we believed. In the beginning, we believed we were fighting for our very existence. There are many thousands of times more Normals than magical folks. The only thing that kept magical folk from being killed by them was our power. But, when they learned how to create light, weapons, and flight without us, we suddenly became irrelevant. We feared their reprisal."

"So you struck first, like children."

"Because if we didn't, we would have been wiped off the planet."

I stood up, disgusted. "And the way you want to make it better is to attack them again? That's so childish."

"What would you have us do?" he said, dropping his face to his hands. "Stay hidden forever?"

"No," I replied. "How about diplomacy? Reach out and try to broker some sort of peace. Like adults."

"They would never hear us out. They would attack us if we ever came out into the open again."

"Sure," I said. "If you revealed yourself right now, but how about…just send a messenger. Tell them you want peace. Tell them you want to live together and build a world together, like rational people."

Lito looked up at me. "You do not understand."

"Sure I do," I replied. "You are playing into their perceptions of you. Since I've been here, I was arrested, my friends were nearly killed, and the only way I was able to do anything was because I nearly brought down the Tuppins through violence. You've had seventy years to grow and change, but you haven't. You're just as selfish and xenophobic as you were in the forties."

Lito stood up. "Watch what you say, child!"

"Or what!?" I replied, stomping forward toward him. "You'll banish me like you did my father. Do it. I don't want to be here among you if you are going to act like jerks."

I spun to leave, but Lito grabbed my arm. "Remember your deal with Fiona. If you do not honor it, your friends will be killed."

My heart broke in that moment. I thought that blood would bond me to my grandfather, but now I knew that I was nothing to him except a thing, a thing that could help him reach his ultimate aim.

"I know what I have to do, Chief Justice, and I plan to honor it, but that doesn't make me any less disgusted in you, or disappointed in how you choose to live. This place is supposed to be magical, but it is rotten, covered with a veneer that makes it seem like paradise. Make no mistake, though, you live in a prison of your own making."

I ripped my hand away from his grasp and turned toward the door. That's when I saw them, standing at the door, smiling at me – Tibor and Anabelle. My heart swelled as I ran toward them, wrapping them in a hug.

They weren't related by blood, but they were my only family now.

CHAPTER NINE

I walked with Tibor and Anabelle out of the house and into the garden outside. The garden was two-tiered and separated by a set of stairs. It was filled with every flower I could imagine and some that only seemed to exist in dreams. Large humming violets swayed to and fro as they danced toward the light. Tulips spun like windmills in the breeze as we strolled past. Marigolds bowed their fluffy flowers toward us. It was weird, and their anthropomorphic bodies made it difficult to believe the secrets I had to tell my friends wouldn't get heard by my nosy grandfather.

Past the garden sat an underground cellar filled with casks of whiskey and wine. We could be alone in the dark recesses of the cellar. It was there that I told them everything, and they hung on each word.

"And she threatened to kill you if you told anybody?" Anabelle asked.

I nodded. "She threatened to kill me multiple times, but yes, I agreed to be their test dummy if they would spare the two of you."

"You shouldn't have done that," Tibor replied. "If they're half as bad as you say, you can't trust them, or their plans for you. They could doom the world."

"Or save it," I replied. "I don't know their plans, but I need to stay close to them to find out what they're trying to do. I can't do that with you in jail."

"So what are you going to do now?" Anabelle asked.

"Now, I become their human pin cushion, and you two…you need to find a way out of Toledo that won't get us caught by the Tuppins."

"I'm still not sure the Tuppins are the bad guys here," Tiber replied. "They have a strict code that…"

"They haven't revolted against Fiona yet," I said, cutting him off. "They are still here, and that makes them complicit in the Council's actions, or too stupid to know what's going on. Either way, I don't trust them."

"You realize you are besmirching my entire way of life?" Tibor replied. "Right?"

"That's because your way of life is dumb," Anabelle replied.

"I didn't have to tell you any of this, Tibor," I said, resting my hand on his shoulder. "I know your duty is to the Tuppins, and if you choose to side with them, Anabelle and I will both be dead, or worse. I'm trusting that you are a better man than you are a soldier, and your better sense will prevail. However, that is a choice only you can make. I risked everything to get you out of that prison, and now you can choose how to repay that kindness."

"Kindness or guilt?" Tibor replied, brushing off my hand. "Don't you forget that. It was my kindness that saved you from the RMP, twice, if I remember."

"And your kindness got me arrested and nearly killed," Anabelle said with a huff. "At best you two are even."

I nodded. "She's right. We're even right now, Tibor. The slate is wiped clean. You can choose what side to take from here on out. Either you can trust me or trust the Tuppins, an organization that nearly killed you."

Tibor grumbled something under his breath, but I couldn't hear him. Fiona's voice overpowered him, as she called for me.

"Rosie!" Fiona shouted sweetly. "It's time to begin your training."

"I have to go," I said. "I trust you both."

Anabelle hugged me tightly. "Be safe."

My eyes hung on Tibor. I could see the conflict eating away at his soul. I only hoped he would make the right choice.

"You know I can't promise that," I said to Anabelle, squeezing her one last time. "I will be as safe as possible, given the circumstances. Meet me in the square outside City Hall in two hours, okay?"

"I'll be there," she said, reluctantly letting me go.

*

My first training session with Fiona wasn't so bad. Mostly, she just made me use the powers I already knew how to unlock. First, I spent time lighting fire with my mind, creating fireballs in my hands, and using my fingertips as torches. Then, I pulled water out of the air, created a flowing river on the cobblestone, and forced a wall of water into the air.

"Very impressive," Fiona said, finally, after a long silence. "Now, it's time to unlock your ground powers."

"I can't. I don't know how I did it before," I replied to her. "It just happened last time."

"Yes, you have said that. It appears your powers are initially triggered by fear. Perhaps, we should dangle you off a cliff."

She said it with such a cavalier attitude, but I understood the implication. It was as much a threat as it was a joke. You will unlock your powers for me, or I will make your life unpleasant.

"I'm trying," I said, squeezing my eyes closed as tightly as I could. "You aren't making it easy on me."

"It's not supposed to be easy. Anything worth doing is hard."

"Please," I said. "I need a break. I'm exhausted."

"Fine," she replied.

Fiona disappeared into the next room. She returned moments later with tea and crackers. We sat against the cylinder as it glowed blue behind us. It was barely a quarter full now, and the liquid inside bubbled a deep blue as it struggled against the sides of the tube to make its way out into the Cathedral pipe around it.

"What is that thing, anyway?" I asked.

"It is what keeps us cloaked, and grants citizens the power to manipulate objects. It is the source of the town's power, drawn from my essence and piped directly into every corner of the town."

"Your essence?" I asked confused. "Like your blood?"

She shook her head. "No. Think of it more like…my soul, I suppose. I fill it three times a week. You can see it is almost empty now. Tomorrow, I will refill it again, as I was doing when you came to me the first time."

"Is it painful?" I asked, taking a bite of my cookie. I was surprised how much I cared about her at that moment.

"It is more painful that you can imagine, but I do it for the good of the city, and its people." Fiona took a sip of her tea. "Does it surprise you that I sacrifice that much of myself?"

I shook my head. "No, what surprised me is how much you expect me to give up for these people as well."

"The magical folk are my mission on Earth; I would do anything to protect them, even if it means forcing suffering on you in order to save the rest. That is the difference between you and me. You would risk the many to save the few while I would risk the few to save the many."

*

Fiona walked me up the dark stairs into the Cathedral after two hours of struggling and failing to unlock my ground powers. Even with focused study, I felt no closer to unlocking my Ground powers. I was too tired to think any more, but even if I could, I'd promised Anabelle and Tibor I would meet them in the square and was already fifteen minutes late.

As we walked toward the heavy, wooden doors, the chorus moaned lowly for us.

"Do they ever stop singing?" I asked.

Fiona shook her head. "I don't know. I've never heard the music stop. I like it though. According to the Bible, a choir of angels constantly sings to praise God. Your religions were dreadfully wrong about the truths of the universe, of course, but I always liked that part all the same."

"Sure, the Bible's fine," I replied. "As long as you overlook the violence."

"Like I said, there are parts I like, but there are also parts I don't like."

"I would think that a warrior like you would appreciate the violence."

"I preferred your God when he was a vengeful type," Fiona replied with a smile. "That is true."

Before she could finish, a messenger dressed all in black crashed through the door of the church and ran up to Fiona. A thick sneer washed across her face. "What is the meaning of this? You have no right to enter my Cathedral!"

"I'm sorry, Your Grace, for interrupting you," the messenger said in an exhausted huff. "However, we've caught another infidel. He claims to know your ward, Roselyn Light. He asks to address her directly. Eustace wants to execute him for lying."

"What is his name?" I asked.

The messenger bowed. "Eduardo, my liege."

My eyes went wide. My friend came to find me. He came here because I said he would be safe, and I was wrong. Now, he would be punished.

"Tell Eustace—" Fiona said.

"—to bring him here," I cut in, understanding I might face Fiona's wrath. She looked at me sternly, but she could hear the eagerness in my voice and acquiesced to it with the softening of her face.

"Fine," she said. "Bring him here."

The messenger ran outside, and the door closed behind him. Fiona snapped toward me. "Never, speak for me again. There are a few things I will never abide, and one of them is insolence."

"I'm sorry," I replied, hanging my head. "He is only here because of me. I am responsible for him."

"Wow," Fiona replied. "You have destroyed a lot of lives, haven't you?"

"Yes," I replied contritely. "I have."

The door swung open again, and Eustace stomped forward with poor, sweet Eduardo, bound in mud chains that dripped all over the floor of the pristine Cathedral. His eyes sunk into his head and his lips receded into his face. His ratty clothes hung loosely off him when they fit tightly just a few days earlier.

He mumbled under his breath as I ran toward him. "Eduardo!"

He looked up at me, his cheeks drooping down his face. I could see the outline of his bones under him.

"I'm sorry," he said. "I'm sorry. I'm sorry. I'm sorry."

"Sorry for what?" I replied, wrapping my arms around him. As I held him close, I felt every vertebrae under his skin. "What happened to you?"

"I'm sorry, I'm sorry, I'm sorry, Rosie," he mumbled. "I didn't mean to."

"It's okay," I said, rubbing his back. As I pressed my hands against his spine, I felt something odd. It was a wire that wrapped around his waist. I pulled back and followed it around to his stomach.

"I'm sorry. I didn't mean to…" he trailed off.

"What is this, Eduardo?" I replied.

"They found me," he said, looking deep into my eyes with cold, dead eyes that once had held so much life. "They found us all. I had to. They have my mother."

I lifted his shirt. There, among the loose ribs, was a timer, surrounded by a thick yellow box. As I watched it tick down to zero, the box began to beep.

"I'm sorry," he said, meekly. "I had to."

I turned from him. "Run!!!"

I rushed toward Fiona, but it was too late. The beeping screeched through the air. Eduardo was pulled apart by the pulse of an orange energy blast that emanated from him and out into the church. The floor thundered as the blast wiped through me, and smashed Fiona against the wall of the church.

I turned onto my back, feeling the pain in my ribs. The blue light that coursed through the church faded until there was nothing but darkness in the church. I rushed to Fiona, who could barely move.

"They found us," was all she said before fading from consciousness. "Check the energy source. Make sure it isn't destroyed. It's all that protects us now…"

"Fiona!" I shouted. "Fiona!!!"

But she fell into unconsciousness. I didn't know for how long, or if it would be forever, but I had to follow through with her final orders. I stood up and rushed downstairs. My eyes were already adjusting to the darkness.

I pushed open the door to Fiona's chambers, and blue liquid flooded out onto the floor. The cylinder was broken into a thousand pieces and lay scattered across the floor.

The cathedral rocked back and forth as a great thunder quaked it. I rushed out of the door and past Fiona, who lay unconscious on the floor. She would need help, for sure, but I had bigger issues, like making sure my friends were safe.

The moment I stepped outside the church I realized they weren't fine at all. Nothing was fine. The field keeping Toledo hidden was gone. We could see out into the forest in front of us. Hundreds of tanks lined the forest. They fired, bombarding the city with hundreds of shells, and destroying building after building as I ducked to avoid the falling debris.

Toledo was under attack, and it was all my fault.

CHAPTER TEN

"ANABELLE!" I shouted as I rushed toward the square near City Hall. She was supposed to meet me there fifteen minutes ago with Tibor, and I just watched it get shelled with a dozen artillery rounds.

The sky lit up with fire the moment Fiona fell into a coma and the barrier protecting Toledo fell. A thousand shells fell through the air and exploded on buildings, homes, and streets all over town. The shelling was targeted at the spire of the Cathedral, knocking holes in the stately visage and setting fires all over the structure.

"Rosie!" I heard Lito shout, hobbling from the rubble of City Hall into the square. "Are you okay?"

Blood trickled down his forehead and down to his chin. A large gash cut across his forehead, and his face was covered with ash from the explosions.

I nodded. "I'm fine, but Fiona. She's in the Cathedral, unconscious. I don't know if she'll ever wake up."

"Good lord," he said, rushing past me. "I have to save her."

It was good to see where his priorities lay, not that I was surprised. I pulled his arm close. "Anabelle and Tibor. Have you seen them?"

He shook his head, and I let him go. He stumbled forward. As his gait turned from a hobbled walk into a slow trot, I turned and scanned the square.

"Anabelle!" I shouted again, pushing myself up. "Tibor!"

There was nothing for a moment except the whimpers of people hiding in the shops around the square.

"Rosie!" I finally heard behind me. I turned to the McDonald's and saw Anabelle, covered in soot, huddled next to Tibor under the overhang of the fast food restaurant. A dozen men and woman huddled behind them in the relative safety of the restaurant.

"Get over here!" Anabelle shouted, waving at me.

I rushed over and wrapped my arms around her. I wanted to cry, but the tears wouldn't come. I was too amped up from the fighting. I felt our hearts pound against each other's chests.

"I was waiting for you," she said. "Tibor wanted to leave, but I knew you would come, and I didn't want you to worry."

"I wanted to leave because we're getting shelled to death!" Tibor shouted.

"Well we can leave now," I said, pushing Anabelle away.

Tibor grabbed us close and closed his eyes. He concentrated on the sky, but his cheek didn't glow. I saw a faded brand of three air wisps, but nothing glowed.

"What's wrong?" Anabelle asked.

"It's not working!" Tibor shouted as the bombs exploded around us.

"Forget it," I said. "We can run!"

I grabbed Tibor and Anabelle's hands and pulled them out of the overhang just as two shells ripped through the cloth and shattered the windows. A second later the shell exploded, taking a dozen men and women with it, blasted out of existence in a second.

"We have to help them!" Anabelle screeched.

She tried to break free from my grasp, but Tibor grabbed her as well. "There's nothing we can do for them."

We all knew it was true. I had read plenty of stories about war, and how people abandoned their fellow citizens to save themselves. I always thought I was better than that, but clearly I was wrong.

"Let's go," I said, stepping toward a narrow, twisty passage next to the burning wreckage of the restaurant. Anabelle fought me for another moment; then she let me turn her toward the street and away from the carnage.

"The order built an underground bunker during the war," Tibor said. "It should be here if my sources are correct."

A shell landed on a building above us, and the debris rained down on us as we ran past it. A red strip of cloth that hung over the street for as far as I could see fell with the debris, along with the lamps that hung under it. The weight of the falling facade caused the cloth to rip from the hangers that held it up and fall in front of us far down the street.

"Where is this place?" Anabelle said. "We're getting shelled to death!"

"Just up ahead!"

The street split into a V and Tibor led us down the right path. Two shells hit above us, and another on the street, which caused Anabelle to jump.

"Would people stop trying to kill me!" she shouted. "I am so sick of it!"

Tibor ripped open a metal cellar door. I heard shouting coming from the bottom of the stairs, but that didn't stop me from rushing inside. Anabelle and Tibor followed me, and he closed the metal doors just as another shell reverberated above us.

"Stay quiet while we are down here," Tibor said. "This is a place for the Order to congregate in times of need, and they don't like us very much."

Tibor led us down the stairs and into a bright hallway. It was much different from the dank, dark corridors I was used to walking through in Toledo. This one was filled with light and tiled with white and blue mosaic chips. On either side of the hallway, torches led the way toward a meeting room.

When we reached the end of the hallway, it broke into a circular room, lined with gray cobblestones and accented with torch lights.

In the center of the room was a round, wooden table, and dozens of men leaned over it and screamed at each other. Some sat, while others stood, but they all shouted just as loudly, waving their ash covered arms at each other, and toward Miguel in the center of the room.

He was the only one not covered in ash and soot. Instead, he was draped in a purple cape adorned with gold and wore a shiny gold crown atop his alabaster hair.

"We should launch a counterattack!" A grimy, tall man said.

"With what?" Eustace replied. He must have run to the shelter right after the bombing. "It's not like we can use magic right now! How about we work about figuring out why that is! Then we can launch a suicide mission!"

"What does Eustace mean?" I whispered to Tibor, who shrugged.

How could the whole town be without magic? I closed my eyes and imagined lighting a fire inside my fingers, and yet, I couldn't, no matter how hard I tried. It was just like when Tibor tried to fly us out and couldn't.

"It is as we feared," Miguel grunted. "The enemy has created a machine to tame us. We have been warned of such a weapon by our scouts. We should have taken their warnings more seriously."

"My god," Tibor replied. "They made it."

"Made what?!" Anabelle said a little too loud, and suddenly, all eyes were on us.

"Yes, Master Tuppins," Miguel said with a sly grin on his face. "What did they make?"

"I'm sorry, sir. My friend talked out of turn."

Miguel held up his arm. "That much is clear, but my question still stands, Master Tuppins. What did they make?"

Tibor glared at Anabelle with scorn before walking forward to address the Tuppins. "There have long been reports that the Normals were producing a weapon that could nullify our powers. Covert operatives even brought us a blueprint of the weapon, but their reports were always met with scorn and derision. After all, something like that shouldn't be possible."

"No," I replied. "It's not impossible. It's very possible. Fiona told me so."

"Why would Fiona, a Valkyrie, confide such confidential information to the likes of you?" Eustace sneered at me, flicking his fingers as he crept forward.

"I don't know. Maybe it's because I can use multiple powers or because my grandfather is the Chief Justice of the city council, but regardless, she told me it's possible to suppress our powers, and that must have been what Eduardo used on Fiona to send her into a coma."

"Our protector is in a coma!" One of the squatter and balder knights said. "We are doomed!"

"Quiet Perniss," Miguel said sternly. "This is no time to panic."

"This is the perfect time to panic!" Perniss shouted. "All hope is lost!"

Miguel nodded at Eustace, who smacked Perniss with his cane and knocked him out. Miguel gave the slightest smile in Eustace's direction. "Well done. That was quite annoying. Now, girl, Roselyn is it? Go on. How was Fiona incapacitated?"

"All I know is that there was a big explosion, and she fell. The explosion broke the cylinder which housed her essence."

"Ah!" Eustace said. "That must have been why the barrier went down."

"It would make sense," I said, looking back at Anabelle for moral support, but all she could do was look on like a deer in headlights and shrug. "But that doesn't help us now, does it?"

"No," Miguel said. "Without magic, we are powerless against this onslaught."

Suddenly, Anabelle came back to life, as if a lightbulb went off above her head. "Not necessarily!"

"So now we're just letting anybody address the council," Eustace grumbled.

Anabelle stood up. "You have my mech still, right?"

"Somewhere," Eustace replied.

"If you can lead me to it, I can go out there and blow up whatever they are using to sap your powers."

"And how do we know you won't use it against us?" Miguel asked. "After all, we did almost kill you."

"So did they," Anabelle replied, "but you never tried to kill my best friend. They did. Besides, it's the best chance you have."

Miguel's eyes roamed from Anabelle to Tibor. "Can that be done?"

Tibor nodded. "I know what the device looks like. I was there when the original plans were delivered to our outpost in Madrid…I…I was the one that said it was impossible. Let me help stop it. If I can find it, then I believe Anabelle can take it out."

"Very well," Miguel said. "Eustace, take her to the Goliath."

"I'm going, too!" I shouted.

Miguel shrugged. "I don't care." He turned to Tibor. "Meanwhile, Tibor, you and a squad of my best spies go and find what that device looks like so we can give this little girl our best shot."

"Seriously," Eustace said. "Are we really trusting our entire future to a little girl and her friend?"

Miguel sighed. "It seems that way."

CHAPTER ELEVEN

Eustace led us out of the cellar as mortars rocked all around us. Dust plumed out of the quaking cobblestones as they shook with every inch we moved. It wasn't until we poked our heads out of the cellar, though, that the true horror of the attack took shape for me.

The pounding of the city had only been going on for a few minutes, but already Toledo was decimated into a hollow husk of its former self. The ancient buildings, erected when the oldest of us was not even a concept in the eyes of the universe, were reduced to ash and rubble.

"Follow me," Eustace snarled, hopping down the street, seemingly immune to the horrors of the bombings.

"This is screwed up, right?" Anabelle said, weaving with Eustace as he turned right down an alley. "I mean, we've been looking for a reason to leave, and now we have it."

"So, we just run right into the arms of the RMP?" I replied, turning with Eustace as he swerved left down a tight alley.

"We could just slip out the back of the city. I take the mech, and we fly away. How are they gonna stop us? It's not like they have powers or anything."

I looked up at the scared faces of men and women in every building we passed. They may live in a horrible city, but it was not their fault. They were just going about their lives, and this horror descended on them…a fate that I brought upon them by bringing Eduardo here.

"I can't just let these people suffer. Not if I can help them."

"Then what's the plan?" Anabelle asked.

"We destroy whatever is suppressing the powers of all these people. Then, we move the city. Then, in the confusion, we leave."

"That's some real hero crap. Do you know that?"

I nodded. "It's going to get me killed one of these days."

"It's going to get us both killed," Anabelle corrected.

Eustace turned around from his perch on a destroyed wall that overlooked an alley. "You know I can hear you right? I have very good hearing."

Crap. "How much of it?"

He shrugged. "Enough to know your entire plan."

"Does that mean you'll turn us into the Tuppins?" Anabelle asked as a cannonball exploded above us, taking out the second floor of a lovely looking bakery nestled into a tight corridor in the city.

"If you do what you say, and help us, I'll bring you out of the city myself. After all, you've given us nothing but trouble since you got here."

"Deal," I said, sticking out my hand for a shake that never came.

"No time for that," Eustace said in disgust. "Now hurry up with your stumpy little legs."

Eustace slid across the street to the other side, as he did, an explosion rocked the building he was under and sent debris falling upon him. Without thinking I closed my eyes. I pushed with all my might, and the debris swung away and crashed into the building across the street.

"Holy crap!!!" Anabelle shouted. "Your magic is working! How is your magic working?"

"I don't know!" I shouted back. "I've never done that before!"

"Oh my god—" Anabelle said, pointing to my glowing cheek. "The mountain."

"Maybe…" I said, touching my cheek. "Maybe I can use powers that were unlocked after I became a Dual?"

"It's possible," Anabelle said. "but--"

"Yes, yes," Eustace said. "It's very interesting. I'm sure eggheads will study it later. But for now, come on! There's a battle going on!"

*

When we reached the main street of Toledo, the Cathedral's burning rubble dominated my vision. The spire was gone, crashed along the ground in heaps of burning stone. The mortars blew holes through the side of the church, leaving nothing but the exposed ground inside. What had survived from the 12th century couldn't survive the RMP bombs for even half an hour.

"This way," Eustace said. "Don't dawdle."

I stepped onto the cobblestones on the main street and hurriedly crossed the road, trying to expose myself as little as possible. I ducked and weaved to avoid the bombs. However, I noticed that the sky was no longer black with shrapnel fire. In fact, the mortars stopped completely.

It should have given me great comfort, but instead, I was filled with dread. It was the calm before the storm. I knew that something much worse was coming.

"Look!" Anabelle shouted. "Goliaths!"

Sure enough, seconds later the sky filled with massive mech suits. Hundreds flew toward us. I had never seen more than a dozen at a time, and that was enough to give you nightmares for weeks. Now, there were several hundred coming at us now, and we had no way to defend ourselves.

I closed my eyes, trying to summon my powers again. I squatted close to the ground and struggled with all my might, but it just would not come.

"What are you doing?" Anabelle said.

"Trying to fight back!" I replied. "Everybody else is powerless, but you saw me. I used my power. I did it. If I can do it again--"

"That's stupid," Anabelle said, cupping my face in her hands. "You can't fight a hundred mechs!"

"And you can? With a busted suit that's got a hole in it?"

"Oh," Anabelle replied. "I guess it does have a hole in it, doesn't it?"

I nodded. "It does. So, if you want to take on a suicide mission, go ahead, but don't stop me from going on one, too."

"Hey!" Eustace said. "How 'bout neither of you takes on a suicide mission. That'd be the right thing to do, I think."

"Stay out of this old man," Anabelle said with a smile. "He's right you know."

"Unfortunately."

"Now let's get out of the street before those mechs come down and destroy us all."

The jets of the Goliaths burned in the sky, and I burned in my gut. I looked over at the Cathedral. They had to know Fiona was in there, and they were coming for her. I thought I would be their prize, but I was nothing compared to a

Valkyrie, and she was with my grandfather who was powerless to help her. I couldn't let them get her, no matter what. With her as their prisoner, the RMP would be unstoppable.

"No," I said. "I won't let them take her. Eustace, hand me that staff."

"But…" he said. "That's mine."

I spun to him angrily. "Just do it."

Eustace moped over to me and placed the staff in my hand. "Don't break it."

A half dozen Goliaths burned their jets above me, about to land on the ground. I turned to Anabelle. "I'm going to do something really stupid because I trust you to do something really stupid, too."

She nodded. "I am always up for something stupid."

"When I tell you, run toward the Goliath. You'll only have a couple of seconds to get inside. Can you do it?"

"I can do it," she replied.

"And what do I do?" Eustace asked.

"Don't die," Anabelle scoffed. "And stay out of my way."

"Get back," I said, making my way to the center of the street. "Out of sight."

They expected us to be hopeless, and helpless. They expected us to kowtow to their superior might, but if I could get one good shot at them with my Ground powers, maybe we'd have a chance to survive.

"Halt!" one of the Goliaths said from the air, pointing its laser at me as it clamped onto the ground. "Do not resist, and we will not harm you."

The mech stood ten feet tall, encased in black metal with red firebolt accents along either leg. The British flag was emblazoned on each of the mech's arms. A blue plastic bubble encased the driver of the mech, who I could barely make out through the polarized lens of the cockpit.

"You've already harmed this town," I screamed. "Why should I trust you?"

"You do not have to trust me," The modulated voice screeched out as it leveled its weapon at me. "You just have to obey me."

It put one foot in front of the other, pulling up the cobblestone ground as it went. As it did, I closed my eyes and stomped my cane on the ground. I thought of ramming a piece of the earth through the bubble that protected the mech driver from the outside. *Please work. Please work. Please work.*

"Now!" I shouted as I opened my eyes.

Anabelle ran forward as I slammed the staff on the ground. My cheek didn't glow, but I felt a flicker in my eyes, and then I went blank for a moment. I felt a surge of power course through my right arm and down into the staff. As I knocked the staff on the ground on more time, I felt the power in my arm surge into the staff and heard the crash of glass in front of me as the orb shattered

Anabelle pulled the driver out of the cockpit and jumped into the driver's seat. She gave me a thumbs up before she turned the mech around and fired at the other five mechs that had landed around it.

Four of the mechs around us blew up, and Anabelle crashed her hand into the final one, ripping the driver out of the seat.

"Get in," she shouted to Eustace, who ran forward and hopped inside.

"I've never driven one of these before!" Eustace shouted.

"It's easier than it looks. Follow me!"

Eustace jumped into the cockpit of the Goliath. After fumbling around for a few seconds, its jets shakily rose into the air. I latched onto the Goliath's arm before she could take off. "I'll let you know as soon as we know where the device is located."

Anabelle nodded. "Take one of the comms from the mechs I blew up and good luck."

"That's an open channel. Everyone will hear."

"I know," she replied with a deep sigh. "Just trust me okay. It'll be fine. Do you trust me?"

"Always."

And with that Anabelle followed Eustace into the air and out of sight. I hoped I would see her again, before the end.

CHAPTER TWELVE

I pulled the radio off one of the downed Goliaths and ran into the church. I flipped the communicator on and heard the chatter between the mechs.

"Goliath seven in front of the synagogue. Five hostiles captured," one crackly voice said into the mic.

"Goliath sixteen, south wall, three hostiles captured. One subdued," another crackled.

"A dozen hostiles accounted for. Returning to base camp," a third shrill voice said.

From the radio chatter, it sounded like they were landing all over town, snatching people, and returning them to camp. If they slaughtered the whole town, it would be a bad look for the government, but if they captured magical folks, traitors to boot, the RMP would look strong. It would send a message to the magical community that the last hope they had for redemption vanished, and it was time to toe the line.

Little did the magic people know the true aims of the people from Toledo. Fiona didn't care about equality. She cared about revenge. She cared about domination. Still, I couldn't let her be taken by the government, either. If they got a hold of her powers, who knows what the government could do with them.

I ran into the cathedral, only to see it was nearly destroyed. The choir pit was broken into a thousand pieces. The altar was obliterated. I could see the sky from the giant hole ripped into the wall by the mortar explosions.

"Lito!" I shouted, flicking off the radio to conserve battery. "Fiona!"

I ran to where I'd left Fiona, but there was nothing there. Where the Valkyrie had been, there was only a giant crater and rubble. *No, she couldn't be dead.*

"Rosie!" A thick voice shouted to me. It was Lito. "Down here!"

I ran toward the back of the church. I crawled over the broken and shattered statue that once depicted Fiona ascending into Heaven above thousands of men begging to join her, and toward the alcove which led down into Fiona's quarters.

"Are you down there?" I shouted at him.

"Yes," he replied. "Please help me. I can't protect Fiona alone."

I rushed down the stairs toward Fiona's quarters. When I reached her room, Lito had Fiona laid across the floor. Shards of the cylinder that once carried Fiona's essence were strewn about the room. He was trying to cup some of the puddled blue water remaining on the floor into her mouth.

"What are you doing?" I asked, disgusted.

"I thought…maybe if she drank, she would come back."

I shook my head, placing the radio on the ground. "No, just no."

He looked up at me. "Well, I didn't know what else to do."

"Does the RMP know about Fiona? Do they know she's here?"

Lito hesitated for a second, then gave a solemn nod. "Yes."

"Then we have to hide her," I replied. "Where is the darkest place in this apartment?"

"I don't know," he replied.

"Is there anywhere we can use as cover?"

"Under the bed," he said emphatically.

"Good," I said. "Help me with her."

I threw an unconscious Fiona around my shoulder and lifted her up. Lito took her other arm, and we headed toward the kitchen, over the shards of glass from the cylinder. Past the kitchen was her cot. I pulled up the mattress and laid her under the box spring. It wasn't easy, but we fit her until only her wing could be seen.

"Pull that table over here, drape it with something, and keep quiet. Goliaths are out there looking for her. I'm sure of that. They are snatching up citizens left and right, but if they know about her, they won't stop until they find her."

"And what if they come for her?" Lito asked pitifully.

"Stay here," I said, grabbing on to Lito's shoulder. "If they come, hide under the table. I will send the Tuppins for you both. They don't have their powers, but they can still do their part to protect you."

"I—I can do this."

"I know you can," I replied, unsure if I was telling the truth. "There is one more thing I need to ask you. How do we move the city?"

"Move the city?" he replied.

I nodded. "Like you did after the war. It's the only way to keep you all safe."

"The last time it took a hundred masters and focused concentration. And we had Fiona then."

"Figure out how to do it without any of that," I replied. "Cuz we don't have those kinds of resources."

*

By the time I made it back up the stairs, there was a Goliath standing in the middle of the downed rubble. I was terrified, and horrified. The only way out was through it, and aside for some patches of rubble, there was nothing I could use to hide myself.

The Goliath turned, and I slid down behind the rubble of Fiona's statue, just as it turned back toward me. I smelled the sulfur emanating from the downed rubble that still smoked from the explosives. The Goliath took another step forward. The servos and motors clamped down on the floor with each step the lumbering behemoth took through the rubble.

The cockpit turned away from me, and I leapt to another small patch of rubble. As I ran, my shoes flicked dirt and debris from the bombing and created a cloud around myself. I was sure the Goliath would see if it turned around, but it never did. I inched toward the door as the Goliath stomped toward the tunnel which would take it down to find Fiona.

I couldn't let that happen. I wouldn't let that happen. Fiona was horrible, but she didn't deserve to be used as a lab rat. She didn't deserve to be a pincushion either. And my poor Lito. He was not innocent in all of this, of course, but he hadn't known anything else besides Toledo for most of his life.

I looked onto the ground and found a decent sized rock from the debris. I gripped it tightly in my hand. The Goliath couldn't fit in the tunnel. If it wanted to find Fiona, the pilot would have to get out of the Goliath and walk down into the darkness, and that's when I would attack.

I took a step forward, as the Goliath stood silently in front of me. It was idiotic to take on a Goliath, even for a fully trained magic user at full power, let alone for me. Still, I was prone to doing stupid things these days. My life seemed to be nothing but stupid mistakes recently, so what was one more dumb mistake?

I took another step forward and hid below the broken choir stable. Bent iron and wood were strewn all over the floor, but a mound of it rested in the center of the room. I didn't have to be quick. I didn't have to rush. I just needed to wait for the room to feel safe, and for the soldier to leave the Goliath. If they didn't dismount, then I would know that Fiona was safe in the basement, at least until I returned, or until troops stormed the city.

I leapt over the mound of choir stables and ducked below a pile of stones that had fallen from the ceiling. The stones had stood for a half dozen centuries, more even, and now they laid at my feet, destroyed and discarded.

Finally, after what felt like an eternity, the cockpit opened, and a young woman with tightly cut brown hair hopped down. She pulled a pistol out of a holster on her leg and started down the stairs.

"Hello!" the soldier said. "If there is anyone down here, come out in the name of the Royal Military Police of the United Kingdom. You are under arrest."

Her voice echoed off the walls of the hallway as I walked forward toward the stairs. I looked down into the darkness but saw nothing, not even the faint blue glow that once lined the walls. There was nothing but darkness.

I inched down the stairs with a knot in my stomach. It's hard to believe that I'd entered Toledo for the first time less than a week prior and then walked down these same stairs for my first meeting with Fiona. I felt like I'd lived a whole lifetime in those short days.

"This is your final warning," the soldier said as she pushed open the door to Fiona's chamber.

I reached the bottom of the stairs just fast enough to watch the soldier disappear toward the kitchen. She crunched on the shards of glass as she moved, and I picked up my gait to meet hers. In a couple of seconds, she would find Fiona and my Lito.

"Okay," Lito said as I heard the table push forward. He whimpered pitifully. "You found me."

"Get down on the ground now!" the soldier shouted.

The sound from the screaming masked my footsteps. When Lito saw me, his eyes went wide. I gripped the stone in my hands tighter as I stalked forward. Just one chance. One chance to save them both.

"I said get on the ground!" the soldier shouted, cocking her gun.

"I don't think so," I said.

The soldier turned, and I whacked her in the face. She spun around at the impact of my swing and slammed into the counter. I pulled the gun out of her unconscious hand and placed it inside my belt.

"What are you doing here?" Lito said as I pulled the camouflage jacket off the soldier.

"Change of plans," I said. "We're going for a ride."

CHAPTER THIRTEEN

Lito helped me drag Fiona up the stairs toward the abandoned Goliath. I hopped into the console, nervous that I wouldn't be able to fly the Goliath. However, I figured that if Anabelle could do it, so could I.

In the cockpit were two foot pedals and two joysticks. Playing with them quickly, I found that the joysticks moved the arms and the foot pedals moved the feet. Twisting the joystick made the arms open and close, and the feet to lock in place. There were also buttons for liftoff, touch down, and transforming the Goliath arm into a gun or other device.

After fumbling around for a few minutes with the joysticks, I was able to move the arms smoothly through the air. I grabbed Fiona with the Goliath's metal arm and cradled her carefully, or as carefully as I could, given the circumstances. Once she was loaded, I opened the other arm of the Goliath.

"I think I have a handle on this now," I said to Lito from the closed cockpit. "Get in the other arm."

"I'm not doing that," he replied. "What if you crush or drop me?"

"Fine, stay here," I said. "But if you don't come, the Goliaths will return, and I won't be here to protect you. Or you can quit being a baby, and I will take you to a safe place filled with Tuppins. Your choice."

Lito grumbled under his breath. "You're not going to cut me in half, are you?"

I shrugged. "I'll try not to, that's for sure."

"Let's just get this over with, okay?"

Lito held up his hands, and I maneuvered the right arm of the Goliath with the joystick. Anabelle wasn't wrong; the Goliath was easy to handle. It was almost like an old arcade game.

I pushed the joystick forward and scooped Lito up into my hand. A turn of the control and the hand tightened around him.

"Not too tight!" he shouted.

"Sorry," I replied, easing off the controls. "Comfortable?"

"As I'll ever be," Lito replied, gripping the mechanical hand for all it was worth.

"Then, we're off."

I pressed a red button to the right of the joystick and the jets in the back of the Goliath rumbled to life. Before takeoff, a steering wheel flipped forward out of the dashboard. I pulled back on it, and the Goliath rose into the air.

"Don't drop them. Don't drop them. Don't drop them," I mumbled to myself.

"What was that?" Lito shouted from in front of me, but I didn't answer. Instead, I pushed the throttle forward and flew upward through the hole in the roof of the Cathedral.

I knew the general direction that Eustace had taken, and I followed it backwards, zigging and zagging through the air, following the downed debris until I reached the downed cloth that once lined the streets of the city. From there, I tracked down, until I found the red rusted door.

"Is something wrong, thirty-five?" I heard through the intercom. "You seem lost. Orders are to fly back now."

I pressed the intercom. "Yes, I just lost one. I'll be along in a minute. Over."

"Roger," the intercom shouted. "Don't take long. We're about to blow this place to kingdom come."

My hands started to shake, and my throat closed. If that was true, I didn't have much time. I had to work fast. I tracked across the alleyway where Eustace led us until I found the downed cloth awning that used to hang over the streets. I followed it down with my eyes until I reached the V in the road and found the cellar where the Tuppins huddled together waiting for us.

I pressed the red button again and the Goliath rumbled to the ground. The steering wheel flipped backward, and I released Lito onto the demolished cobblestone. Once he was back on the ground, I dropped Fiona into his outstretched hands.

Then, I jumped out of the cockpit and flung open the doors to the cellar. I braced Fiona around my shoulder while Lito did the same on the other side. The hallway was still bright, but there was no longer arguing from the end of it. When I finally reached the end of the hallway, all eyes turned to me.

"Welcome back, Roselyn," Miguel said. "I thought you would have surely died by now."

"Me too," I replied. "Where is Tibor?"

"Nobody has heard from him or our spies. He was supposed to be back by now."

"Where did you send him?" I asked.

"To the west entrance," Miguel replied. "It's closest to the troops so he could get the best look. There is a guard tower that overlooks the battlefield which should have given him a good look at the whole line to find the weapon the RMP are using to subdue us."

"Keep them safe," I said. "I'll be back."

I ran back out of the hallway and shut the cellar behind me. I hopped into the Goliath and pulled down the cockpit. In a moment I was airborne, headed back toward the front with the rest of the Goliaths.

As I neared the Toledo's wall, I noticed two busted, falling apart mechs fighting a team of Goliaths in the ruins of an old church. It had to be Anabelle and Eustace. Behind them was a group of men, and one of them looked like Tibor from a distance. I pressed the red button on my Mech, and it lowered me down to the battlefield.

"Reinforcements!" the intercom squawked. "I thought they were going to leave us to take care of these traitors ourselves."

I slammed my hands on the controls to make my mechanical arms become lasers. "They are."

With one shot, I blew through both Goliaths that were fighting my friends. Anabelle smiled at me.

"About time!" she shouted.

"Sorry. I was on a rescue mission," I replied. "Did you find the device that's screwing with the magic here?"

"No," Anabelle replied. "We've been protecting Tibor this whole time. He's in bad shape."

"Thank goodness you came along," Eustace said from the other suit. "I can't believe I'm saying that."

I jumped out of my mech and ran over to him. Tibor was bloodied from a knock to the face, and his body was half covered in debris.

"What happened?" I asked as I laid down next to him.

He struggled to breathe. "Mortar shell. I couldn't—I'm sorry."

"It's fine. It's fine," I replied. "Rest. Rest."

"No," he said. "The city depended on me. You depended on me."

I looked over at Anabelle, who had every reason to worry, as concern wrinkled her brow. It was my stupid idea to save the city. We could have just left. We could all run away and leave this city to burn. I could find Tibor a healer somewhere outside the range of the transmitter, and he would be fine. He had come back from worse.

"You still in this?" Anabelle asked. "Or are we gonna flee?"

"You can't flee!" Eustace shouted from his mech. "I won't let you."

Anabelle spun her gun at him. "Don't tell me what to do."

I sighed. "Are you willing to let this whole city be destroyed because that's what they are going to do."

Anabelle nodded. "I know, but at some point, it's not your problem. You have to think of yourself."

"I've been thinking of myself this whole time, Ana," I replied. "That's how I got into this spot. I couldn't live with myself if I turned my back on this city now."

"So what do we do then?" Anabelle asked. "Take on the whole RMP?"

"No," Tibor replied. "Lift me up into the air. I'll show you what the transmitter looks like."

"Are you sure? What if I pull this thing off and you're nothing but a torso under there?"

"Then at least I can do one good thing before I die," he said, smiling.

I nodded. "Alright, Anabelle and Eustace, get ready to attack when I give the word."

I jumped into my Goliath and throttled forward toward Tibor. My mechanical arms made quick work of the rubble that covered him. He writhed and screamed in pain as I pulled the debris off him. It was clear to me that the pressure was stopping the bleeding.

When Tibor was free, I picked him up with my left hand and squeezed him tight enough to make sure to simulate the debris.

"Not so tight!" he said, screaming in pain.

"This might be the only thing keeping you alive. Quit being a baby!"

I pressed the red button in the cockpit and rose me into the air. We could see the entirety of the battlefield. A hundred tanks lined the valley, and five hundred Goliaths lay in wait behind them. In the back of the battlefield, stood a large beacon that rose from a craggily bit of metal on the ground. It was locked into the ground with big metal legs that looked like spider leg and guarded by a dozen Humvees with turrets on the tops of them.

"There it is," Tibor said. "The beacon is high in the air. It looks just like the blueprint."

"Are you sure?" I replied. "We have to be sure."

He nodded. "Yes, I was there when the plans were delivered to our outpost in Madrid. I'm sure of it. I studied the schematics for hours."

I floated back to the ground and opened my cockpit. Anabelle and Eustace turned to me. "It's sitting in the back of the battlefield. It looks like a big spire with spider legs."

Anabelle nodded. "Consider it taken out."

"Ana," I replied, solemnly. "They have so much firepower. Even if you somehow can get there… You'll never…"

Water filled my eyes. I couldn't tell my best friend she was about to die.

"Hey," she replied. "I got this, alright? Trust me."

I shook my head. "We can go. We can leave and never come back. It'll be okay."

"No," she replied. "You're right. I could never live with myself if I abandoned this city now. Besides, if we don't stand up and fight, then they'll use this technology on every magical person in Europe, maybe the world. Anywhere we run, you won't be safe. Nobody will be safe."

"I can come with you," I said. "Another mech could turn the—"

She shook her head. "Take care of Tibor. I'll see you in no time. Let's go, Eustace."

Anabelle and Eustace flew into the air and out of sight. I knew I was watching my best friend fly away for the last time, and I wish I had more to say. I just hoped against hope that the odds were in our favor.

CHAPTER FOURTEEN

I spared one last look for Anabelle and Eustace, but I couldn't worry about them anymore. I had my own mission. I had to help Lito move the city somehow. I spun around in my Goliath and started heading for the bunker. It wasn't long before my guidance system lit up with a Goliath on my tail.

"Goliath thirty-five," I heard over my radio. "You are headed in the wrong direction with that prisoner. Return to base."

I pressed down my intercom. "Negative. I have orders from the Commander to take this prisoner somewhere else."

"That's funny," the intercom buzzed. "Because I am the commander, and I gave no such orders."

Crap. I stepped on the pedal under my feet and pushed forward with the wheel until I was going at top speed. Tibor fought against the force trying to push him down as I struggled to keep the mech flying forward.

No matter what I did though, the Goliath stayed on my tail gaining on me with every second. He had years of training to my none, and everything I tried to do wasn't enough.

Wings flipped out of the sides of the Goliath. I didn't even know they had wings, nor that the wings blasted their own rockets. He would be on me in a second with the extra rocket boost. I spun around and slammed the button to turn my right arm into a laser.

I fired frantically into the air, but it was no use against the Commander. He spun easily to avoid my blast, as it cut through the air on either side of him. He raised his arm, and

I dipped down to avoid his blast, but he didn't fire. He was waiting for the perfect moment.

His mech stopped in midair, and I heard the beep of my readout as it turned red and read TARGET LOCKED. I didn't hear the laser fire, I only felt its aftermath, as the Goliath lurched forward toward the ground. I spun around and cradled Tibor in my mechanical arms as I fell through a building and crashed onto the ground.

*

"Taking…heavy…fire…" Anabelle said through the intercom.

"Near…target…" Eustace replied. "Hang…tight…"

I popped my eyes open to the knowledge that my friend was about to die, and she wasn't even going to be successful. This would all be in vain.

"Be safe," I said through the intercom, knowing it was an impossible task. "Love you."

"Ditto," was what she responded after a long silence.

I don't know how long I was out, but when I came to the oil had leaked out of the mech and all around the suit. Fires raged in every direction. If I didn't pull Tibor to safety, he would be blown up or burnt to a crisp. However, if I let go of him with my mechanical arm, there was a good chance he would bleed out. I had to take the risk. I unlatched my cockpit and released my left hand.

Tibor fell to the ground, and I pulled him free of the mech suit. "Stay with me."

His eyes fluttered as I tried to sit him against the wreckage of the building. His head drooped down, his neck unable to stand the weight of his head. "Go."

"I'm not going anywhere!" I replied. "We've been through worse than this."

He wanted to smile, but he had lost a lot of blood. He had lost too much blood. There was nothing I could do. Nothing I could do. All I wanted was to touch his pain and make it go away. I closed my eyes and pressed hard against the gash in his leg. *Please, please, please, please…*

I felt a pinprick in my cheek, and suddenly it glowed a bright blue. My hands pulsed orange, and after a moment the hole in Tibor's leg closed up. I moved my hand to his stomach, and the cut across his abdomen closed as well. I was crying so hard I was laughing as I placed my hand on his head and watched it clear up as well.

Tibor's eyes finally came into focus. "What…happened?"

He caught the last of my glow, but I didn't have time to explain. "A lot. Can you walk?"

He pushed up from the ground, shaky and wobbling. "I lost a lot of blood."

"I know," I replied, grabbing his arm. "At least you're not going to lose anymore."

"I need a hospital," he said. "Blood transfusion."

"There'll be time for that later, but right now, we've got to get down to the bunker and help move this city."

"Move…the city…why?"

I didn't have to answer his question, because a bullhorn rattled over the whole city and echoed through every corner of it before I could open my mouth.

"Any inhabitants of Toledo still inside the walls of the city. We will begin our final bombardment in ten minutes, which will destroy what is left of your city. If you wish to survive, come outside the city and surrender. A life in captivity is a far better fate than death."

"That's why," I said.

In front of me, I saw the downed lined of cloth which had led me to the bunker earlier, and would do so again. I just had to follow it to the bunker.

"Left or right?" I asked Tibor.

He thought for a moment. "Umm…"

"Not fast enough! Come on!"

"Left," he said. "I think it's left."

*

It only took us three minutes to get down the street and into the bunker, and another minute to hobble down the hallway toward the meeting room with the rest of the Tuppins, but by the time we got there 40 percent of our deadline had ticked away.

"What have you found?" Miguel said. "Is the magical suppressor destroyed yet?"

I shook my head. "We're working on it."

"So you've done nothing since you've been gone?" Lito said, scoffing. "I should never have trusted a girl to do the job of the Council."

"Yeah!" I replied. "Well, where is the council now? Dead, probably, or captured. At least I did something!"

Suddenly, every cheek in the room lit up at once. The room was aglow with squares, mountains, suns, moons, plus signs, and in the center of them all, my cheeks glowed with all four signs that I unlocked, which brought apprehension to all the people in the room. They recoiled from me in fear but kept their eyes affixed on me in awe.

"She did it," Tibor said, grabbing my hand. He was the only one who didn't question me and who wasn't fearful of my power.

As he clutched my hand, Fiona took a deep, heaving breath and sat up. That brought all the attention to her. Scowls turned to smiles as they looked upon their awoken savior.

"My lady!" Miguel said. "You've returned."

"You must warn everybody. Evacuate the city—"

"They've already come," I replied. "They are about to bomb the city."

"You!" Fiona shouted, clawing toward me. "You did this to us!"

"Stop!" Tibor shouted, getting between her and I. "She's been trying to save this town while you've been asleep, but we can't do it alone."

"I will fly out and—"

"It's no use now, Fiona," Lito mumbled. "The only option left is to move the city."

She snapped at him. "Move the city! Do you know what kind of toll that would take on us all?"

"We do, my lady," Miguel said. "However, I see no other way. They will destroy us in moments."

"Me either," Lito added. "It's unfortunate, but it is the only way."

"I won't be at full strength until tomorrow," Fiona said. "Surely we can fight until then."

I shook my head. "We are outgunned and outmanned. Goliaths have taken thousands of captives and bombed what they couldn't capture. The only option is to move the city and to do it now."

Fiona sneered at me. "You've really fouled up our paradise, haven't you?"

I eyed her intently as she stared me down. She wasn't wrong, of course, but I wasn't going to give her the satisfaction of telling her so, and she wouldn't give it up until I cowed before her.

"We could keep this up for the next five minutes," I said, "And watch the whole city burn. Or we could put aside our differences and work together."

"Child," she growled. "You have no idea what you have unleashed."

"You can tell me all about it AFTER we move the city," I said.

"We could never move the city in five minutes. That kind of focus takes—"

"You have five minutes," I snarled. "That's it. So, figure it out."

"We wait for your instructions, my lady," Miguel said. "The Tuppins are at your command."

Fiona didn't have time to argue. We had less than five minutes before the shelling started. "Grab hands, in a circle now. Hurry."

The Tuppins shifted around until they formed a big circle. In the center Fiona stood with her arms open, head tilted back to the Heavens.

"Close your eyes," she continued. "Picture the ocean. The waves crashing down. Picture the cliffs overlooking a bluff. Picture vacating this plane and entering that one. Picture every house in Toledo. Picture your house, and picture it all vanish and reappear far away from here. Do you have it?"

"Yes," the Tuppins chanted in chorus.

"Good, now reach forward with your mind and give your power to me. Imagine touching me with your hand and transferring all you have to me. Good, good. I feel it flowing through me."

"Come on," I grumbled. "Hurry up."

Fiona's eyes opened. She was no longer an angel of the flesh but one of pure blue light. She stared at me with her bright eyes, and shot forward, placing her hand on my head. The fire burned the top of my head down into my chest and through to my legs until my whole body burned.

I had to get it out. I had to move, but I couldn't break the chain. I stared up at the Heavens and screamed. From my mouth, a torrent of blue fire spat out, burned through the ceiling, and shot into the sky far above. I couldn't see the sky with my eyes, but I saw it in my mind's eye. I saw the fire shoot up into the heavens, and cascade down around the city. A second blue light from Fiona rose up with me and merged with my light.

Outside the city, Goliaths swerved to avoid the blue fire, and the soldiers gawked at it. I saw the beacon, broken, and destroyed; a Goliath charred in its ashes. I saw close up on the face of the Goliath driver, expecting it to be Anabelle, but it wasn't. It was Eustace, smiling in his sacrifice as he fell motionless.

I looked further into the woods and saw three men surround Anabelle and pull her out of the heaping wreckage of her Goliath. I saw them lead her to a pen with a thousand other magic users, who all stared up at the sky with the soldiers as my blue light cascaded down and enveloped the city.

I saw the cheeks glow on each Toledo prisoner. I watched them break through their cages, fighting against the army. I watched them attack, and I watched the army fight back.

Suddenly, I was above the city, looking down as the city was enveloped in white light. Then, it was gone. A quake rippled through my body, and I fell backwards. Fiona fell the other way. My eyes tried to retain focus, but they couldn't. I couldn't see. I couldn't move. I could only fade away.

CHAPTER FIFTEEN

When my eyes fluttered open again, I was back in my room in Lito's house. Fainting and then awakening there seemed to be a habit for me. Lito sat in one corner of the room, watching me, as he did when I got here so few days ago. However, then I had hope that he was the good kind of witch. I harbored no illusions of that now. No matter why he was watching over me, it wasn't for my own good; it was for his own ends.

"You're awake!" he said, palpably hiding his excitement.

"Did we do it?" I asked, groggily. "Did we move the town?"

"Yes," he said. His eyes had none of the luster they once did. "Everyone is safe. As safe as we can be, at least."

"Good," I replied. I had done it. I had helped save the city. Now I could leave.

"I'm glad you are okay. I was so worried."

I sneered at him with scorn in my eyes. "Yeah, I'll bet you were."

"What are you talking about? I thought we were past this after you helped save the town."

"I didn't help save the town because of you. I helped because I couldn't live with my conscience that my friend helped blow this town up. I couldn't have that on my conscience for the rest of my life, eating me alive, festering away at me. I don't know how you do it."

"That's not fair," he said. "What I do is for the good of my people."

"I'm sure you believe that," I replied. "But war is never the answer."

"You really believe that," Lito replied. "After today? That there is no reason to wage war on somebody, even when the other option is genocide."

"I think both of you are stupid. You and the government. There's no difference in my eyes. You hate them. They hate you."

Lito lowered his eyes. "Only one of us is trying to wipe out the other."

"No," I replied. "Only one of you tried today, but you would wipe them out to save your people, too. Do you think it's any different for them?"

Lito looked up and stared into me, steely-eyed. "Yes. I do. Get dressed. You are needed downstairs."

"I still don't feel good," I replied. "I need to rest."

"None of us feel good, nieta, but there is work to do regardless. Get dressed. Do as I say."

All the warmth was out of his voice now, and his true nature bled through. "Fine. Get out so I can change."

Lito left without another word, leaving the door open behind him. When I stood up, I was still in my dirty clothes from the battle. I desperately wanted a bath to feel normal, but what was normal anymore? What was anything? I swung open the shutters on the room and looked out onto the vast horizon.

The ocean stretched far into the distance. I didn't know where we were, except on the vast blue water. Below me, the smoldering wreckage of the town filled my eyes. Everywhere was destruction and damage. When I looked out, I was violently angry. I was aghast. I was furious. I could only imagine the anger that bubbled up in the residents of Toledo.

I had no love for the RMP, but I was once a Normal, and those without magical blood weren't all bad. A war would do nothing but destroy all of us. I had to make them see that. I had to make them understand that destruction for destruction was no way to live. It was only a way to die.

"Are you ready?" Tibor said from the doorway. "Are you ready for what's coming next?"

I turned to him and smiled. "No. I don't think any of us are ready for what's coming next."

BOOK THREE

"Hunted"

PROLOGUE

"You don't have to do this," I screamed from the edge of a sewer pipe that emptied into a river below it. Sewage gushed under me, creating a waterfall of disgusting sludge that dumped into an otherwise pristine lake.

Four soldiers drew their guns and aimed them at me, the laser from their sights hovering on my chest. I placed my hands behind my head and took a deep breath. The Royal Military Police had chased me for the better part of a decade and finally found me living in Berlin under the assumed name of Hans Lieber. I shed my past and the name Thomas Abalos and led an unassuming life, working as a butcher in the northern-most part of the city.

I tried hard to tamp down my magic use. However, every once and a while, in the cold of the German winter, I lit my hand on fire and used them to warm my cheeks. I was human after all, no matter what the United Kingdom of Europe thought. Somebody must have seen, and the RMP came down on me with fire and fury. I was used to them finding me by now and had grown accustomed to leaving at a moment's notice.

I didn't have loved ones anymore; not since I gave my baby up to the nursemaids to raise as a Normal, and not since my beautiful wife Susan was taken by the Royal Military Police. I didn't live anywhere long enough to put down roots, so there were no roots to pull up when it was time to flee.

"That's where you're wrong, Tommy!" A booming voice shouted through the tunnel.

Out of the darkness a man with a handlebar mustache, bright red hair, and soulless, emerald eyes walked into the light. Even though I had led them on a chase through the disgusting sewers of Berlin, General Michael Sullivan didn't have a stain on him. Even his boots shone brightly in the dank darkness.

"I just want to live in peace!" I screamed back, peering over the hundred-foot drop into the freezing water below.

"And I wish that was an option for you, mate. I really do, don't cha know. However, you are an enemy of the crown, and we can't just have ya runnin' all around, like yer one of us and not a disgusting Shiner. Now, you can either come back with me peacefully or meet your end here, ya see."

I was an enemy of the crown for nothing more than using magic and being born in Toledo, the last great stronghold of magic users in the world. The United Kingdom of Europe didn't like that, as it was the final holdout of England controlling the whole of the continent.

"What's the point of going with you?" I shouted. "Either way I'm going to die."

"Yer not tellin' a lie, I hate ta say," General Sullivan said with a proud smirk. "However, if ya come with me peaceful, at least you won't die like a dog. Have some pride, man."

I didn't have any pride left. Living like a nomad for the last eight years took all of it out of me. I found work just long enough to make it to the next town, and the next town after that. There was always a mark on my chest, all because I wanted to live free, and the UKE didn't like that one bit.

Living free as a magic user was tantamount to heresy in The United Kingdom of Europe, which blossomed after England's victory in the Second World War. If you wanted to be a magic user in the UKE., it meant living in squalor and being treated like an animal. It meant letting go of the last vestige of your humanity, and I wasn't ready to do that. I wasn't ready to be a second-class citizen. I was worth more than that, even if everything in the universe conspired against me.

"I would rather live free and die hard, General, then spend one second under your thumb."

"That is disappointing ta hear, mate," General Sullivan said. "I hoped for a better end than this, I really did, you see, but I guess every good hunter gets his prey eventually, ay?"

Now, it was my turn to smirk. "Not always, general."

I spun on my heels and dove out of the tunnel, into the waterfall of putrid waste flowing into the river. Bullets careened out of the tunnel above me as I fell, but I was already halfway down to the water before they'd pulled their triggers. I was lucky that it was early enough in the year that the river hadn't frozen solid yet. In another month, I would have cracked my neck on the ice.

Still, pockets of frozen water bobbed up and down in the river. A large ice chunk floated under me as I neared the water, and I prayed to whatever god still existed for it to move before I crashed onto it. Luckily, at the last moment, the ice moved onward, and I crashed into the water right behind it.

My first thought upon entering the water was that maybe I wasn't so lucky after all. The water was bitterly cold and moving rapidly, making it hard for me to surface. I fought against the onslaught of the water as it pounded me hard with every stroke I took.

I crested over the water just as a large rock slammed against me, tearing a gash in my leg and spinning me furiously back into the water. Every stroke I took was agony, but I refused to give in. I refused to die. With one last push, I gathered all my strength and broke through the water and latched onto an icy pancake moving past. I pulled myself onto the frazil pan, struggling to catch my breath.

*

Eventually, the river stopped its restless movement and settled into a light current. As it did, I unlatched my fingers from the frazil pan that saved my life and rolled onto the shore. I had lost all feeling in my legs as I pulled myself onto the river bank. I closed my eyes and imagined myself on fire. As I did, I felt a burning in my cheek as it started to glow with a dull blue sun that denoted my powers to control fire.

When I opened my eyes, my body glowed with a red flame crackling across every inch of my body. I focused my thoughts on the blaze, and the fire cascaded off of my body into a roaring fire next to me. My hands shook as they tried to control the fire, but soon enough I could feel the tips of my toes again, and then my ankles, shins, knees, and finally my thighs.

I pulled off my jacket and placed it next to the flames, as well as my boots and other clothing until I'd stripped down to my boxers. Then, I brought the flame up into my body, and laid it on top of me, like a thin layer of protection, crackling across my skin, warming me, without burning me alive.

It was a trick I'd learned from a friend of my father's back when I lived in Toledo, before my old man became Chief Justice of the City Council, back when he was still half pleasant to be around. Sometimes, I wondered if he'd ever changed his ways in the years since I ran away, but mostly the city never entered my mind, except to dream about returning one day. That could never happen though, as I renounced my citizenship when I left with my wife and unborn child so many years ago.

With my leg bare, I finally saw the depths of my cut. It was worse than I imagined. The rock gashed my leg deeply, nearly to the bone. I needed a hospital, quickly, but I couldn't be seen at a government facility. They would turn me over to the RMP. Immediately. There was no time for first aid either, and I would bleed out before I ever found a doctor. I wasn't a healer. The only thing I knew was fire, and that would have to be enough. I closed my eyes and concentrated the flame engulfing my body toward my leg wound. At least I could cauterize the wound, and stop it from bleeding.

When I opened my eyes, the fire pooled around the gash in my leg. I knew it would hurt like the dickens, but I forced the fire to singe my leg anyway. I nearly passed out from the pain, but when the fire finally stopped, my leg no longer bled, and the flame burned it shut. There were similar scars all over my body from where cuts turned to burns and healed awkwardly. I should have been born a healer. Then, maybe I would look like a human, instead of like Frankenstein's monster, carelessly cobbled together by an incompetent creator.

Still, it allowed me to keep my secret, the secret of what happened to my child. If they knew I left her to be cared for by the nursemaids, and that she was being brought up in Ambrosia without powers until she was eighteen, they would arrest her right now. They would kill her before she could infiltrate their puritanical world, which was one devoid of magic users altogether.

If they only knew how many magic users worked their way through the system, found jobs in their ministries, fed them, and only used their magic in secret if at all, their entire society would crumble.

I sat on the cold ground, heating myself with flames licking my body, for another two hours, until my clothes were dry and my stomach ached for food. I put on my clothes and tamped out the fire. Nobody knew where I was, but it was getting dark, and I didn't want the fire to be a beacon for the RMP to find me. The Goliaths could seek out heat, and they would surely be tracking these woods for me.

I was sick of running. My father was right, the world was cruel, and I had to try going home, back to Toledo, even if I would likely be turned away, or worse.

I couldn't avoid it anymore. I tried to run from it for a decade, but it was time to go home, to Toledo. At least there I would be safe from the RMP. At least there I would be safe from the constant hunt.

*

I looked different now than I did when I left home. When I ran away from Toledo, I was just a boy with a clean-shaven face and perfect skin. Now, I returned with a thick beard, dark circles under my eyes, and scars all over my body.

It had been nearly a decade since I left, but I still knew the way from Germany, through France, and past San Sebastian in the north of Spain. I knew the woods from where I left, and I knew that Eustace would be guarding the entrance for my return, just as he did when I left. He was unyielding in his protection of Toledo.

"Halt!" Eustace said with his shrill, shaky voice as I walked toward the illusion that hid Toledo from the rest of Spain. His beard was longer than when I left and filled with strands of white hair. He was old now, but still powerful, and he growled when he talked.

"I mean you no harm," I said, holding up my hands.

"State your business," he replied, pointing his walking stick toward me.

There were plenty of fire users; it was the second most common magical power next to Eustace's mastery of the Earth.

"I seek entrance into Toledo."

"For what purpose?" Eustace said, hesitantly. "Be you a spy?"

I shook my head. "Long have I heard stories of Toledo's greatness, and I wish to see for myself. I have spent my life being hunted by the RMP, and the government, being forced to live in squalor like an animal. I wish to live like a human again."

I didn't know how much I meant those words until they came out of my mouth. I longed to be home, where I could be free, and where I could live without looking over my shoulder every second of every day. I wanted peace. It was all I wanted from the moment I left Toledo until now. I thought I could find it somewhere else, but my father was right, his city was the only place where magical folk could rest peacefully at night.

"A likely story," Eustace said. "You are a traitor and a coward. You wish to undermine us with your ways of the outside."

"No, Eustace," I bellowed. "That's not true. I wish to come home."

Eustace looked closely at me. "Do I recognize you, stranger? You seem familiar as if we knew each other in a different time."

I sighed. "It is I, Thomas Abalos, son of the Chief Justice. Here to reclaim my place among you."

Eustace sneered. "You are sick, usurper. Everyone knows that Thomas is dead. The Chief Justice presided over the funeral himself."

"No!" I said, limping forward. "I am alive! I have returned!"

I grabbed onto Eustace, but he flung me asunder. "I am feeling particularly generous today, traitor. Leave this place, and never return. If I hear the name of a dead man escape your tongue again, I will rip it out."

I opened my mouth to speak, but it was no use. I was homeless, abandoned to the wilderness, and cast aside from the only place I ever felt safe.

Now, what would I do?

CHAPTER ONE

I never wanted to be a hero. That was a truth I still held even after I saved Toledo and effectively became one despite myself. I never wanted to be the chosen one, even though lots of people seemed to think I was destined to save all magic kind. I never wanted to save the world or even a small piece of it. I never wanted to be a beacon for magic kind, and yet, here I was, facing that destiny.

I was never negative, like ever, but war will do that to you. Plus, my best friend was taken from me, and now she's a prisoner at some government facility who knows where. Usually, Anabelle countered any negative energy I had, but she had been captured by the RMP right before we removed Toledo from their grasp. Now, she was in prison somewhere, all because of me.

That kind of thing jaded you up quickly. It's one thing to know war is horrible intellectually, and another thing to be in a city where civilians were being shelled to death.

Maybe other people faced with the same fate as me would welcome the savior path, or at least have something positive to say about it. Anabelle would have something nice to say about it, but she wasn't the chosen one, I was, and I hated my destiny. I wished I could put a positive spin on what's happened to me in the past couple of days, but the truth was that I just…couldn't. Not just because what happened was crap, but because I lacked the tools to see the light through the darkness without my friend.

I'm not quite sure how long I had been staring out the window of my newly un-estranged grandfather's house, but during my time sitting there I watched the sun move over the horizon from midday to nearly dusk. Downstairs, the city council of Toledo waited for me to join them, but I couldn't force my legs to move toward them.

"Are you ever going to join us?" Tibor asked, pushing open the door to my room which I purposely closed a half dozen times before after others had tried to rouse me. The door didn't lock, which meant people could nag me endlessly and there was nothing I could do about it.

I suppose I could block the door with my bed or something, but that meant moving, and I lacked the will to move from my perch near the window. Besides, I didn't really mind them interrupting me, if they understood it was a futile pursuit.

"They're asking for you," Tibor added.

"They can keep asking," I replied. "I'll be down when I'm ready."

Tibor was the oldest friend I had in Toledo, if only because I only arrived in Toledo a few days ago. He was strong and muscular, with a shaggy beard and dark eyes. He could control the air, and his power of flight had saved me more than once since we'd first met.

He rescued me from the Royal Military Police after I learned that I had magical powers. The RMP chased me mercilessly through Spain as he brought me here, almost dying in the process.

The RMP hated magical folks. That wasn't uncommon, though. Everybody who didn't have powers hated us. There was a time I wasn't hated, though. For the first sixteen years of my life, I thought I was a Normal, without any powers at all.

Everybody knew that magic presented on your thirteenth birthday, and I'd passed that marker three years ago. Lucky me, though, my powers were just being suppressed until my eighteenth birthday, and even luckier me, I missed curfew one day and my powers burst out in front my boyfriend two years earlier than intended…well they presented to my ex-boyfriend…and he told everybody. The power of social media ruined my life, but I'm not bitter. At least not much. Not about that at least.

After my powers presented themselves, I'd nearly died a half dozen times making my way out of Ambrosia and across the countryside to the mythical city of Toledo, last stronghold of magical folk, hidden from the rest of the world by illusion magic, since before I was born.

"I don't think you should keep them waiting much longer," Tibor said. "The sooner you join them, the sooner you can be done with them for the day. They need you to come up with a plan."

I spun around to him. "They don't need me to come up with a plan. I'm sure they already have one ready to go."

He nodded. "They have part of an idea, at least, and I'm telling you, as a friend, you want to hear it."

"Is it stupid?" I asked.

Again, he nodded. "Just come and talk to them yourself."

I sighed. "Fine, but I'm not going to change."

He shrugged. "I don't care. And if they care…who cares, right?"

I pushed off the chair. "Alright, I'm coming. I don't know how much longer I could have looked out into the looming darkness anyway."

"Unfortunately, kid," Tibor said with a sad sigh. "Most of life is looking out into the darkness."

"Don't call me kid, alright," I said with a snicker. "I'm the chosen one, remember?"

It was a joke, of course, but I really was the chosen one, or at least that's what Fiona believed. She was the Valkyrie who guarded Toledo. She came down from Heaven, or Valhalla, or wherever, to protect all magic kind from Normals. Once, I lived in awe of Fiona, and magic of all types, but this place took the luster off everything I once admired.

Fiona did a piss poor job of saving magical folks too, what with the prosecution of our kind after World War 2, and our subjugation under the boot of the United Kingdom of Europe's rule. She could have done more to protect the magic people of the world, but instead, she chose to hole up in Toledo and hide for several decades until the chosen one came along—until I came along.

I don't know what she planned for me, because the RMP had bombed us into oblivion before she could tell me her plan. I knew it wasn't good, though. Nothing in Toledo was very good. It was probably why I didn't have any interest in hearing her plan.

"They are pretty pissed at you," Tibor said, weaving through the tight corridors of my abuelito's house. I called him Lito, but he was better known as the Chief Justice of Toledo's city council. He was the most powerful single figure in town, next to Fiona.

"Well, the feeling is mutual," I grunted. "Maybe they should be grateful, instead. After all, I saved them all."

Once the RMP started bombing Toledo, there was only one choice to make…move the city. Moving the city had only happened once before. After the war, the city council moved the city from south of Madrid, which was its name before the English conquerors renaming it to Ambrosia after they defeated Franco, up to the north of Spain, just south of San Sebastian. When they discovered us and started bombing, we did it again.

"They appreciate you moving the city," Tibor said. "They just think you also led the RMP to their doorstep."

"It's hard for me to argue with that," I sighed. "I did lead them here, but I saved them, too. At least I'm a net neutral."

Currently, the city of Toledo hovered over the Bay of Biscay, in international waters, north of Spain and to the west of France.

"You're more than a net neutral, Rosie." Tibor hurried down the wooden stairs of the courtyard which led out into the garden. "Come on. They are just outside."

"Do I have to go out there?" I asked, grabbing Tibor by the wrist.

Tibor nodded. "Yeah, you have to go. You moved a friggin' city, Rosie. I think you can handle a couple of pompous windbags."

"I could, but what if I don't want to?"

"Life is all about doing crap you don't wanna do, my friend. Get used to it."

I sighed. "I'm starting to figure that one out."

I followed Tibor through the archway of the house and out onto the lawn. I expected to see a dozen or so people out front, but there was only my Lito, Fiona, and Miguel, the leader of the Tuppins, a group of magical soldiers who had protected the city since before Fiona had landed on Earth in the thirteenth century. Tibor was a Tuppins, but I didn't hold that against him.

Fiona looked as radiant. Her long blond hair glowed and shimmered as if it were plucked from the sun itself, and as a Valkyrie, it might have been for all I knew. You couldn't tell she had just been in a battle, or that she got knocked out during it by a magic zapping bomb that put her in a coma for hours during the worst of the attack. That was how the RMP got the drop on us, by using a magic nullifying bomb and transponder to quash our powers.

Miguel looked as weathered as he did when I first met him, but during our previous encounters, he carried himself regally. Now, he was nowhere near as well put together. He wore a purple cape and ornate golden adornments when I saw him before. Now, he was draped in a simple black robe. Granite flakes spotted his salt and pepper beard as if he hadn't washed it since the bombing.

"I told you to shower," Lito said, forcefully. "What were you doing up there all this time?"

Lito showed no kindness to me. Not after I so blatantly told him off the last time we spoke. I wondered if he'd ever felt kindness for me, or if it was just a ploy so I would do his bidding. He was a very powerful man in Toledo, and powerful men knew how to manipulate people to their whims and show only what they wanted others to see.

"Be kind," Fiona scolded. "It is not Rosie's fault she is how she is. It is a symptom of her upbringing as a Normal. They are the worst. Isn't that right, Roselyn?"

I snarled under my breath at the subtle way in which Fiona chose to insult me. I preferred my insults out in the open, where I could respond to them with anger, instead of couched in pleasant platitudes.

"We are all a product of our upbringing, Fiona," I replied, growling every word. "I am, as are you, and my grandfather, and even the warmonger next to you."

"Warmonger!" Miguel shouted. "I have kept the peace here since before you were born, and you have destroyed it in less than a week."

"Miguel!" Fiona shouted. "She's just a child. She knows not what she says. Besides, you act as if warmonger is an insult. Some of the best people I've ever met were warmongers."

"It is an insult," I growled. "I know exactly what I'm saying, Fiona. Now, why did you need me here?"

"Straight to the point," Fiona replied with a smile. I didn't know how she could smile at a time like this, but then again, I wasn't adept at the games Fiona played either. "I like that about you."

"Interesting. I'm still trying to find something I like about you."

"Well, you will like this, I hope. Or maybe not. Luckily, it doesn't matter."

"Get on with it," I replied, staring deep into her eyes.

She sighed. "Unfortunately, we have found the bodies of the other two members of the City Council. They…did not make it through the unpleasantness…let us say for the sake of polite conversation."

"So, they're dead," I replied, refusing to be polite about it.

Lito nodded. "Quite dead."

"What does that have to do with me?" I replied.

"Well, we're in a pinch and need a replacement body to fill in until we can appoint new members to the Council, and I thought it would be nice to give the chosen one a place on the Council to show that we are united in the struggle against the United Kingdom of Europe."

The United Kingdom of Europe included everything England occupied and annexed after the Second World War, from France across through Poland, only stopped by the western tip of Russia.

"Are we united against them?" I asked in a huff. "I feel like you will have very different ideas on how to deal with what happened."

"Well, that is why we have a Council," Fiona said in a rare moment of levity I wasn't comfortable with, which might have been the point.

"I think it's a bad idea to allow you on the Council, personally," Lito said. "You are only a child, and know nothing of the ways of governance."

"And I begrudgingly agree with the Chief Justice," Miguel said. "However, I defer to the wisdom of Fiona, as always."

"I appreciate that, Miguel," Fiona said with a smile before turning to Lito. "As for you, Rosie is still bound to her agreement to help us, lest she wants her friend to die, of course."

Tibor smiled an uncomfortable grin as he looked at me. "That's the thing here, Rosie. They expect you to cooperate, and they're wagering my life you'll play along to help me."

"Why even come to me?" I asked. "There are plenty of crusty old men who would do a better job."

Fiona stood. "Perhaps, but Toledo is at a crossroads. We need to show that we are unified against our common adversary. However, we must also give hope to the city, and you are the perfect encapsulation of that message. You ooze hope, don't you? Look at you. Young, beautiful, vibrant, as if you've never felt pain."

"Trust me," I grunted. "I've felt my share of pain."

"Oh, I'm sure you think that. However, that's neither here nor there. I only need you for a moment. Once the city sees we are united, I can appoint another feckless whelp to the Council and govern as I see fit. However, I cannot do so without you to cast the deciding vote."

I stepped forward to her. "And then I leave this place, yes? I leave, and you don't stop me. Got it?"

"Think about this for a moment," Tibor said. "Fiona will have complete control over Toledo. Is that what you want?"

Fiona wanted to keep me here, as her indentured servant, until I fulfilled whatever purpose she set forth for me, but right now, in this moment, I had her over a barrel, and I had to take advantage of it.

"I don't care about this place," I said. "I never really have. She can have it, as long as I can leave."

Fiona nodded. "Then we have a deal. You get what you want when I get what I want, a big, grand show that proves my power was attained legitimately."

"Why does that matter? You're an angel—"

"Valkyrie."

"Whatever. What does it matter if a bunch of humans believe you or not?"

Fiona scoffed at me. "My reasons are my own. Will you help me or not?"

I nodded. "If it gets me out of this city, I will walk through fire and crawl over glass."

Fiona stood and took a step toward me, staring deep into my eyes. "Let's hope it doesn't come to that. Though, I would get great pleasure out of seeing you suffer, personally."

"Sane to you," I replied, with a steely stare.

CHAPTER TWO

Fiona led Miguel, Lito, and me out of the front yard and up the crumbling streets of Toledo. Stepping out of the perfectly kept garden of Lito's house, I was immediately struck to tears with the carnage in front of me.

The adrenaline of the attack caused me to forget just how horrible the damage was to the entire city. Every building along the cobblestone streets laid collapsed upon themselves. In their rubble, haggard citizens worked to clean the broken pieces of buildings from the streets and organize them into piles, like a horrible jigsaw puzzle nobody asked for nor wanted to finish.

The cheeks of each citizen glowed as we passed, illuminated with one of the seven signs of magic. The Sun showed its bearer controlled fire and light. They helped warm the citizens with flames and cooked food for them. Those whose cheeks lit with the Moon controlled liquid and brought water from the ocean to quell the smoldering rubble. Those whose cheeks lit with a Mountain controlled the Ground and earth. They helped clear the streets of rubble. Three wisps of Air meant you could control the sky, and those citizens flew around rescuing those stuck in the rubble who needed help. The glow of a Plus Sign was the symbol of a healer, who bustled to and fro trying to mend wounds and broken bones as fast as they could.

Meanwhile, the illusionists, who were branded with a Square on their cheek, huddled around the edges of the city trying to rebuild the barrier which protected us from being seen by the rest of the world. The barrier stood for sixty years, and now that it was down, the city was vulnerable to more attacks.

The final sign was the all-seeing Eye, which lit on seers, those who could look into the future and the past. I didn't see any of those glowing anywhere.

"Where are the seers?" I asked Fiona as we walked.

"They are probably asking themselves why they couldn't see this coming," she replied. "I know I've asked myself that question since the attack."

"And how did you not see this?" I asked.

"Seeing is not a perfect gift, my dear. Seeing the future is an imperfect science. You must know exactly what to look for, and when to look for it, or it will lead you astray. Even if you can see the future, the further you look increases the chances of failure. Mostly, we see and then guess the most logical conclusion."

"A seer helped me to rescue Tibor once. It worked fine."

I didn't tell her that the seer was Eduardo's mother…poor Eduardo. He helped me free Tibor from jail once, but the next time I saw him, he wore a magic nullifying bomb which ripped him to shreds. He set this whole attack off to save his mother. I wondered if he would've thought it was worth it, seeing how it turned out and how many died.

"Then you were lucky. Every time a seer entertains a new variable, there are more chances for them to be wrong. It is a powerful gift, but a fickle one as well. Still, they will likely never be able to forgive themselves for missing this attack."

"Should they be able to forgive themselves?" I asked.

Fiona shrugged. "I don't know. I will not be able to forgive myself either."

As we walked, more and more citizens gathered to look at us. Fiona had not been out of the Cathedral in some time. Many citizens had never seen her before. It became clear with every step we took, and every fascinated eye she drew, what she was doing. She was trying to show stability for the citizens as they watched us, and that the powerful were in control of the situation, even though they weren't.

Fiona stepped into the main square of the town. All around us, the once ancient buildings that had stood for centuries were nothing but rubble and soot. The City Hall, jail, restaurants, and apartments around the square took heavy damage during the attack. Not one stood undamaged. Only rubble remained. Dozens of citizens pored through the rubble, looking for survivors.

"Citizens!" Fiona shouted, flapping her wings to rise into the air. "Gather around."

Everybody stopped their work to get a look at the angel floating through the sky. Sad eyes filled with wonder at the look of Fiona rising into the air.

"I know you are downtrodden. I know you are sad. I know you are angry. I know, because we are as well. You may not have seen me for a long while, but I know you have heard of me. I am the great Valkyrie that protected this city, and I have failed you."

"No. No. No," the citizens chanted in protest at her failure, even though she was right. She had failed them.

"I have protected you for eons, and now…this has happened, and I am sorry. However, we are still strong. Stronger than ever. We now have a secret weapon. The chosen one has come at last!"

The citizens murmured to each other, as if they didn't know what a chosen one was, or why they should care. I wouldn't be surprised if they didn't know me, or my destiny.

Fiona pointed at me. "She will be the key to us rising up, overthrowing the United Kingdom of Europe, and restoring balance to the world. She is the key to magic returning to its place atop the social order!"

People liked the sound of that and started nodding their heads. Fiona bent down to me. "Do the thing with the multiple powers. Show them. Make them believe."

"Fine, but I'm not a trained monkey."

"You are what I say you are. Remember that, if you want to leave this place."

I closed my eyes and thought of a fire burning in one hand, and a ball of water in another. When I opened my eyes, my cheeks glowed with the Sun and the Moon. A ball of water pooled in one hand, and a fire in the other.

The citizens oohed, ahhed, and whispered amongst each other.

When I closed my eyes again, I thought of raising a boulder into the air, as I hid my left arm in shadow. When I opened my eyes, a piece of rubble floated into the air as my left arm vanished from view. My cheek glowed, not with the sun and moon as before, but with the square and the mountain.

I dropped the boulder to thunderous applause. I bowed for a moment, then smiled. It felt good to be liked.

"As you can see, this child is not a Dual, but so much more. She is the key to righting this horrible wrong we suffered at the hands of the Normals. I have asked her to join the City Council to help us plan for what's next, and she has agreed!"

Fiona's words crescendoed at the last word, and the people went crazy. Fiona floated down to the ground and turned to me.

"See, I knew they would love you."

I nodded. "Now what?"

"Now, we actually make a plan."

*

"We have to attack!" Miguel shouted from the makeshift City Council chamber Lito made out of his art room. Along the walls, dozens of paintings from the Spanish masters hung…and I hated all of them.

Well, that's not fair.

I nothinged all of them. I liked art just fine, but how many times did I have to look at an old, sad painting of Jesus or a mean-mugging rich dude? Lito once tried to show me the difference between the styles of the old greats, but they all looked the same to me. Equally boring.

"We have to hold tight!" Lito shouted back. "Our numbers are too low to mount an effective attack on the Normals."

Lito had moved a circular wooden table into the art room for us to sit around, and every slam of the wood by one of the Council's hands reverberated through the room.

"That's because half of our citizens are dead or captured!" Miguel grumbled. "They attacked us. We will look weak if we don't retaliate in kind."

"And what do we retaliate with, Miguel?" Lito said, grumbling. "If we attack, we will be outnumbered and outgunned. Not to mention they could use that dastardly, magic-zapping weapon on us again. We'd be powerless!"

Anabelle destroyed the weapon that had nullified our power. She risked her life to pilot a Goliath out of Toledo and blow up the device, and now she was imprisoned for her efforts. Even though that device was destroyed, we didn't know how many more they had at their disposal.

"He makes a point," Fiona replied, calmly. "That is a concern."

"I understand, your grace," Miguel said with a level of deference he lacked with my grandfather. "There are always reasons not to attack, and the risks are often high, but if we do nothing then we will be seen as weak, and more attacks will come."

"And what if we start a war?" I said.

Miguel turned to me. "They have already started a war. The only question is if we rise to the challenge and accept their declaration, or cower like children."

"Those aren't the only two options," I scoffed.

"And what do you know?!" Miguel shouted, flailing his arms in the air. "You are only a little girl. You know nothing about the ways of the world."

"Don't talk to my granddaughter that way," Lito bellowed. "She is a member of this Council same as you."

"No," I replied. "I'm not the same as you. I've lived on the outside. I'm the only one here who has lived among Normals."

"She's right," Fiona said with a wry smile. "What would you have us do, then?"

"I don't know," I replied. "But I know attacking is foolish."

"That's what I said," Lito replied with pride. "You really are a chip off the old block."

Pride, but only when I agreed with him. What a coward. "I don't think you should stand back and do nothing though."

"Ha!" Miguel shouted, pointing to Lito sarcastically. "Some block that is!"

"Children!" Fiona yelled, stamping her feet on the ground. "Oh, I'm sorry. You are fully grown adults. I thought you were tiny children from the way you were behaving."

"I'm sorry," Miguel said, eyes hung low. "I lost myself for a moment."

"Me too," Lito added, sheepishly.

"I'm just saying," I replied. "We can't beat them in a fight, and we can't stand back and do nothing."

"There is no other way," Fiona said. "At least not as far as I can see."

"Then you don't see very well," I replied, shaking my head. "There is another way. Diplomacy."

All three of them burst out laughing, and I was immediately offended by their idiocy. Diplomacy was a tried and true way to alleviate conflicts, dating back even before Fiona's time on Earth. We learned about it in world history, during our lessons about the time before the Second World War.

"I think Hitler showed that diplomacy has no place in the new world order," Fiona chuckled.

"And he lost like the horrible piece of garbage he was!" I replied forcefully. "He lost. Franco lost. Mussolini lost. They all lost. All the people who started the Great War lost. Now, there is no Germany or Spain, and all because their citizens listened to horrible men telling them to abandon diplomacy and become mass murderers. Are we really no better than them?"

"So what?" Miguel asked. "You're saying we just go out there and try to make peace?"

I stood up. "I'm saying you go out there and try to lead our people. There are millions of magic users out there who have known nothing but suffering their whole lives. They don't know what it's like to be free. They don't know what it's like to live and work in whatever job they wanted. And you…we…could be the beacon for them. We could show them that magic isn't something to be feared. We could show them Toledo is nothing to be feared."

"I don't think anyone fears us anymore," Lito said. "If they ever did. Not after how they decimated us."

"They did fear you. Normals fear things they don't understand, just like you do. I don't think you understand them any more than they understand you, but you could if you tried. You could go out and try to be the light. You could show the world that just because Normals attacked you, does not mean you have to attack back."

"That sounds pretty idealistic," Fiona said. "Normals began this, and it is our duty to end it."

"They didn't though. Hitler invaded Poland first; the Normals only attacked after our aggression. We started it. Hitler and his horrible, militaristic, jingoistic attitudes about the world."

"They escalated it, though!" Miguel shouted.

I slammed my hands on the table. "Fighting a war is no way to bring about peace! Look, Normals don't understand us. We are different. You are different. This place, it might have been a beacon of hope to magic users, but to Normals it was resistance. It was fear. And we can end the fear by extending an olive branch to them. If we go out there and start a war, we're going to get slaughtered. We're going to get our people killed. Then, we are no better than Hitler, and please, God, let us be better than Hitler. It's such a low bar. It's maybe the lowest bar there is. Can we at least reach over it?"

Lito, Miguel, and Fiona were silent for a moment as their eyes ping-ponged back and forth between each other.

Then, Fiona shook her head. "No. I don't think we'll be trying peace. I think it is time to attack."

"Agreed!" Miguel said with a hearty and booming voice.

"It was a good attempt, sweetie," Lito said, extending his hand onto mine. "But I think it's a little naive."

I pulled my hand from Lito's and turned from the table. "You're the naive ones."

"Mature," Fiona said.

"I never said I was mature," I replied. "Just more mature than you."

The three of them blustered and moaned, but I didn't listen to their words. I just stormed out.

CHAPTER THREE

Why was the first inclination of every adult in Toledo to fight, scream, and argue? I went through ten years of school, and my teachers always told us to resolve our disagreements with words. Then, I got magical powers, and everybody changed their tune and said all we could do was fight or cower in fear?

I ran out to the garden, away from the bickering of the council, and sat on a bench in peace, surrounded by hundreds of varieties of flowers. I didn't know how Lito's house didn't get destroyed by the bombings, but it was nice to get a respite from the disaster that smoldered all around us. Outside, everything was bleak, gray, and smoking. In the garden, the flowers were bright and vibrant, and the fragrant smell put me at ease.

"Don't you have a meeting?" Tibor asked behind me.

I turned begrudgingly to him. "Don't remind me."

He sat down next to me, even though he was both uninvited and unwelcome. "Not going so well."

I shook my head. "No, it's not. I was just coming out to get some peace, alone. Tell me, do all magical people just rudely do whatever they want, or only the ones I've met?"

Tibor stood up. "Sorry. I didn't—"

I placed my head in my hands. "No. It's not you. It's this place, Tibor. I thought things would be different in Toledo, but they are so much worse."

"How so?"

"At least at home, you knew where you stood. You may not like where you stood, but you always knew where you stood. Here, there are so many people trying to get things from you and for themselves. It's impossible to figure out what is right. I used to be…so clear on what people wanted…much clearer than I am now, at least."

Tibor bent down and smelled a marigold blossom. "That is a function of getting older and acquiring power. Nobody wanted anything from you before, because you were a nobody from nowhere, so it was easy to spot what people wanted. Now, you are the chosen one. I don't think it's a function of this place, but of the human condition."

"Well, humans suck. I've been walking around with a pit in my stomach for days."

Tibor laughed. "I agree with you there, but I don't think you can blame this place for the horrible feelings you have in the pit of your stomach…you just have to blame humans as a whole."

"Yeah, well, I can't help humans everywhere. I can help humans here, though."

"Rosie!" Fiona shouted from the bottom of the steps in the garden. "Are you up there?"

I spun to her. "Yes. What do you want now?"

"I called the city council off for the day. I want to show you something."

I looked to Tibor. "This is clearly a trap, right?"

He nodded. "Clearly."

"But we should go, right?"

Again, he nodded. "Right. Otherwise, we would never do anything."

"Because everything is a trap now."

"Exactly."

*

Fiona led me up the hill of Toledo, past the main square where people still ogled me with deep adulation and admiration. Tibor tagged along, against Fiona's wishes, because I refused to be alone with her ever again.

As we passed the cathedral, she stopped. The church had been her home for the better part of six centuries, and now it was gone. Nothing but rubble and a slanted steeple listing toward the ground was left.

I placed my hand on Fiona's shoulder. "Are you okay?"

I would have sworn that Fiona sniffled, if I thought she had the ability to feel anything. "It's nothing but rock. It was always nothing but rocks. Little has changed, except its form. Pity and sadness are human conditions. I have neither."

I knew that wasn't true. Her friends, cardinals dating back to the thirteenth century, lay buried under the main floor of the church. I knew they mattered to her because she told me once when I thought better of her.

"It's okay to feel sad," I replied. "Being sad is human."

"Yes," Fiona replied, sneering. "It is a very human emotion, isn't it? Disgusting."

"If you don't like humans," Tibor said. "Why have you lived among them for so long?"

"Orders," Fiona replied, brushing past us. "Come, we have a ways to go yet."

Something caught in my throat as I walked up the hill behind Fiona. I thought she was a bit of a callous monster for caring so little about the place she was from, but at the same moment, I barely spared a moment for my own home, which was raided by the RMP the night I left Ambrosia forever.

I didn't like to think about home. My memories of Ambrosia were filled with confusion, sadness, anger, and pain, all spiraling and swirling around my head simultaneously. Perhaps it was because my entire childhood was a lie, having been brought up by somebody who said they were my mother, but in reality was just a nursemaid hired to help me scam the system. Still, I should have worried about her more. After all, she did raise me. Yet, I couldn't bear the thought of her betrayal, so I stuffed my emotions down and trudged along. *Was I no better than Fiona in that respect?*

"Up here!" Fiona said as she crested the top of the hill, which looked out on the water of the bay in every direction. I rushed to join her and was met by a sheer cliff which looked as if it was broken from a mountain.

"That's because it was," Fiona said. I forgot she could read minds, in her way. "This was the place Toledo broke off from when it rose into the air and claimed its independence. Ripping this city from the earth exposed my underground laboratory, which I created with my bare hands after I landed to act as a laboratory. There was an entrance under the Cathedral, too, but that has been destroyed now."

"You have an underground lab, like a supervillain?"

Fiona laughed. "You have a wildly active imagination. Follow me."

Fiona rose into the air and dove down toward the sea below her. I turned to Tibor, who was already staring at me quizzically.

"So, like a super villain, right?" I asked.

"Totally like a supervillain," he replied. "Should we follow her?"

I nodded. "Seems like the thing to do."

"Can you fly yet?"

"I haven't tried yet. In all the commotion..."

"Here," Tibor said, holding out his hand. "I'll be your training wheels. The secret to flying is to be at peace, if only for a moment."

I placed my hand inside Tibor's and closed my eyes. I took a deep breath and felt my cheek glow. The light felt cool on my cheek, like a light autumn wind.

I felt myself rise into the air. My cheek glowed in time with my lift off. It was shaky at first, but after a sputter or two, I rose slowly into the sky. I opened my eyes to see Tibor smiling at me, like a proud teacher.

"I think you got it."

"Me too, but don't you dare let go."

"I won't."

I tilted myself down and followed Fiona down toward a cave entrance below us. Tibor gripped my hand tightly to prevent me from falling, but every second I was airborne made me more comfortable with the experience.

*

There are very few times when somebody with an underground lair ended up being a hero. Superman had a fortress of Solitude, and he was a good guy. Batman had the Bat Cave, and so was he, at least nebulously. I had a hard time believing somebody with billions of dollars who chose to punch petty criminals was a hero, but that was the lore.

On the flip side, every bad guy has a secret lair they keep hidden from the world. There were already plenty of reasons not to trust Fiona, and a secret underground cave lair only added to the list.

Tibor and I landed in the mouth of a wide cave. In front of us was a huge door carved with battle scenes and angels drifting off to Heaven.

"Come," Fiona said, pushing open one half of a hundred foot high arched wooden door with her bare hands, exposing a great cave as the door gave way before her.

Except that it wasn't much of a cave at all, at least not in the way that I imagined a cave. This cave looked like it was carved with a huge drill, not by nature over thousands of years. It was a circle all the way around, except for the perfectly level floor, and both sides of the cave were symmetrical. On either side of the cave hung the tapestries—Fiona fighting a chimera stretched the length of a football field on one side, and Fiona holding up a bloody dragon head on the other.

If nothing else, it was ornate. The steps down to the lowest level of the cavern were made of marble, and the walls were lined with square stones which looked to be chiseled by hand by a master craftsman. It like the burial crypt of an emperor mixed with a modern library. As we passed through the cavern, my footsteps echoed and vibrated off every wall. Torches lined our path, and a dozen candelabras each bigger than the last hung perfectly from the center of the cave.

"Ostentatious, isn't it?" I asked.

"Somebody is compensating for something," Tibor whispered back.

"No," Fiona replied. "I just like pretty things. There's nothing wrong with that."

We walked up a set of stone stairs carved into the mountain. At the top of it, the ground was carved in a circular pattern with the letters of the Latin and Norse alphabets. Across the room, Fiona stood in front of a large wooden door.

"This is my favorite part of Toledo," Fiona shouted toward us, giddy as a school child, as she pushed open the door and disappeared behind it. "Come, come!"

It was as if she was sharing a long-held secret for the first time in a millennium.

"How did you make this?" I asked, walking forward toward the wooden door.

"The machinations of its creation are inconsequential," Fiona said, from the other room. "But it was built to house the most powerful device in the known world."

I pushed open the door with all my might. Inside was a metal chair, much like the one that sat in Fiona's residence. It was sleek silver metal, with tubes that fed into a rock wall behind it. In her room in the Cathedral, the tubes fed into a blue cylinder housing part of her essence, which she had to refill every few days to keep the city's protective barrier from failing.

This chair fed into the wall, and I couldn't see where it fed once it disappeared beyond the rock.

"It feeds back into the source," she replied. "The source is what draws magical folks here from all over the world. It is what allows us to manipulate the world differently than magical people everywhere else."

"What is this place?" I asked.

Next to the chair was a computer, like you would find in old pictures from the 1970s. It took up the entirety of one wall next to the chair. Wires hung from it, like a switchboard, and fed from one side of the computer to the other. On the side nearest the chair, a large lever sat, waiting for someone to pull it, while other knobs and pulleys adorned the rest of the face. Lights of yellow, red, and green lit up and blinked throughout the computer, but gave no indication of what they were for if anything at all.

"This device is a gift, from the gods. They gave it to me when I left Valhalla, as a final solution if you will. With it, I have the power to destroy all non-magical life on this planet."

"I'm sorry. What?" I said, trying to parse the monumental news she'd just casually told me.

"This device will kill all Normals. Isn't that incredible?"

"What! I don't think that's incredible at all. It's horrible!" I shouted at her. "You can't do that!"

"Oh, I know I can't. I've tried, for many eons I've tried. Since they brought me here, I have tried, but I cannot do it…no, not without killing myself at least, in the process, and I like life a bit too much to do that."

"Seems like a silly thing for gods to want, to kill a bunch of their creations," Tibor said, furrowing his brow.

"Well, they didn't want to kill you, of course. They wanted you to live in harmony with each other. Naive fools the gods were. I know that now. Back then, though, I was just as naive as them."

"Why are you telling me this?" I asked.

Fiona shook her head. "And you are supposed to be smart. At least you have a smart mouth. I suppose that belies your other failings. You are as dumb as the rest of them. I need you, Rosie. You are the key."

"What do you mean?" I asked. "And before you treat me like a child, yes I know what a key is, but I don't see how I fit into your little scheme."

Fiona spread out her wings. "Why you are going to be the power for this device, so I don't have to be, my dear. You will be a great power source. I've waited all my life for you, Rosie. Now, you will die so that the magical people can inherit the Earth."

I knew it; never trust somebody with a secret lair. Ever. At least I wasn't surprised she turned out to be even eviler than I thought. I wasn't even shocked. I was just disappointed.

CHAPTER FOUR

"I'm getting a little sick and tired of people trying to kill me," I grumbled as Fiona spread her wings and launched into the air to attack me. Seriously, even though my adrenaline was pumping, I wasn't even angry about it. After a dozen attempts on my life, I was over it.

"My sweet," Fiona said. "You should be happy. You will help usher in a new world order, where Normals can no longer subjugate magical folks…because they don't exist."

"Why don't you just use that little machine to turn Normals into magical folks?"

When we first met, Fiona told me that everybody had the ability to use magic. Normals, though, had a blockage in their brains that prevented them from developing magical powers.

"I could do that," Fiona said, her body shimmered blue as her skin evaporated into her body. "But they haven't earned magic. They have picked their lot, and they will die because of it."

Fiona wasn't flesh and blood, like a human. She was made of something else, and her skin was just for show. Under it, she was as bright, blue, and translucent as the light gushing up from the other room.

Tibor balled up his fists and jumped in front of me. "If you want her, you are going to have to go through me first."

Fiona shot forward and whacked Tibor into the wall with enough force to knock him out. He fell onto the ground with a thud, like a pile of rocks.

"Okay," Fiona said. "But that wasn't much of a challenge."

I stepped backwards, shaking with fear. Fiona's blue aura radiated out of her as she flew toward me, leaving a streak of light behind her.

"Stay back!" I shouted.

"Or what?" she replied, continuing forward slowly.

My left check lit up with a mountain, and I heaved the heavy wooden door off its hinges and across the room. "Or that!"

Fiona caught the door with her outstretched fingers, eyes glowing brighter than her body as she placed it on the ground. "Little sweetie. I have spent eons mastering my powers. You have had them what, less than a week? There is nothing you can do to hurt me."

Fiona came to Earth with the ability to use all seven of the powers. I had only learned how to use six of them, and only a few days ago at that. The one power I didn't have was the ability to see into the future, so I had no idea what was about to happen, whereas Fiona could predict my every move.

Still, I couldn't let her take me without a fight. Predicting the future was still just a guess, even if it was an educated one. I could still beat her. I just had to be unpredictable.

I squeezed my eyes shut until my cheek glowed with a fiery sun. I opened my eyes, and my whole body flamed brightly. I held out my arms and smacked my arms together until the fire cascaded off me across the floor toward Fiona.

Fiona flashed her eyes and pulled water out of the air to dispel the fire, before flickering her eyes again and throwing a tornado toward me out of her fists.

I turned and sprinted out of the room and past the gushing blue light that flowed from the middle of the room. I jump down the stairs as fast as I could, but the tornado spun faster as it closed it on me. It caught up with me in midair and lifted me up toward the ceiling.

Fiona flew toward me and pulled two metal brackets off the wall that held a tapestry in place. They flew around my back and locked my arms into place as the ancient tapestry fell to the floor.

When I was immobilized, the tornado dissipated and dropped me to the ground. Fiona landed and stomped toward me.

"You will help me," Fiona said, grabbing my legs and pulling me forward. "Whether you want to or not."

"You're a monster," I squealed, trying to kick free.

Fiona nodded, proudly. "I can live with that."

Then she snapped her fingers, and a large marble slab ripped out of the wall smashed against my head, knocking me out.

*

When I woke, Fiona was hard at work plugging wires into the computer next to me. My thoughts were cloudy, and my head was on fire. It throbbed and ached as I turned it from side to side.

"Can you stop knocking me out?" I asked, trying to rub my head before realizing I was chained tightly to the metal chair next to her. "It's gonna cause brain damage."

I tried to lift my head despite the pain, but a metal brace locked my head to the chair, and I couldn't move except from one side to the other. I kicked my legs, but they were equally locked in place.

"Oh good," Fiona said. "You're up. Just in time too. I'm going to start soon, and I wouldn't want you to miss your death."

Fiona fiddled with the control panels, knobs, and buttons. Her hands moved in a blue blur, faster than I could follow. Behind Fiona, Tibor rocked back and forth in the corner, waking up, but Fiona paid him no mind. I needed to keep her focus on me and hope Tibor could save me.

"I wouldn't want to miss this," I replied, groggily. "After all, these might be my last moments of life."

Fiona shrugged. "This life, but you will have died a warrior's end, and you might even win a place in Valhalla."

"What's it like up there?" I asked, half trying to stall and half genuinely curious.

"I'll tell you…it's kind of dull. It's mead for breakfast. Mead for lunch. Then, a less than sensible dinner. People sit around telling stories of their hunts all day, and after a few hundred years those stories get old and repetitive."

"Is that why you don't want to go back?" I asked.

Fiona shook her head. "Partially. I generally like it here. But in truth, I'm not sure I would go back if I died. You kill a human, and they end up in the afterlife. What happens though, when you kill a Valkyrie? We're supposed to be immortal. What's the afterlife look like for us?"

"For what it's worth," I replied. "I hope it looks like Hell."

Fiona flipped three switches on a big metal board. "Well, I hope you go to Valhalla. It's the least they could give you for saving the world."

"I'm not saving the world. I'm dooming it."

Fiona chuckled. "I hope that's not true, or you'll go to Helheim for sure. You won't like it there."

I closed my eyes and tried to summon my powers. A sharp, searing pain coursed through my body. I screamed up to Heaven at the unbearable pain, until it subsided several seconds later.

"I wouldn't do that if I were you," Fiona said, wagging her fingers at me. "This machine sucks up all your magical energy and uses it as fuel. It takes an incredible amount of energy to function, which is why only I could turn it on…until now."

She said it with such passion and satisfaction I wanted to retch. There were close to seven billion people on this planet, and only a small percentage were magically inclined, which meant she was about murder almost the entire planet with the flick of a switch. Mass genocide on a scale I couldn't fathom. I couldn't let that happen.

I struggled against the metal latches buckling me, but they wouldn't budge. Then, I tried again to use my powers until I was in so much pain I couldn't even whimper. I sagged against my restraints, weeping.

"You really are quite the fighter, aren't you?" Fiona said. "They normally don't fight like this."

"There were others?" I said, groggily. "How many others?"

"Dozens. Hundreds. It's hard to keep track." Behind her, Tibor woozily wobbled to his feet. I didn't know what he was planning, but it was too late anyway. "No matter. The calibrations are done. Goodbye, Rosie. I wish I could have said it was a pleasure, but you are the worst."

Fiona slammed a lever down on the switchboard, and the machine whirred to life. The tubes on my head pulsated and throbbed, and a blue, electric charge shot from the control panel into my body.

"AHHHHH!!!!!"

I screamed louder than I ever had before. Every joint, every cell of my skin, pulsated and burned, down to my very core. My cheeks filled with white-hot energy, and my eyes radiated with blue light. In the last instant of my consciousness, Tibor rushed Fiona, gaining on her. I wanted to watch, but my eyes went white.

Still, I heard the shriek from Fiona as my body fell out of the device and collapsed onto the floor.

"Get up!" Tibor screamed at me. I felt him yank on my restraints until my arms fell free.

"Peon!" Fiona screamed, and suddenly Tibor's hands were ripped from me.

When my eyes focused, they saw a dazed Fiona pick up a lifeless Tibor and throw him asunder. I didn't wait for her to turn toward me. I pulled off my head restraint and unbuckled my legs. When I was free, I darted toward the entrance as fast as my weak legs would carry me.

"Get back here!" Fiona shouted, the electricity flaming behind her as the chair went up in smoke.

She grabbed at me, and in my mind, I saw her next movement. I spun away and rose to my feet. I felt my right cheek ignite with the glow of the all-seeing eye. I had finally unlocked the power to see into the future.

Fiona rushed forward, and I witnessed her kick in my mind, moments before she did. I rolled forward to avoid it and ran out of the room and down the stairs.

"You can't escape me!" Fiona shouted as I rushed down the hallway.

Fiona ripped a chunk of marble from the floor and shot it at me. My cheek glowed with the Mountain. I caught it with my hands and threw it back at her. She was more powerful than me, but she didn't expect me to survive or unlock my last power. I had caught her off guard, and now I had to use it to my advantage while I still could.

Fiona shot a fireball out of her hand, and I saw a glimpse of it in my mind. I dove to avoid the blaze and ripped a piece of stone off the wall, kicking it toward her. In front of me, the two wooden doors blocked my exit. I flung them open as I ripped them off the hinges and sent them flying back to her.

As I did, my cheek turned from a Mountain to three wisps of Air. I rose up into the sky and headed the last meters toward the door. Fiona snapped her fingers and a hurricane formed outside the cave, blowing wind and rain inside the cave as it bellowed outside. Teaming rain gushed inside and pushed me backwards.

"You will not leave!" Fiona screamed. "I have waited too long for this moment!"

"Shut up!" Tibor shouted from behind her. He had a torch in his hand and lit Fiona's toga on fire. For a moment she was distracted, and the wind stopped. I flew toward the opening of the cave. I turned back once more to see Tibor's mouth form the word "go" before Fiona slapped him across the room.

She turned back to me with fire in her eyes. She sped toward me at full speed. Without thinking, I pulled a tapestry from the wall and wrapped her in it, crashing her to the ground.

Spent and exhausted, I tumbled out of the cave and down into the water. I wanted to fly. I wanted to move, but I couldn't. In one last fit of energy, I pulled the water up to reach me and used it to cushion me into the briny deep below.

*

I swam as fast as I could, but the current was too strong for me to make much headway. I tried to close my eyes and calm my mind so that I could control the ocean, but it crashed against me relentlessly every time I tried to focus for even a moment.

Please. Help. I prayed to somebody, anybody for help, but there was no one. I was utterly and completely alone in a way that I had not been in my whole life. Sure, often the people who helped me were out for their own ends, but at least there was help available for me when I needed it in the past.

When I scraped my leg when I was a kid, my mother bandaged it up. She worked three jobs to keep a roof over our head. She laughed with me, cried with me, and lived with me. I have been so mad at her this whole time, but the truth was, she was as much a mother to me as Anabelle was a sister, and I would never be able to tell her how much she meant to me.

When I found out I had magical powers, Tibor saved me from the Royal Military Police. He whisked me away from trouble and stayed by my side…even after I nearly killed him.

And Anabelle, she'd been by my side through thick and thin since we were children. She was a true friend, who came with me when everybody else would have abandoned me. She helped me even when it was against her basest instincts. She came with me to Toledo, even though she was told the people there would hate her — and they did. She fought against the RMP, even though she could have run away, and for her bravery, she was captured.

Even when Tibor and Anabelle were locked away in the dungeons of Toledo, my Lito was there, guiding me forward, telling me what to do, and showing me how to navigate the city. When he wasn't there, Fiona, the Valkyrie, who just tried to kill me and destroy the world, was there to show me how to use my powers.

Up until the moment I jumped into the ocean, there was always someone there to save me, to help me, and to guide me. Now, there was nobody. For the first time in my life, I was truly on my own. Every choice I made was my burden to shoulder…and I could only count on myself to save me.

As the current of the tide crashed against me, I vowed that I would survive. I promised myself I would rely on my own instincts from here on out. Even if they were bad at least, they would be my choices.

I would not die today.

I ducked under the current and stopped battling the waves. I closed my eyes under the water and imagined a bubble pushing out from me. When I opened my eyes, an air bubble formed around me. My cheek glowed with the three wisps of air. With another blink, I imagined shooting through the water like a dolphin. When I opened my eyes my other cheek glowed with the Moon, and I shot forward like a fish through the tide, fighting for the shore. I was going to survive. I was going to make it, even if it was the last thing I did.

*

By the time I reached the shore, I was barely able to move. I coughed water out of my lungs for a full minute before I finally laid on the soggy ground. I turned my head to look up at the floating city of Toledo, once a beacon of hope, but now a harbinger of my doom.

Fiona would be after me before long. I would be hunted everywhere, and anywhere I turned. If not by her, then by the RMP who wanted me for their own ends, as both a Dual and someone who helped Toledo escape their clutches.

They would not have to look far to find me, though, because I knew my next move. I had to save the people of Toledo and Anabelle from the clutches of the RMP. Fiona would not save them. Lito would not save them. That task fell to me. If the magical people the RMP captured couldn't count on Toledo, I had to rescue them myself. I had just unlocked my seventh and last power. I could see into the future.

Still, I didn't need to see into the future to know that entering the belly of the beast was a bad idea. Even a non-magical Normal could figure that one out. That didn't change the fact that I owed it to Anabelle to try and save her, and the people of Toledo deserved a savior they could be proud of, and I was determined to be that for them, and for magical folks everywhere.

I closed my eyes and focused all my energy on Anabelle. In a flash, I saw an underground bunker in the woods. I blinked again, and I was inside, watching Anabelle hum to herself in a small, metal cell, rocking back and forth.

I opened my eyes and smiled. It wasn't much, but it was a start. *Hold on, Anabelle. I'm coming for you. I'm coming for all of you.*

CHAPTER FIVE

It took me forever to find the prison that housed Anabelle and the rest of the prisoners from Toledo. I had a really hard time controlling my Seer powers. The rest of the powers were relatively simple, honestly. I closed my eyes and thought of what I wanted to do, and it was done.

Whether it was healing somebody or throwing fire, what I envisioned in my mind's eye happened moments later. Seeing was a lot different than my other powers, though. When I closed my mind's eye to see into the future and imagined what I wanted, all I received were incoherent flashes in return.

For instance, I wanted to figure where Anabelle was being held, but every time I closed my eyes I saw something different. Once, I could have looked through Anabelle's eyes, which didn't help much since she was blindfolded when she entered the facility, or I could have seen through the eyes of a guard, but every time I tried that I saw a different base in another country. It could have meant seeing into the past, or seeing the future, or seeing both at the same time, layered on top of each other in a jumbled mess.

Usually, it meant seeing a little of each of those things every time I closed my eyes and trying to decipher what they meant. I felt bad for anybody who was suddenly endowed with the power of sight, like I was, and had to stumble through learning, like I did, without any help, as was my plight, especially if they were being hunted my magical folks and Normals alike. Though, I doubted any of that happened to people besides me.

My visions took me all over Spain, but eventually, I ended up north of the city that was once called Avila, and was now called Victory since it was where the Allies signed the victory accords with Spanish representatives after the war officially ended in 1960. It's not much of a city, except that it was ancient and meaningful to the people of Spain, and was close enough to Madrid that ambassadors could make a day trip out of it.

An hour north of the city was a government facility and RMP base, in which there was an underground bunker on the west-most side of the facility. Inside that bunker was where Anabelle and the others were kept…at least, I hoped.

To the best of my ability, my visions over the past two weeks led me there, to the fence line outside the facility. I watched through various guards' eyes as they had lunch in the walled city of Avila. I watched Anabelle exercise in the prison yard that looked out on the same tree line that dotted the area around the facility.

I watched as the prisoners were led into the prison camp and marched downstairs into the underground, behind a metal fence which bore the words: "Warning: Stay Out," in English and Spanish, on a metal sign with a dent in the lower left corner and rust along the top, in just the same way the sign for this facility did when I arrived.

Yes, I was as confident as I could be, given the circumstances, that my friend was being held prisoner inside this complex. Now, it was a matter of sneaking into the facility undetected, finding Anabelle and the others, and sneaking them out, a feat which would be impossible without the power of sight.

Except, I didn't know how to use the information the vision granted me in any useful way. I needed help.

I figured I could find help in Victory, assuming I could get into the city without being spotted. I remember when I feared flying, but now I excelled at it, and every one of my powers, except Seeing.

When I finally landed near a stream outside of Avila, I closed my eyes and imagined myself as an old woman with a hunch back. The Square of the illusionists glowed on my cheek. When I opened my eyes, I felt my nose grow in front of me, and my skin sag around me. I looked down at the stream underneath me and smiled at the old hag staring back up at me.

*

I hobbled toward the town slowly and awkwardly. I was careful not to act too spry, as my "old bones" shouldn't move as quickly as my young ones. I wanted to move fast, but my haggard and hobbled persona wouldn't allow me to run or hop as fast as I wanted.

The city of Victory was, like Toledo, surrounded by a wall on all sides. The only way in was through gates surrounding the city. I slowly hobbled toward a gate on the east part of town. Several RMP guards milled outside its walls, talking to each other. The guards who have surely been sent a picture of my natural face, so I hoped I was at least a competent illusionist.

"Good morrow," I shouted in a shrill, squeaky voice, raising my hand into the air.

One of the guards waved at me. "Morning, ma'am. Enjoying this fine day?"

I smacked my gums together. "Very much. Thank you. Perhaps, you can help me?"

The guard nodded at me. "Perhaps. What can I do for you?"

"Have you a ghetto for magic users in this city? I want to be sure to avoid it at all costs. Dreadful, they are."

"Agreed," the soldier said. "It's on the west side of town, south of the Cathedral. If you stay away from there, you'll be safe."

"Thank you, young man. They really are the most dreadful things, you know."

The soldier nodded. "You don't have to tell me, ma'am. We have them under control, though. This is a very safe city. Have a nice day."

I shuffled past the soldier as fast as my "old bones" would have reasonably allowed, careful to contain my hatred for the soldiers. Now, all I had to do was make it through the city to the magical district where I hope to find the help I needed.

*

Victory reminded me a lot of Toledo, from the old rustic buildings that looked as if they stood since the dawn of time, to the quaint cobblestone streets, to the pretty little shops that lined the streets. However, while Toledo celebrated magic users, Victory vilified them. Everywhere I walked were signs about the dangers of magic use. Televisions blared with propaganda about the dangers of using magic in public. I hadn't seen such focused hatred since I left Ambrosia.

"Don't forget," one commercial said. "If you or anybody you know sees somebody using magic in public, run, don't walk, to your nearest magistrate and tell them. It's your duty to report unlawful magic. After all, if somebody is injured by a magic user, do you want it on your head? It's your responsibility as a proud citizen of the UKE. to do your part."

I wanted to sneer and scream at the television, but I knew that would give away my secret, or at the very least bring unwanted attention. I didn't need that, so I stuffed my feelings deep inside.

*

It took me a little over an hour to shuffle across the town and make it to the Cathedral. The moment it came into view, so did the decrepit slums in its shadows.

"Excuse me?" I asked a middle-aged woman strolling down the street. "But why would they put the magical slums next to the church?"

The woman shook her head. "Not from around here are you? The church insisted on it being close to them so they could do outreach. Stupid Catholics and their need to help those poor and wretched Shiners. Let them die, I say."

She looked like such a polite woman, dressed head to toe in a finely pressed suit, and yet, she spewed vileness and venom. I was taken aback by how casually she spouted her magicism. I suppose, thinking back on it, I had been part of many such conversations in Ambrosia, and I was suddenly appalled and ashamed of my complicity in the way Spain functioned.

"Alms!" A sweet voice shouted from in front of the church.

A meek-looking priest with short hair and a white robe clanged a bell in front of the church. A wicker basket rested under his foot, half filled with coins.

"Alms!" he said again, looking at me. "You ma'am. Can you spare a pound to help the poor, unfortunate magic users suffering in the ghetto?"

I shook my head as I tried to putter past. "No. I can't. I'm sorry."

The priest slid in front of me, blocking my way past him "No, you can't, can you? After all, you are one of them."

I shook my head. "That is a disgusting accusation, and I won't hear another word about it."

The priest held up his hands. "Very well. It's just…you get very good at spotting an illusion when you spend your life helping magic users, don't you know?"

The right side of my lip curled up. "I would not say such things if I were you. I'm just a little old lady."

"Fine," the priest said. "However, you're making a beeline for the ghetto. There aren't many who would do that. Most people turn the other way. I've done this for a long time, and I can only name a handful, besides me, that aren't magic users."

I poked him in the chest. "Are you trying to get me caught?"

The priest shook his head. "No, I'm trying to help you."

"If you want to help me, bring me to a Seer and don't say anything else about it."

Without a word, the priest picked up his basket and threw his bell inside. "Follow me."

That was easy, I thought to myself. And easy things were usually fraught with difficulty before too long. I had to keep my guard up. Every person who's ever helped me ended up screwing me over before long, and I couldn't imagine a priest would be much different. After all, honest to god angels screwed me over quickly enough, and he wasn't one of those. He was just a man and a stranger at that. I couldn't trust even family; I couldn't trust him either.

*

The priest led me through the narrow streets of the Avila slums. He zigged and zagged quickly in front of me through the tight alleys, but with my experience in Toledo, and navigating the darkness there; I had little trouble following him. Still, I trailed him quite considerably after a couple of minutes.

"Follow me," the priest said. "Move those stumpy legs."

"They're not all that stumpy," I replied, momentarily forgetting that I was a short, old woman now. A quick look into the mirror across from me reminded me of the truth. "Maybe they are a little stumpy."

The priest stopped for a moment, looking back at me. "Yes, they are. Do you know how hard it is to find a Seer anywhere? What you are asking isn't easy, or safe."

"Why is it so hard?" I replied, breathlessly.

The priest started again, more quickly this time. "Seers are the least common of all the signs. Don't you know that? One out of every thousand magic users are born with that power, and with fewer magic users being born every year, it is almost being bred out of existence."

"That's sad."

The priest stopped in front of a bright blue door. "There are many things about these times that are sad."

The priest knocked on the door three times. "It's Father Harold. Open up."

"No!" a shrieking voice replied. "Go away. I won't be lectured by you, today."

"Regina! It's not about me. Somebody is here to see you." Father Harold turned to me. "I'm sorry. She really is quite nice. Sometimes."

"I don't want to see anyone!" Regina screamed from behind the door, even as I heard her stomp toward it. "Go away!"

"Tell her yourself! She's looking for a seer, and you're the only one in town. If you want her to go away, be courteous enough to look her in the eyes when you tell her."

"Ugh!" the woman cried from the other side of the door. "I'm not doing any magic tricks today."

The woman opened the door. Her long nose and wrinkled face looked like the spitting image of my illusion as if I was looking into a mirror.

"What!" Regina screamed at Father Harold.

He pointed at me. "I thought you would get a kick out of this. Apparently, you are what this person thinks of when they think of old."

Regina turned to me and started to chuckle. "Well, I'll be. That is funny. It's been a tough day, and that helps."

"I appreciate that you appreciate it," I said, stepping forward. "But I need your help to teach me to see."

"I don't know about that, girly. You already have a power. I can't teach you another one."

I didn't have time to tell her how wrong she was, so I just lowered my illusion. My cheek glowed with a square. I closed my eyes and imagined a fireball in my hand. When I opened it, my other cheek glowed with a sun, and the fire lit up my hand.

"Well, I'll be," the woman said. "A Dual. Haven't seen one of those in years. Least not as young as you."

I looked at her in the eyes. "I wish that was all."

I closed my eyes again and imagined floating into the air. When I opened my eyes, I lifted a foot off the ground; my cheek now glowed with three wisps of air.

"I could keep going if you want," I replied.

"Fascinating," the woman said. "I have never seen anything like it."

I stepped back onto the ground. "Nobody has. I don't know if there has ever been anything like me before, and I need your help. I need to learn how to See. How to really See. Not just parlor tricks, but look into the future and see the truth."

"You shouldn't be doing that outside. There are cameras everywhere." The woman looked over at Father Harold. "You really know how to pick them, huh?"

"I am good at that. The more hopeless, the better."

Regina beckoned me inside. "Well, come in then."

I walked past Harold and inside. I didn't trust either of them, but I did appreciate his efforts to help me.

"I should get back," he said. "I hope you find what you need."

I smiled at him. "Thank you."

CHAPTER SIX

"Would you like an orange snow cone, sweetie?" Regina asked as she walked me down her foyer and into the house.

Her house was less a place to live and more a warehouse, full of bits and bobs, a massive hoarder's den with things and stuff everywhere. Newspapers stacked high on top of socks on top of cans of beans, which teetered precariously back and forth. Every surface of her house was covered with crap and smelled like it, too.

I passed four litter boxes on my way through the main hallway of the house. There were cats everywhere, which meowed and cried out to the Heavens for somebody to feed them, or save them, or let them run free. I'm not sure how many cats were in that house, but I counted six on my sojourn through the maze of junk, and there were at least a couple I could only hear through the chorus, and never glimpsed.

"No, thank you," I replied.

What a weird question. Who had the ingredients to make orange snow cones just laying around their house?

"I know what you are thinking, of course," she said, riffling through her fridge. "And the reason I keep the ingredients around is because most people really would like an orange snow cone if they thought about it for even a minute. However, they are so lost in the jumble of thought in their head they don't take a second to think clearly. Are you sure you don't want one?"

I thought about it for a minute, and she was right. The more I thought about it, the more I really did want an orange snow cone.

"Actually, you're right," I said. "Yes, I do want an orange snow cone, if the offer's still on the table."

Regina popped back up instantly with a little plastic cup filled with a scoop of ice drizzled with orange syrup.

"I knew you did, honey," Regina replied. "That's one of the first lessons about Seeing, my dear. Once you know what people desire deep down in their soul, my dear, it becomes a lot easier to see their future."

"Do you See my future?" I said, sucking on the ice.

She smiled. "Of course, I do. I wouldn't be much of a teacher if I didn't, but I don't think you want to know it, honestly."

"Why? Is it bad?" I replied.

She shrugged. "Nothing is either good or bad, but knowledge makes it so. It's why I don't like Seeing, personally. You are burdened with so much knowledge. It's hard to know what to believe, what to act on, and what to let float away."

"I know!" I said. "I've been trying to—" I stopped myself before I revealed why I needed to figure out my seeing powers. Even if she should see the future, I needed to play my cards close to the vest.

"You want to save your friends," she replied. "Well, your friend, and all the others taken from Toledo."

I nodded. "That's right. You are good." I could have denied it, but there wouldn't be much point in that. "Yes. I need to figure out how to get them out, but my brain keeps getting scrambled. I can't see anything clearly."

"That's because you let emotions into your visions, my dear, and that clouds what you're seeing. You are trying to see your future, or at least your place in it, but in seeing the future, you are changing it at the same time."

"That's not true. I've looked at Anabelle and the guards in the past, the present, and the future, and I'm nowhere to be found."

"Yes, but your mind is, dear. You are focused on how you can change things, instead of seeing things as they are."

I took another lick of my snow cone as the juice ran down my arm. "That makes sense. How do I change that?"

"You must look into the future as a dispassionate observer. You must clear your mind of what you wish would happen, and see only what will."

"How can I do that, if I want so desperately to help, though?"

The woman grabbed the snow cone from me and took a bite. "I hope you don't mind. I am old and don't mind the germs, but I couldn't eat a whole one."

"It's fine, but it doesn't answer my question."

"I know, because the truth will be something you don't like, and you will fling your arms in the air, getting orange syrup all over my carpet, and that will be very messy."

"No, I—" I realized it was useless to argue with a psychic.

"Now, I can tell you. You must take it one step at a time. Find one part of the path, navigate it, and then move onto the next. You cannot hope or wish, you must only see, slowly, and dispassionately, in order to be a powerful seer."

I flung my arms in the air. "That's crazy! I can't do that! I need it all right now."

Regina chuckled. "I'm afraid it is the only way, with what time we have."

"I can stay here, and train until I've learned it, though, can't I?"

Regina smiled. "I'm afraid not. Father Harold is a fine man, but he is a flawed one. He wants to help this slum so badly that he made a deal with the RMP. He informs them of intruders, and in return, they leave him alone to do his work. And that means—"

I gasped. "It means he told them about me, and they are coming for me right now."

Regina nodded. "I'm afraid so. Luckily, there is a trap door under this table, which can bring you outside. I had it put in special just last week."

"You knew I was coming."

She smiled, lifting up the trap door. "I had a feeling, which is why I turned off the cameras outside, so they would not see your display. Now, hurry. Like the wind. You are in grave danger here."

The front door slammed open with a loud crash. "RMP!"

As the guards rushed inside, the stacks of papers teetered over and fell on them, burying the first wave of officers in a pile of refuse. A second wave stepped over the pile, only to be buried in a stack of plates and clothes, knocked over by a hungry cat.

"You did this all on purpose," I said lowering myself into the hatch. "Building up the horde. To help me. Didn't you?"

"I don't know what you are talking about dear. I'm just a cranky old woman." Regina winked as she lowered the door on top of me. I heard her slide a pile of trash over the top of the door to hide it, as I rushed down the tunnel toward a light at the end of it, then kicked up into the air to escape the city.

*

I landed outside the RMP base that held Anabelle prisoner. By the time I got back to the compound, it was dark, and the lights flickered in the darkness. Large pockets of shadow loomed in the darkness, which would be perfect for sneaking inside the facility without being detected.

I couldn't wait for the break of day. By then, the compound would be swarming with guards. It didn't take a genius to figure out why I was in Avila. Even the densest RMP general would connect the dots sooner or later. My only chance was to make my move now or risk even more guards protecting the compound come morning. I wasn't anywhere near prepared, but that didn't matter. It was now or never.

I crawled through the darkness and inched up close to the chain link fence that protected the facility. I closed my eyes and imagined my finger as a blow torch. When I opened them, a white-hot fire shot from my index finger, and I used it to cut open a little hole in the fence for me to crawl through into the complex. Luckily, I was quite small and nimble and could hide in the shadows.

A searchlight swept left and right as I moved across the grass toward the bunker. I waited for it to pass and then ran forward into the cover of another patch of darkness afforded by the corner of a barracks building.

"Alright," I whispered to myself. "Let's see if this works."

I looked up into the guard tower above me. Two guards watched over the complex. I focused intently on one of the guards and closed my eyes.

"Show me his future," I whispered to myself as dispassionately as possible, as if I was saying some incantation. "Don't think about how this affects you, just see the truth."

A vision came upon me in a rush, and clearly. The phone rang in the guard tower, and he turned away from his post toward it, while his friend stood next to him, eavesdropping on the conversation.

I opened my eyes again and waited for a few moments. Sure enough, the soldier's head popped up, and he turned around. As he did, I rushed around the barracks onto the other side, where the latrines were, and hugged the wall.

"Alright, that was good," I muttered. "More of that please, vision."

I inched along the wall until I came to the end of a long building and crouched next to it. Across from me stood the entrance to the underground bunker which I had seen in my earlier visions. Even as a jumbled mess, I knew that was where they kept the Toledo prisoners.

A young man, clean shaven and doe-eyed, guarded the door to the bunker. I closed my eyes and thought about his future, trying my best to see the truth, not my hope for it. I thought about the soldier typing in his key code, going inside, and suddenly I was inside his head.

"Soldier!" A white-bearded man with emerald eyes shouted. From his uniform, it was clear he was a general or high ranking officer of some type. "Let me inside now!"

"Yes, sir, General!" The boy soldier shouted, fumbling with the rifle in his hands.

The soldier looked down at the keypad and typed in 96423871. The keypad made a chime and turned green. The lock clicked open, and the general stomped inside.

"How far into the future was that?" I whispered.

It was impossible to know. I just wanted to see him open the keypad. It could have been a minute or a year from now. Who knows how often he used that pad?

"Now, I need to see when he leaves. Show me the next two hours. Fast, I guess."

I didn't even know if that's how it worked. I closed my eyes, and sure enough, I was there, going ten-speed through the machinations of the guard's day. Every six minutes he made a loop around the bunker, and for one minute nobody was guarding the entrance.

I opened my eyes and waited. Sure enough like clockwork, the soldier looped around every six minutes. The next time he moved out of sight I ran forward across the muddy ground and typed in 96423871.

The door clicked open, and I slid inside, just as the soldier's foot came around the bend. I pulled the door closed. Now, I was locked inside a facility. It was the most dangerous place for me to be at the moment. I was in the belly of the beast, and there was no turning back now.

CHAPTER SEVEN

I crept carefully down the metal stairs of the underground bunker until I reached the bottom. The stairs led into a wide corridor. On each side of me, long glass windows lined the pathway, filled with white-coated scientists working on experiments behind the windows. I slid down under the windows, careful not to be seen, and peeked my head over slowly to see what was going on inside.

"Don't move so much," One of the scientists said in a thick, Belgian accent. "This will hurt either way. If you stay still, it will hurt less."

The wild-haired scientist walked across the room and placed a pair of goggles around her eyes. On a lab table in front of her was a young red-haired woman, crying and pleading for her life as she struggled against the leather straps that held her down.

"Stop! Please!" the red-haired woman shouted. "Let me go!"

I sympathized with the woman. I had been there, and not long ago, either. I knew what it was like to be a rat in somebody else's experiment. I wanted to break through the glass and punch out the scientists, but that would have given away my position. If I wanted to help that poor woman, I had to leave her to suffer a little while longer, even if it made me sick to my stomach.

I crawled along the metal wall to the other side of the room. The screams of the woman echoed across the hallway. In front of me was another hallway, guarded by an unlatched metal door like you would find in an old aircraft carrier. The hallway was dark, save for dim red bulbs that lit the corridor.

I closed my eyes tightly and imagined the scientist. I asked my subconscious to show me where the scientist went to get the red-haired woman from in the first place. When I opened my eyes, I was there. The scientist walked backwards down the hallway, turning left, then right, and then two more lefts, before she ended up in the cell block.

No guards blocked her way as she snaked through the halls, but I couldn't be too careful. Guards could pop up at any moment. I crept carefully through the room and into a hallway lit only with red lights. It reminded me of a submarine from an old movie, with cramped hallways and metal, sterile walls.

If she turned left, I was supposed to turn right to mimic her backward path, and I did so, down another cramped hallway. I recognized the next turn from my vision and turned left. I still heard her patient's screams in my head, and the guilt of not helping her ate at me with every step I took deeper into the dark bunker.

"You're crazy!" A male voice boomed down the hallway. "No way Manchester City is better than Chelsea."

A woman's voice cackled. "Ok. How about twenty pounds on who finishes higher in the Premier League this year?"

Two soldiers, a plump, oily man and a rodent-like woman with buck teeth and a ponytail, walked into the hall as I dove into an open, dark doorway.

"You're on!" The man said as they walked past me. "You are so gonna lose."

"We'll see about that."

I peeked my head out of the door in time to see the fat soldier and his rat-like friend waddling away. I closed my eyes and imagined his path. Time spun back and showed me the same two lefts that the scientist had taken with her victim. Again, no guards were in the hallway, but they could come at any time.

I poked my head out a second time, and heard no sound, except the light whirling of an engine. I crawled out into the hallway and turned right at the end, and then made another right, just like the soldiers had done. When I did, I was at the top of a flight of slatted metal stairs that looked down into a cell block coated with white plastic. Everything was clean and precise. Hundreds of prison cells lined each side of the block, and a dozen guards paced up and down the cells carrying rifles, ready for a fight.

In the middle of the room, a tall, statuesque blond woman stood behind a console with her back towards me. She fiddled with hundreds of brightly colored buttons in front of her that glowed green, red, and yellow, as she watched the monitors above her.

How was I going to get down there and rescue my friends? I could sit up here for days and never find a way through their security from here. Then I remembered that I had the power of illusion. I closed my eyes and thought back to the tubby guard. He came from here, which meant they expected him to come back.

I closed my eyes and thought of him in as much detail as I could. When I opened my eyes, my cheek lit up with a Square, and then it vanished as my body molded into his proportions, and he engulfed me.

I pressed myself to my feet and lumbered forward down the stairs. It wasn't easy to balance the new mass around me, but I managed to slowly make my way forward until I was finally at the bottom of the stairs.

"Back already, Billy?" A dark-skinned guard asked. "Did you already eat the whole mess hall?"

The rest of the guards snickered together as if Billy was a great joke to them. I felt a little sad for Billy. Sure, he worked for the RMP, but he was clearly an outcast among them.

"Knock it off!" The statuesque blond said. She must have been in charge by how forcefully she commanded the others. "It's not his fault he was raised by elephants."

The snickering turned into full-on laughing, and I bowed my head in shame. It wasn't even my shame, but I couldn't help but feel wounded by the taunting.

"Well, aren't ya gonna say something?" A woman soldier with a shaved head asked.

"He can't," a square-jawed soldier said. "His mouth is still full of pizza!"

Again, the entire squad went up in laughter, and now I was angrier than I was sad. I walked forward toward the command station. As I neared it, I got a clear look at the buttons and knobs on the console.

They were as easy to read as the ones on the Goliath. A different button controlled each of the cells, and they were labeled with the same number as the one above each cell door. Two of the cells were empty, and those were lit with a green light, while the others were lit with a red one.

I craned my neck from side to side as I walked past the cells. Every prisoner wore a thick metal collar around their neck. Some of the prisoners I recognized from Toledo. Others were new to me. They stared at me with a combination of contempt and sadness. They didn't know I was there to save them, and I couldn't tell them to stay strong for just a couple minutes more without blowing my cover.

"H-h-h-h-hi," I said in my best Billy voice.

"Look!" the dark-skinned soldier shouted. "He's making another pass at Sarge!"

"Am not!" I replied, somehow defensive even though it has nothing to do with me. "I was just wondering if you wanted a break, ma'am."

A smile came over the sergeant's rough face. "That would be nice, Billy. Go find me somebody qualified to operate these controls, and I'll take one."

"Well…" I said. "I thought…"

"What? You thought YOU could do it?" She started chuckling. "Oh, Billy. I like you, I do, but you're dumb as rocks."

"I've been studying," I replied, lying through my teeth.

The sarge sighed and looked at her watch. "You know what? Antonia isn't set to bring any prisoners back for another thirty minutes. Don't touch anything okay, and you can't screw it up."

I shot her a wide smile. "Can do!"

I saluted her, and she saluted back. She came down from the control console, and I stepped up onto it. I looked down at all the buttons and found one that said, "FIRE RELEASE."

"Hey, Sarge!" I shouted. "What's this one that says fire release do?"

"It releases all prisoners in case of a fire. Don't press it, Billy. Don't press anything."

I grinned even deeper as my hand hovered over the Fire Release. Billy's hand inched down further and further. I readied myself for a firefight. I didn't want to fight, but I had to fight, and I certainly knew how.

"Enough, Roselyn." A thick Irish voice boomed through the cell block over the speaker system. "This has been fun to watch, but you are quite surrounded."

I went to press the button, but the entire command console turned black and shut down. I slammed my hand on the console, but nothing happened when I pressed the buttons. The squad raised their guns at me. Even Billy, from the top of the stairs, dropped his brown bag and pulled out his gun.

"You can fight all you want, but I am quite sure you will die, ya know?" the voice said over the speakers.

"I'm going to die anyway," I shouted back.

"True, but at least if you come quietly, nobody else will be harmed, including your friends. If ya care about that at all, that is."

I didn't have any other choice. I failed. I couldn't risk my friends being harmed in any way, so I held up my hands and surrendered.

"Fine," I said. "I'll come quietly."

"That's a good girl," it replied, as the soldiers descended upon me. "Bring her to me."

CHAPTER EIGHT

Five guards, including Billy and the rat-faced woman, led me down the circuitous halls of the bunker. It smelt of sweat and rusted iron, like playing on an old swing set on a sweltering summer afternoon. The metallic taste fell onto my tongue and filled my nostrils until I nearly gagged. I smacked my tongue against the roof of my mouth, trying to rid myself of the taste, but it lingered there, in the air and on my breath, and became more insufferable the further I descended into the facility.

I quickly lost my bearings, which was probably the point. I couldn't tell which way was left or right, and our quick turns made me dizzy and disoriented by the time we descended our third flight of metal stairs. With every level we descended, the bunker got darker and colder, until I was engulfed in pitch blackness when we finally stopped.

"Explain to me this," a loud voice shouted, echoing off the metal walls around me. "Once you got your friends, how were you gonna get out of here?"

I answered despite myself. I didn't know who I was talking to, or why I was compelled to answer, but I did anyway. "I…hadn't thought that far ahead."

"No, I suppose you hadn't. I figure you musta gotten spooked by your encounter in Avila, and just, went in head first, didn't cha love?"

"Don't call me that," I grumbled.

"Oh, I'm sorry," the voice continued. "Is it distressing you for me ta call you that? More distressing than the fact yer gonna die?"

"No," I mumbled. "I mean. I don't want to die, either. I would like you not to call me that, and not to kill me. They are not mutually exclusive."

"Hmmm," the voice said, mocking me. "I'll take it into consideration, but it doesn't look good for you, don't cha know?"

As he said the last word, all the lights in the hallway turned on, and the brightness blinded me. I closed my eyes to prevent the light from burning my eyes, but it still singed the air around me, leaving a burning smell wafting through the hallway.

After a moment, I opened my eyes again, and they adjusted to the light. In front of me, the spotlight revealed the outline of a figure, short and squat, but muscular in form. I barely made out the tips of handlebar mustaches and the tufts of curly hair sitting atop his head.

"Who are you?" I asked.

"I'll ask the questions 'round here, lass, but I'll tell you for my own humor. Name's General Sullivan. I run this here facility, and I've been hunting your kind since I was a wee lad. Get a might bit of pride from it too, don't cha know?"

"No," I replied, squinting through my burning eyes, trying my best to acclimate to the darkness. "I don't know."

"That was a rhetorical question, of course. You weren't supposed to answer that. 'Course, you'd know that if you were a little older, or if you hadn't grown up in such a dirtbag country. Did you know, they used to call themselves PIGS, with a might bit of pride, too?"

"What's a pig?" I replied.

"It's a short, fat, little animal you use to cook bacon. But that's not what you mean, is it, dear? PIGS stands for Portugal, Italy, Greece, and Spain—the greasy, bottom feeders of Europe. We called 'em that as an insult, but now they say it with pride, like a badge of bloody honor. don't cha know?"

There was a long silence, uncomfortable and hollow. "Am I supposed to answer that?"

"Of course not, ya daft child. I already told you that yer not supposed ta answer that, didn't I?"

I nodded. "You did."

The shadow moved closer to me. As he did, I made out the red freckles all over his round, pale face. "We are gonna have trouble if you answer the things ya aren't supposed to, but I can forgive it if you do answer they things I ask ya to answer. Are we clear?"

I shook my head. "No, sir. I'm sorry, but no."

Sullivan slapped me with the back of his hand, and I fell onto the floor. I'd never been hit so hard before, especially by somebody so slight, and the pain in my eye made me want to cry out in pain, but I couldn't. I couldn't let him break me, not until I was alone.

"Take her to solitary. Let her think about what she's done. Soften her up a bit."

"Yes, sir," one of the biggest guards replied.

Sullivan bent down to me. "Though, I must admit. You are pretty soft already, aren't ya?"

I didn't answer him. I didn't know if I was supposed to, but even if I were, I wouldn't give him the satisfaction.

*

They threw me in a dark room and slammed the door. There was no light. There was no bed. There was only the cold, metal floor, and the sounds of the bunker. Water dripped through pipes, steam hissed through the chambers, and footsteps ambled along the hallways above me.

Perhaps I should've been scared, but I had long since grown out of my fear of the dark. Too often evil people conducted their business in the cold light of day, and that is what I truly feared. Those that worked in the darkness feared being found out, and that fear meant they still had shame.

Sullivan. I could hear the shame in his voice. I smelt it in his rancid sweat. It oozed off him. In polite conversation, he could never admit he hunted people, nor that he enjoyed it, but here in the darkness, he was free to satiate his animal instincts, even revel in them.

The true horrors in this world acted in the light of day. They acted without fear of reprisal, or shame of their actions. Fiona had no shame. Statues were carved to celebrate her atrocities. People worshiped her not despite her actions, but because of them. My grandfather was no better, and there was no shame in either of their eyes. Those were the true monsters of this world. Those that operated in the darkness, I could handle them.

Besides, the darkness brought clarity. I'd been going non-stop for longer than I could remember. It was only a matter of weeks that I'd been gone from my home, but it felt like years. I felt as though I had grown into an adult since I left, but the truth was I was still only sixteen years old. I was not much more than a child, and less than an adult. Yet, I tasked myself with doing the extraordinary…the impossible.

What was I going to do if I fought through all the guards and got Anabelle and the others out? Was I just going to walk out of the bunker? Would Sullivan really let that happen? Sure, I could fly, but how many of the prisoners could fly with me?

If we couldn't fly, were we all going to fight? Most of those people were civilians. Did I really think they could fight trained soldiers? Heck, could I fight trained soldiers? It's not like I have ever tried before, except for once, and let's face it, most of my success against the Goliaths came because of luck. Luck and sheer bravado. I wasn't about to kill a soldier with my bare hands. Who had the stomach for that?

I was so gung-ho about taking responsibility for my actions, and now this was the consequence for me going off half-cocked, like a child. I thought I was all grown up, but the truth was that I couldn't have been naiver if I tried. Even with everything I'd been through, I was still nothing but a stupid kid.

Now, everybody would suffer because of me. Poor little Roselyn Light, dragged from a comfortable life of privilege to a world of fantastical magic, and now brought back to reality. She would be responsible for inflicting even more pain on innocent people who didn't deserve it.

I wanted to have a pity party for myself, but I didn't deserve one. I had brought this all on myself.

*

There was nothing but time in the dark, time to think, and my brain didn't like to stop moving. Facing your own mortality puts a lot of things into perspective. Ever since I left home and found out the truth about my mother, I'd demonized the woman who raised me. However, the longer I stayed in solitary, the more chance I had to remember and reflect on my life.

The truth was, no matter whether we were related or not, my adoptive mother was there to mend every cut and comfort me in time of need. She never shied away from her responsibility, even though I wasn't her child, and that was commendable.

I had to know what happened to her. I'd put it off until now because I couldn't deal with the pain of knowing, but now the pain of not knowing ate at me more the longer I sat by myself. I loved her, no matter what I said or thought, and her safety was important to me.

I closed my eyes and felt the heat from my cheek of the All-Seeing Eye. "Don't feel. Just see."

Flashes of light rushed through me, and I was suddenly back in my old house. Tears fell down my face as I watched it as it once was, the last time I was truly happy, and felt truly safe.

"RMP!" A voice banged on the door. "OPEN UP!"

The RMP didn't wait before they smashed down the door. A group of twenty soldiers clad in body armor rushed into the house in every direction. The trampled our carpets, destroyed our table, and smashed up our counter, as they tore through every room.

I moved through the house with them, but there was no sign of my mother. I walked back down the stairs and into the study. A force drew me toward our drafty brick fireplace. Suddenly I was flushed through the wall, under my house, and through a dirt tunnel, before smashing through the other side in the alley behind my house.

A taxi cab rolled through the alley, away from the house. In the back window, I saw my adoptive mother's rosy, plump face crying ugly tears. She pressed her hand to the window, and I flew forward to touch her.

"Goodbye, my love. May we find each other again."

I pressed my hand next to hers, across the glass, and I cried. Suddenly, the vision was gone, and I was back in the cell, in blackness, but the crying continued long after the vision stopped. She was safe, and a weight lifted from my heavy heart.

*

I don't know how long they held me in the cell, but eventually, two burly guards flung open the metal hatch and the light from the hallway streamed in. I was disoriented and confused, but I understood now that was the point. The darkness was for fear, and the light was for confusion. That was the game General Sullivan played, and he played it well.

"We meet again, don't we, lass?" Sullivan said when the guards threw me into his office.

Much like the rest of the bunker, Sullivan's office was sparse and clean, almost antiseptic. There were no papers on his desk or human touches of any kind. Instead, hundreds of monitors glowed around him, showing him images from around the facility. A computer was all that adorned his desk, save for a long, serrated knife which he thumbed from across the desk.

"It would seem that way," I replied, trying my best to hide the fear in my voice. It was hard to tamp down the dark thoughts of what he would do to me if I didn't bend to his will, but I knew that even if I helped him, I would not save myself.

"It's time that I presented you an offer and see if you're a smart girl or a dumb one."

"I can tell you; I'm not that smart."

"Well, I can see that," Sullivan said, gripping the handle of his knife and spinning it in his hand. "I guess the question really should be whether you are a dumb girl or a stupid one."

"That's a lot harder to answer," I replied.

"And that's why we're gonna test it and find out. Now, a smart girl wouldn't have come here, but since you did, we can move on to the important question. I need you to help me."

I smiled. "That's not a question."

He chuckled. "You got me there. Maybe you aren't as dumb as you look."

I nodded. "I'm probably dumber."

"You see, you're a bit of an anomaly. You are more than a Dual. It's the first time I've ever seen that, which means you can be the voice of reason to a lot of magical folks out there, show them the way and the like. I need somebody like you. You could save a lot of lives if you played your cards right."

"You want me to work for you?"

"In a matter of speaking. That is to say, in all manners of speaking. I need you to be the mouthpiece of the RMP, and tell the magical folks of the world that Toledo is not here to help them."

"That I can do, but I assume you also want me to tell them that the RMP is here to help them, which I won't do, because you are both the worst."

"Ah, well at least we are halfway there. I suppose I should sweeten the pot then. If you help us, then I won't kill ya."

"I don't believe you," I replied. "I think you're gonna kill me either way."

"That's an interesting thought, and I appreciate your moxie. You know, you've really turned me around. If I'm gonna kill you anyway...I might as well kill ya now. Guards!!!!"

"Wait, what?" I said, stunned as guards grabbed me by both arms. "No, stop. You're just kidding, right? This is supposed to be a—"

"It's not supposed to be an anything, love, except what I want it to be. Take her to the yard and execute her. Don't make it pretty. She doesn't deserve it."

Sullivan walked around his desk and strapped a thick metal collar around my neck. "This will prevent you using any of your powers when you get outside, which would be quite a bother to us, ya see."

"NO!!!!" I screamed as the guards pulled me out of the room kicking and screaming. "Stop it!!!"

But they wouldn't stop it. I had already sealed my fate, and now I was going to die.

CHAPTER NINE

Every step my guards marched toward my execution was a hard-fought one for them, and for me. I struggled and squirmed against their thick arms, but the guards pinned me to their sides and wouldn't let me go, no matter how much I resisted their procession.

And I cried.

I cried for my mother and father, lost to me for my whole life, and my adopted mother, who tried her best to raise me right, yet clearly failed. I cried for Anabelle, who would likely die in prison, and for Tibor, who'd died to save me. Through my tears, I realized how few people truly mattered in my life. I could count them on one hand, and that made me cry even harder.

I closed my eyes and tried with all my might to summon my powers, but Sullivan was right, the metal collar he locked around my neck prevented me from accessing anything, except more tears.

I bent my head backward as we climbed up the final set of stairs which led out of the bunker. The metal door clicked open, and the goofy guard who protected the entrance sneered at me with a stone face. I had made him look like a fool, and he was none too appreciative of it.

"I'm sorry," I shouted as they dragged me past him. "I didn't mean to get you in trouble."

And I didn't. Frankly, I didn't even think about getting him in trouble. I just wanted my friends back, and he stood in my way. Maybe I would be better at this if I was a better person, but I doubted a rational explanation would have yielded much better results, except to halt me before I could ever get inside.

I wished he had stopped me, especially since I'd failed spectacularly. If I'd known I was going to fail spectacularly, I might not have even tried in the first place.

No, I probably still would have, because I'm the kind of person who didn't believe in fate and actively worked to change it, no matter how high the odds were stacked against me. I couldn't believe that Anabelle was trapped and there was nothing I could do to save her, because then I would have to admit that I failed her. She only helped save Toledo because of me. She only left Ambrosia because of me, and I had condemned her to a life in prison.

She was only a child. Heck, we were both only children, still in school. We thought we knew about the world, but the more I learned, the more I realized that I didn't know. I didn't know about Toledo or their war against the UKE. I barely recognized that there was a problem between Normals and magical people. Sure, I played a bleeding heart, but I didn't actually do anything. I didn't actually know any magical people, not until I became one. And now, what? I was going to be their savior?

Pitiful.

"Let me go!" I shouted at the guards as the cold night air hit my skin. I smelt honeysuckle wafting on the air, combined with the light hint of gunpowder.

I closed my eyes and focused on the wind. I couldn't float on the wind, but I could enjoy it blowing against my hair. If there was nothing I could do, at least I could take solace in my last moments of life.

I stopped my struggle and listened to the wind blow through the grass. It was almost peaceful. In a different time and place, this base might have been a pleasant meadow for children to play in. Maybe I would have played in it, in a different life. Unfortunately, this was the only life I knew, and in this life, I was moments from death.

"Don't move!" One of the soldiers shouted as the guards threw me into the cold grass.

I looked up and another man, cold-eyed and clean shaven, stared down at me. There was no soul behind his dead eyes. His face contorted into a wicked smile as if he took some sick pleasure in murder.

"Well, well, well, girlie. What do we have here?"

I want to say I was brave, and that my heart was strong, but the truth is that I blubbered like a child. "Please...please...don't...kill...me."

The man's smile grew ever wider as if his mouth wasn't bound by the corners of his face. "Well, now. That's a lot of sadness, ain't it? I guess you shoulda thoughta that before ya done wrong, ay?"

I scooted away from him as he lunged toward me, but the burly guards blocked my escape. With one hard shove, they toppled me over until my face was in the grass. The soldier with the wicked smile grabbed me by the metal collar around my neck and stood me up, as I kicked and screamed against him. As he lifted me, I caught a look at his uniform, and the name Edwards stitched above his right breast pocket.

"You are a little squirmy one, ain'tcha?" Edwards said with a spring in his voice. "I know just how to deal wit' you."

In one smooth motion, Edwards spun me around and clasped my hands behind my back with a pair of handcuffs. Then, he kicked his foot into my knees, and I buckled to the ground.

"I don't like my victims ta be all blabby about it, so yer gonna get a gag. Now, this is my sock, and it ain't clean, so I'm sorry 'bout that, but I ain't too sorry about it if you catch my drift."

I bent forward, trying to wriggle free, but Edwards slung his sock around my chin and pulled me backward. Then, he grabbed my forehead and wrapped his sock around my mouth, tying it off with the tight knot in the back. I smelt ten days of hiking as I gagged from the stench. Gone were the pleasant honeysuckles. All that remained was the rancid stench of sweat that stung my nostrils and dripped down my throat.

"Now," he said, dragging me to my feet. "We can do this the easy way, or the hard way. It's up to you, but either way ends the same, with you dead. The question is how you wanna live out the next few minutes. Writhing in agony from a beatin', or nice and easy. Heck, if yer a good girl maybe I'll even take that sock out yer mouth for a last breath of fresh air before you go. Wouldn't that be lovely?"

I nodded my head. It was enough to die. I didn't need to catch a beating too, especially if it wouldn't do any good. I closed my eyes again and tried to use my powers, but it was useless. No matter what I did, my cheeks would not glow. Finally, I dropped my head. I wasn't ready to die, but it was a fact of life.

"That's a good girl," he said, pushing me forward toward a pole in the middle of an empty field surrounded by cheap, brick buildings. The pole and the brick wall behind me were covered in bullet holes, and it didn't take a genius to figure out what was going to happen to me there.

"Now," Edwards said. "I ain't gonna lie. This is gonna hurt, quite a bit, and you might not die straight away. We try to aim for the head, but sometimes the boys miss and hit yer stomach, or your ear, or your thigh, and then we gotta wait for you to bleed out. Nasty business that, but it's the way of things."

As he spoke, five soldiers carrying rifles marched into the field. They walked in lockstep, carrying wooden handled rifles in their right hands, stiff against their shoulders.

"Those are the boys now. So, they all know this, but only four of 'em have bullets in 'em. The other has blanks. That way, each soldier can go to bed tonight thinking he didn't just kill a little girl. That kind of thing weighs on yer head, don't it?"

Edwards led me to the wooden pole and tied me to it around the chest, stomach, and legs. Finally, he placed a rope around my neck and pulled it tight behind my metal collar until I could barely breathe.

"We don't want ya to move, ya know. That makes it bad for everybody. Plus, if you don't die straight away, this gives us a backup. Kill yourself with your own body weight and all. That way, everyone's conscience is clear, yeah?"

I wished I could clear my conscience. There was so much I wanted to repent for. When I was five, I punched a little boy in the nose because I wanted to play with his G.I. Joes, and he wouldn't let me. The fracture never healed right, and people had made fun of him ever since. At least he was alive though.

When I was eight, I told my whole class that Jenny Thompson peed the bed at a sleepover because my mom said I couldn't hang out with her anymore. That was a lie. Jenny was a nice person, and I saw how deeply my lie wounded her.

When I was ten, I saw a little bird dying in the street, and I did nothing to help it. Not a thing, except watch it die and smile when the last ounce of life escaped the bird's mouth.

When I was sixteen, I left my adopted mother. I didn't know where she was, or if she was safe. I didn't know if she was dead. God help me, I would kill for one more minute with her. She lied to me for sixteen years, and it broke my heart, but now, all I wanted was to squeeze her again one more time.

The more I thought about it, the more I realized that I probably deserved to die. *What kind of human does those sorts of things?* The bad kind. That's who. The kind that caused most of Toledo to be wiped out or captured because they trusted a boy.

"You've been a good girl, ay? If you promise not to scream, I'll take that stinky sock out ya mouth, yeah?"

I nodded. I hated to admit it, but I was slightly grateful to this horrible man for taking out the sock, even though he put it there in the first place. More, I was marginally relieved, truth be told, that it would be over soon. Being a human was hard, and I had done nothing but muck it up for sixteen years. Who knew how bad I would make things with sixteen more? I was almost glad the world wouldn't have to find out how bad an adult I would be.

"You got anything to say fer yourself before we get on with it? Any more beggin' you wanna do."

I shook my head. "No, just do it already."

"Oh, well that's nice, always a bit sad when they beg, you know. As if we had any power to do anything about it, ya know?"

I didn't know. I had never been in this situation before, and still, I nodded at him as if I understood his plight, and he smiled at me as if he knew mine. It was a caring smile, not like the one I saw before, and I appreciated it, even if he would be the harbinger of my doom.

"Just do it. I'm sick of listening to you."

He chuckled. "Your wish is my command, love. I wish more people were as eager as you."

He spun on his heels and walked behind the line of men. "Ready!"

The soldiers pulled the guns from their shoulders and clasped it with both hands. The synchronicity of their hands hitting the barrel of their guns caused me to break out in tears again. It's one thing to be brave when death was an abstract concept, but now, in the last moments of my life, I began to shake and quiver in fear.

"Aim!" Edwards shouted.

The guns leveled at me. I could see down each barrel as it pointed at my head. Even from fifty meters away, I could tell their aim was true. I appreciated that it would at least be quick, even as I looked up to the heavens for a final prayer. Even Fiona, clad on a white horse, would be a welcome sight right now.

Unfortunately, there was nothing, except the smell of honeysuckle and the hoot of an owl in the distance. A peaceful and serene last moment.

"Fire!"

The guns went off, and the world faded to black.

CHAPTER TEN

I opened my eyes and sucked in air as hard as I could. I must have been dead, but then, why did it smell so bad, and why was the air so brutally cold that it hurt to breathe?

The cold from my lungs washed over me quickly, and I began to shiver. Under me, a metal table held me off the ground. I clenched my fist together tightly, trying to keep in as much body heat as I could, as my breath slowly escaped through my nose and drifted into the air.

"You're awake," a man with a thick Irish brogue shouted from the right of me. I turned and saw Sullivan, clad in a thick coat, standing in the corner by a metal door.

"Where am I?" I replied.

"Well, as I'm sure ya figured out by now, we didn't kill ya. No, we didn't. That was just a bit of a scare, to show you what we're capable of, ya see. Don't get me wrong, Corporal Edwards was a might bit pissed that we filled all his guns with blanks, but ya just can't tell that man anything without him blathering it to everyone, and we needed it ta look good, so we could put the fear of God into ya."

His gamble worked, in a sense, but as scared as I was at my death, I also had a great sense of relief in my waning moments, as I came to terms with my own humanity.

"And why did you bring me here?" I asked.

"Well, that was my own little showmanship, ya see. I figured when ya came to; I could show you the alternative if ya don't help, bein' as this is the morgue and all."

I looked behind me and saw dozens of drawers with latches on them, like what you would find in a cop show.

"The morgue? So all of these drawers are filled with—"

"Dead bodies. Yes, well, not all of 'em. Good to have the room, but bless the lord they haven't been filled since the war."

I pushed myself up and swung my legs off the table. A shudder trickled up my spine, and I let out a great gasp of air.

"Now what?" I asked, trying to stay as nonchalant as possible. I lifted my head to look into Sullivan's beady, little green eyes and show him I wasn't scared of him, though that was an outright lie.

"Well, now you have two options. You help us, or you don't. I know that's a little simplistic, but it's the truth."

"I assume things will be bad for me if I say no."

"There's only one way to find out."

"And if I say yes?"

"Well, that would be a horse of a different color, as you can imagine. Dream up all the things that might happen if ya said no, and then the opposite of that would happen if you said yes, ya know?"

"So you'll help me and free my friends if I help you?" I asked.

"There's only one way to know for sure."

"I don't believe you," I replied.

Sullivan stepped closer. "I thought you might say that, so I went about setting up a little demonstration for you, just in case of this eventuality. Come wit' me, will ya?"

It wasn't like I had much of a choice. It was either go with him or freeze to death. Some other death awaited me outside, for sure, but at least it was a known unknown, and I was willing to take my chances with that.

*

"I'm not a monster, just so ya know," Sullivan said as we rounded a corner toward his office.

"I never said you were," I replied.

"But I know what you're thinkin'."

"I highly doubt that."

"You're wondering if you are fast enough to take that retaining brace off your neck and knock me out before I killed you, aren't you?"

"Oh my god, no," I replied. "What sort of people do you deal with?"

"Well, even if that's not what you're thinkin', I needed you to know I'm not a monster, because when you see what I'm about to show you—" Sullivan opened the door to his office and gestured me inside. "Well, I got a wife and kids. My eldest, she's not much younger than you."

"I hate to tell you," I replied, walking past him, "but if you can do this to me and not see your kid in me, even a little, means you have no empathy at all, and that makes you…a monster."

"But I'm not," he replied.

Even if I believed him before, I couldn't after what I saw inside his office. On the monitors, every single one, was a line of ten blindfolded men, women, and children, with braces around their necks.

Edwards, I could tell his evil grin even from a hundred meters away, through a grainy screen, stood in front of thirty soldiers, standing at attention, with guns at the ready.

I spun around to Sullivan. "Please, don't do this."

Sullivan shrugged. "I'm not doing anything. You're doing it, by hesitating. You could have helped them. You could have saved them. All you had to do was say yes."

"Yes!" I shouted. "Yes! I'll help you. Just stop all this."

Sullivan shook his head. "I'm not a monster. Just remember that. I take care of my friends, and I punish my enemies, like anybody that loves their family and country."

My eyes watered as Edwards spun around and walked behind the line of men and the soldiers leveled their guns.

"Please…don't…"

And then it was over in a puff of smoke. The men fired their rifles, and the prisoners dropped like sacks of bricks, each of them, hanging limp as blood oozed down their chests and dripped onto the ground.

"Why?" I growled, spinning to Sullivan. "Why would you do that? They were innocent!"

"Nobody is innocent!" Sullivan shouted back, stepping toward me. "That is what you don't understand. They lived in Toledo. They were complicit with the enemy. You have seen her. You have seen what she can do, have you not?"

I had seen what she could do. She could destroy all the Normals in the world, and all she had to do was die in the process or use me to enact her plans. Once she fired up her machine, she would snuff out all the Normals on the planet in one moment.

"You don't have to tell me," Sullivan continued. "I can see it in your eyes. We know what she can do, and anybody that doesn't stand up to her is an enemy of free people everywhere. All these people are traitors to the United Kingdom of Europe, and so are you. Now, I will ask you again, will you help me or not?"

I took a deep breath. "Do you promise to keep your word?"

He nodded. "I'm not a monster. I need you to believe that."

"I don't know if you are or not, Mr. Sullivan. But I'm not inclined to believe you, given what I've seen. Still, she is a monster, Fiona, and I think it takes a monster to catch one, so part of me hopes you are a bit of a monster, cuz that's what it will take to bring her down."

"That's not a yes."

"I'll help you, as long as you give me your word, your word, that I can see Anabelle before I do, and that once this is all done, you'll let all of your prisoners go free, and that if I die, somehow, they are gonna be let go too, cuz if I'm gonna die for you it's gonna be for something. It's gotta be for something. Now, you give me your word, and I'll give you my yes."

Sullivan stared me down for a long moment, but I did not break from his glare. If I could stare down an all-powerful Valkyrie and have her lose, then I could do the same with an egomaniacal soldier.

"Fine, Ms. Light," he said, grumpily. "You have my word."

"Then yes, I will help you," I replied with a smile. "That wasn't so hard, was it? Now, take me to my friend."

Sullivan nodded. "Follow me."

CHAPTER ELEVEN

I wished I could happily skip down the hall to meet my friend. I wished we lived in the same world we left just a couple short weeks ago when seeing each other meant nothing more than walking down a street.

I guess we always lived in this world, though; it's just that we were blissfully ignorant about it. In my first sixteen years of knowing Anabelle, she spent less than one day in jail. That is to say; she spent no time in jail – a grand total of zero days. In the last two weeks, however, she'd spent almost every day in jail, and not just a single jail either. First, she was an enemy of Toledo, so they put her in their jail. Then, she was an enemy of the UKE., so the Royal Military Police put her in their jail as well.

Anabelle was in this jail because of me, and I hoped she would not hold too much of a grudge. I was ecstatically excited to see her again, and I hoped she felt even a fraction of that excitement for me.

Even though I was thrilled to see her, I was equally worried. What if she blamed me for her capture? What if she hated me? What if they tortured her until she couldn't see straight, and now she loathed me for my part in her capture?

"You can see her," Sullivan said, walking down the stairs to the cell block. "But she ain't getting out until you help me, you savvy?"

"Savvy," I replied, sneering at him. "God forbid you lose the high ground, after all."

"Yes," he nodded. "God forbid that."

The cell block bustled with soldiers just as it had the first time. However, now instead of being picked on, I was scowled at as an enemy of the state. Even Billy, doughy, sad-eyed Billy, stared me down. Billy had the devilish eyes and thick forehead of a man who would kick a puppy if it stared at him wrong. I hadn't noticed it before, because I pitied him, but he was no better than the rest of the soldiers. Animals, each of them.

Sullivan pointed to the end of the cell block. "She's at the end, to the right. Don't you be makin' any sudden moves or you know what'll happen. You do know what'll happen right?"

I nodded. "You won't use fake bullets next time."

"That's sure shooting. Also, I'll make sure your friend suffers worst of all, got me?"

"I got you."

Every step I took echoed through the halls of the prison. Before I saw Anabelle, all things were possible. I could remember her as she was, and she could think of me as a care-free child. The minute I caught her eye, the last shreds of our innocence would be lost, and only reality would be left – cruel reality.

Some of the prisoners recognized me as I walked through the cell block. They pointed and stared, whispering amongst themselves. Hope swelled in some of their voices, but bitterness oozed out of others. I didn't know which emotion was right, but I had a feeling they both were equally justified.

As I approached her cell, I heard her humming. "And that's *Baby Got Back,* from Sir Mix-A-Lot," she said. "Do you want me to do more?"

"NO!" the guard in front of her cell shouted. She was a tall, thin, gawky woman with thin blond hair. "Just shut up!"

"That's not the game," Anabelle replied. "The game is to hum things."

"How do you win?" the guard said, exasperated.

"Duh," Anabelle huffed. "You hum things."

"I don't want to hum things."

"Then, I guess I win."

The guard stomped away from the cell as I neared it. Behind bars, Anabelle looked every bit herself except that her hair was darker and her skin was paler. Black circles under her eyes made her look ten years older, and her cheekbones showed through her limp face making it look like she hadn't eaten in weeks.

"You always win," I said with a smile, walking up to her. This might be the last time I ever saw her, and I wanted to make it count. "She should've known."

"Oh my god!" Anabelle shouted. "Rosie!!!!"

Anabelle leapt out of her cot and shoved her arms through the bars until her face smooshed against them.

"I can't believe you're here!" Anabelle shouted, squeezing me close to the bar. "What are you doing here?"

"This is very painful," I replied.

Anabelle let me go, and I pushed back from the bar. "That's not an answer."

"It's good to see you."

All the joy went out of Anabelle's face and with it the happiness in her voice. "I made you promise not to come looking for me, Rosie. What did you do?"

I sighed. "Something stupid."

Anabelle nodded sympathetically. "Yes, I can imagine. I would probably do the same if my best friend were captured."

"I couldn't let you rot in here. Not when I was out there."

"Wait, how did you get out of Toledo?" Anabelle asked breathlessly.

I sighed. I didn't want to tell her, but I couldn't lie to her, either. "Tibor…he sacrificed himself for me. Fiona. She's planning something bad, Anabelle. She needs me to finish her plan, but if she gets me…if she gets me, it's going to be bad."

"And why are you out of a cell? Why do they let you walk free?"

I sighed. "Come on, Anabelle. Don't make me say it."

"So you made a deal with the RMP to protect you from her? That's stupid. Why would you trust them?"

"That's not why I'm here," I said. "I made a deal with them…for you."

Anabelle sneered at me. "That's an even dumber reason. I'm fine here. I can do ten years here standing on my head. I'm a Normal. I'm a nothing. They don't want me. They want you. And you came right to them. And I was the bait."

I nodded. "It seems that way. I never said I wasn't stupid. I'm pretty sure I am, actually, but I couldn't do nothing."

"I get that, but did you have to do such a stupid thing?"

I shrugged. "I guess so."

She laughed. "You always were an idiot."

"Enough," Sullivan bellowed from the other end of the cell block. "You had your time."

I placed my hand on the bar of the cell. "Be strong. It will be over soon."

Anabelle placed her hand over mine. "I don't like the sound of your voice when you say that."

"Me either," I said, sliding my hand down the bar and turning away. "Take care of yourself."

"You too!"

I wanted to smile at her, comfort her, but I didn't think it would be fair to give her false hope, so I just waved one last wave and walked away.

*

"I have something else to show you," Sullivan said, walking through a corridor on the top floor of the center. "I want you to remember; I am not a monster."

"And I want you to remember, that I don't care," I replied. "Keep telling yourself that and maybe someday you'll even believe it…"

Sullivan sighed. "You will. About sixteen years ago, we captured a woman in Ambrosia, bending water, trying to protect her daughter from our Goliaths."

I didn't need to hear any more before my stomach dropped, and I lost my breath. I knew exactly what he was about to say before he said it, but I wanted to hear it from his mouth before I allowed myself to get excited.

Sullivan stopped before a sealed door like you would find on a submarine. There was a wheel to turn to open it, and a sealed glass window to look inside.

"Her name is Susan Abalos," he said. "We believe her to be your mother."

I stepped forward; breath held tight. I couldn't reach the port window on the flat of my feet, so I rose to my tiptoes, and there she was, awash in blue light. Her hair was shaved off, and her face was longer than in the images I saw in my Toledo vision, but there was no doubt it was her.

"Mom…" I whispered.

"Yes, well…"

"What have you done to her," I asked, scared of the answer.

"She was one of the first we used…we used to find out how magical folks worked, Rosie. She—"

"You experimented on her," I said. "You really are a monster."

"No, I am not," Sullivan said, raising his finger. "And the proof is this. If you help us and help us with all your might and effort, never hold anything back, and do your very best, then I will reunite you with your mother as well. It will be my carrot."

"And what is the stick?"

Sullivan flicked a switch on the side of the door, and the entire room lit up with electricity. My mom shook and convulsed. In a second it was over, and she fell onto the floor.

"Mom!" I shouted.

Again, Sullivan held up his finger. "Consider that the stick."

I snarled at him. "I'm going to help you, but when this is done, I better never see you again, or I will split you in half."

"Oh, I would absolutely love that," he replied. "I have no interest in seeing your mug ever again either."

Just then, a loud siren blared through the hallways. The lights turned red and soldiers filed into the hallways from every direction.

"What's happening?" Sullivan shouted. He pressed a radio transmitter on the wall. "What's going on down there?"

"It's Toledo, sir," the radio crackled back. "The Shiners are attacking."

The ground shook above us a swarm of soldiers ran out of the bunker and onto the base above. We followed the soldiers until we reached the top of the stairs. When we did, Sullivan started to run out, but I held him back.

"Wait," I said.

"Are you daft, lassie?" Sullivan replied. "I got to help my men."

I slammed the door closed in front of him. "Trust me. Take this stupid thing off my neck."

"That's not gonna happen. I—"

"They're not just after you! They're after me, too! Take this off, or we're all as good as done for!"

Sullivan waved his hand over the collar, and it fell to the ground. "Fine, but you better not screw me, ya hear?"

"That's funny, coming from you."

He didn't have a chance to reply before Fiona slammed down a hundred meters in front of us, wings outstretched and blue fire burning in her eyes.

"How strong is this door?" I asked.

"Strong enough to stop a tank shell from point-blank range."

"Let's hope that's enough."

I closed my eyes and thought of the ground. I saw it rip up in front of me and encapsulate Fiona around it. When I opened my eyes, the ground surrounded Fiona like a pod and held her in place…for a moment at least.

Then, she slammed through the rock and kept walking toward us, as if it were a stroll in the park. I imagined rain, and sure enough, rain came down on the battlefield. I closed my eyes and imagined lightning, and it struck her twice, but she just kept moving.

"Do you have any more of those bombs?" I asked. "The ones you used last time that zapped my powers?"

"No? Are you kidding? Those are experimental. It'll take months to have another one ready."

"Do you have any way to stop this Valkyrie?"

"Nothing comes to mind; I'm afraid, love, 'cept you maybe."

The rain fell harder outside, and Fiona inched closer to the door. As she did, Air magic users from the Tuppins picked off soldiers and carried them off into the eye of the storm.

"I quite like this rain," Fiona said. "Do you have any more?"

She was mocking me. She was mocking me because she knew I was nothing but a little girl compared to her. Even at my best, I didn't stand a chance against a Valkyrie. The last time I escaped due to sheer luck.

"Don't worry," Fiona continued. "I'm not here to break down this door and take what is mine. I will leave you to do that for me."

"You're daft, love," Sullivan replied.

"I am not. You will bring my people to the edge of Toledo by tomorrow mid-day, and you, Rosie, will surrender to me willingly."

"Or what?" Sullivan replied.

"Or you will see what I can do at full power as I rip every one of your soldiers in half on live television and announce my war against Normals like you. I swear to you, I will not be like the imbeciles I groomed to lead my revolution."

"You mean the butcher fascists who started World War 2?"

"Yes! They were weak, and I should have never trusted them. I should have dealt with you myself. I will not make that mistake again. You have until midday tomorrow before I unleash my full power to the world."

With that, Fiona snapped her fingers, and the rain stopped. She smiled at me through the glass and then gave a playful titter. Finally, she opened her wings and flapped into the air. Just as quickly as she came, she was gone, with a hundred Air magic users carrying soldiers under their arms as they followed her.

"What do we do now?" I said.

"Well, she's got the upper hand, I would say. I have to talk to my superiors, and then have a plan of attack. If we give you to her—"

"What?" I shouted. "You're thinking of giving in to her demands?"

"I don't know. I don't know what else to do, ya see. They're just one little city, but full of magic users, who knows how far they could take this fight and what kind of army they could raise from magic users around the world."

If I let the general bring me to Toledo, then I would be risking the lives of every Normal I've ever met, including Anabelle. However, it would mean that everybody would go free. However, if I told him the truth, I would doom everybody in prison to a life behind bars, and who knows what else.

I nodded and took a deep sigh. I didn't know what would come out of my mouth, but I figured it would be the right move, or at least I was willing to trick myself into believing it was, for my own sake.

"General, there's something you should know about me."

CHAPTER TWELVE

"So what yer tellin' me," Sullivan said after I finished my story about how I escaped Toledo. "Is that if I bring you back to her, then she's going to use ya to destroy all of humanity?"

"Not all of it, just the non-magical bits," I said. "That's what I'm saying."

"Wow," Sullivan scratched his head. "That's a bleak picture you paint. Kinda screwed if you do and screwed if you don't kind of stuff, isn't it?"

I nodded. "It would seem that way. Either you sacrifice your men and start a war with Toledo, with possibly the whole magical world coming to their aid, or you bring me in, and you risk the whole world falling apart."

He nodded. "A bleak picture, for sure."

"If you'll hear it, I do have an idea though."

He sighed, loudly. "Sure, this I gotta hear."

"Well, before Fiona captured me in her cave, she told me that the device could be used for another purpose which could save everybody, but I don't think you're gonna like it."

"I haven't liked anything you said in the past hour, so I would say there's a good chance this will be the same. Go on."

"She told me that the device could be used…to give everyone magic."

"Give everyone magic!" Sullivan shouted, slamming his fists on the table. "That's crazy. I can't even deal with the magical folks we got running around right now, and you want even more of 'em. No, that's gotta be worse than dyin', I must say."

"Well, you are in a no-win scenario. You just gotta find out which loss is most palatable."

"I think we should just blow up the whole thing," Sullivan replied. "If I brought enough C-4, I could blow Toledo to kingdom come."

"No!" I shouted. "You wanted my help, and if you want my help, you have to accept that we're not blowing up Toledo."

Sullivan reached into his holster and pulled out a shiny, silver pistol. He raised it into the air and pointed it at my head. "Or I could just kill ya, kick your body into the sea, and be done with it. Then, what is Fiona gonna do?"

I nodded. "You could do that, but I took it on faith that you wouldn't, given that I told you the truth. You said if I helped you, I would be safe, and so would my friends."

The gun shook in Sullivan's hand. "Deals change all the time."

I closed my eyes. "Then do it already."

I wasn't ready to die, but I was sick of suffering fools. I was sick of arguing in circles. I was sick of listening to megalomaniacs telling me what I had to do. It was just easier to call them on their bull and if they really wanted me dead, well so be it.

"I ain't gonna shoot ya," Sullivan said, exasperated.

I opened my eyes and watched him put the gun back into his belt. "Good. Now we're getting somewhere."

"I ain't gonna help you turn the world into magic users, either though."

I nodded. "Then you have a tough decision to make unless you can magically send a bomb to blow up that device, all while delivering me to Fiona, I don't know what to tell you."

Sullivan smiled. "That's exactly what we'll do."

"Excuse me?"

"We'll use you as a distraction, and send a squadron of Goliaths to blow up that cave while Toledo's backs are turned. You are one smart lady, did ya know that?"

I shrugged. "If you're happy, I'm happy, I guess. I have a few more requests, though, before we go."

"I think you're plum outta requests, love," he replied.

"Not if you want my help, I'm not."

*

Sullivan walked with me to my mother's cell. I stood on my tiptoes and watched her pace back and forth, muttering to herself, biting her nails.

"She's not gonna know you," Sullivan said.

"I don't care," I replied. "I want to talk with her."

"Whatever," he said, spinning the wheel on the door. "Make it quick."

Air whooshed out of the door as the seal broke. Sullivan yanked it open with all his might. I stepped onto the steel grates which made up the floor of my mother's room. I crept closer to the wild-eyed woman that birthed me.

"Who are you?" she said, her voice cracking with each word. "What do you want with me? They told me if I did what they said they would leave me alone. That's what they said. Be a good girl, and you'll get a cupcake. Be a good girl. I'm a good girl. I'm good. What more do you want!!!?!!?!"

I held up my hands and slowed my pace. "Easy, I'm not here to hurt you. I'm here…I don't know if you'll believe why I'm here."

"You're here to take my brain away, finally. You're here to make me, make me a monkey with a top hat."

I shook my head. "I'm not here to do anything to you. I'm here…I'm here because…I'm your…I'm your daughter."

The tears flowed as I finished speaking. I didn't know if she would lunge at me, turn away, or embrace me on the spot, but it didn't matter. I just needed her to know. I needed her to know I was alive, that she got me out alive."

Mom looked at me with a quizzical look. "My…daughter…"

I nodded, tearing up even more. I could barely see her through the tears in my eyes. "Yes, mom. It's me."

I closed my eyes and imagined a ball of water in my hand. When I opened it, a small trickle of water filled my hands from the bunker hallway. More importantly, my cheek glowed with the moon, which was her power.

Mom's quivering lip stopped shaking, and her frown curled up slowly on each side. Tears filled her eyes.

"Yes, yes you are, aren't you?"

I nodded. "I am. I'm here, mom. I'm here."

Mom rushed forward and wrapped me in a big hug. She squeezed me tight like she would never let me go. I never wanted to let go, either. Together, we collapsed onto the floor, crying tears of joy.

*

My second request was easier on me than the first. It didn't involve me seeing a person who I didn't know existed until a few weeks ago. This one was about Anabelle. I needed her help if I was going back to Toledo since I didn't trust the RMP. Sullivan brought her to his office in the bottom floor of the bunker, unchained. The minute she saw me, her arms flung wide, and she ran toward me.

"Buddy!" Anabelle said, wrapping me up in a big hug. "I missed you so much."

I quickly started sobbing again as I held her in my arms. I don't know how long we held each other, but eventually, after a long while, she released me.

Anabelle wiped the tears from her eyes. "I knew you would get me out of there. I mean, I hoped you wouldn't be so stupid about it, but once you came to the prison cell, I knew you wouldn't give up."

I smiled at her. "Well, if you think I was stupid before, wait until you hear this. I made a deal with Sullivan so he would release all of you."

"That doesn't sound stupid."

"That's not the stupid part. The stupid part is that to do it; I have to lead him to Toledo, and meet Fiona again."

"Shut up. That is so stupid. Wait, you are working with one enemy to bring down the other. Oh, that is so, so, so, so stupid."

"I know," I couldn't do anything but laugh. "Which is why I need your help."

Anabelle sighed. "Of course you do."

"I don't trust any of them, Anabelle," I said, grabbing her arms. "I only trust you. If you don't have my back, nobody does."

Anabelle smiled. "Well, I guess it can't be any worse than the prison, right. And heck, maybe I'll die, and then this'll all be over."

"Good," I said. "They are going to fix you up with a nice, new Goliath. State of the art. If worst comes to worse and this all goes south, I need you to find me, and help me."

She shrugged. "It actually sounds kind of fun."

"Because you're as crazy as I am."

And with that, we embraced again, two idiots, about to risk our lives yet again for a mission we were confident wouldn't work. At least at the end of it, though, we would be free.

*

My final request was the hardest to accomplish for the RMP. I wanted to talk to my adoptive mother again. It took nearly the whole night, but eventually, Sullivan brought me to an old-fashioned corded phone at the entrance to the bunker.

"I couldn't get yer ma on the phone, I'm afraid," Sullivan said. "But this is an answering machine we have tapped fer years. It used to be one used by the nursemaids, and best we can tell it still is, ya see. If ya want to get yer ma a message, this is the best way."

Sullivan typed in a number and handed me the phone. It rang three times and then went to voicemail. "Hello, you've met Marvelous Matilda's Nanny Service. We are not here to take your call, but please leave a message at the beep, and we'll get back to you as soon as possible."

I took a deep breath before the phone beeped. "Hi. My name is Roselyn Light. One of your…people…helped me for a long time. I need to get a message to her. Tell her that

I loved her…that I love her…and that I'm fine. She doesn't have to worry about me. And thank her for everything she did for me. Nothing I could ever do could repay the gift she gave me."

And with that, I hung up. "It's done."

"And that's yer last favor, lass. It's yer turn to live up to your end, don't cha know?"

"I'm ready," I said, wiping a final tear from my eye. I'd gotten my affairs in order, in case the worst happens. Now, it was time to look ahead to the future, and the mission at hand.

*

It took the rest of the night to unlock the prisoners and ready them for transport, locking them in collars that nullified their powers, and placing them on the backs of transport trucks. By the early morning, we were on the road.

The general rode with me in a Jeep at the front of the convoy. I no longer had my power nullifier around my neck. I suppose I'd proved my worth to him the previous night when I didn't crush the bunker to the ground.

"This is a daft plan, you know," he said as we drove.

"It's your plan," I replied.

"Yeah, and so I know how daft it is. We're going to meet the enemy, on their turf, where they have all the power."

I looked behind us at a dozen tanks and then craned my neck up above us at a hundred Goliaths flying with us. "I don't think they have all the power."

"I hope we don't have to use it, Rosie, but it's there if we need it, don't cha know. You can never be too careful, with the enemy at your doorstep."

It took us another three hours before our convoy met the bay. Past the edge of the bay, the outline of Toledo hovered in the air. A dozen warships surrounded the city in every direction. Goliaths dotted the sky all around Toledo. None fired, even though their weapons were aimed at the heart of the city.

"It's just a precaution," Sullivan said. "We aren't gonna fire unless they do."

Several squads of Goliaths guarded our route, which dead-ended at the edge of the sea half a kilometer in front of us. A hundred of Toledo's Tuppins guards stood stoically on the edge of a mighty cliff overlooking the water, their cheeks glowing the symbol of a blue Mountain. In front of them, the prisoners that Toledo took in their raid the previous night knelt on the ground, they arms and legs bound with rock and mud.

Sullivan held up his hand, and the convoy stopped. He leapt out of the jeep, and I followed suit. Together we walked toward the cliff as the Goliaths parted for us. It was so weird to be on the side of the beasts that had hunted me for so long.

Miguel walked through his troops and smiled at us. "So nice of you to make it." He looked down at his watch. "And so close to being late, I see. Like to cut it close."

Sullivan shrugged. "It takes a long time for us to get these people ready to move. Plus, midday is a kind of nebulous term, don't you think? What does it even mean?"

Miguel said. "It's meaningless. The time was mere theatrics, you see. They have their place, but they are not without their problem. Do you have our citizens?"

"I do, "Sullivan said. "And you have my men, I see."

"These are most of them. Fiona has a few with her in Toledo, hoping that she can entreat you to come into the city yourself and fetch them." Miguel smiled coyly at me. "And deliver our prize as well."

Sullivan huffed. "You expect me to go to Toledo and meet with her? Are you as stupid as you are ugly, mate?"

Miguel laughed. "That is her request, not mine. She would like you to deliver the girl personally. Or you don't get your last prisoners. In good faith, we will let our prisoners go first."

Miguel snapped his fingers, and his troops' cheeks stopped glowing. The earth receded, and Sullivan's men were freed. They ran forward toward us.

"Go to the truck, boys. Help our prisoners off, and exchange them with this fine gentleman. I'm sorry. I don't know your name."

"No," Miguel said with another big smile. "You don't. Shall we?"

Three Tuppins soldiers walked forward and then rose into the air. One grabbed Miguel around the shoulders, and another came for Sullivan.

"No thanks," Sullivan said, turning around. "I have my own way."

I held up my hands as a final soldier came for me. "Me too."

Sullivan turned to a Goliath. "Get out of there."

A slight soldier popped open his bubble and hopped out. Sullivan jumped into the driver's seat and pulled down the cockpit like an old pro.

"No fighting," Miguel said, lifting into the air with his carrier. "Or this will all be for naught."

"I'm not gonna fight," Sullivan said, blasting off with his Goliath. "There's no reason. We're gonna do this all peaceful like, don't cha know."

I rolled my eyes, joining them in the air as they headed toward Toledo. Men and their shows of strength. Whatever, soon this would all be behind me, I hoped, and I would either be free, or dead. Hopefully, the former, though the latter had a certain appeal to it.

CHAPTER THIRTEEN

We landed in the main square of Toledo a half hour later. The city hadn't remotely recovered from the bombing. It was just as derelict and falling apart as when I'd left a few weeks ago. I don't know why I expected more. After all, it had only been a couple of weeks since my escape. Even for magical folks, it would have been hard to rebuild a city so quickly. Still, watching the few remaining citizens work to lift the rubble of their lives was a little heartbreaking. After all, they didn't deserve to suffer just because Fiona was the worst.

Fiona, clad in a silver breastplate with golden bracers on her arms and greaves on her legs, waited with outstretched wings in the middle of the square when we arrived. In her hand, she clutched a long sword which I'd previously seen only in images around the city. It glowed with a blue fire that projected high into the sky. Behind her, a dozen of Sullivan's soldiers wearing metal chains on their arms and legs knelt with black bags covering their heads.

Next to her, my grandfather cowered and prostrated himself to her. He was once a powerful man, and now he groveled like a childish sycophant.

"Greetings!" Fiona said to Sullivan as he unlocked the cockpit of the Goliath and stepped out. "For a moment I thought you might be here to declare war on me."

As I landed next to him, I noticed a dozen cameras, floating above the square with stickers on them from Al Jazeera, BBC, Fox, NBC, CANAL, and more. She wasn't lying about televising the event for the world.

"Nothing of the sort, lass," he replied. "I just don't like being carried by grown men. I'm sure ya understand."

She nodded. "Of course, I understand that. What I don't understand is what a Goliath carrier group is doing a mile off shore, waiting for the order to strike. That is not something friends do, which must mean, we are not friends."

Fiona turned around and cut the heads of every one of the soldiers behind her in one strike of her sword. "And if we are not friends, then we cannot entreat together."

Sullivan went for his gun, but by the time he pulled it out, Fiona had spun back around, and with the flick of her wrist she cut off Sullivan's gun hand.

"Ahhh!!!!" Sullivan screamed. "You dumb—"

But he didn't finish before Fiona cut off his head as well. Blood pooled around the square, as magical folks turned from their chores and opened fire on the carrier group with everything they had in them.

"This was your plan all along!" I shouted at her.

"Of course!" Fiona shouted. "You can't get into a good war without killing a few notable people, Rosie. Look up there! This has been broadcast on every news source on the planet."

All around the square were cameras, set up to catch the slaughter on tape. "Listen here," Fiona shouted. "This is a call to arms for every magical person in the world. You have been oppressed far too long. Today, fight with me to regain what we have lost!"

Fiona raised her sword into the air and dropped her head toward mine. She was quite proud of herself, I could tell, but that pride did not translate to my Lito.

"How could you!" Lito shouted. "We have a plan that would lead to no more bloodshed. You swore—"

Fiona slapped him across the face. "Quiet! Your usefulness is at an end. Come to think of it, it ended when your seed gave me this child to fulfill my destiny and destroy all the Normals in the world."

"Whoa," I replied. "Who says I'm going to help you?"

Fiona grinned. "Who says you have a choice?"

Miguel clenched his fist into a ball, and a dozen Tuppins flew into the square, surrounding me. I planted my feet under me. If they wanted a fight, I would give them one.

"Do you know what she's trying to do?" I shouted. "Do you know she's trying to kill everybody without magical powers?"

"Know it," Miguel said. "I am giddy about it!"

"You fool!" Lito said as he rushed toward Miguel. "That's genocide!"

The move took both Miguel and Fiona off guard. With Lito's momentary distraction, I turned to the Goliath. I jumped inside and closed the hatch. When I put my hands on the controls, I watched Fiona slice my grandfather in half.

"NO!" I shouted from the cockpit. I didn't like my grandfather, but he was still my blood. Aside from my mother, he was the only blood family I had left.

Still, the fact that she killed my grandfather made it much easier to open fire, and I shot vigorously against the Tuppins guarding my exit. As I did, I slammed on the jets and blasted off.

I rose into the sky and shot a burst of fire into the air to warn the nothers of the attack, but they were already too aware. A hundred Goliaths descended on Toledo. This time, it would be a fair fight, but there would be no innocents. All the citizens of Toledo were complicit in the war now.

As I flew away, firing at the Tuppins soldiers chasing me, Fiona smiled at me. She knew where I was going, and I would see her again before the end.

"Rosie?" I heard through my communicator. It was Anabelle flying in with her Goliath. Thank god I got her one because I needed her help now more than ever.

"Anabelle! Thank god! Did you hear what happened?"

"We all heard everything," she replied. "Get down to the device, destroy it, and make sure she can't make another one. Salt the earth if you have to. I'll take care of the Tuppins."

True to her word, a cavalcade of bullets swarmed through the air, and the Tuppins soldiers following me dropped off to chase the one who was following them. Meanwhile, I broke free and glided toward Fiona's cavern.

*

I unlatched the cockpit on my Goliath and set it to autopilot. Then I jumped out and floated down into Fiona's cavern. I couldn't let the Goliaths destroy the cave. It wouldn't be enough to stop her. Fiona was smart. She would find a way to rebuild, and one day, maybe a thousand years from now, another person like me would be born, and she would have another chance to end it all.

No, the only way to stop her was to make the machine unlock everybody's magic power, and then…turn it on…even if it meant I was going to die. I was willing to take that risk, for the greater good. After all, it's not like the world would miss me much. My mother was a broken husk of a woman. My father didn't know I was even alive. Perhaps my surrogate mother would miss me, but no more than she already did. The only person left was Anabelle, and I put her through enough in the past month to last a lifetime. One more tragedy wouldn't push her over the edge.

*

I landed on the edge of the cavern. The wooden doors that guarded the cave hadn't been replaced after I'd ripped them off.

"You came alone," Fiona's voice echoed through the wide, empty chambers of the cavern.

She stood in the middle of the cave, surrounded by the rubble created when we last fought. Last time, I had fought her trying to escape. Now, I fought to enter deeper into her sanctuary.

"Let me through, Fiona. It doesn't have to be this way."

"You know nothing, child," she said with scorn.

"For a child, I've sure done enough to mess up your plans."

"Are you kidding?" Fiona replied. "I've wanted war against the Normals for ages. It was your grandfather and the rest of the Council that fought me…but now they're dead and look; the war has come. My children will rise up and defeat them."

"How?" I replied. "Hitler, Mussolini, and Franco had well-trained armies at their side, and they lost. Technology has only gotten better since them. You'll be lucky if you last a month. It's going to be a massacre."

She grinned a maniacal grin. "That's why I have you. The Final Solution, as it were."

I shiver went up my spine. No sane person could hear the words "Final Solution" without it knotting up their insides.

"I'm going to turn on that machine, Fiona," I said, floating around the cavern. "And I'm willing to die doing it, but I'm not doing it to kill everyone on this planet. I'm doing it to save them."

"Look at what people do without powers, Roselyn. They still fight, and kill, and torture. What do you think they will do if you put the power of gods in their hands?"

"I don't know, but it can't be any worse than killing them," I replied, stepping down the stairs into the main hallway which led to Fiona's machine.

Fiona circled me as she spoke. "Couldn't it? The population is far beyond the carrying capacity of this planet, Rosie. If it keeps going, the world is going to die, and humans will be the cause. Killing the Normals…well, it gives you all a second shot. Think about it, Rosie. A second shot for humanity to live their best lives."

I inched forward into the gap that Fiona left when she moved around me. It was a straight shot to the computer, but Fiona didn't leave anything to chance. I knew she was playing me. She took the time before I arrived going through every scenario she could find in her head. If there was an opening, it was by design.

"So how does this end?" I asked.

"I have seen many ways, but the most likely is with you dead, either from me throwing you in the device or from me snapping your neck. Trust me; either one is fine with me. I would rather kill each human myself with my bare hands anyway. It's bloodier and more satisfying that way."

"There's something I don't get. If you hate it so much here, why don't you just go home?"

"Oh, I would if I could," Fiona replied. "Now, this conversation has gotten stale and boring, my old chum. I think it's time we settle this once and for all…"

Fiona flew forward as fast as she could. My cheek glowed with the mountain. I pulled up the ground and slammed her into the wall with it. Fiona pushed it off. Her eyes glowed blue.

"Pitiful human," She laughed. "You will never match my power!

Fiona cloaked herself in darkness as she flew toward the ceiling. Invisible now, rocks flew at my face. I broke them apart with my hands as I inched backwards toward the device at the other end of the cavern from me.

"Give up!" She said, her voice drawing closer to me.

I spun around just as a whoosh of air whizzed by me. I blinked, and my cheek glowed with the mirrored square of an illusionist. I cloaked myself in my own invisibility as I flew into the air with the wisps of air glowing on my other cheek.

"I don't have to beat you, Fiona," I said. "I just have to outlast you."

I shouldn't have said anything, but I couldn't help myself, even if it gave away my position. Out of the wall a marble block collapsed upon me.

I uncovered myself and used the power of the Earth to rip it apart before it slammed me into the ground. I closed my eyes and imagined the rock as dust. When I opened them, the pulverized dirt blew across the cavern, revealing Fiona's form. I blinked again, and suddenly both my arms were on fire.

I flung the fire bolts at Fiona as I rose up the steps toward the device's anteroom. She didn't even bother dodging the fire. Instead, it engulfed her, causing her to burst into flames.

"Foolish mortal," she snickered.

Fiona grabbed the fire from around her and flung it across the ground at me. It created a fire trail, and the ground beneath it boiled and popped. I rushed up the stairs and dove away from the fire as it chased me.

I closed my eyes again and felt the wet dew from the cavern. I pulled it all to me, every last drop, and when the fire trail was on top of me I threw the water on it, and the water dissipated the fire completely. Steam rose from the fire's ashes.

"You are more impressive than I thought," Fiona said, floating up the platform to meet me. "You have been practicing."

"Not much else to do on the run," I replied, gasping for air. "Besides, I've always been impressive. I just didn't know it until recently."

"Relax, kid. I said you were more impressive. I didn't say you were impressive. It just means I'll actually have to try this time."

She rushed towards me. This was the moment I was waiting for since we began the fight. I remembered the woman from Lito's office who saw into my past by placing her hands on my face. I needed to do the same. I needed to see Fiona's past. I closed my eyes and imagined seeing into Fiona's past. She told me she changed the settings on the device long ago, and I knew the answers were locked in her mind.

I tried to See her past without touching her, but no matter what I did, she locked me out. All I saw was blackness when I looked. I hoped that physical contact would unlock the information I needed.

As Fiona reached for me, I grabbed her by the face. When I opened my eyes, they glowed as blue as hers. Fiona dropped to the ground, and I did as well. In a flash, I was inside her mind.

CHAPTER FOURTEEN

I dropped into a cloud and slammed into the ground so hard I bounced back up like a rubber ball. When the clouds parted, I stood in front of Fiona's device, except it was pristine, new, and being polished slowly by a tall, statuesque woman with a crown on her head. Fiona knelt next to her. She looked pale, meek, and small, very unlike her confident bravado.

"Do you understand, Fiona?" the woman said.

"Yes, my queen," Fiona replied.

"Repeat it back to me then."

"I am to go down to Earth, make the heathen humans realize that they can all unlock the powers in the universe by mastering their own minds. Should that fail, then I will use this device to unlock the power for them, killing me in the process."

"Very good, Fiona. Do not bother coming back if you do not do this correctly. Understood? We can't have another Gomorrah on our hands."

Fiona nodded. "Yes, my queen."

The clouds rose into the sky and washed the scene clear. I pushed through and watched Fiona sit on the edge of a cloud. Two Valkyries with long, flowing hair and elegant wings, walked up to her.

"You, barely a Valkyrie. What do they call you?" one shouted.

Fiona sneered. "You know my name, Haas."

"Yes, but we dare not say it," the other replied. "For fear of having it contaminate us."

The men laughed and walked away. Fiona sneered, but couldn't respond, wouldn't respond. The scene washed away, and suddenly I was in the cave. Fiona shook with fear as the queen, glowing a transparent blue but no less beautiful, hovered next to her.

"Please, my queen. I just need more time."

"There is no more time. I grow tired of your tomfoolery. Turn on the device. Do it tonight. The least you could do to complete your task and wipe your failure from the universe."

The queen vanished, and Fiona sulked back to the device. I followed behind her as she sat in front of it.

"If she just gave me more time. Just a little more time."

Fiona pulled open the control panel. "If she loves her precious humans so much, let's see what happens when I wipe them from existence."

Fiona cut two wires in half, a red wire and a blue wire, and stitched them together with each other so that the red wire was tied to the blue, and vice versa.

"At least I will die wiping her mistake from the universe," Fiona grumbled.

Fiona sat down in the chair and placed the helmet on her head. She closed her eyes for a long minute, breathing heavily, building up the courage to pull the switch. Just then, a little girl walked into the room.

"Fiona," the girl said.

Fiona looked up, sneering, and then her face softened. "Yes, sweetheart. What is wrong?"

"I had a bad dream. Can I sleep here?"

Fiona thought for a moment; then a light bulb went off in her head. "Sure, sweetheart. Why don't you come over here and sit down for a second?"

Fiona took the helmet off her head and stood up. The little girl hopped onto the seat, and Fiona put the helmet on her head.

"Now, this device can take all the bad dreams away. Did you know that?"

The little girl shook her head. "No."

"Would you like that?" She asked sweetly.

The little girl smiled. "Yes, please."

Fiona gripped the switch in her hands. "Then lay back. This will only hurt for a moment."

*

I fell back onto the ground, and Fiona skidded across the floor away from me. I regained myself and stood to my feet just as she did.

"You're a monster," I said. "A monster. You killed that poor child, and who knows how many others!"

"I am not a monster!" she shouted. "I'm just doing what I have to do! What I was told to do!"

"You weren't told to do any of this!" I shouted. "This is all you! All of it!"

Fiona opened her wings and flew toward me. As she neared, the wall next to her exploded, and it sent her flying across the room. From the rubble, a Goliath emerged. I looked into the cockpit, and Anabelle smiled at me.

"Hey buddy!" she said. "Sorry, I'm late."

"No problem. I knew you would come!"

"Did you figure it out?" she said. "Did we win?"

I looked over at Fiona, who was righting herself. "Not quite, but we're about to. Keep her busy."

Fiona rushed toward me again, but Anabelle grabbed her hands. "Can do!"

Anabelle's Goliath flung Fiona across the cavern toward the entrance. Then, she jumped into the air and landed next to the Valkyrie. Meanwhile, I rushed through the door and came face to face with the machine.

I ran up to the switchboard, and flipped open the command console, just as Fiona had so many eons ago. The insides were a mess of wires, dust, and cobwebs as if it hadn't been cleaned in a thousand years. I reached into the device and rooted around, just as Fiona had until I found a knot in the wires.

I pulled them out and found an old, frayed blue wire and an even more frayed red one. My cheek glowed with the three wisps of air, and I used my breath to blow off the dust.

Sure enough, the red wire was attached to the blue, and vice versa. "Well, this seems easy enough. Only betting the entire human race that I'm right about this. No pressure."

I unfurled the wires from each other and tied them together correctly. Blue on blue. Red on red. Then, I slammed the console closed and sat down in the chair. I placed the helmet on my head and took a deep breath.

"Look out!" I heard from the cavern, just as Fiona flew through the door at full speed. This was it; it was my last shot to stop her, all I had to do was believe in myself, believe that I was in the right. Believe that I was going to save the world, instead of end it.

Yet at that moment, it was so hard to believe in myself. I'd made so many mistakes getting here. *What if I saw the wrong memory? What if I saw only what Fiona wanted me to believe? What if I doomed the entire world to destruction?*

No. I had made mistakes, and each one of them led me here, to this moment, so I could make the right one.

My eyes caught Anabelle's lumbering, broken Goliath enter the room as I flipped the switch. Anabelle looked on in horror through her shattered cockpit window, screaming out to me to stop. As the lightning flowed through my skin, Fiona grabbed me tightly, and I watched as the blue lightning filled her eyes as well. Together, we screamed into the abyss as the light exploded out of us, and I became one with it.

The light crested over the city, out of the rubble of the church, and fluttered across all the plains of Earth. I watched the beam travel to London, Paris, Perth, Harare, New York, Los Angeles, Toronto, Mexico City, Buenos Aires, and every city and little village in the entire world all at once.

The light slammed into every person on the planet simultaneously, and I was inside them all. I was with them as the light traveled through their veins, into their brains, and electrified them. I watched new synapses form where there were none before, and I watched the blue light shoot out of their cheeks, bursting forth, as they unlocked their power.

There were people of every type of magic, and many forms of magic I had never seen before. There were cheeks with skulls, and with bulls, and with three rings. There were blades of grass and hundreds of other signs which boggled my mind.

There was everything, and then…darkness. In the nothingness, I found peace.

CHAPTER FIVETEEN

"You can open your eyes now," someone softly whispered into my ear.

"I didn't realize I had them closed," I replied in a daze.

I popped my eyes open and recognized the place immediately. I was in the cloud city from Fiona's dream, filled with mist and rainbows, and in front of me was the most beautiful woman I had ever seen, glowing blue and smiling at me.

"Is…this Heaven?" I asked.

She shook her head. "No. This is where I live."

"And where Fiona lived once, as well."

She sighed. "Please do not speak that name to me. I made a huge mistake in trusting her. She had one job to do, and she failed epically."

I looked up at her. "Did…I…mess it up?"

She smiled sweetly and touched my shoulder. "No. You did wonderfully."

"So, I didn't kill everybody?"

"Not everybody, no. You saved quite a few lives. The fighting over Toledo stopped after the blue light turned everyone magical. After all, once everyone had magic, what was the point of war anymore?"

"What was the point of any of this?"

She chuckled. "I suppose you have a point. Unfortunately, I cannot tell you, for I do not know. I wish I had a more satisfying answer than that, but we are all doing what we can do while we can do it, and I am no different."

"Why did you send Fiona to Earth? She seemed unqualified for this mission."

The woman smiled. "I wanted Fiona to be better than her nature. We all deserve that. Some, like you, rise to the challenge. Others, like Fiona, fail, but we all deserve a chance."

"And you were willing to risk it all, the whole human race, on that?"

"I risked more for less," she said. "Unfortunately, you can only do so much, even as a god. You need trust."

"That bit you in the butt."

"Quite."

"And why…when it bit you in the butt…didn't you just…bring her back?"

"You ask a lot of questions."

"Yeah, it's pretty annoying, I know."

"I actually like it. Nobody questions me around here. The truth is, I do not have time to worry about every little thing on every little planet. Sometimes, things fall through the cracks. I hadn't even realized it had been seventy years. Time flows differently here."

"I see," I said, quizzically. "So…am I dead now?"

"Do you want to be dead?"

I shrugged. "I don't know. Is it any easier when you're dead?"

"I'm not sure," the queen replied. "I've never been dead. But I would think it's not much easier than being alive…just different…and longer. You are dead much longer than you are alive."

I thought for a moment. "Then, I think I would like to be alive again, if I could, at least for a little while longer."

"A wise decision," she said. "All you have to do is open your eyes."

*

I fluttered open my eyes, and I was back in the command room. The device was flaming and sparking all over. Fiona's hands were around my throat, but she wasn't moving. Her eyes bugged out of her head as she stared at me motionless. I brushed her arm away, and her hand turned into dust at the force of my blow.

I emptied my lungs out onto her, and she broke apart, floating away like ash into the air, gone. I stood up, feet wobbling, as Anabelle ran over to me.

"Rosie!" she shouted. "You fool! You stupid, idiotic, ridiculous fool! What were you thinking?"

I threw my arms around hers. "I was just trying to save the world."

"Did you?" she asked.

"I think so. We'll find out soon, I guess."

"Yes, I suppose we will," Anabelle said, walking toward her mech. "The most wonderful thing happened. Check this out."

Anabelle closed her eyes, and three wisps of air appeared on her cheek. She could fly now, and that made me happy. Anabelle always seemed happiest in the air, and after being a prisoner for so long, having the ability to fly meant she could visit anywhere at any time.

"That's wonderful," I said, cradling her neck as she walked, unable to stand unaided myself. "Can we go home now?"

"Yes," she said. "I would very much like that."

"And get some hot cocoa?" I replied.

She nodded, laughing. "Yes, we can do all those things and more."

"Awesome."

I limped forward, toward the entrance to Fiona's cavern. Everything in the world was different now. There was so much work to do, and we were just getting started.

*

If you liked this book, please go check out *Invasion,* about a boy who falls in love with an alien and together they have to save with world from a hostile race of aliens trying to take over Earth.

*

Now, here is a preview of *Invasion.*

Chapter 1

Joshy Carter didn't much like the idea of spending his summer traveling across the country with his parents. Not that he had much going on back home. He'd never had much success making friends, so there was nobody to miss. Still, his room had his PlayStation and his sleep—his precious, precious sleep—and solitude.

On the road there was nothing except for his family, his sister, and—

"The open road, Joshy!" his father, Bill, said. "There's nothing like it."

"Actually, there are tons of things like it. There's nothing literally everywhere. This is the part I hate in video games. Endless nothingness until you reach a town. At least in games, you can fast travel. Can't do that here, though. We gotta endure every excruciating second."

Josh folded his arms across his chest. "And I hate being called Joshy," he added. "I'm eighteen years old. I'm not a child anymore. Like literally, I am no longer a child in the eyes of the government, even. Pretty much everywhere, I am an adult by any measure of the word."

Joshy squeaked when he talked, and it made his mother Carole laugh. After all, that was the kind of child…adult…that Joshy was…the kind that people didn't fear. He was kind of meek, and frankly uninteresting. The only thing he cared about was playing Fortnite.

Joshy played all day and night, hardly leaving his room except to eat. He dreamed of being a professional video game player, which was the kind of thing that wasn't even possible a few years ago and now consumed the thoughts of millions.

"Would you lower the volume of that music," Joshy said, looking over at his sister blaring K Pop from her phone. "I can hear it all the way over here."

"Suck it up," Leslie said.

"You're gonna go deaf," he replied.

"That's future me's problem," she replied.

K Pop was a thing Leslie loved, so of course, it was stupid to Joshy. That didn't make it any less fun or catchy. Most people couldn't listen to it on repeat like she could, but to each their own. If Joshy could spend hours rotting his brain with computers, then Leslie could rot hers with Korean pop music. That was the American Way.

"This blows," Joshy said with a deep sigh. "America is boring."

While Joshy was dull and uninteresting, his sister was spectacular. Not only did she graduate two years early from high school and take an accelerated track at Stanford, but she was going to be the first in her family to graduate law school. If all went to plan, she would be the first in her family to be governor of California, too, though that would be true for most families.

"That's a horrible attitude mister," his mother said to him. "You should take a second to stop and enjoy these little moments. I would have killed to go on a road trip with my parents as a child."

"That's a lie, and you know it, mom," Joshy scoffed. "Nobody has ever wanted to go on a road trip with their parents in the history of the universe."

Leslie raised her hand. "I did. I mean, I took time off from summer school to be here, so your point has been disproven inside this very car."

"You're a bit of a know-it-all, did you know that?"
Joshy said. "It's really annoying."

The voice inside the GPS blared through the car before
Joshy and Leslie had a chance to argue more. "In two
miles, stay left on Interstate 15 North."

"We're getting close, Joshy!" his father exclaimed.
"Can you smell it? Vegas baby! Vegas!!!"

"No," Joshy said. "Just no."

"I don't see why you think Joshy would be excited
about Vegas," Leslie said. "It's not like he can drink or
gamble."

"As long as the room has internet and AC, I'll be fine,"
Josh said.

*

While there were many outrageous hotels in Vegas, made
up like New York City or a glass pyramid or the Venetian
canals, their differences were generally aesthetic. Inside,
they all performed the same functions. There was a casino
area, a shopping area, a restaurant area, and then the hotel
itself, which depending on where you were in Vegas took
on a different look.

At the Elara, it meant elegant white marble everywhere.
The Elara was a timeshare complex attached to the
shopping center of the Planet Hollywood Resort and
Casino. It didn't have a casino of its own and wasn't
affiliated with Planet Hollywood, though it glommed onto
its popularity. The Elara, much like David S. Pumpkins,
was its own thing.

Bill Carter pulled his minivan up to the front of the
hotel and stepped out of the car. His bones ached from five
hours of driving, and his back cracked as he arched it.

A valet in a red vest and bright smile ran up to him. "Your keys, sir?"

Bill pulled his keys close to his chest. "No. I'm sorry. I'm going to…self-park."

"It's complimentary, my friend," the valet said with a smile. "There's no charge for valet."

Bill liked that idea. He was thrilled about it, actually. He never valeted his car in Los Angeles. After all, who had an extra $10 to pay the valet? Forget about it. But a free valet, well he could indulge in that. Those are the best types of splurges, Bill thought, the free kind.

"Quit talking with the valet and open the trunk!" Carole called to him, cranky from the long drive and ready to relax by the pool.

Bill reached into his car and pushed the button to open the trunk. He thought it was quite extravagant to buy a car where the trunk opened by itself, but it was included in the base model price, so who was he to argue?

Before the truck finished opening, a bellboy pulled up a luggage carrier to the car and loaded a large suitcase onto the carrier. It was heavy, and the bellman struggled with the massive weight, but he didn't say anything, except to let out a soft grunt.

"I'm sorry," Carole said. "Do you want any help with that?"

"It's their job, Mom," Joshy said with a scowl. "Let them do their job."

Joshy hadn't yet learned the concepts of compassion or empathy. That was something that solidified with time, work, and sacrifice, none of which were things Joshy ever had to deal with much in his privileged life.

"I'm fine, ma'am," the bellman said. "Please go to the front desk. I'll meet you there."

Joshy pulled a tattered backpack out of the trunk and flung it across his back. Then, he walked inside and up the escalator toward the front desk.

*

By the time Joshy's parents joined him in the lobby of the hotel, he was already halfway through his fifth level of Angry Birds. It insulted his skill to play casual games, but his Nintendo Switch had lost power halfway through the trip, and he'd forgotten his car charger at home, so he was stuck until he got into his room.

"About time!" Joshy said in a huff when his parents stepped off the escalator.

"You could have helped them unload the car," Leslie replied. "It would have gone a lot faster if you did."

"Sure," Joshy said, standing up. "But I can follow directions. He said to go to the lobby, so I went to the lobby."

Now, you have to imagine Joshy, an eighteen-year-old human male, saying this, with all the sarcasm of an eighteen-year-old human male, dripping with testosterone and filled with the kind of wisdom only a teenager could confidently show, devoid of any irony in the fact that he truly knew nothing.

Bill stepped up to the front desk and pleasantries were exchanged. Once the keys were given and the platitudes traded, Joshy and his family were on their way up to their room, a rather luxurious suite filled with nice beds, cozy towels, and the like.

"You and your sister get this room," Bill said, gesturing toward the room on their right as they walked into the suite.

There were two queen beds inside, and little else. Then, he pointed toward a much larger room across from them, beyond the couch and dining room table. "Your mother and I get that one."

"Not fair!" Joshy said, walking inside to see a kitchen, couch, and big screen TV mounted on the wall. "Why can't I have my own room?"

"Because life isn't fair," Leslie replied. "It's not like I'm happy about this either. You snore."

"Do not," Joshy argued, except he totally did. If he had any friends, they would all agree with Leslie.

"Well," Carole said with a smile. "I'm ready to do a little lounging around. Who wants to go down to the pool?"

"Sounds nice," Bill said, thumbing a wad of money in his wallet. He knew the odds of hitting it rich in Vegas were low, but that wasn't going to stop him from trying. "I'll come for a little bit. Then, I want to walk around."

"Not me," Leslie said. "I plan to lounge by the pool until dinner."

The doorbell to the room rang. Bill ran to the door to welcome in the bellman, who pulled his luggage carrier inside and took all their suitcases off it. Once he was done, he stood there, smiling, for a good ten seconds without saying a word. It was quite awkward.

"I think he wants you to tip him, hun," Carole said.

"Oh!" Bill replied. "I thought it was free. Isn't this free?"

"Yes, sir, technically."

Bill slapped the bellman on the shoulder. "Perfect! Then I'll see you again soon. Have a great day."

The bellman left, grumbling to himself. Bill was the third person in a row to stiff him. He hated his job and looked forward to the day he finished night school with a computer science degree. Nobody would stiff him then.

Chapter 2

Joshy didn't join his family at the pool when they filed out of the room. He wanted to get in some gaming first, so he plugged in his laptop and handily won three Fortnite battles. Then, he put on his swim trunks and went to the elevator that would take him down to the pool.

Joshy wasn't a fan of most elevators, and he didn't like this one any better. It was one of those fancy glass ones which looked down on the strip. He could see all the way down to Mandalay Bay at the bottom of the strip if he cared to look, which he didn't.

His suite was on the fifteenth floor, which meant that he risked running into humans thirteen times before he reached the bottom. Of all the things Joshy disliked, humans were at the top of the list. They were rude, annoying, and smelled horrible. He hated elevators because it meant being trapped with humans in an enclosed space, and that meant he might have to interact with one. It was bad enough that humans existed around him, but the thought of having to engage with them was a fate worse than death.

Luckily, nobody entered the elevator while Joshy road down to the pool. He took the circuitous route around the lobby of the hotel and toward a side door guarded by a burly security guard. Thumping techno music echoed through the glass.

His family was already at the pool and had been for some time, but Joshy needed some alone time before he joined them. He needed the serenity only video games could bring. Playing video games relaxed him. That was what his family never understood about his passion. It was quite hard being Joshy, but when he played video games, all of that melted away and he was able to be somebody else for a while.

Joshy's main problem was that he hated himself. He hated other people as well, but nobody as much as he hated himself. That was what stopped him from joining clubs, or flirting with girls, or existing like a normal human…he was always in his own way.

Of course, sometimes other people were in his way too. In this instance, it was a tall, bearded, Black man with a three-piece suit and rippling muscles who guarded the entrance to the pool area.

"I'm gonna need to see some ID," the guard told him.

"Why? I'm a guest at this hotel," Joshy said, pulling out his keycard.

"Gotta be twenty-one to use the pool."

"Really?" Joshy said, raising his voice half an octave. That kind of thing happened all the time. It wasn't the manliest thing in the universe, and it didn't make him seem older than his eighteen years.

"Yeah," the guard replied, holding up a clipboard. "Now, I'm really gonna need to see some ID."

Joshy hadn't cared much about using the pool when he left his room. He was doing so to placate his mother so she wouldn't nag him later about not hanging out with his family. He was ready to turn around and head back to his room, until a group of bikini-clad, bronzed women pushed passed him and into the pool area.

Joshy peered into the pool area, past the glass and saw dozens of beautiful women dancing rhythmically, gyrating, and…well, it was enough to make Joshy believe that while most humans sucked, those particular humans were fine with him.

"Come on," he said, flinging his arms in the air. "I left it in my room, but I'm twenty-one, I promise I'm twenty-one."

The bouncer chuckled. "Yeah, and I'm Otis Redding. Get lost, kid."

Joshy couldn't believe that he was trying to get closer to his parents, but he desperately wanted to get into that pool. It wasn't enough to creepily stare at the bikini girls from the other side of the glass.

As the wheels started to turn in his head, Joshy watched his father stand up from his lounge chair, place his sunglasses in his pocket, and walk toward him.

"Look," Joshy said. "That's my dad right there. He's got a bad heart, and I need to give him his pills."

"Show 'em to me," the bouncer replied.

"Well, I don't have them on me!" Joshy said.

Joshy's father walked out of the pool and past the bouncer, smiling at him as he passed. Bill then made a beeline for the lobby that would lead him out of the hotel toward the casino. He had already wasted enough time on pleasantries, and now he needed to get down to business.

"Dad!" Joshy shouted.

Bill, startled, turned to him. "Oh, there you are, kid. I thought you were still upstairs."

"No. I'm trying to get into the pool," Joshy replied. "This guy won't let me in. Says you have to be twenty-one to get inside."

"To use a pool? That sounds stupid."

"Rules are rules," the bouncer replied. "I don't make the rules. I enforce 'em. We got a kiddie pool around back he can use."

"The Gestapo had rules too!" Joshy replied, furious.

"Alright, alright," Joshy's father replied, grabbing his arm. "Wish you had used a little more of that knowledge in history class, last year. Maybe then you wouldn't have nearly flunked. You can come with me."

"What!" Joshy whined. "Come on dad, I don't want to go with you. Do you see what's in there? Come on. Tell him that I can go in."

Bill looked through the glass toward the pool and saw the women dancing, the drinks flowing, and thought about how desperately he would have wanted to go inside if he were Joshy's age…and knew he couldn't let his son anywhere near that.

"Guard," he said. "My son is eighteen. Don't let him into that pool if you see him again."

"DAD!"

"Will do, sir," the guard said with a smile. "You can count on it."

"Come on," Bill said, pulling his son along. "You can ogle women later. That'll be about all you do when you get to be my age."

*

Outside of the Elara sat a strip of shops and restaurants that lined the "miracle mile," which was supposed to be a play on the Miracle Mile in Los Angeles, except that, well it didn't look like LA at all.

For instance, smack dab in front of the hotel there was a bar where you could buy premade margarita slushies. Nothing like that bar existed in Los Angeles. Plus, if you craned your neck up at the right place, you saw a ceiling lined with stars, which is something you would never see in the Miracle Mile in Los Angeles. Maybe Griffith Park, but not in the heart of Los Angeles. Then again, that wasn't really the point, was it? People didn't go to Planet Hollywood for the authentic experience. Vegas wasn't built on authenticity.

"Alright," Joshy's dad said when he got to the casino entrance. "Can you keep a secret?"

Joshy shook his head. "No. You know I can't keep a secret."

Bill grabbed his son tightly around the arms. "Well, I need you to try son. I need you to try really hard, because I'm gonna do some things in that casino, and your mother can't know about it."

"What kind of things?"

"Just—" Bill stuttered. "Things. Okay. That's all you need to know."

Bill held the money in his pocket tightly. He wasn't used to holding over a thousand dollars in cash on his person. He feared it would be stolen, or worse, fall out onto the ground for some other lucky sucker to collect.

"You're scaring me, dad," Joshy said. "Not much, but a little."

"Don't worry about it. Look, I've got a system. Everybody's got a system, but I got a system, a real good one, okay?"

"Systems don't work, dad," Joshy said. "I've watched enough TV to know that."

"Yeah, but you haven't seen this one yet. Follow my lead, okay?" Bill said. "And stop being so negative."

Bill walked past the security guard and into the casino. Joshy sighed. He didn't know if his father was having a nervous breakdown, but he knew enough to know that a casino was a dangerous place to go nuts.

"Wait up, dad," Joshy replied.

Joshy barely took a step into the casino before a short, squat woman with cheap hair and long fingernails grabbed him. "No way, honey. Not today. You gotta be twenty-one to be on this floor."

Bill turned to Joshy, wanting to help his son, but less than he needed to gamble. So, he turned away, confident that Joshy could take care of himself, even though Joshy had never proved he could do so, not even one time in his pathetic life.

The security guard pulled Joshy out of the casino and plopped him down outside the casino entrance. "I'm watching you."

Joshy didn't know what to do. He couldn't find his mother and sister because they were at the pool and wasn't allowed to go with his dad into the casino. He was alone in Vegas. Then he realized, he was alone…in Vegas…and a devious smile crept across his face.

*

If you liked this, go pick up *Invasion* today.

ALSO BY RUSSELL NOHELTY

THE GODVERSE CHRONICLES
And Death Followed Behind Her
And Doom Followed Behind Her
And Ruin Followed Behind Her
And Hell Followed Behind Her
Katrina Hates the Dead
Pixie Dust

OTHER NOVEL WORK
My Father Didn't Kill Himself
Sorry for Existing
Gumshoes: The Case of Madison's Father
The Invasion Saga
The Vessel
Worst Thing in the Universe
The Void Calls Us Home

OTHER ILLUSTRATED WORK
The Little Bird and the Little Worm
Ichabod Jones: Monster Hunter
Gherkin Boy

www.russellnohelty.com

www.wannabepress.com

www.ingramcontent.com/pod-product-compliance
Lightning Source LLC
Chambersburg PA
CBHW051000180726
48291CB00006B/1913